Yet none of the scents  him as that

Even now he could smell her, could still feel the wonder and the heat of her soft flesh against him. The hunger she had aroused in him still pulsed so strongly that with every beat he had to fight the desire to turn back and explore the fire until he burned alive, which was likely why he'd been unable to shift into his spirit form. He needed to rid the woman from his mind and spirit before shifting again.

Glancing back at her dwelling a brief moment, he wondered about the voice that had frightened her. It still disturbed him. He'd heard every word the man had whispered. A very deep pain lay hidden beneath the mortal woman's fiery warmth, and the man had made the pain worse.

Aragon took three steps back, drawn toward the woman, then swung away with his hands fisted. He couldn't allow himself to get involved in the mortal realm. Time was running out. . . .

———————

"These days, readers have a rich range of paranormal worlds to choose from, and St. Giles adds another powerful one to that list."

—*Romantic Times,* about The Shadowmen series

The Lure of the Wolf is also available as an eBook

"With its dark, dangerous hero and sexy storyline, this historical romance will appeal to contemporary romantic suspense fans who enjoy danger and intrigue."

—*True Romance*

"Teeming with menacing atmosphere. . . . St. Giles captures that Gothic essence with a sinister plot complete with unusual twists and turns, while maintaining a strong sexual tension between the protagonists."

—Fresh Fiction

The Mistress of Trevelyan
Winner of the Daphne Du Maurier Award

"Full of spooky suspense. . . . [St. Giles's] story ripples with tension. This tension and the author's skill at creating the book's brooding atmosphere make this an engrossing read."

—*Publishers Weekly*

"[An] intriguing, well-crafted romance."

—*Library Journal*

"[An] excellent debut novel. St. Giles does a masterful job of evoking a Gothic atmosphere, and updates it nicely with smoldering sexual tension. . . . The story is compellingly told."

—*Affaire de Coeur*

Also by Jennifer St. Giles

Touch a Dark Wolf
The Mistress of Trevelyan
His Dark Desires

JENNIFER ST. GILES

The Lure of the Wolf

POCKET BOOKS

New York   London   Toronto   Sydney

An *Original* Publication of POCKET BOOKS

POCKET BOOKS, a division of Simon & Schuster, Inc.
1230 Avenue of the Americas, New York, NY 10020

First Pocket Books paperback edition August 2007

POCKET and colophon are registered trademarks of Simon & Schuster, Inc.

For information about special discounts for bulk purchases, please contact Simon & Schuster Special Sales at 1-800-456-6798 or business@simonandschuster.com.

Cover design by Anna Dorfman
Illustration by Franco Accornero

Manufactured in the United States of America

10 9 8 7 6 5 4 3 2 1

ISBN-13: 978-1-4165-1333-9
ISBN-10:   1-4165-1333-7

Come what come may,
Time and the hour runs through the roughest day.

—William Shakespeare,
Macbeth, 1:3

This book is dedicated to all those who have helped
and prayed for me during my difficult year.
You made writing possible despite the problems.
I send you my many heartfelt thanks and love.

Prologue

A SPIRIT WIND *as powerful as Logos's right hand moved over the mountain, whipping through the trees and twisting through the misty maze of souls that hovered in the twilight between heaven and earth. Dawn broke across the bleak horizon of the night, its light slicing through the shadow, ferreting out the darkness, seeking to wipe it from the face of the mortal world.*

"You must stop Jared, Aragon, before it's too late! He may still have time left for redemption," Sven said, pain lacing every word.

Aragon turned from the outcropping of rocks where he watched Jared running up the mountain to the Sacred Stones. "No," Aragon said harshly. "He is doing what must be done. He cannot become what Pathos is. Jared should be allowed to die a warrior's death."

"What if you're wrong, Aragon?" Navarre asked. "What if your anger toward Pathos and the betrayal you've always felt that he'd disgraced all Blood Hunters has weakened your judgment? What if Sven is right?"

"Navarre speaks true," said York. "Your anger against Pathos has burned for an entire millennium. Why? Your compassion should be greater that one once so mighty has fallen so tragically."

Aragon turned his back, refusing to let his mind travel back to what was too painful to accept. He shook his head, determined. "Jared cannot become what Pathos is."

"We all agree upon that," said Sven. "But the time to assure Jared's death is not now. Navarre and York agree. You must act with us, for the Blood Hunters are nothing if they cannot fight together."

"A warrior must lead even though none may follow, or he ceases to be one," Aragon said harshly.

"And a leader who cannot see the wisdom of the council of those whom he trusts and fights beside might be leading all the wrong way. Stop Jared from doing this."

Was he wrong? Aragon reached deep inside himself, yet could not see any light or truth. Then he heard Jared's scream echoing in the blinding light of the dawn. It was a scream of a warrior dying, not of one damned beyond hope. In that cry, Aragon saw his error.

Sven fell to his knees, groaning, as did York and Navarre.

Aragon planted his sword into the mortal ground before Sven, causing the earth to violently shake. "You must lead now. I am unworthy."

Sven looked up, horror on his face. "I cannot lead."

"You must."

Another death cry ripped through the air, and Aragon turned. "Jared!" He turned his back upon his Blood Hunter brethren and ran to the Sacred Stones. Reaching the stone pillars, he found Jared suspended in the air within the center of them, his mortal body convulsing with pain as if every fiber of his being was suffering unimaginable torture.

"Jared. No! I was wrong." Aragon fell to his knees, his own pain and Jared's agony ripping through him. He had made a horrible mistake in believing nothing good remained in Jared. He was unfit to lead the Blood Hunters, or to be a true warrior. He tore Logos's amulet from about his throat and flung it into the air, praying that his spirit would die with Jared's.

Chapter One

"NO!" ARAGON YELLED, leaping from his knees. Jared couldn't die. Shifting into his were-form, Aragon had to save Jared or die trying.

Breathing hard, his fangs and claws clenched with frustration, he threw the full force of his massive were-form at Jared, desperately trying to free him from the Sacred Stones' killing hold. But Aragon hit an invisible wall before reaching the powerful force that held Jared's dying body captive.

"By Logos! Let him live!" Aragon cried, clawing at the barrier. The spirit wind gusted in response and slammed into him, throwing him back twenty feet. He sat up, dazed, shaking his head, finally realizing that it wasn't his lack of might that was blocking him from Jared, but a force greater than any power he'd ever fought.

Before he could react, he heard a mortal woman screaming Jared's name.

She appeared at the opening to the Sacred Stones, fighting the wind that had just thrown him as she plowed to the center where Jared hung in the air, twisting in agony.

Aragon started toward the mortal woman to rescue her from the same blast of power that had thrown him. What had dazed him would kill her. But she flung herself at Jared before he could stop her—and penetrated the barrier with ease. She wrapped her arms around Jared's convulsing wereform.

Jared recoiled as she clung to him, desperate to save him; but the love pouring from her, one as powerful as the wind, had come too late.

Aragon watched in horror as Jared's spirit separated from his body and rose toward the heavens. The mortal woman held Jared's lifeless body to her and pressed her mouth to his. Her cry of pain ripped through Aragon like a knife, rendering his heart in two. He'd not only caused Jared's death, but he, who'd sworn to protect the Elan, had just caused great sorrow to one of Logos's chosen.

Instead of accepting Jared's death, the woman pressed upon Jared's heart hard with her hand and gave him the very breath from her lungs. Again and again she repeated the motions, refusing to give up, fighting with a valor worthy of any warrior. Then suddenly, Jared's spirit came diving back down from the heavens, and his body shuddered back to life to feel the full force of the mortal woman's love.

Jared was saved.

Aragon ran from the Sacred Stones, his soul burning from the pain and the damage he'd caused. To have sent his brother to his death, to have been so wrong about Jared, made Aragon unworthy of anything. It didn't matter that love had saved Jared, that Jared had found salvation from the assassin's poison corrupting him. That only proved how mistaken Aragon had been. He didn't deserve to live, much less lead the Blood Hunters.

He'd had no choice but to leave the Guardian Forces. His fate should be far worse than the punishment decreed by Logos for such an act—to be exiled as a faded warrior, one whose spirit would remain trapped in time for eternity, having substance neither in the spirit world nor upon the mortal ground.

He didn't know how much time he had before Logos stripped him of his warrior's powers and threw him into the torturous void, but he knew there was one last thing he could do for his brethren: execute Pathos. The former Blood Hunter was a bane upon the mortal world and had shamed the honor of all Blood Hunters. It would be breaking Guardian Forces law to seek another's death outside of battle. But Aragon had little doubt that he and Pathos would fight to the end, so bitter was the draught in Aragon's soul.

In the spirit world a warrior's honor became entwined with that of the man who trained him. If he fought well, he brought honor to the one who'd done the training. But if he were cowardly or traitorous, he shamed his mentor as well as himself. When Pathos had become purely evil, taking up with Heldon within two short days of being poisoned by a Tsara, one of Heldon's spiritual assassins, the betrayal cut like a knife that went deeper as Pathos became leader of one of Heldon's most vile vampyric rings—the Vladarian Order. Pathos had led them to slaughter the Elan in a bloody reign of death that still echoed in the nightmares of mortals. Now Pathos led the Vladarians on an even more destructive path by making the ravenous beasts into an organized and deadly force. The souls of all mortals, not just the chosen Elan, were now in danger.

Pathos must be stopped. And Aragon would be the warrior to do it.

The rising sun chased the night chill from the Tennessee mountain air, but left Dr. Annette Batista shivering as if she stood in an arctic void. Too cold inside to accept the sun's warmth, and too isolated in her pain to rejoice with friends, she stood on Spirit Wind Mountain with her heart silently crying.

Around her, Emerald Linton, Sheriff Sam Sheridan, Erin Morgan, and Jared Hunter spoke softly, relieved that Jared had survived. But their tentative snatches of humor were tense; Jared's near death, along with the cloud of evil hanging over them, weighed heavily on their hearts, etching lines of strain upon them all. For Annette it was worse.

The pain she constantly carried sharpened to an excruciating point at the Sacred Stones cresting the deserted mountain. In the six months that had passed since her sister disappeared from the ancient worship site, she'd learned nothing more about what might have happened to Stefanie. Nothing had surfaced anywhere despite the numerous searches, the posted flyers, and the half million in reward money offered. Stef had come to the mountain to hike with her coworkers and disappeared without a trace.

Amid the Druid-like pillars, Annette always felt as if she stood in an open doorway from this world to the next, at the threshold of a dark, vast void into which she wanted to jump to find her sister—even if the black abyss was bottomless. The morning mists lingering over the dew-dampened ground twisted eerily around her ankles, swirling about the Stones like lost spirits searching for a soul to hear their cries.

I'm here. Talk to me, Stefanie! she silently beseeched her sister. *Where are you? What happened to you?*

Fisting her hands, she squeezed her eyes shut against the brightness of the fresh day. She prayed for an answer with her whole being, just as she had many times before, but the Sacred Stones remained silent. She heard only the whispering kiss of a breeze, the voices of her friends, and the wrenching "what if" tearing her apart.

Stefanie had called the night before she'd disappeared and left a message for Annette to call her back; that she had something important to talk about. But Annette had been in surgery when the call came and didn't get out until well after midnight. With patients in the Cardiac Intensive Care Unit still to see before going home, Annette had put off returning Stef's call until the morning. By then it had been too late. Stefanie was gone.

What if Annette had called just as soon as she'd left the OR that night? What if she hadn't let her career take precedence over her family yet again? What if she had acted as fast with Stefanie as Erin had done this morning when Jared left? Would Stefanie still be alive?

Annette had no doubt that Erin's love and quick response in rushing to the Sacred Stones had saved Jared Hunter. Though Annette had never seen Jared's Blood Hunter—aka werewolf—form, she no longer doubted that he was who and what he claimed to be.

Nor did she doubt that there was a host of supernatural beings in the world. Since meeting Erin and Jared, she had learned that vampires were finding human victims at free health screenings offered by the Sno-Med Corporation and its twisted head, Dr. Cinatas—the very company Stefanie had worked for. A company whom Annette hadn't questioned—she had even volunteered to help during their health expo last week.

God! She'd placed the blood of so many children into the hands of those monsters. She shivered again as a flood of pain and self-disgust washed over her.

"Please!" she prayed. "Please let me find Stef. Let me find something, anything." Chest almost too tight to breathe, Annette slipped to her knees and pressed her palm into the leaf-strewn soil where Stef's backpack had been found the day she disappeared. But all she could feel was the damp chill of the ground. Odds were that her sister's body lay somewhere in the cold earth of the surrounding forest, somewhere close, but hidden.

Emerald had tried to keep her optimistic even though everyone else had given up hope of finding Stef alive. The volunteer searches had ended several months ago, and every time she spoke to the people in town, she could see the resignation in their eyes—if they spoke to her at all. Some avoided her, starting to turn down the grocery aisle before seeing her and quickly moving to the next, or crossing the street before reaching where she walked. They weren't being cruel, but a tragedy hanging in limbo with no hope of closure was hard to face. She saw it in her nightmares and walked with it every day.

Yet she couldn't seem to resign herself as completely as Sam. Twilight's sheriff never sugarcoated anything and always pared truth down to the bone. He believed Stef was dead, and had believed it within days after she disappeared. He still did his job, though—ran a crime scene investigation of the area, personally searched every nook and cranny within miles, tracked down every story of a woman found or a body discovered that buzzed along the law enforcement's national and international wires, and questioned every stranger or vagrant found within a hundred miles.

Blinking hard against her tears, she saw something shimmering in the sunlight next to her hand on the ground and gasped as she recognized the golden-bronze amulet as Jared's. She reached for it. Before she even touched it, she could feel the warmth radiating from the metal into her fingertips. As she grasped it, a tingling shock danced from her toes to her scalp, and its heat went bone-deep into her hand, intensely comforting. With it clutched in her hand, she automatically brought the amulet to her chest and felt for the first time a fissure of warmth penetrating the cold that had imprisoned her for so long.

The ends of the chain dangled loose, their thick links broken. No wonder Jared had lost it. The amulet felt very important to her for some reason, and she was reluctant to give it back, but she knew from Erin how much Jared's badge as a Blood Hunter in the spirit world meant to him. She started to call him, but her voice died in her throat.

Erin was just slipping Jared's amulet over his head. It was impossible to miss, considering that's all he wore besides a yellow towel wrapped around his waist. Annette wasn't sure what the ins and outs of the spirit world were, but apparently either clothes and it or clothes and shape-shifting didn't mix. Jared always ended up naked.

If Jared had *his* amulet, then whose amulet had she found? Had another Blood Hunter appeared?

Clutching the symbol in her fist, she rose to her feet and swept the area with a sharp, searching glance, seeing only Emerald, Sam, Erin, and Jared.

"Nette?" Emerald turned. The compassion and concern settling over her delicate features reached out to Annette just as they had many times over the past six months. Emerald had found Stefanie's backpack that day and had called Annette, using the contact information Stefanie had carried in it. From then Annette's life had been an unfolding horror. Now that Annette knew about Sno-Med, she'd have to start searching there for a reason for Stef's disappearance. Thinking Stef had fallen prey to vampires made Annette ill. She shuddered again. If only she had called when she left the operating room that night . . .

"What is it, luv?" Emerald asked. "Something more is wrong today. I can feel it."

Without thinking, without even really knowing why, Annette hid the amulet from sight, clutching it tightly in her palm. She cleared her throat and forced herself to take a deep breath.

"I'm okay. It's nothing," she answered, too raw to share how much she'd failed her sister. And even though keeping the amulet secret made little sense, especially considering how much Emerald and all of her new friends had done for her, she couldn't share it just yet. And she didn't want to take the chance that Jared might want to keep it. She'd prayed for an answer, and finding the amulet exactly where Stef's backpack had been left seemed like a special message just for her.

"You canna give up hope on Stef. You just canna," Emerald said. Her endearing Irish brogue always thickened with deep emotion. With the morning sun lighting her moon-blond hair and glinting in her green eyes, she appeared even more magical and elfin than ever. Her petite size and sprightly allure enhanced her mystical image as much as her talk of crystals and her visions of the future.

"It's hard to hold on," Annette said.

"I'm sorry. I wish I could see something more about Stef, but the Druids are silent. Yet the sense that she lives is with me." Emerald moved closer, wrapping her arm across Annette's shoulder and squeezing tight.

"Don't tell her that," Sam said under his breath as he too moved closer, his dark countenance as rugged as a mountain peak. He zeroed his arctic gaze on Emerald. "Can't you see that all of this Druid and mystical bullshit about Stefanie being alive is only making it harder for her?"

The sparks that flew between Sam and Emerald had always been hot, but lately they'd been blistering. Emerald inhaled sharply, looking as if she was about to blow her gasket completely. And Annette couldn't blame her. Sam had been a real bear lately, and nailing Emerald with a speeding ticket for rushing Erin to save Jared this morning hadn't been one of his smoothest moves. She doubted Sam would file the ticket, but he'd been steaming mad, believing that Emerald had unnecessarily endangered everyone by not stopping when Sam caught up to her and letting *him* speed them to Spirit Wind Mountain. He was a macho guy who liked to be in charge, and Emerald was a woman who stood alone—no matter what.

"We'll talk later," Annette whispered to them both as she returned Emerald's hug. "Now's not the time." She forced a tight smile, knowing that when later came, she'd delay talking again. Only once in the six months since Stef disappeared had Annette let go of the firm rein she held on her emotions. Giving in to them meant losing control and being vulnerable. The surgeon in her avoided the first, and the woman in her avoided the last—at all cost.

After a long, hard stare passed between the two, Emerald's BlackBerry tinkled and Sam cursed.

"Do your clients ever take a breather?" he asked.

Emerald rolled her eyes. "Do you? You're like a dragon who breathes nothing but fire, scorching everyone in his path twenty-four/seven."

"Better than being the call girl of the twenty-first century."

Ignoring Sam, Emerald turned away to type her response to whatever crisis one of her patients was in the midst of. Being an online sex therapist put her in high demand. It was the best way Emerald could be in America and continue to help the patients she'd been treating in her established practice in Ireland.

Annette left them to duke it out and joined Erin and Jared.

She'd met them only a few days ago, when Emerald brought them into her clinic for treatment. Since then, danger and a shared enemy had plowed through normal barriers, making her feel as if she had known them for years, but she still felt a little uncomfortable around them.

Maybe it was because the love and passion between the couple was so strong, it was like a bright light you couldn't help but gaze upon, but couldn't look directly at either. Or maybe, she thought, it was Jared's all-knowing air. Could werewolves read minds? Could he see her darkest secrets? Did he know how she'd failed her sister? Did he know she had a Blood Hunter amulet hidden in her hand?

She'd learned the hard way that there was a whole lot more to Jared Hunter and his silent he-man-warrior manner than met the eye. Besides his werewolf strengths, like running and jumping with inhuman ability and healing from injuries rapidly, he could read faster than a speeding bullet and process information quicker than a data geek's dream machine.

Then again, the all-knowing look could come from the fact that Jared's spirit was a couple of thousand years old.

He would know whose amulet it was. She should tell him about it.

Annette held her tongue, refusing to give in to the niggling voice inside her head. If he could read her mind, then he'd have to be the one to out her. She didn't breathe until he shifted his gaze at Sam's approach.

"I hate to rain on anyone's parade, but we've got some major talking to do," Sam said, joining them. "I can handle the FBI and the Arcadia Police Department, who are most likely parked in my office right now wanting answers about the fires at the Sno-Med clinic and research center. But this Vladarian vampires shit—masquerading as rich men, playing God with people's lives, torturing them—"

Something bad had happened to Sam in the past, something he'd left the Delta Force over. Something he never talked about. Annette and Emerald had pieced together that something had happened in Belize, that Sam had been blamed for something and nobody had believed the truth. Yesterday they'd gotten another clue in the mystery when he'd read one of the names off the list of Vladarian vampires Erin had compiled—Luis Vasquez.

"You realize that siding with us puts you on the wrong side of the law you serve," Jared said.

"Yeah," Sam replied. "But as I see it, there's only one side to take. After being kidnapped and put on ice yesterday by Cinatas, I'd be a fool not to believe Erin's story. Only I think Cinatas has murdered more people than the four she found drained of their blood in Manhattan. I'm still trying to absorb the fact that he's feeding vampires with it, but I'm catching on fast."

"Faster than I caught on," Erin said. "I worked for Cinatas for three months thinking he was curing cancer with the specialized blood transfusions." She visibly shuddered. "Instead I was helping vampires."

"What I'm having a hard time facing is the number of rich, influential men that are on that list you gave us," Annette told Erin, then shook her head. "Hell, let me rephrase that. Not men. Vampires pretending to be men."

"Well, as I see it," Sam said, "Cinatas, Ashoden ben Shashur, and the rest of those bloodsuckers are about to meet their judgment day." He smiled hard at Jared. "We may be a two-man army, but if we're smart and plan right, we'll get the job done."

Jared nodded.

"Make that a two-man, three-woman army," Annette said. "Stefanie worked for Sno-Med. Now that we know what they are, I'm betting they're behind whatever happened to my sister."

"Jared and I will check it out. That I can promise you, but there's no way you three are going to put yourselves in harm's way," Sam said. "Not while I'm alive."

Erin rounded on Sam. "I've been framed for murder, chased, shot at, and kidnapped. I'm currently wanted by the FBI, and I'm prime food for vampires. I'm already in harm's way, and I refuse to sit in a corner and twiddle my thumbs. I'm fighting back."

"Count me in," said Emerald. "We'll meet at my place to plan. Sam, unless you're interested in dying today, you'd best get over your bleedin' self."

Emerald didn't wait around to hear Sam's reply. She marched ahead down the path leading to the cars. This time it looked as if Sam was going pop his piston. All things considered, Annette thought it was pretty miraculous Emerald and Sam hadn't done each other in by now.

She clutched the amulet tighter, pressing the warm metal deep into the flesh of her palm as she followed Emerald away from the Sacred Stones. *A miracle,* she prayed. She really needed a miracle.

Mozart's *Eine Kleine Nachtmusik* floated through Pathos's state-of-the-art war room in Zion, the Austrian estate from which he directed the lives of his many offspring and collected data on every creature on earth and among the damned. His plan to rule both Heldon and Logos was taking shape nicely. Another century, and he just might clinch the prize.

Trouble was, he didn't know if he could stand dealing with the Vladarian vampires for a hundred years more. As much as he needed them to gain the power he wanted, their

petty infighting was becoming more and more tedious—
and now they were showing signs of insolence. They needed
to be taught another lesson. But doing so would set in motion things Pathos wasn't ready to let happen yet. Since
Pathos had led the Vladarians from being mindless beasts,
they'd aligned themselves with different demon factions. To
punish them now would lead to a war within the Fallen
realm he wasn't prepared to fight.

Pathos glanced over at Nyros. The red demon had been
serving him for the past century and was quickly proving
that the red were the most intelligent of Heldon's demonic
factions. The blue and green demons who'd served him prior
to Nyros had been a disappointment. Pathos hoped that
when the time came to take control of the Fallen realm, the
red demons would side with him.

"Did I ever tell you about Amadeus, Nyros?"

"I don't recall the name," Nyros replied.

"Wolfgang Amadeus Mozart is the genius composer of
the serenade you're listening to. In a single night I killed half
of the existing Vladarians over him."

"Why?"

"I'd forbidden the Vladarians to harm certain humans
who had Elan blood. Amadeus was one of my protected."

"I thought all Elan would be prey to one from the Fallen
realm," replied Nyros. "I've heard of how pleasurably excit-
ing their blood can be. Makes me wish I drank blood."

Pathos smiled indulgently. "When I first joined the
Fallen, I too thought nothing of eliminating all Elan from
the world. That was before I realized how necessary it
was to have a number of them among the world's masses,
especially those of unique achievement. It took almost five
hundred years before the world recovered from our mass
annihilation of the Elan. The Dark Ages were a dreary time

of few creature comforts, and I do so enjoy those. So, I started a list of Elans that were not to be touched and the world was 'reborn.' Amadeus was on that list. His musical genius was beyond compare."

"What happened?"

"A number of Vladarians hated living under a were-being's rule and one in particular hated me. Drakulya. Upon learning that I took great pleasure in Amadeus, Drakulya secretly had Franz von Walsegg commission a requiem mass from the composer. Amadeus never imagined he was composing his own funeral. Every night Drakulya drank Amadeus's Elan blood a little at a time until Amadeus breathed his last. I found out too late. And that night I tortured half of the Vladarians into extinction. What do you think would happen were I to chastise the Vladarians like that again?"

Nyros shifted and settled his gaze on the floor.

"Come, I asked for the truth. Feel free to give me your opinion."

"I think you'd have a war in hell. All I can say is that the red demons would fight for you rather than against you."

"That would be a good choice for your faction to make, one with everlasting rewards. And you're right about the war. I'll have to come up with another way to bring the Vladarians back to heel, which is a shame. Extinction is such a simple solution."

"I'm sure genius will strike you, Pathos. It always does."

Pathos smiled. He liked having his ass kissed. "Perhaps by tonight I'll have an answer. Plan on a guest for dinner. Make it special. Hire a full ensemble of classical musicians. Fly in a gourmet chef for each course and I want a case of Chateau Petrus's finest reds here as well."

"And roses for the lucky woman as well?"

Pathos couldn't remember the last time a woman had interested him enough to share a meal or anything else with her. That was the trouble with long-term overindulgence—all pleasure faded. "Roses will be fine, but they'll be for my son. It's time Dr. Anthony Cinatas met his real father."

"As you wish," Nyros replied.

It always is, Pathos thought, utterly bored with his existence. With a sucking pop of air, Pathos left Austria for the United States to invite Cinatas for dinner.

Since moving to Twilight, Tennessee, Annette had come to the conclusion that the darkest hour wasn't before dawn, but the creeping twilight that sneaks up and bites you in the ass at the end of the day. That's when the gears of life in Appalachia ground to a screeching halt and small-town USA hunkered into its cozy homes, belonging places bulging at the seams with the essence of kinfolk—an elixir distilled from generations of shared history and love.

She didn't have to smell the home-cooked meals on the tables or hear the conversation to feel her isolation. And it wasn't hard to see how she'd ended up all alone in life either. She'd buried herself in schools and then in big metropolitan hospitals, where it had been easier to rev up on caffeine and pull another six hours than to have a relationship. Easier to work until she dropped for a few hours before starting the cycle again than to have any sort of personal life at all. Her drive had made her a good cardiac surgeon on the cutting edge of robotic medicine, but it had taken away everything else.

At thirty-five she could count on one hand the number of relationships she'd had *and* the number of years they'd lasted. Worse yet, she'd put the people she loved on hold, and now it was too late. Even after the sudden death of her parents two years ago, and her vow to bridge the gap between her and her sister, she hadn't done it.

Habit had Annette walking through her empty cabin without turning on the lights as she came home from work. Though having the Blood Hunter amulet in her pocket kept her from feeling as alone as she usually did, she still went to her lounge chair on the back deck where the fireflies could keep her company.

Tonight, even her closest neighbors weren't in. Annette had stopped by the Rankins's place across the road before coming home. She'd been trying to reach Celeste Rankin all afternoon, ever since the woman's blood work had come back from the lab with disturbing results. Surely there had to be some mistake. They'd have to redo the test, but Annette could assure the woman that she wasn't pregnant and that she absolutely was not anemic. Quite the opposite. The lab had never seen such a high concentration of red blood cells, and said they would need to repeat the test before they could give Annette an "official" level. It was almost impossible that the lab report was right. Celeste's polycythemia was so high that her blood was worse than sludge, making blood clots imminent and putting the woman practically at death's door for an embolism or a stroke.

Annette owed Celeste and Rob Rankin a lot and felt bad that she hadn't spoken to them in a while, not until Celeste had come in for a pregnancy test a few days ago. But the situation had been difficult. Celeste had been a friend of Stefanie's, and Rob had worked at Sno-Med with Stef. When Stefanie went missing, the Rankins had spearheaded organizing the volunteers to search for her. When those searches ended, it had been hard for Annette to accept that Celeste and Rob had given up.

Almost as hard as the outcome of the meeting at Emerald's this morning. The men had decided to wait, to keep the half-burned Sno-Med Center under surveillance until tomorrow, giving the various authorities time for their investigations before disturbing the area. Annette was more of the mind to get in there now and destroy any surviving patient records or blood samples from the health expo. She also wanted to see if any information about her sister was in the computer systems. Sam had pointed out that because of the fire, the place had no utilities, and one day to avoid running into the authorities wasn't going to hurt.

So investigations would have to wait. After the meeting, Annette had gone to the clinic to see patients for the rest of the day, and she was tired. There'd been little sleep over the past few days. Make that months. She hadn't slept well since Stefanie had disappeared.

Pulling out the Blood Hunter's amulet, she let it rest in the palm of her hand a moment, studying the beautiful, almost iridescent quality of the metal and the intricacy of the twelve-point star engraved upon it. The thing had consumed every spare minute she'd had during the afternoon. Though the tingling sensation she'd had when first touching it was gone, the amulet had stayed warm, as if still being heated by a bright sun. Even after she'd stuck it in the refrigerator, its temperature didn't change.

Then she'd worried about radiation, but a quick check with a gamma-detecting device from her old offices in Atlanta had ruled that out.

After that, she'd spent a lot of time thinking about how she might use the amulet herself. It had to belong to a warrior, a Blood Hunter like Jared, most likely. So how would a warrior be able to help her? She didn't have a murdering doctor after her. She didn't have vampires wanting to suck the life out of her. Jared would have said something if any of them had had the same special blood as Erin. So how could a warrior from the spirit world help her find Stef?

Or better yet: How could she find him?

Agitated, she sat up on the side of the lounge chair so abruptly that she lost her balance for a moment. As she caught herself on the edge of the chair, the heavy chain slipped from the amulet's loop and fell to the deck.

Picking it up, Annette slid the necklace back in place and studied the ends of the chain. There were no broken links and no visible clasp. A jeweler would have to cut open a link and weld it back together. She held the amulet up in front of her, studying it in the fading light as she pressed the two broken ends together.

Suddenly a bright light blinded her and a jolt of energy shot through her, electrifying her nerves. The moment her vision cleared, her pulse raced. She felt different in an indescribable way, and the chain had fused itself together; the broken ends were now connected by seamless links.

How? What had happened?

As she stared at it, the disk grew warmer than ever before. Surprised, she pressed the metal to her cheek, testing it. But the temperature intensified so quickly she had to jerk it away fast. Seconds later she needed to use the hem of her lab coat to protect her fingers from the increasing heat of the disk.

The atmosphere about her changed, becoming charged with a strange energy that cracked like a whip snapping in the air. She jumped up from the chair. Her breath caught in her throat, and sweat beaded her brow. *She was no longer alone.* The sensation rippled down her spine and pumped into her heart like injected adrenalin, making the hair on her arms and at her nape stand on end.

Jerking around, she saw a large shadow across the yard, ten feet below and twenty yards from where she stood. Partially covered in mists, the hulking shape stood along the darkened tree line of tall pines and twisting oaks.

A second's glance showed her that the amulet was scorching the hem of her lab coat. Were the shadow and the amulet connected? Was it a Blood Hunter like Jared? She moved a few steps closer, trying to peer through the mists and shadows.

What she saw was too large to be a man. At least, she thought so. She moved toward the railing, her heart hammering with expectation, but the shadow slipped deeper into a low-lying patch of thick fog on the forest's edge, mingling into the mists.

"Who is it? Can you speak to me? Can you help me?" she called into the eerie silence, gripping the railing and biting her lip to stem the raw excitement racing along her nerves. Her breath lay trapped and burning in her lungs. "Please, can I see you?"

The shadow emerged from the mist and moved toward her now. His pace was slow, almost predatory. She took a step back, wishing like hell that she could see better, but night had fallen during her reverie, darkening the evening to an inky black. The fireflies had abandoned her.

Lightning streaked sharply across the night sky, revealing a wolf-man whose ferocity stole her breath. Blacker-than-black hair covered Incredible Hulk–sized muscles that bunched with menace as he stepped her way. He growled, low and deep, flashing what had to be fangs.

Good God! She backed away from the creature, becoming sharply aware of a sudden hunger filling the tense void between them. The beast's primal lure snared her like a deer caught in the headlights of an oncoming truck. The air pulsed with danger, but she couldn't seem to move or look away. Heat radiated across the distance, almost scorching in its intensity.

Suddenly the creature charged toward her, moving faster than she thought anything could move. Whatever safe distance she thought she had up on her deck vanished in a second. She scrambled back, her scream locked in her throat as her pulse roared in her ears.

You're dead, she thought.

Chapter Two

THE BRIGHT BEAM of headlights arced into view, sweeping across the cabin and part of the yard as the car revved up the drive. Annette recognized the sound as Emerald's Mini. The beast turned toward the car, standing in the shadowed night beyond the reach of the headlights. With the lightning gone, Annette could no longer see its features, but she still felt its primal menace and heat filling the air. She could hear its low growl of warning.

Oh, God. Emerald was closer to the beast and would be getting out of her car at any second, where she'd be even more vulnerable. Annette dropped the amulet and started waving her arm wildly, rushing toward the deck's railing.

"Hey! I'm up here. Come up here," she called to the beast as she dug with her other hand for her cell phone to warn Emerald. Instead of moving her way or Emerald's, the wolflike beast backed slowly away. In a patch of moonlight, she saw it pause and look directly at her, as if making a point of remembering her, before it disappeared into the black of the night, moving toward the deeply forested area higher up the mountainside.

With it went the energy and power charging the air, making her feel as if the atmosphere around her had been sucked into outer space by a huge vacuum. She exhaled, almost doubling over from the force of her relief. As her eyes focused, she saw the amulet lying on the deck at her feet and tentatively reached for it, careful to check the degree of its heat before clasping it in her hand again. An edge of excitement coursed through her fear. Had a Blood Hunter come to her? Had she just seen a real werewolf?

Gaining her feet, she hurried back inside and through the cabin to meet Emerald at the front door. Her mind raced with questions. Was the beast she saw how Jared appeared as a werewolf? Part of the man whom Erin loved?

Annette gulped, trying to wrap her mind around that idea.

She knew darn well that something that big and primal hadn't been frightened off by her or Emerald. It could have attacked and killed within minutes, but it hadn't. So did that mean it wasn't as dangerous as it looked? Had it understood her?

Opening the front door, she flipped on the porch light and saw Emerald and Erin emerging from the Mini. She expected both of them to be home, getting some much-needed rest, and she thought Erin especially would be with Jared tonight. Instead, neither of them looked happy.

"What's wrong?" she asked, hurrying across the porch where they met up with her.

"We're bleeding mad, is what we are!" Emerald answered. Irritation flashed in her green eyes and her hair had been finger-combed to spikes of worry—or anger, it would seem. "Sam and Jared are up to somethin'. Bleedin' investigatin' without us, I say."

"Jared left without saying a word," Erin said, adding more steam to the stew pot. "He left a note. Did it while I was asleep! He said he and Sam had to take care of something and he'd be back by morning. Can you believe it? If I'd done the same thing, he'd have torn the world apart by now."

"And if you or I pulled a stunt like this, Sam, the gack, would have a cow," Emerald added. "Men are clueless when it comes to wearing the shoe on the other foot."

Irritation stabbed Annette as she marched back inside her cabin, turning on the lights. The amulet in her pocket and the beast in her yard took second seat to her being duped. "Damn. Do you really think they're sneaking behind our backs and searching Sno-Med without us? Was all that talk this morning about waiting nothing but a smokescreen?"

"What else are we supposed to think?" Emerald asked. "Sam's cell phone switches automatically to voice mail. He's not answering his home phone." Emerald pursed her lips. "And according to the dispatcher, he's off duty and bleedin' unreachable."

"Sam is never unreachable," Annette replied, frowning. "It does sound suspiciously as if they went without us, but there could be another reason." Sometimes in the mountains cell reception sucked. "We have to do something, though. First, I need some caffeine to think by." She motioned for them to follow her to the kitchen, barely suppressing her wince at the powder blue curtains and soft pink rosebud wallpaper.

The previous owner had overindulged in country pastel decor, and Annette had yet to change anything to the bolder colors and more modern patterns that fit her comfort zone. Her whole life had been suspended since Stef disappeared, and she saw no reason to change it.

Annette smacked the coffeemaker on. "It's my sister who is missing, and I'm the one who drew innocent children's blood for those bastards. I should be there." The heavenly aroma of her favorite Swiss almond mocha blend filled the air, grounding her for the first time all day. There was something about coffee that made any situation manageable.

Bringing out three mugs and the sugar, she fished the cream from the fridge. "Sam's conscience doesn't allow for him to be out of touch. Twilight is his baby to care for, and he's obsessive about his duty. Are you sure the dispatcher isn't giving you the brush-off, Em? The woman has her eye on Sam, even if she *is* married."

"You call and see if you can get more out of her." Emerald poured a bit of straight cream into her cup and downed it with a cat-licking sigh.

Annette shuddered as she dragged her cell from her pocket. Her fingers brushed the warm amulet, and she paused, setting her gaze on Erin. How did she go about asking what Jared looked like as a werewolf?

Erin was looking at a sketchbook of Stef's Annette had left open on the counter, one that Annette hadn't even bothered to really look at until learning that Jared was a werewolf. That had been another way Annette had failed her sister. Stef's dream had been to be an artist. She drew fantastical creatures and made up stories about them. Annette, who'd been twelve years older than Stef, had taken their parents' side, insisting that Stef get a *real* education and a *real* job. Annette had pushed Stef toward something in the medical field, which landed Stef a job at Sno-Med, which was likely responsible for her disappearance.

Shaking off the thought, Annette bit her lip. Did Annette really need to ask Erin? Did she really have any doubt that the hairy Incredible Hulk–like wolf wasn't a Blood Hunter? What she really wanted to know was, how dangerous were the beasts, and how did she talk to one?

She dialed the sheriff's office. The dispatcher answered. "Hey, Myra," Annette said. "This is Dr. Batista from the clinic. I have a situation and need to speak to the sheriff as soon as possible. . . . No. Deputy Ross can't help me. This has to do with what *Sam* is doing tonight. Do you understand now? I can only speak to him alone." Annette smiled as the answer came through and she disconnected the line.

Emerald and Erin glared at her.

Inwardly grinning, Annette leisurely poured everyone's coffee and brought a cupful of the fragrant black liquid to her lips. She relished the hot bitter bite and the fire that tried to warm the cold inside she couldn't ever seem to shake. At least, until she'd touched the amulet. She'd been warm then. What happened with the amulet seemed personal, as if it was meant just for her. And if she shared it with anyone, she was afraid the magic would go away.

"Unless you expect this to be your last bleedin' breath, then you had better tell us now!"

"After the week I've had, I'm ready to pound something myself," Erin added.

"Tell you what?" Annette asked innocently, toying with her friends.

"About Sam!"

"And Jared!"

"Annette! By the bloody Druids, where are they?" Emerald shouted.

"Oh!" Annette said. "Patience, ladies." Smiling, she shoved a cup of coffee under Erin's nose, then pushed one at Emerald. "Drink your coffee, ladies, and relax. Sam and Jared haven't been anywhere and aren't going anywhere. The gossip according to Myra is that Sam has locked a man in the station's cell and then has shut everyone out of that section of the station with orders not to intervene no matter what they hear."

Erin groaned. "Jared's still afraid that he's going to hurt someone."

"Hurt someone as a werewolf?" Annette asked, snatching the opportunity. "Has he?"

If the beast she'd seen was like what Jared had become as a werewolf, then how had Erin learned to love and accept him? Yet when she saw Jared as a man and the love he had for Erin, how could she ever doubt that Erin would love him back?

"Yes and no. And yes," Erin replied in answer to Annette's question. "It's hard to explain. The poison affected Jared's werewolf side. Made him feel like a bloodthirsty beast out of control. He thought he was the greatest threat to me, but I didn't believe him, and I still don't."

Annette shivered. She'd felt that in the beast tonight, the primal hunger, the predatory hunter. Base desires uncontrolled in such a strong creature would be worse than frightening.

"Because of the poison, right?" Annette asked. "If it weren't for the poison, his werewolf side wouldn't be dangerous to a regular person, right?"

"I'd trust Jared with my life, but it seems he doesn't trust me," Erin said. "Why didn't he just tell me that Sam was going to lock him up tonight? That he was still worried?"

"Just might be a man thing, luv," Emerald said.

Erin sniffed the coffee, then picked up the sugar spoon.

Emerald frowned at the coffee. "I'm not much on sludge, Nette."

"Think of it as chocolate with a high-octane kick," Annette said and pushed the cream Emerald's way. "Pollute it if you must, but you can't miss the experience."

"What do you mean, a man thing?" Erin stirred in more sugar until Emerald snatched the spoon away, then grabbed the cream and nearly overfilled her cup.

"Would you have let him go?" Annette asked, wincing at the desecrated coffee.

"No." Erin sighed as if her whole heart rested on that breath. "You don't understand. I've seen what changing into a werewolf does to him. He almost lost his soul before. And he needed me then. What if it's just as bad now? Why didn't he take me with him? It's just stupid."

"Get used to it. He's male, luv," Emerald said. "Experience has taught me that women get a bit irrational and men get a bit stupid in situations. Lucky ducks for you, Jared's a wee bit wiser." Emerald reached over and clasped Erin's hand. "Part of lovin' is letting another walk the way they need to and not the way you want them to."

"Words you're going to need to keep in mind as your daughter gets older," Annette said, then watched Emerald's eyes pop wide. "Speaking of which, where is your angel now?"

"Megan's at Bethy's again." Emerald sighed. "They're still trying to beat the Dark Lord on Fairy's Fantasy X." Her smile didn't quite reach the shadows in her green eyes.

"What are you not saying, Em?" Annette searched her friend's face for an answer. "After the meeting this morning you couldn't wait to pick Megan up from Bethy's and bring her home."

"I did."

"And?"

"We did a reading, and I decided that Bethy's is the safest place Meggie can be right now. Unfortunately, the Druids weren't kind enough to reveal why."

Erin set down her cup with a thump. "We escaped from Cinatas yesterday, and part of me keeps hoping that the reason he hasn't come after us again is that he died in the Sno-Med fire even though his body wasn't found. Still, I keep wondering why the other goons behind Cinatas haven't shown up on our doorstep yet. Jared thinks it's because

Cinatas kept us secret from the rest, either because he was too ashamed to admit that I'd bested him, or because he didn't want anyone else to know what his plans for Jared were. The lunatic wanted Jared to help him take control of the Vladarian Order from its current leader, Pathos."

Emerald waved her hand, making her bracelets tinkle like fairy bells. "Might be that, but keep in mind, luv, you're in the Twilight zone."

As if on cue Emerald's BlackBerry rang. "Hold on," Emerald said as she read the message and typed a reply. It didn't take long, so whoever it was, their sexual glitch mustn't have been too bad. Annette shook her head with a half smile. Only wonderfully wild, wacky Emerald could be an online sex therapist and get away with it. Just as she pulled off all of her other mystical predictions and made you want to believe her even if you couldn't quite bite into the dish she was offering. Erin didn't know whether to take Emerald's Twilight zone comment seriously and hummed the TV *Twilight Zone*'s theme tune a moment before speaking in Rod Serling's ominous tones: "You are protected by the . . . Twilight Zone."

Emerald blinked a minute after she finished with her BlackBerry, looking confused. "No, luv. You've got it all wrong. Not that *Twilight Zone,* but Twilight's real zone. It's a bit difficult to explain, but there are a few places on earth that are . . . magical. It has to do with the magnetic and electric fields being scrambled, which creates a fog, if you will. The atmosphere makes it very easy for them to enter our world, but makes it a wee bit harder for them or anyone with powers to 'see.'"

"By *them,* you mean—"

"Spirits from all dimensions. Heaven and hell and in between."

Annette started to shake her head in denial, then stopped.

"That's good to know," Erin said, rolling her eyes. "We're sitting in the middle of a demon highway crossing with nothing but fog for cover? We can only hope that Jared is right."

"The crystals don't lie, luvs. Bloody hell is on its way," Emerald said, then drew a deep breath. "And Stef is still alive, no matter what Sam says."

Annette met Emerald's gaze head-on, wanting to have that same kind of belief burning inside of her. "Then where is she?" Annette whispered, slipping her hand into her pocket, absorbing the warmth of the amulet into her fingers.

"Doona know, but I have a feeling the answers are on their way."

Annette nodded. *Or she was on her way to them,* she amended Emerald's prediction. "Tomorrow I'm going to Sno-Med to search for answers, no matter what Sam and Jared say."

"And we'll be with you. What time?" Emerald asked.

"Dawn," said Annette.

Emerald pushed herself back from the bar with a grimace that clearly revealed her aversion to early hours. "I was afraid of that. That means we'd better get moving to the sheriff's station."

"Both of you have gone way beyond the call of duty in helping Jared and me out," Erin said. "Why don't you drop me off at the station and go home and get some sleep while you can? I want to be where I can get to Jared quickly just in case something goes wrong, but you don't have to stay up all night with me."

Emerald shook her head and gently pushed Erin toward the door. "Sorry, luv. We're partners in crime. I'm camping out at the station with you. Jared and Sam will muck things up without us."

Annette followed, already seeing the sparks fly. Sam and Jared were in for it. Hell was about to descend on them via a red Mini. "You two tackle the men. I'm soaking in a hot tub and then sleeping in my own bed tonight." For the past few nights she'd slept at Emerald's.

She waved them off from the porch and stood absorbing the night. Though no lightning flashed or thunder rolled at the moment, the brewing energy of a storm hovered in the mountain-chilled air. The wind had picked up its pace, briskly twisting through the trees as it bullied the sun-weary leaves.

She'd try and call Celeste Rankin again to make arrangements for her to come in and have more blood drawn. She couldn't tell the woman at this point how off her red blood cell count was, since the lab hadn't given an "official result," but she had to tell her enough to get her to come in quickly.

She also wondered if she should say anything to Rob about Sno-Med. Thousands of people worked for the company worldwide. The corporation had a philanthropic reputation akin to Mother Teresa's. Funny. Spelled backward, the firm was nothing but a bunch of deM-onS.

Would Rob Rankin even believe her? *Hey! You work for a company that uses free health screening to find special blood to feed vampires. They employ unsuspecting people to help kill innocent people.*

Doctors were sworn to heal and protect, not to prey upon the innocent. She was sure that most of the people who worked for Sno-Med, like her sister Stef, were unaware of the evil, but there had to be many who were willingly helping these horrible creatures.

How could they even begin to stop this group or discredit Sno-Med?

After a long while, she realized that she was staring out at the night, letting her thoughts roil, because she was hoping to see something. A movement in the shadows, a crackle in the air, a primal energy, something—

Was she crazy? Hadn't she been frightened enough? Erin trusted Jared with her life. But it was obvious Jared didn't trust himself. He'd had Sam lock him up. And wouldn't a man know himself better than anyone else?

She needed to forget about the amulet and the Blood Hunter for tonight and face it all tomorrow.

Turning from the darkness, she checked and locked all of the cabin's doors and windows twice, then made her way to the kitchen, where she poured three fingers of Bailey's Irish Cream in her second cup of coffee—the only cream she ever used in coffee, and only at bathtime when she indulged herself. Coffee in hand, she headed to the tub.

When the Rankins had mentioned the cabin was on the market, Annette had at first been completely against living anywhere beyond a stone's throw from town. But then she'd seen it, and bought it for two reasons. She'd always lived comfortably in the city, with people stacked as tightly as layers of colored sand in a terrarium around her. Coming this far out from the small town of Twilight was like a punishment in some ways. If Stef was lost in the forest, then Annette would be, too. The second reason was the jetted, freestanding Roman-style tub in the center of the bathroom, big enough for two.

The only indulgence she'd allowed herself over the years was a luxuriant bath. It had been a once-a-week ritual when she'd lived in the grind of hospital life. Since coming to Twilight, she guiltily took one every night.

Within fifteen minutes she'd polished off her Bailey's-enhanced coffee and filled the tub with steamy water drenched to a milky white with gardenia bath oil. Her clothes hit the floor and she sank into the welcoming heat, letting her senses absorb the heavy perfume. She closed her eyes, ignoring the garish contrast between her red towels and the pale lavender wallpaper, and let her body and mind relax from the rigid confines she kept them in throughout the day.

After a moment one eye popped open, then the other. She couldn't relax. She kept thinking about the amulet.

Irritated, she rose, dripping silky suds across the floor as she fished the medallion from the pocket of her lab coat. Her fingers were hotter than the metal now, and she carried it back to the tub, sliding deep into the water, closing her eyes. What would have happened if Emerald hadn't interrupted when he'd appeared outside her cabin?

Aragon fought against the sensation pulling at him again. Head bowed, he strained to stay on track, chasing the trail of Pathos's scent that he'd just picked up.

Did Pathos sense that Aragon was after him? Aragon hoped so. He hoped the vile being was just waiting for Aragon to catch up to him. Though with the company Pathos now kept, he might be hiding like the coward he'd proven himself to be.

Teeth clenched, he forced himself forward as another wave of energy pulled harder against him. What in Logos's name was going on? Earlier he'd been racing through the forest of the mortal ground, feeling his essence hover between that and the spirit realm, when suddenly he'd shifted across the land and found himself running toward a mortal woman sitting beneath the stars. Something about her was drawing his being her way as strongly as Logos's magnetic core spun the world. And something was causing his essence to solidify within the mortal realm in a way he'd never experienced before, as if he were actually becoming more mortal than spirit. He sucked in air, absorbing the smell of the damp forest, feeling as solid as a rock.

He wondered if it had anything to do with the fact that he'd thrown his amulet upon the mortal ground. He always thought he'd lead with a mighty and sure sword of truth, never causing another to falter, but he'd failed.

He wouldn't fail now. He'd restore the Blood Hunters' reputation and the honor that Pathos had blackened so long ago. This was his one chance, and he couldn't let the mortal woman's witchery distract him. The trail he chased suddenly intensified, telling him he was very close to his prey. Pathos's unique scent was now rotten with the stench of evil. After a millennium of waiting, Aragon finally had the chance to face his old mentor and put an end to the traitorous existence.

Raising his sword, he barreled ahead with a Blood Hunter's howl meant to cower all of the Fallen's craven cowards.

"Hell." Annette clutched the amulet in frustration, irritated that she couldn't get her question about its owner or the impressions the beast left with her out of her mind enough to enjoy her bath. Who was he? She wanted to see his mortal form, not his werewolf form.

The amulet instantly heated, and a howling yell echoed off the bathroom walls as a naked, sword-carrying, enormous man suddenly appeared, barreling right at her.

She screamed and stood frozen, totally terrified. Her mind demanded that she run even as she registered his long black hair and harsh features. She saw his dark eyes widen in shock, as if he was as horrified as she. He lowered his sword and appeared to try and change the direction of his charge, but he hit the patch of oiled water she'd dripped on the floor and hydroplaned. His sword clattered across the tile floor as the side of the tub wiped his feet out from under him, and he plowed right into her chest face-first. She lost her breath and precarious balance, sliding to smack her ass hard on the bottom of the tub. Water erupted everywhere. The amulet fell from her grip and wedged hotly against her hip beneath the water. His body was as heated as the amulet and connected with hers . . . everywhere.

At that moment she knew she should be feeling outraged. But her entire existence boiled down to the feel of a scruffy jaw planted between her breasts and her hands clutching the broadest shoulders she'd ever seen. That her legs were splayed wide with a hard body intimately between them was too earth-shaking to even register on her Richter scale.

Chapter Three

A T THE BLOOD HUNTER'S howl, Pathos swung around with his fangs and claws bared, aching to rip the world apart. His long black coat whipped in the rising wind, and his leather-and-steel-booted feet dug into the soil, bracing for a fight. When the enemy was suddenly sucked away, cheating him of even that small satisfaction, Pathos's rage boiled even hotter.

The incompetence surrounding him had reached an intolerable level. No one could find Cinatas or Shashur, the Vladarian he'd been seen with last. If his idiot minions weren't already dead, he'd murder them himself and take Heldon out as well. The conceited fool was the worst of the lot, sitting upon his craven throne, letting demons and underlings and subpar shifters go wild, sure that the more chaos and mayhem they created, the more easily he would win the battle for the world. In Heldon's book, as long as every man was looking out for himself and screwing everyone else, figuratively and literally, then Logos would lose.

Pathos had figured out long ago that Heldon would lose too, and that's when he began his attack on the throne. Using the Vladarian Order was just part of his plan, but the schizophrenic sect with delusions of grandeur was fast becoming a thorn in his side. Especially if they'd cost him Cinatas.

Before long, Pathos would have the means to put the Vladarians in their place. Soon Pathos would activate more of the seeds he'd spent decades planting. He'd supplied sperm to a great many sperm banks around the world as well as making fruit-bearing use of every mortal woman he could seduce. The first of his offspring he'd brought into service had been Cinatas, and everything had been going well until Ashoden ben Shashur, the pissant vampire king of oil-rich Kassim, had arrived at the Manhattan Clinic for a transfusion.

Pathos would bet his fangs that Shashur had something to do with Cinatas's disappearance. Shashur, along with several other oil-rich Vladarians, Vasquez and Samir to name two, had been sowing seeds of dissent among the order. Pathos knew it, but had chosen to ignore their little games.

Now he was faced with two burned-out centers and a host of Vladarians demanding to be reassured about their next fix of Elan blood. And his son was missing!

If he didn't get answers soon, he'd raise hell from Heldon's putrid bowels and unleash it upon the mortal ground.

Before Annette could do more than blink and gasp, the man wedged his hands on the side of the tub and reared back enough to look her in the face. He was similar enough to Jared in his presence that she had little doubt she was staring at a Blood Hunter, one that she'd called to her by the amulet. Nothing else could explain what had happened both times she'd concentrated on the owner of the amulet while holding the disk.

The dynamic alphaness of the man matched Jared's, except that this man was rougher. The only thing that softened his warrior-sharp features was the black silk of his long hair and the luxuriance of his water-spiked lashes. Dark-coffee eyes flashed with irritation and confusion above a nose that, though perfectly straight, seemed so bent with badass attitude, you'd swear it had to have been broken in a fight or two. His full mouth and the knock-'em-dead cleft in his chin were set too grim to ever be sensual, but that didn't stop the stomach-clenching thought of feeling his lips on her. Or was it the rising hardness between their intimately pressed bodies that sent her thoughts south?

Breathe! She sucked air into her burning lungs.

His nostrils flared as he too breathed. Then he leaned down just a fraction and inhaled deeply, his gaze dropping. From the chill of the air upon her breasts and the teasing lap of water against her ribs, she knew without looking what he found so interesting. He looked like a bull choosing between two targets he'd never seen before.

She gasped and dropped her hands from his shoulders to cross her arms over her breasts, an act that brought his gaze back to hers. He moved back even more; confusion etched deeper into his frown as he shifted his weight to his knees. Her relief at gaining some distance from his hard body was short-lived because as his thighs widened to balance his weight, he spread her legs wider apart, pinning them to the sides of the tub. Though the milky water hid her exposure, the vulnerability of being so splayed and trapped by Mr. Rough and Ready rendered her incapable of . . . almost anything.

"What magic do you wield upon me, mortal woman? Are you a witch?" The depth of his voice vibrated everything that he hadn't already shaken. "How am I here in a fleshly form that's more mortal than spirit with such desires pulling upon me?"

She swallowed, her mouth too dry and her mental and physical synapses too overloaded to ask any questions or make any confessions. She, who'd handled hundreds of medical emergencies during her career and who had the balls to operate on people's hearts, couldn't even get her tongue rolling.

"Wh—?" she croaked, trying to ask him who he was.

He frowned.

She pulled against her trapped legs, trying to sit. "M-m-move," she whispered, forcing a coherent word from her lockdown.

He grunted before gripping the tub's rim and standing. His frontal assault below the waist was just as powerful as above. There was nothing soft about the sculpted six-pack, jutting erection, and granite thighs facing Annette. Droplets of oil-slick water slid along the trail of hair bisecting his abs, around his sex, and down his long legs.

As a doctor, she'd thought she'd seen it all. Had been there and done that many times over when it came to the body. She was wrong. She'd never been *here,* and she sure as heck had never seen anything like *this* before.

"Can you not move?" he asked.

When she didn't promptly respond, he grasped her arms and hauled her up to her rubbery knees. His hands slipped a little from the gardenia-scented oil drenching her, but he managed to hold on, and she finally regained some of her cognitive abilities. She grabbed a towel from the nearby rack and wrapped the red Egyptian cotton around her body, then stepped onto the bath mat.

She pulled another red towel from the bar and handed it to him as she determinedly kept her gaze on his safest feature, his badass nose. "Here," she said. "Get out of the tub and *then* we'll talk."

He took the towel, and she put a safe distance between them by walking to the door of the bathroom. When she turned to speak to him, she found that he'd dropped the towel on the floor and had retrieved his sword. He studied the sword as if checking it for damage, then glared at her. "You must send me back. I have an important task to complete, and no time to talk."

"Me," she yelped. "Back where? Who are you?"

"I am Aragon Hun—just Aragon. I must return immediately to the forest from which you summoned me. Much will be lost should I fail in my quest before my time upon the mortal ground is over."

Before his time was over . . . What did that mean? "Aragon, what quest are you on?"

The phone rang. Aragon spun adeptly with his sword raised, looking for a threat.

"I'll be right back," she said and exited the bathroom, quickly reaching the phone in the hall. She would have let it just ring except that Emerald or Erin might need her help.

"Hello," she said as she pressed the receiver to her ear. The caller ID flashed "unknown," making her frown. No answer met her greeting, though she could hear the rasp of breathing. "Hello? Who is it?"

"Don't hang up, not if you want to know where your sister is." The muffled whisper was nearly indistinguishable.

The blood drained from Annette's head and she gasped. Her back hit the hallway wall as she sought support to remain upright despite the swirling dizziness. "What did you say? Who is this?"

"Meet me in the Infectious Disease Department of the Sno-Med Center at midnight. She's in the computer there under 'X-files.' " He chuckled as if he'd heard a great joke. "Tell no one and come alone, or I won't show."

"Wait!" she cried. "Where is she? Is she aliv—" The blaring dial tone cut off her question. Was Stef alive? Where? Midnight was hours away yet! She cried out in frustration.

Suddenly the receiver was snatched from her hand, and Annette screamed before she realized that it was Aragon. She'd momentarily forgotten him. He'd followed her to the hall, naked and holding his sword at his side.

"Does this harm you?" He shook the receiver, glaring at it, looking very much as if he'd gladly subject it to the blade of his sword.

She pressed her hand to her chest, forcing herself to a calmness she did not feel. Her distress had disturbed him. "No. The phone did not harm me. The message I received upset me."

"Why?" he demanded.

She made the split-second decision to keep the call a secret. She wanted answers, and to get them, she might have to take a few risks, but she didn't have to be stupid about it either. She'd get there well before midnight and find what she could before Mr. X made an appearance, maybe even get the data from the computer herself. Until then she wouldn't even let herself consider what this meant about Stefanie. Infectious diseases ran the gamut from a cold to the plague and worse.

"It's nothing," she said, taking the receiver back from him and hanging up the phone. She was probably the first woman ever to look at a naked hunk like Aragon and wonder how fast she could get him out the door. Well, maybe not, considering he was an armed naked hunk . . . and not exactly human either. She had to remember that.

He lifted a brow and slid his thumb beneath her jaw to shift her gaze to his. "Why the need for untruths?"

She winced at the pure honesty in his voice even as the gentle warmth of his warrior's touch did something inside her that outrocked everything that had already happened between them. She wrapped her hand about his wrist, not even covering half its circumference, but enough to feel the throb of his pulse and the penetrating heat of his skin. If there was something inhuman about him, she sure as hell couldn't feel it.

"Sorry. You've a quest to take care of, and so do I. I don't know how to send you back or even exactly how you came to be here." Which was essentially the truth. She had an educated guess that the amulet was key, but she didn't know for sure. "What forest were you in? Can you tell me anything about the area? Anything different or unusual about it?" Her touch seemed to do something to him, because his gaze was riveted to her hand clutching his wrist. Then he slowly moved his gaze to her face.

"Different? Unusual?" he asked softly, staring at her intently, as if seeing her for the first time. The harshness of his features eased within moments as a sensual light warmed his gaze.

"You are so soft," he said. "Your touch and your skin." He slid his thumb down her throat to her collar bone and traced its ridge, making her heart pound and her body heat. She released his wrist and let her hand fall to her side, pressing her palm to the cool wall.

"I've never known things such as this fiery interest you ignite inside of me," he said, brows drawing together. He didn't look exactly pleased with his attraction.

She could have stopped his exploration, but her senses screamed too loudly for her to do anything but feel. How long had it been since she'd let herself feel anything but determination and guilt?

He leaned in closer and breathed deeply, making her impossibly even more aware of him. "What scent do you cover yourself in?"

"Gardenia," she whispered, catching her breath as his fingertips splayed across the rise of her breasts, just above the edge of her towel. She arched to his touch before she could think, causing the tucked end of her towel to loosen and dip lower across her breasts, barely covering her nipples. Seemingly awed by the feel, he followed the towel's edge down, caressing the cresting curve of her breasts as his fingers pressed gently into her skin.

The erotically slow exploration had her trapped in a wave of edgy expectation. Her heart hammered with desire and fear, of him, of who and what he was, and of herself. She fisted the bottom hem of the towel in her hand, trying to keep from running her fingers through the silk of his hair or along the hard contours of his chest . . . and below. The six-pack tapering down to his impressive sex and thighs needed to come with a warning label.

She'd always lived her life under rigid control; yet here she was, a breath away from exploding. Whether it was the unexpectedness of the situation or the man himself, she didn't know. She only knew she'd never been this sexually excited in her life.

He could have easily jerked the towel down farther, but he didn't. Instead, he slid his hand up to finger a long curl that had loosened itself from her customary tight knot. He rubbed it between his fingers, slowly, savoring the feel and driving her need even higher because she wanted that sensual, alluring touch . . . oh, just where she burned. If he'd just . . . a vision of her dropping the towel and backing him to the wall to drive him past this lazy control rushed through her mind.

No. You have no idea what you're getting into, or who or what he is. This isn't like you, Annette! You're disciplined, logical, rational . . . you're—

The room flashed white, and she blinked, slowly registering from the crack of thunder that lightning had struck somewhere very close by. She could relate. She felt as if a bolt had hit her right between the legs—eyes, that is.

Aragon froze, then shook his head as if surfacing from a dream. He backed away from her. "What power do you hold, mortal woman?" he demanded.

"Annette," she said. "My name is Annette, and I don't know much more about this than you do." Then she recalled what Emerald had said. "Perhaps it has something to do with Twilight's scrambled magnetic fields." She waved her hand in the air, and lightning struck again as thunder immediately boomed, making her jump. The storm had arrived.

Strangely, Aragon swung around to face the window with his sword raised. "Enough talk. Show me the way from this mortal dwelling to the forest." The heavens exploded with a loud rumble.

"You're going out there naked into that?"

"We must hurry," he said, then marched in the direction of her bedroom.

"Wrong way," she said, her voice squeaking high at the thought of him naked in there. "Come this way." She motioned for him to follow as she tightly clutched the towel. Had she seriously contemplated backing He-Man to the wall? She'd truly lost her mind. She led him from the cabin and pointed at the woods.

He nodded and grunted, then turned to look at her. He seemed about to say something, but then a bolt of lightning ripped across the sky and hit a tree directly across the yard from the porch. She gasped, backing into the cabin, feeling the hairs on her arms and neck stand stiffer than her knees were able to at that moment. Aragon swung around and ran into the forest, howling like . . . hell, she couldn't even think of anything that crazy.

The hottest buns north or south of any worldly or other-worldly Mason-Dixon line just happen to belong to a mad-man.

She slammed the door shut, shoved the deadbolt into place, then ran to the bathroom. Groping around in the tub, she found the amulet. Careful not to touch the disk, she picked it up by the chain and swung around, looking for the darkest place to hide the thing. Too bad she didn't have a garbage disposal.

Three steps down the hall, at the same place he'd tried to rescue her from the phone, she came to a halt and drew several deep breaths. He really didn't know what a phone was. She closed her eyes and tried to recall everything Erin had said about Jared.

Then Annette groaned as a swell of guilt knocked her flat. There'd been a number of things Jared hadn't known. It had to be the same for Aragon. How could she have been so insensitive, so stupid? And she'd let him go running naked into a thunderstorm.

Snatching a pair of sweats from her drawer, she pulled them on with a pair of sneakers and ran back. Always pre-pared for any emergency as a doctor should be, she grabbed the heavy-duty flashlight from the plug and unlocked the door.

"Aragon!" she yelled, but the whipping wind sucked away any sound. The rain had started, and the night still flashed with the fury of lightning and thunder. Biting her lip, she glanced up at the sky, and after only a moment's hesitation ran to the trees where Aragon had disappeared. Rain stung her head and face as it pelted down, but she pushed forward, worrying more and more about what could have happened to him with every step. "Aragon!" she called again, delving into the prickly branches of the thick pines. Here, amid the trees, the force of the wind eased and the rain sluiced down from the needles in rivulets, giving her some relief from the storm. Every way she turned, she saw only trees and brush and no sign of Aragon. He'd apparently moved on with his quest. Something the man looked more than capable of handling. Why in the world was she worried about him out in a storm? She had a quest of her own.

Deep within the heart of the spirit world, a whispered cry of disbelief echoed from realm to realm. For amid those who served Logos, it was unthinkable that a Shadowman so elite as to hold the title of Blood Hunter had abandoned his duty as a protector of Logos's Elan.

The act had brought about a special meeting of the Guardian Forces Council, one that Sven had been summoned to attend. Shoulders burdened with the heavy weight of the council's judgment, he shifted to where York and Navarre waited. Within one moon's cycle they'd lost both Jared and Aragon, leaving a gaping hole among their band and a wrenching sorrow in their spirits—a sorrow that was only going to deepen when Sven relayed to the others the council's decision.

As expected, York was pacing, his fiery countenance exuding a great power barely held in check. Navarre sat quietly, a rock-solid force no matter what battle was waged, even the unprecedented turmoil with Jared's poisoning and now Aragon's defection. No, Sven couldn't put so strong a word upon what Aragon had done. Aragon hadn't turned to evil, hadn't joined the Fallen. So defection was wrong, but Aragon had sought his own way rather than Logos's. Instead of seeking the wisdom of the Guardian Forces Council for direction, Aragon had punished himself, and now that punishment would have more severe consequences than anyone imagined.

The council refused to see Aragon's choice as the misguided action of a spirit in turmoil. By acting on his own and forsaking his post, Aragon had made a choice that could not be permitted. If others followed, then the structure, order, and integrity of the Guardian Forces and their shapeshifting Shadowmen would disintegrate.

Before Sven could speak to his brethren, York clenched his fist with a passionate cry, and Navarre bowed his head.

"What do they want us to do?" York demanded. "I see the despair in your spirit, Sven; your very soul is crying out in sorrow."

Sven sighed, letting his shoulders slump under the burden he'd stoically borne without a flinch before the council. "Aragon cannot be redeemed, nor will they allow his spirit to eternally hover between heaven and earth, as we all believed his fate would be. Should he cross the spirit barrier, he is to be captured and executed."

"Though no evil poisons his spirit? Why? How can they choose so harsh a punishment?" York's outraged cries matched those within Sven's own heart, but they were questions that as leader of the Blood Hunters he couldn't give voice to.

Navarre rose and set his hand upon York's shoulder. "It is as I feared. The council must act to preserve Logos's order. Even though he didn't mean to, by going against Logos's rule, Aragon set himself as a higher authority."

"So now we are to hunt our own and see him executed?" York had his back to him, but Sven didn't have to see York's expression to know how greatly he doubted the wisdom of the Guardian Council.

Sven didn't speak, for the burden of his answer was too great, and the glaring fact that Aragon had stood in almost this same place with Jared was too stark a truth to face.

"We've our duty to attend to," Navarre said into the dark silence, and shifted to make good his word. Sven followed, praying that York would find the strength to join them.

Aragon hit the trees skirting the mortal woman's dwelling, ready to shift into his spirit form. He ran, completely forgetting that he'd turned leadership of the Blood Hunters over to Sven. All he thought about was the call to battle in the heavens roaring in his spirit.

Though shadowed in a way they'd never been before to him even from the mortal realm, he could see the Guardian Forces fighting against Heldon's Army in the heavens, their weapons flashing fire, hitting the ground with fiery destruction. The swiftness of their attacks and counterattacks whipped the air into a frenzied whirl, doubling the force of the carnage raining down upon him.

That he'd forsaken his amulet, decreeing himself no longer worthy to serve, didn't enter his mind as he raised his sword and leapt, focused on shifting to his spirit form and joining the battle. Instead of fading into the air, he smacked into a thick tree and fell back to the ground, his sword embedded in the trunk. He lay stunned a second before rolling to his feet. *What in Logos's name had happened?*

Lifting his fist, he unclenched his fingers and stared at his hand. The sense that his mortal form was more solid than ever before washed over him again, and this time he couldn't blame it on the mortal woman and her magic. At least, he didn't think he could. Was more time or distance needed to fade the effects of her magic? His desire for her still rushed hotly through him. Though he knew of mortal desire, having read of it in *Logos's Lore of the Ages*—something all Shadowmen who work within the mortal realm had to study—as a spirit being, he'd never experienced such.

The effect of desire was as disorienting as hitting the tree and as binding as the physical world, and he chafed under its pull upon him. His instinctual dash to join the fight didn't make sense either. He'd left his duty behind to eliminate Pathos and needed to put his mind and body back on track with his quest. He snatched his sword from the trunk of the tree, smelling the pungent sap that seeped from the gaping hole, and realized that an entire world of scents and sensations was opening up to him. As a Blood Hunter, he'd only known the scents of Elan blood, those of other spirits, and the stench of evil. Now other scents rushed at him from every direction, the pines, the rich oaks, the decaying soil, and the purifying rain—the blood of the spirit warriors spilled in the battle raging above.

Yet none of the scents made as deep an impression upon him as that of the mortal woman. Even now he could smell her, could still feel the wonder and the heat of her soft flesh against him. The hunger she had aroused in him still pulsed so strongly that with every beat he had to fight the desire to turn back and explore the fire until he burned alive, which was likely why he'd been unable to shift into his spirit form. He needed to rid her from his mind and spirit before shifting again.

Glancing back at her dwelling a brief moment, he wondered about the voice that had frightened her. It still disturbed him. He'd heard every word the man had whispered, and it wasn't so much what the man had said, but what Aragon sensed it had done to the mortal woman.

A very deep pain lay hidden beneath her fiery warmth, and the man had made her pain worse.

Aragon took three steps back, drawn toward the woman, then swung away with his hands fisted. He couldn't allow himself to get involved in the mortal realm, or he'd lose his chance at Pathos. Time was running out. He shifted into his were-form and set his acute senses on detecting one thing—Pathos.

Chapter Four

"CALL YOU BACK." Sam hung up the phone, abruptly ending the call from his deputy, who had the Sno-Med Research Center under surveillance. The "all is well" report was great, but Sam couldn't talk longer. Hearing Nick Sinclair's voice was only making Sam's brewing situation worse. Nick sounded way too much like his father, and that brought back memories of the last time Sam had heard Reed Sinclair's voice. Belize.

Two hours until midnight. Eight until dawn. Son of a bitch. Before anyone could see how badly he shook, Sam clenched his fists and shoved his hands into the pockets of his sweats. He'd like to think that the shakes were due to too much caffeine, and the sweat breaking out over his clammy skin to a dysfunctional thermostat, but he knew better.

Heart pounding, he sucked in a deep breath and tried to stave off what he knew was coming.

Breathe. Find something to concentrate on.

The flashbacks always hit him at night, and were like unstoppable seizures. He was the one that needed to be locked up. Not Jared. Only Sam's cell needed white padded walls.

Panic attacks. Psychosomatic pain. What kind of pansy-assed shit was that?

At home he'd get on the treadmill and run full-out until it hit. It used to be half a mile before he was incapacitated;

now it was ten. Nothing stopped them, though. But here, having to watch the monitor showing Jared in a holding cell and Emerald and Erin parked in the chairs on the other side of his desk, flipping through magazines, he was trapped.

Why in the hell did they have to show up? Why in the hell didn't they just go home?

He should have expected something like this. Planned for it. Emerald had a knack for making his life difficult. She'd been trouble since the day she and her little girl had sailed into town, driving that pea-sized death trap she called a car. Little cars were fine when everyone else around had them, but on curvy mountain roads full of big-ass SUVs, pickup trucks, and logging semis, being the smallest thing out there was just asking for it.

He didn't give a crap what the Druids did or didn't predict—another thing about her that irritated him to no end. How could any sane human being live her life based on some mumbo-jumbo crap with visions and crystals and who the hell knew what else? The woman was nuts.

Glancing at her from beneath his lashes, he watched her flip through the pages of a magazine, occasionally slipping her tongue out just enough to lick her finger to separate the pages. Just enough to drive him wild.

Why her? Why after years of nothing, not even a glimmer of interest in sex, did she suddenly interest him? Was it because she was a sex therapist, and his subconscious was grabbing for help? Did he think he'd be like all of the other patients she helped with her little BlackBerry, thumbing out advice in their moments of desperation? Nobody must be getting any tonight. The blasted thing hadn't gone off since she and Erin arrived over an hour ago.

That had to be it, though. The only reason he had the

hots for her was because his subconscious wanted him to be normal again.

But you had it going for her before you even knew what she did for a living.

Hell, she didn't just interest him.

He wanted to kiss her so badly he couldn't even see straight whenever he looked at her.

He wanted more than a kiss. He wanted to get all over her, inside and out. Her pale, silver-blond hair was spiked into a just-made-love mess, begging for him to put that same look on her face.

At least Jared could pace. He rambled in his cell like a caged beast. Every now and then he'd pause, flex, and stretch his muscles as if something bothered him, but he wasn't busting out of his clothes or turning into a hairy, fanged beast. Maybe what happened at the Sacred Stones had purged him of the poison inside him.

Sam envied Jared. Nothing could get the poison out of him. Nothing could cure him. Luis Vasquez had scarred him for life in Belize. Inside and out.

Sam was still trying to wrap his mind around the fact that Vasquez was a vampire. He'd always known the man wasn't human, to do what he did to other human beings, but to hear that he wasn't even *Homo sapiens* had been unbelievable. When he'd seen the bastard's name on the list of men Erin had given transfusions to, men she was certain were part of a powerful group of supernaturals known as the Vladarian Order, he'd nearly had a flashback right there in front of everyone. Luckily, he'd made it out of Emerald's house and down a secluded dirt road before it hit him. It had been the first time he'd had an attack during the day.

The pain always started at the top of his spine and descended with paralyzing agony. He could already feel the burn begin. It would seem that hearing Vasquez's name and knowing Sam just might get a go at him after all had shot the hell out of his coping mechanisms.

He had to get the hell out of there and find somewhere to hide. Fast.

He stood. His knees were already shaking. Both Emerald and Erin looked up. "I'll be back. Why don't you two keep an eye on Jared for me?" He nodded at the monitor. "Whatever happens, don't go in there, and don't let anyone else either. I gave Jared my word on that. Okay?"

Emerald nodded. Erin only gulped in air. She didn't look too steady about the instructions. In fact, she looked as if she were about ready to bolt into the cell right now. Not good. Jared would be torqued if he knew they were here.

Sam narrowed his gaze at Erin. "He wouldn't be able to live with himself if he turned and hurt someone. You hearing me? You want to keep your man, you let him do this his way. Got it?"

"I got it," she said.

"Good." His voice already sounded like jagged glass, cutting his own ears. At the last second, Sam grabbed his coat off the hanger next to the door. He had to be prepared if this was going to be a rough one.

Thank God the hallway was empty. Ten feet down and to his left was the utility closet. He made it almost all the way before the first stab of pain ripped down his spine. His left leg buckled, and he went down hard on his right knee. The groan escaped before he could stifle it. Stuffing the sleeve of his coat in his mouth, he bit down on the soft material and grabbed for the doorknob of the closet just as another pain shot through him. His shoulder slammed the door open, and he fell inside. His body spasmed. Rolling, he managed to shut the door, closing himself into the darkness, before he lost the use of his legs.

The next pain had his back arching off the cold floor, slamming his head against the cement. His teeth clenched down tight on his coat, and a gut-pulling moan escaped. Son of a bitch. This was a bad one.

The door opened. Sam blinked at the brightness before he registered the fact that Emerald stood there.

"Holy bleedin' hell, Sam. What's wrong?"

He jerked his coat sleeve from his mouth. "GET. OUT," he managed to say before another spasm tore down his spine.

"Fook that," she said. She shut the door, bringing back the darkness, but he knew without a cringing doubt that she'd just shut herself in the closet with him. The feel of her palms on his cheek and on his chest confirmed it.

God. He couldn't handle this. But he couldn't stop it. He was no longer with Emerald in the closet. He could no longer feel the cold hard floor or smell the cleaners. He was in Belize, hanging upside down in a tree, naked. The soles of his bloody, swollen feet were being beaten with a hard stick. And that was just the preshow. Vasquez and his whip came next.

Annette pulled onto the shoulder of the road about fifty yards from the obscure utility entrance to Sno-Med's research center and drew several deep breaths. She'd removed her car tag and had replaced it with a Tag Lost and Applied For sign, making her about as anonymous as she could with so little time to plan.

Her hands shook, and her mouth was so dry she could barely swallow.

You can do this, she told herself . . . repeatedly. The world had turned black and miserable since the thunderstorm

Aragon had disappeared into. Dark clouds and drizzling rain had snuffed out the moon and stars, leaving an eerie fog chilling the mountain air.

Two hours had passed, yet she still felt the imprint of his hand against her chest. Still had the image of his body rising up out of the tub. Still sensed his power and his strength. And she could still see the question in his deep, dark eyes when he'd asked, "Why the need for untruths?"

Something in that look, something in his voice, got to her as much as his heated touch. She'd obviously jerked him from something very important, something he had been in a hurry to get back to, and yet he'd shown concern for her. And she'd treated him . . . badly. Had indeed lied to him.

But what was she supposed to say? The phone call tonight had been the first crack in the black void that had swallowed Stef. It could be a setup—it seemed way too coincidental that the fire at the center had been just yesterday, and now, after all this time, she'd heard from somebody. And if it was a setup, they sure wouldn't be expecting her two hours early and going in under the radar, so to speak. She prayed she could get into the center without anyone seeing her.

On the other hand, it was possible the fire had been a catalyst for the call . . . especially if Cinatas was dead. Annette's pulse sped as she realized that this could be a real lead at last.

Grabbing her backpack, Annette rechecked her stash of things she'd collected from her office in Twilight just a little while ago. She wore all black with her hair tucked into a black cap that she'd pulled close about her face. She'd collected everything she'd thought she needed, plus more. As the utilities at Sno-Med were shut down because of the fire, she'd brought the twenty-five-pound battery-powered generator she kept for medical emergencies. Besides the pepper spray she kept in her desk drawer, she had gathered a lighter, a spray can of disinfecting alcohol, and a scalpel. Around her neck, she wore a one-gig flash drive to store computer data on, and before she left, she'd dumped a detailed note into Emerald's mail slot. Their offices were next door to each other near the town of Twilight's main crossroads. In case something went wrong, Annette wanted to make sure she didn't just disappear without a trace, as Stef had.

She'd started out confident and determined, but now that she was out in the night all alone, she was having second thoughts. Breathing deep, she focused on her goal—finding Stef. Every surgeon was a risk taker—it took that to open up another human being and cut—but every *good* surgeon weighed the odds and chose the safest route possible. Had she done that?

She'd come early and armed. Somewhat.

If the building was as they had shown it on the television video clips, then the damage from the fire would probably make getting into the facility fairly easy. Firemen had hacked down doors and busted windows in their battle to access the blaze. According to reports, only the fourth floor and part of the third floor had suffered severe damage. And from what she remembered of the building's layout, the Infectious Disease Department was on the north end of the first floor.

No doubt there'd be a couple of guards. Or an army of them. She gulped in another breath, her palms growing damp beneath her black leather gloves. What then?

She could always wait on the edges of the forest and see who showed up at midnight. It was worth a try. Exiting the car, she slid on her backpack and made her way into the mist-shrouded woods, her cell phone clutched in her hand. Having the sheriff on speed dial was a precaution. Having

Aragon's warm amulet stuffed into her pocket was a reminder that . . . anything was possible. And with it, she wasn't quite so alone. It wasn't rational or logical, but it worked.

Fifteen minutes later, she sat against a tree and wondered what in the world she was going to do next. There wasn't one guard walking the perimeter of the center. Nor was there an army. There were four guards, each patrolling one side of the building, pacing up and down in the rain, looking miserable. If there had been one or two, she would have felt confident in trying to sneak in. If there had been an army, she would have immediately given up. But four . . . at that number, she had to try, but it was going to be hard.

She needed a good distraction.

When you need it fast, use Moe's To Go.

She slipped a little back into the thicker part of the trees and pulled out her cell phone. A quick 411 call got her the Arcadia number, and she punched it through.

"Moe's goes all the way to you! Whaddaya need?"

"Four large coffees and four steak sandwiches with fries. I need them delivered to the Sno-Med Center."

"Whoa. Didn't that place burn?"

"I've got a crew working late in cleanup. They're wet, tired, and hungry. How soon can you get it here?"

"Thirty minutes. Will that be cash or credit?"

"Cash. Get it here in twenty, and I'll give you an extra twenty. When you drive up, beep your horn six times, and I'll meet you out front."

"Okay, lady. What's your nam—"

Annette hung up the phone, then moved around the perimeter of the building to line herself up with the closest, easiest route inside, which happened to be in the back. After that, she waited and prayed the guards at least would go look at the honking delivery guy.

Twenty-one precious minutes later, the first horn blast had her perched in the shadows at the edge of the woods, watching the back guard run to the corner of the building to get a peek at what was happening out front. Two more horn blasts had the guard moving toward the front. Annette slipped from the trees and ran like hell, pulse roaring in her ears and lungs burning because she refused to gasp for air. She made it to the door, found it locked, and blinked against the dizzying wave of panic that gripped her. She ran along the building in the opposite direction the guard had taken and nearly fell to her knees with relief when she found a broken window.

Gripping the glass-riddled sill, she lumbered ungracefully inside, hitting her shoulder as she met up with a chair. She teetered off balance a second before she fell onto her back on the floor, arched over her backpack like a flipped turtle. She didn't think her heart had ever beat as fast and hard as it was beating now.

That, plus a giddy elation that she had actually gotten inside, had her feeling more alive than she'd felt in . . . *two hours and thirty-two minutes, when Aragon had his hands on her.*

Hell, honesty wasn't a girl's best friend. She rolled to her side and eased to her feet, keeping a close ear out for anything. The place was completely black, as she knew it would be. With the entire electric system shut down, there'd be no alarms to worry about. Only locked doors—something she'd forgotten to consider.

Dragging out her penlight, she quickly moved through the room and luckily found the door to the hallway open. Once the guards figured out that none of them or anyone they knew had placed the order, they would likely search the building. Hurrying, she saw that all the doors were open along the corridor, so she randomly shut some as she passed. She didn't want the room she planned to invade to be the only door shut if the guards came looking. She reached the department in less than five minutes, and leaned against the door once she closed herself inside. She was almost too afraid to move.

Surely the guards would investigate. She had to hurry. The room was undamaged and in complete order. So if there was information to be had about Stefanie as the caller suggested, then it should still be here.

Annette set her mind to surgical mode—the place where she shut everything else out but exactly what had to be done and how quickly she needed to do it.

There were five computers in the room, four at what appeared to be data-logging stations for lab techs and one at an official-looking desk in a glass-walled office on the left. Everything that could possibly be white was: floor, walls, counters, chairs, and ceilings. And from what she'd seen so far, the entire facility followed suit, as if it were one big padded room for the insane.

She set up the generator and connected the computer to that, successfully booting it up, only to stare at the screen asking for her password. She thought she heard a door close, and her heart doubled its beats, making her body break out in a cold sweat. *Breathe. Focus.*

Another noise had her switching the monitor off and ducking beneath the desk as she stretched her black shirttail over the tiny light denoting that the computer was on. Then she held her breath as the door opened and a light beam swept the room.

How could they fail to find her? Surely her fear alone had to be a shuddering beacon, waving madly through the airwaves. But the light disappeared, the door closed, and somehow she found the intelligence to breathe and move again, and to face her biggest hurdle yet.

She was an idiot! Of course the computer was password-protected. Everyone these days protected their files. But she couldn't give up now; she had to try. What had the caller said?

Meet me in the Infectious Disease Department at the Research Center at midnight. She's in the computer there under X files. Tell no one and come alone, or I won't show.

It was a long shot, but at the moment, she didn't have anything to lose. She typed "X-files" and was denied access, then typed "X files" and "files X," and then just an "X," with the same result. It was eleven fifteen. Sweat beaded her brow, but her mind stayed sharp. The man had laughed after his X-files comment, as if it were a private joke. People didn't do and say things without meaning. She tried "Fox" and "Mulder" and "David Duchovny" and its variations. Nothing. "Gillian Anderson"—"Dana Scully"—came next. She hit pay dirt with just "Scully."

The user's personal settings appeared on the screen, but she couldn't make heads or tails of the desktop icons, and she had little time to explore. She typed "X files" into the search window and pressed enter.

When X-files1, then 2, then 3, and on and on, popped into the window, she located a USB port and inserted the flash. By then the computer was at a hundred X-files and counting. It was now eleven thirty. Time to secure a position to observe who arrived at midnight to meet her.

Five minutes later, on the two-hundredth found file, she stopped the search, highlighted what she had, and copied them to the flash. She was out of time. Still, she refined the X-files search to include the keywords "Stefanie Batista," but nothing came up. Her stomach twisted with pain and disappointment.

Had this been nothing but a wild goose chase? A lure to get her out here and alone? Way out of time, Annette disconnected the flash and shut down the computer. She repacked everything except the drive, tucking it beneath her shirt, and the alcohol canister, which she slipped into an outside pocket on the backpack. The lighter went into her jeans pocket, and her scalpel into her gloved hand.

She searched about the desk and inside its drawers, looking for anything to identify the operator of the computer, but came up with zilch. No business cards, pictures, name tags, cartoons, nothing personal. But as she stood up from the chair, she realized that a lab coat hung over the back of it, with a name tag. Dr. Steven Bryers.

At eleven forty she slipped from the room, automatically heading for the room directly across the corridor. She changed her mind at the last second and dashed down the hall to the ladies' restroom. She had a glimpse of white marbled walls and floors, white paint, and a row of white-frosted windows lining the outside wall before she snuffed out her light. Moving to a window, she unlatched one, making sure it would pop open with a touch, then wedged a handful of paper towels in the door to keep it open enough for her to see down the hall.

With the Infectious Disease Department in her sights, she sat down to wait, feeling like she'd just completed a successful operation. Any second Mr. X, possibly Dr. Steven Bryers, would make an appearance. She'd identify him, then make her escape.

The muffled sound of booted feet upon the carpeted hall had her anticipations high until she discerned more than one person coming her way. And they were making no attempt to be quiet either. Had the guards returned?

"Nyros, I am putting you in charge of this facility. Until I find Cinatas, no one is to have access to this building. No matter what mortal authority attempts to enter, you stop them by whatever means you find necessary. Just make sure those means aren't traceable."

"I understand."

"That order includes all members of the Vladarian Order as well, except for me, of course. Is your team prepared to enforce that?"

"With pleasure, Pathos."

"Then we understand each other. Since one of them was with my offspring when this happened, I want the facts before anything can be altered. In the morning, I will have trucks waiting at the tunnel's entrance. Any and all sources of data are to be loaded onto the trucks. With all the blood and laboratory samples already airlifted to Corazon de Rojo, by noon tomorrow this facility should be a shell, empty of anything but equipment."

Damn! She was going to chew Sam out. The blood samples were already gone! And tomorrow the computers would be too! Some surveillance.

The men came into view, and Annette pinched herself to assure she wasn't having a weird nightmare. A reddish aura surrounded the smaller of the two men. His features had a macabre edge to them that made them inhuman in appearance, completely unlike the large man who strode at his side. Wearing a black leather coat, black pants, and black shirt à la *The Matrix,* that man exuded a power that radiated brighter than the other man's glow, even though he stood in shadow. All that Annette could make out was an impressive physique and what she thought might be long blond hair.

"I will see that it is done," the glowing man said. The larger man turned and paused, bending toward the red light and revealing the most beautiful male face she'd ever seen. Perfectly sculpted, perfectly set features, perfectly—? She shook her head. How could she know that when she could hardly see him?

"The red demon faction is proving to be very valuable, Nyros. Don't give me cause to—" The larger man fell silent and sniffed the air.

Before Annette could even blink, he moved like a blur down the corridor and flung the restroom door open. She fell back against the tiled wall with a scream that didn't even have a chance to echo before he hauled her to her feet and pinned her to the cold marble with an iron hand clamped against her throat.

Chapter Five

WHAT WAS WRONG with him?

He felt out of control.

He'd thrown his sword away.

He wanted to taste blood, smell its salty sweetness as he ripped into flesh with his fangs.

Aragon swung around, slashing at the night air with his claws, howling at the moon in frustration at what it was doing to his were-form. Too many scents were bombarding him. Too many thoughts and sensations were intruding into his mind, stealing his focus from his prey, turning his Blood Hunter abilities into nothing more than animal cravings that were hard to fight. Yet still he battled with himself, determined to overcome this new hurdle, determined to find Pathos. No matter what.

The battle that had waged overhead with the Guardian Forces and Heldon's Fallen Army had charged on to a different part of the heavens, giving the moon free rein to exert its full power upon the mortal ground. With its strengthening had come this change within him and his were-being—change that had never occurred before.

At first he couldn't keep his mind on Pathos because of the mortal woman. He kept thinking about her, the man who'd upset her, and the pain she'd tried to hide from him. He wasn't sure if it was that pain, the seductiveness of her scent, or the sweet, alluring glow of her soft skin that had urged him to touch her. But he hadn't been able to stop himself. And once he touched her and felt the vibrant warmth of her softness, he'd become lost within the desires she evoked, almost driven to delve into the fire erupting between them.

If the battle hadn't suddenly raged overhead, he'd likely still be there touching her, giving way to the mortal desire she'd brought to life.

Though he'd gained time and distance from her magic, he'd lost more of himself instead of recovering the balance in his spirit, as if she'd taken a part of him and kept it. Then the longer he ran beneath the moon's brightening light, the stronger other primal, almost overwhelming desires pulsed through him as well, things he'd never felt before.

He didn't want to track down Pathos or follow through with any quest. He wanted to run wilder than the wind, until the blood pulsing within him drowned out anything but the urge to satisfy his growing wants and burgeoning needs. He could smell the hot, juicy blood of the creatures that ran scurrying from his path. He wanted to grasp them with his claws and tear into their warm flesh with his teeth so strongly that he tossed aside his sword, ready to attack with his bare hands. He could taste their fear and relished in the power that—

By all that is Logos's Will! What was happening to him? He clenched his fists in frustration, forcing himself to focus on Pathos, what Pathos had done, and why Pathos needed to be eliminated.

Frightened from its hiding place, a fawn leapt across Aragon's path, and the raw desire to sink his fangs into hot blood and taste the flow of life over his tongue coursed through him. He raced toward it even as his howl of self disgust reverberated with bone-chilling depth through the dark of the night.

The gloved hand splayed menacingly around Annette's throat held an unforgettable icy chill.

"Nyros, shed a little light on this situation," her captor said to his companion, sounding unpleasantly amused.

The smaller creature obliged by shifting his aura from red to a dull yellow-white, lighting the area as a dim bulb would. Her captor's hair wasn't blond, but a rich silver that contrasted startlingly with his deep tan. He smiled slowly, coldly, striking more fear into her heart with that one gesture than with the hand that pressed slightly harder against her trachea. His eyes, an arctic blue, pierced her.

"Why are you here?" His tone of voice clearly said she'd die if she lied.

"My sister." Annette gasped. "She's missing. I must find her." She'd lost the scalpel when she fell, but she doubted it would have done any good against his deadly force.

He pressed her throat harder. "Why are you here now, at this time of night?"

A dizzying buzz rang in her ears, and her vision dimmed. She needed more air. She slid her hand into her pocket, searching for her lighter, anything to help. "A man . . . called . . . meet him . . . here . . . midnight . . . he didn't say who . . . he was . . ."

Her fingers touched the amulet, and she pressed it against her palm. Her heart pounded with fear, and her mind immediately recalled Aragon, his power, his strength, and his touch. She wished she was back, in her cabin with—

A primal scream shattered the night as a black, hairy, wolflike man appeared in the restroom, rushing at her and her captor. It was the beast she'd seen before. The were-wolf . . . the other part of . . . Aragon.

Releasing her throat, the silver-haired man swung around and thrust himself at the black wolf with a chilling cry. The window glass rattled with the force if it.

In midair, right before her eyes, her captor turned into a wolflike creature, grotesquely different from Aragon's form, but similar in its upright movement and deadly presence. An elongated snout housed this other wolf's fangs, and a thick tail burst through his pants and flicked like a whip. Aragon had neither snout nor tail. The other werewolf's leather coat and shirt hung by shreds from its body. Its hair was dull and patchy, nothing like the sleek gleaming black of Aragon's coat.

The werewolves plowed into each other with bone-crunching force, knocking each other off their feet. Though the other wolf was taller, maybe seven feet to Aragon's six and a half, Aragon was broader, more muscular, and more agile.

They circled each other, fangs bared.

"Pathos, at last," the black werewolf said with disgust. His voice rang deadlier and colder than before, but was un-mistakably Aragon's.

The gray wolf shifted its immense head questioningly, then smiled, if one could call the stretching of his fleshy snout to expose more of his fangs a smile. "Aragon, my son. You've changed over a millennium. Did a Tsara bring you to the mortal realm to join my party?"

"No, I've not been poisoned. Even if I had been, I'd kill myself before I became what you are. You coward. Don't call me son again. Ever. I renounce you as my mentor. You're a bane upon the honor of all Blood Hunters and an abomi-nation to all Shadowmen. I am here for one purpose: your execution, Pathos."

The gray wolf, Pathos, cocked his head with interest. "So Logos is desperate now? He's turning to assassinations to win his war?" He jerked off the shreds of his leather coat and shirt, tossing them aside, revealing more of his dull, patchy pelt. It looked sickly beside Aragon's pantherlike sheen.

"No," Aragon said, broadening his stance. "I alone chose this path. I left the Guardian Forces to see you to your end."

Pathos gave a humorless snort. "My elimination? Was such a foolhardy goal worth your eternity, Aragon? You surprise me. I thought I trained you better than that."

"I will restore the honor of the Blood Hunters or die."

"Hell," Annette muttered. What had she landed in the middle of? Aragon was either going to win or die right here. And there wasn't anything she could do about it. She let go of the amulet and dug for her lighter.

"So be it. You've sacrificed yourself for nothing." He suddenly launched himself at Aragon, claws slashing.

Using his bulk to his advantage, Aragon dove low in response, knocking Pathos's feet out from under him. Pathos managed to rake a claw across Aragon's chest as he went down. Aragon arched, grunting with pain. Pathos rolled to his feet.

Annette winced, squeezing the lighter against her palm. She didn't see what happened next because Glow Man grabbed her arm, dragging her attention his way. Up close, his features became even more inhuman. His soulless eyes were desolate, devoid of any compassion or human feeling. Where he held her, an icy burn rushed painfully up her arm, and she tried to jerk free. Reaching behind with her other hand, she wrenched the disinfectant spray from the side pocket of her backpack. The man needed warming up, and the alcohol-based spray would help.

He smiled at her. "Let's go. Tonight I'm your chill pill,

baby. By the time I finish with you, you'll be begging for more, and Pathos will join us then."

"I don't think so," she said. Flicking the lighter on, she brought the can up and sprayed it in his direction through the flame. A fireball shot at Glow Man's face, and he backed away, screaming as if she'd fired a machine gun. Another blast, aimed lower, caught his suit coat on fire.

Turning, she found Aragon and Pathos at each other's throats, locked in a death grip. It was a battle of strength to see whose fangs were going to rip into the other's carotid first. Pathos was closer to Aragon's. She rushed forward with her makeshift torch, sending out a blast of fire before her, praying that the flames wouldn't eat a trail back to her and blow the can up in her face. Her third blast hit Pathos in the back, and he flinched, but didn't let go of Aragon.

"No!" Aragon yelled, but she didn't stop. She pressed the spray button harder. The fireball, larger than before, singed Pathos's long mane of silver hair to a frizz, emitting a rank smoke.

Wrenching from Aragon, roaring with an icy rage, Pathos came at her unafraid of the fire she wielded, and Annette realized her mistake too late. She'd taken the situation from fifty-fifty odds that she and Aragon would live and turned it into a sure thing that she was about to die. She turned to run, but had nowhere to go. Four walls hemmed her in, and Glow Man was still smoking at the door.

Pathos's claw made excruciating contact with her back. She screamed, turning sideways to escape him and the pain. The alcohol slipped from her grip. Out of the corner of her eye, she saw Aragon knock Pathos aside. One second she was on her feet, the next she was caught up in the arms of the black wolf-man. Aragon's arms. Strong arms. Warm arms. Hairy arms. Hairy everything. With fangs and claws and like Wolverine on *X-Men* . . . Oh, God, she felt faint.

He leapt toward the windows, clearly planning on smashing through the beveled glass.

Annette saw the glass coming right at her and cringed into Aragon's shoulder, but he twisted in midair. His back hit the window, shattering it. Glass rained down for a second, then the damp night air blasted her face.

Unbelievably, not only had he protected her from the glass, but he'd managed to land on his feet and didn't even pause before he pumped into a sprint that should have broken the sound barrier. In fact, she thought he had when she first heard a crack, but the shouts from the guards and several following pops made her realize they were being shot at through the swirling mists and drizzling rain.

As he reached the edge of the woods, Aragon grunted and seemed to stumble, then lurched into the cover of the forest, where the rain slowed to a damp mist beneath the shelter of the leaves.

"Let me run now," she said.

"No. I must . . . danger—" His voice, more guttural than earlier, rumbled through her, touching her inside. He pulled her tighter into his arms and ran harder, cutting to the left then right. He ran upright, his movements so aggressively fast and animal-like that there was no mistaking his feral nature, but there was also a cunning intelligence driving him. She had no doubt he would be the most deadly predator any man or beast could ever face.

Yet she sensed amid his feral countenance a protectiveness toward her that would see her safe at all costs. And she was afraid it was costing him as he ran farther, determined to carry the burden of her weight. His breathing became labored, and the pound of his heart against her right shoulder made her hurt to do something to help.

"Please," she whispered to him, squashing her trepidation enough to touch his hair-covered cheek. "Let me run. Let me help."

He paused a moment, as if her touch confused him, surprised him. Then he shook his head and rushed forward. Only his apparent will was greater than his waning strength. Minutes later, he stumbled and fell to his knees.

"Let me help," she said, pushing from his arms. He released her. She rolled to her feet and faced him. Her back burned from where she'd been clawed, but the rest of her instantly felt the loss of his heat in the chilled mountain air, making her want to burrow back against his warmth. She stiffened her shoulders instead and tried to take stock of where they were.

Aragon had moved so fast through the forest that her head was still spinning. His speed had carried them a good distance from the guards and whatever beings Glow Man and Pathos were, but they still had to hurry. She had no doubt that if Pathos was in pursuit of them, he'd be on them in minutes.

The deep woods surrounded them, and a misty rain continued to fall. She listened hard for sounds of pursuit, but could hear nothing beyond the rasp of their breathing and the pound of her own heartbeat in her ears. Even the night creatures seemed to be holding their breaths.

Aragon had landed in a patch of moonlight, his body shuddering as if racked by pain. She started to step toward him, but he flung his arms out, stretching them toward the sky as he looked up at the heavens. His body strained and trembled as if suffering greatly. "Must get out of the moonlight," he cried, thrusting himself into the deep shadows of a large pine tree.

"Aragon?" Annette moved closer to him. "What is it? Are you hurt?" She reached for him.

"No!" he shouted. "Stay away. Must change before I harm you."

He was so strong, so deadly, that she had no doubt he could kill her in an instant. And he hadn't harmed her. "You saved me," she said. "Now, let me help." In the brief second it took for her hand to connect to his hairy shoulder, he changed form, becoming a man with smooth skin and muscles that tightened and quivered beneath her fingers. The shift was so sudden that she almost pulled away from him, shocked. But the temperature of his skin registered, and the doctor in her took over. His skin burned hot and deep and bleeding slash marks gouged his chest, a condition that carrying her had to have aggravated.

"You're hurt, fevered," she said softly. He didn't seem to hear her. He kept his gaze fixed upon the night sky and breathed heavily as if he couldn't get enough air into his lungs.

"What is this weakness that I cannot fight? What are these hungers that drive me to do things no Blood Hunter would ever think of doing? If my fate is that of a faded warrior, then why do I gain substance?" He shouted his questions at the heavens in an angry rush.

When nothing happened, no answering sound or even rustling breeze, he grabbed her hand, urging her closer, his face a dark shadow, his voice ragged. "How do you call me to you at your whim? What magic do you cast, mortal woman? And what is your connection to Pathos? Why were you with him?"

She had a lot of sympathy for him, but she didn't like feeling his anger. Nor did she like the accusation in his tone.

She pulled her hand free and spoke just as emphatically as he had. "My name is Annette, not 'mortal woman.' There's no magic. I wasn't 'with' Pathos. He just appeared, and I don't know from where. Now you're hurt and need help. So sit still and let me take a look at your injuries," she told him, standing to listen for signs or sounds of someone following. The shouting she and Aragon had done would have been a beacon to anyone after them.

"There's no need," he said harshly. "We must talk. What does Pathos have to do with—"

"I'm not saying another word about it until I see if you're all right," she said firmly. When it came to medical attention, men were the worst at accepting the need. Her back ached sharply from the scrape, and his chest wound appeared worse than hers, so he had to be in pain. "I promise that I'll be careful. You can trust me."

He set his palm against her cheek and looked deep into her eyes, and that connection she'd felt before came roaring back, barreling through her isolation and pain. It almost seemed as if he had the ability to get inside her somehow.

Don't be ridiculous. Don't go looking for excuses for your libido.

"Do what you must, but hurry," he said softly. "I must know of Pathos."

See. He can't read your mind. Otherwise, he'd know there was nothing about Pathos to tell.

Shaking off her thoughts, she set to work. When she touched his shoulder to angle him toward the light, she felt warm, wet fluid on her hand. Moving around him, she cried out at the amount of blood covering his back. She grabbed her flashlight, training the beam on his injuries, wincing at the chunks of glass embedded in his back. Then she saw ripped flesh and a dark hole in his shoulder. A constant flow of blood streamed from the injury.

"Dear heaven. You've been shot. And you carried me while hurt like this?" Her chest squeezed tight.

She had to get him to her car fast before any of the goons they left behind found them, and especially before he became too weak to walk. First she had to stop some of his blood loss.

"Hold still." Yanking off her backpack, she propped the flashlight on the ground so that she could see in the shadows. He seemed to want to avoid the moonlight, as if it had a bad effect on him. She removed her cotton and lace bra under her shirt and doubled the cotton cups into a thick pad that she tied together. Then she pressed the bandage against his bullet wound and wrapped the elastic around his broad torso, unhooking the bra's straps to be able to stretch around him enough to create a pressure bandage.

Every breath he took, every look he gave her as she worked, seemed to ratchet the tension he created in her higher and higher. She'd never been as aware of a man as she was of him, and his intent scrutiny of her as she worked wasn't helping matters at all. When he focused on her hands, they went numb and she'd fumble. When he looked at her mouth, her lips would tingle and her breath would catch. And God help her, when her bra-less breasts accidentally brushed his arm, she burned right to her center, feeling as if she were back in the hallway of her cabin with his hand exploring her skin about the towel and her libido ready to back him to the wall. He completely unhinged her professional detachment and left her open, vulnerable, and wanting.

His sin-dark eyes, shadowed stubble, and angled features made for a deadly combination, a primal mixture of roughness and wildness that lured her closer to him. Made her want things—not just the sensual either; she wanted that connection he made her feel when he looked so deeply into her eyes.

"Come on." She urged him up. "My car's on the highway, which should be south of here. Once we're safe, I'll tend your wounds, and then we'll talk. You can tell me about Pathos and what connection he might have to my missing sister." Just to be sure she still had the computer data, she pressed her hand against the flash drive nestled between her breasts under her shirt.

Aragon stood, seeming stronger than she expected he would be under the circumstances. Now that she had him up, she had to collect her bearings. She'd parked her car west of the Sno-Med Center. They'd exited the building from the east and had cut to the left once under the cover of the bushes. He'd run in a straight line, so she guesstimated that if they were to cut to the left again, they'd go south and arrive at the road where she'd left her car. How far they were from it she didn't know, but once she got him to the road, then she could go after the car.

"My car should be this way," she said, turning away from him and moving ahead. She wished the drizzle would stop. Maybe she wouldn't be so chilled and in turn so hungry for the feel of Aragon's warmth against her. She reached into her pocket to feel the amulet with her fingertips. She should tell him about the amulet, but if she did and he took it back, would she ever see him again?

Aragon stared at the mortal woman's back a moment, his head swimming from the inundation of sensations that had been flooding through him. He'd felt such a primal hunger when he was carrying her that he feared if he stopped running, he'd devour her. It was a different kind of hunger than what had driven him in the forest before she pulled him to her, but it still had been so sharp that his wavering control on his were-form had nearly crumbled. The scents of the forest had been overpowered by the smell of gardenias and her blood. He drew a deep breath, smelling more of the gardenia now, but still feeling an almost overwhelming need.

He didn't know what to do with it either. It was as if he wanted to consume her essence within him, make her a part of him.

Pathos had caused her injury, yet she'd only seen to his hurt. The fact didn't sit well with him, nor the fact that she had taken on Pathos even though he'd warned her away. She'd barreled ahead without the slightest clue as to what she'd cost him and almost lost herself. His quest had been in his grip, and she'd snatched it away.

But once Pathos had turned on her, Aragon had had no other choice but to abandon his quest and save her.

She was right. They had to leave the area. Had to leave Pathos behind, rather than retrace his steps and finish the one thing that would restore honor for him and for his brethren. For now he had to stay with the mortal woman until he learned how she was able to summon him to her side and why Pathos had been with her. Even then, he might not be able to leave. She'd garnered Pathos's wrath, and would need a Blood Hunter's protection.

If he'd had his full strength about him, he'd just pick her up and carry her to wherever *he* decided, and they would talk until *he* was content with the answers. As it was, this unaccustomed weakness of his body and the fact that his wounds continued to drain life and energy from him urged him to follow her lead.

That, plus the change she seemed to effect within him. Her nearness diminished the feral state the moon had been pulling from him. And he had no wish to return to that near-mindlessness. He'd been so consumed with the primal lust for blood that he'd forgotten Pathos and tossed away his sword in favor of the hunt. A warrior never left his weapon behind. That he had showed him just how broken a leader he truly was. He'd have to retrieve his sword in the light of the sun. For now he'd stay within the realm of her influence.

She was a puzzle—soft and vulnerable, yet firm in her determination to stand alone amid the pain and trouble he sensed she was in. She'd also been resolute in her desire to minister to him, but this repeated delay to the questions he wanted answered would not work. First she'd put him off until she saw to his injuries. Now she wanted to wait until they were someplace else, and she'd tended his wound, after which point it was supposed to be he who answered questions.

Crossing his arms despite the biting pain in his back, he waited. He could hear the guards approaching. Their muttered curses and heavy breathing let Aragon know they were getting closer. Since Pathos hadn't overtaken them yet, that meant he wasn't following now. Years of training under Pathos had taught him that the were-being would wait, giving his prey plenty of time to sweat before death. After about ten steps, she realized he hadn't moved. She turned, nearly blinding him with the light she carried. "What's wrong?"

"You."

"Me? Whatever it is can wait. You're bleeding. You've got a bullet in your shoulder that needs to come out, and you need stitches. If you pass out from blood loss before we get to my car, I'm not going to be able to carry you. I took an oath to save your alpha rear, and it's going to kill me if something goes wrong."

He moved toward her. The closer he got, the more he liked being within the radius of her body heat, within the saturating range of her scent. It made him hungrier, but it soothed him in some way, too. Though he hadn't planned to get so close, he couldn't seem to stop himself until the warmth and softness of her body brushed his. Her eyes widened, her mouth parted as her breath hissed from her, but she stood her ground. Her dark hair was hidden beneath a cap. Water had spiked her lashes and dripped from the edge of her jaw.

He slid his fingers along her cheek as he had before, wanting to know if the feel of her now was just as potent as it had been before. It wasn't. It was even stronger. His pulse sped, and the fire inside him grew hotter. By Logos, how did she have such power over him? He wanted to heal her wound as well, and tried to send his energy into her, but either he was too weak at the moment from his own blood loss or her mind was too closed off from him, because he couldn't get past the stiff barrier she seemed to hold against the world and everyone in it.

He shook his head. They were out of time and needed to move on. For some reason the guards were now running. Maybe they'd seen the glow of her light.

"Turn off your light quickly," he said.

She did. "What is it? What's wrong?" she whispered.

"There are two guards after us, and they are approaching from the direction you were going." He took her hand in his and moved to the left, thinking that she was a lot like him. "You know, if you always charge ahead, then you will often walk alone and into trouble."

Sam writhed under the memory clawing through his mind. The whip landed, slashing pain down his back, across his chest, and over his thighs. The panic inside him grew with every lash, because he knew what was coming next. He tasted his blood and sweat. He felt the jungle heat and smelled the stench of dirt and death. He heard Vasquez's amused laughter, and his heart pounded to the bursting point, knowing where the whip would land next. The lash cut into his groin, into his genitals, just enough to make him scream and jerk wildly at the end of the rope. Again and again the agony came—

"Sam! Stop! You canna do this!"

Cold water hit his face, going up his nose and shocking him. He choked and sat up, gasping for air. He was back in the utility closet. The light was now on, and Emerald was standing next to him with a metal bucket in her hand. She looked horrified and in agony, too. At least he hadn't hurt her in his delirium.

"Sam," she said, dropping the bucket and falling to her knees beside him. Her voice and eyes were full of pity as she reached for him.

He cringed. Dear God! What had he said? He must have communicated what had happened to him in some way, because she looked as if she knew.

"Get out," he gasped. He jerked away from her. "Don't touch me, ever."

"Sam. You canna push me away. What happened to you—"

"Is my business. Now get the hell away from me." He rolled to his feet. Every muscle he had ached. Water dripped down his sweat-drenched clothes, and his pulse was still racing out of control. Oh, God. She did know. He couldn't take her pity.

She stood up. "I canna leave you—"

Her BlackBerry chimed.

"You're not wanted. Period. Now leave and go answer your damn slave masters."

"At least they're smart enough to accept help and aren't prisoners of their problems," she said opening the door.

"Doona think that this is over, Sam, because it isn't." She slammed the door, and he ran his hands through his hair, pulling so hard on the ends that his scalp hurt.

It *was* over. And he was damn glad he'd never really started with her.

Coward, his mind shouted.

He couldn't go back to his desk and sit in the same room as Emerald. He had a change of clothes in the car, and he headed that way. He'd grab a three-minute shower and then figure out what to do. But no amount of bravado or soap and water washed away his cowardice.

Vasquez's tortures rarely killed a man, just made him want death more than anything else. Sam had prayed for death, especially after the others had died. One by one Vasquez had tortured them beyond their ability to survive. Not that Vasquez had killed them. They'd killed themselves. But Sam hadn't been able to do it.

The road couldn't be much farther, Annette thought. As soon as she saw her BMW, she was going to kiss its tailpipe. She was wet, chilled, miserable, and dog tired. The journey through the foggy woods had worn her to a thread. Pathos's scrape down her back burned, and they'd been walking seemingly forever, twisting in and out through the trees, stepping over downed logs, moving more silently than she thought possible. He'd told her to follow his every step, and she'd done that, all the while keeping close tabs on the flash drive hanging around her neck, worrying about the guards after them, about Aragon's injuries. She felt as if she would explode at any second.

"We can talk now," Aragon said. "The guards have headed off in the wrong direction."

"How do you know that?" she whispered. "And how do you know there are only two of them?"

"I can hear anything that moves or breathes for a good distance. And depending exactly how close they are, I can smell them as well. That helps in discerning who I'm hearing."

"Oh," she said, wincing at how inane her response sounded, but her mind was trying to grasp all the implications of what he said. She already knew he could see in the dark.

"What oath and to whom?" he demanded suddenly, as if he too were sitting on the edge of an explosion. "I must know the source of this magic that gives you control of my being."

"What?" she said, stumbling on one of the roots riddling the forest floor.

He caught her arm and drew her closer to his side as he brought them to a pause. The heated firmness of his grip made her tingle from her toes up, erasing the discomfort of the rain. "You said you'd taken an oath in regard to me. To whom?"

She shook her head, wondering what in the world he could possibly be talking about. "I don't—"

"To save me," he clarified.

"You're talking about the Hippocratic oath." She smiled. "I'm sorry. I didn't mean to confuse you. Upon graduating, all doctors take an oath to preserve the sanctity of life, alleviate suffering, and follow a moral and ethical code in the practice of medicine. So it wasn't an oath I took specific to you, but one that states what I will do to help everyone."

"Like a warrior," he said after a long moment. "All warriors take an oath to protect that which they must."

She bit her lip, deciding to plunge ahead into what she'd heard him say to Pathos. "But that's not why you are here?"

"No. I'm here for a different reason."

"To kill Pathos?"

"Yes." He set his hands on her shoulders, urging her to meet his gaze. "What is he to you? How do you know him? Why were you with him?"

"I told you before, I—"

He suddenly pressed his fingers to her lips and shook his head, telling her to be quiet. Then he turned, thrusting her behind him. Her unbound breasts made contact with heated muscle, instantly flaring her senses into alert. Never in her life had her breasts been so sensitive, so aching for touch. She almost pressed harder against his back rather than pulling back.

Was there someone close by?

After a moment, he turned to her and mimed for her to stay put, then disappeared into the night. She didn't like it. If anything, he should be waiting while she searched the area. He was the one who'd been shot. He was the one bleeding.

The sound of a painful grunt followed by several thuds were more than she could ignore, and she hurried through the woods at a run. She burst from the cover of the bushes to find herself at the side of the road. Her car sat there in the mists, and she could hear the sound of Sam's voice. "Nick? Give me a damn answer now, or I'm calling out the troops."

Heart thudding with dread, Annette ran to where Aragon stood over a body on the ground. It was Nick Sinclair, one of Twilight's deputies—she considered him the best of the lot. He did double duty for the county by flying the LifeFlight helicopter when needed. He'd saved one of her patients by getting the elderly man to the hospital in time.

"Oh, God! Did you kill him?" She rushed over, picking up the cell phone lying next to Nick on the ground with one hand as she checked Nick's pulse with the other.

"Sam!" she said into the receiver as the blessed beat of Nick's heartbeat rushed across her fingertips.

The pregnant pause gave way to a string of blistering curses that ended in, "Put Nick on now, Annette! You're under arrest."

"For what?"

"Reckless conduct and endangering others. What in the hell are you doing there?"

"What did you do to him?" she asked Aragon, craning her neck back to see his face, but the deep shadows of the night made it impossible.

"He but sleeps for a time," Aragon said. "Do you know this man?"

"Yes, he's one of the good guys. Or at least I think he is." What was he doing here, near her car at Sno-Med at this time of the night? Surely he wasn't her Mr. X.

"Where's Nick, Annette?" the sheriff demanded very loudly.

"He's busy," Annette shouted back. This was all she needed now. She had an injured werewolf at her side, not to mention a pissed-off one after her ass, along with his "glowing fiend." Now she'd added an unconscious deputy and an irate sheriff with his badge in a wad. "Everything is fine. We'll call you when we get to the clinic," she told him, and calmly hung up. It started to rain, hard.

The night just could not get any worse. Could it?

Chapter Six

W ORSE CAME IN the form of Deputy Nick Sinclair waking up a few minutes after they'd handcuffed him to the door in the back seat of her car. She'd had no choice but to assure he couldn't do anything to harm Aragon, and she didn't have time for any complications Nick might cause. She needed to get to the clinic to tend to Aragon's bullet wound. His injury wasn't life-threatening, but any wound that bled so much wasn't good.

Sam kept calling Nick's cell phone. It was in the car somewhere—she'd tossed it in before they'd cuffed Nick inside. At least it was set to its lowest ring.

"By Logos! What is that constant noise?" Aragon asked, covering his ears.

Nick gave Aragon his uncensored version of what it was.

"It's Nick's cell phone, and it's probably Sam calling. If you can find it, we can turn it off," she told Aragon. He must have very sensitive hearing.

"It comes from here." Aragon reached down between the seats and pulled up the cell. He looked at it as if it were the creature from the Black Lagoon. "What do the lit numbers mean?"

"What are they?" Annette asked. "That's Sam's number," she told Aragon after he read the number off to her. "He is

Twilight's sheriff. Nick's boss. If you want to talk to him, you call that number, and he will answer."

"Do all mortals have a number that you can speak to them at?"

"Yes, usually." She explained to Aragon how the phone worked and how he could turn it off. He listened intently and shut the phone down.

Nick asked very colorfully if Aragon was for real.

The deputy was her biggest problem at the moment. His choice of expletives was fast changing her good-guy opinion of him. Not that she could blame him that much, given that she'd just more or less kidnapped him with the help of a huge, naked stranger. The man probably didn't believe that they were heading to the clinic and that Sam would meet them there.

"What does that mean?" Aragon finally demanded when Nick said the word several times in succession just to blow off more steam. "It is not a word I remember from my studies of mortal language."

Nick laughed. "Good try, but I'm not buying your ET crap."

"ET what?" Aragon asked.

"Crap!" Nick shouted.

"If you don't shut up, Nick," Annette said, "I'm going to have him shut you up, and you'll be out even longer than before."

Aragon asked what the expletive meant again. Every second of her explanation, Annette kept telling herself that this wasn't happening. She was *not* explaining an overused euphemism for sex to a werewolf from another dimension. Surely she'd fallen asleep in the hot bath she'd made for herself hours ago, and this whole thing was a nightmare.

Nick expounded upon her definitions as only a guy could, making it all too real.

"So it's a word used to describe mortal mating," Aragon said after a moment. He then gave Nick a puzzled look. "How does a phone or a car or handcuffs mate as mortals do?" Aragon said, listing some of the things Nick had used the euphemism for sex with.

"What loony bin did you dig him out of?" Nick asked, rattling the handcuffs again. "Listen. If this has anything to do with me and your sister, you have to believe me, it was just one date. No big deal."

Annette slammed on her brakes in the middle of the street, throwing everyone forward. Luckily the rural road running between Twilight and Arcadia was deserted at one in the morning, and nobody plowed into her rear. Nick had been out with her sister?

In his early to mid-twenties, with dark brown hair and gray eyes, Nick had enough good looks and sex appeal to have tumbled in more than his share of haystacks. But he was so totally not the type of guy her sister went for. Why hadn't anyone mentioned this to her before? Why hadn't *he* mentioned this to her before? He'd had plenty of opportunity. She had a flash of all those detective shows where the date had killed the girl.

"What did you say?" She turned to look at Nick with an eagle eye, thinking that if the SOB had had anything to do with Stef's disappearance, she'd become a werewolf herself just so she could torture him.

"Hell," he said, sinking back into the seat with a puzzled frown. "That isn't what this is about?"

"You'd better start talking, or this will damn well *become* what this is about, deputy," Annette said between clenched teeth.

"Listen. It was no big deal. A friend of hers from work—you remember Sharon Wills?"

Annette nodded, recalling the teary-eyed woman who'd searched for Stef. Annette had spoken a number of times to the woman in the first few weeks after Stef's disappearance, but then, as with all of Stef's other colleagues, Sharon stopped keeping in touch after the search parties had ended.

"Sharon set us up on a date. I chose the restaurant, and Stefanie chose the show. I took her to a steak house, and she ate a salad because she doesn't eat meat. Then we went to see some subtitled film that I fell asleep in. We ended the date planning to do it again, only this time she was going to pick the restaurant, and I would choose the show. She had a mystical quality about her that I didn't know what to do with, but it intrigued me. I called her the next week, and she said that she was hung up with a project from work and couldn't go out, but would call me as soon as she was free. I took it as a brush-off, or that she had come to the conclusion that our karmas didn't mesh. Only . . . she disappeared that weekend, okay. And I feel like shit, which is nothing to what must have happened to her. . . . Sam knows about it."

Annette didn't know whether to believe Nick or not. She'd like to think that she was a good judge of people. She'd like to believe in the honest emotion of frustration and guilt on his face. But what if he was another Ted Bundy? What if he was some psycho who didn't like to be told no?

"Did she say what the project was?" she asked.

"The project?" Nick's brows knitted with surprise. "She didn't say anything more than it was something she was working on at Sno-Med. Sharon would know though. . . . You think that it might have something to do with her disappearance?" he asked sharply. "What's going down at Sno-Med anyway? The fire yesterday. Sam's insistence on keeping it under tight surveillance. And why in the hell are you sneaking around looking like a Charlie's Angel nightmare?"

"Thanks," she said, putting the car in gear and speeding to the clinic. "I can't tell you anything about Sno-Med. Not until we talk to Sam."

"Then let me loose," Nick demanded.

Annette shook her head. She couldn't trust Nick just yet, and Aragon didn't need to do any fighting.

They'd just hit Twilight's outskirts when the sheriff pulled in behind her, lights flashing. Annette wasn't about to stop and have an argument with Sam. She needed to get to the clinic, and she wasn't going to let anything slow her down. She turned on her flashers and kept going.

Sam hit his horn and his siren.

Annette kept going.

She arrived at the clinic with the sheriff riding her ass. The trip had been a nightmare, and she was sure Aragon's first impressions of mortals ranked subzero, all of which ratcheted up her irritation. She'd been spinning her wheels for six months, searching the forest and focusing on spreading flyers, hoping someone would have information on Stef. She should have stopped beating the bushes and started on the people that Stef knew, so to speak.

The sheriff jerked her car door open before she could kill the engine.

He reached into the car, either for her or for the car keys. "What in the hell are you doing?" he demanded.

Aragon didn't give the sheriff an inch. He leaned in front of Annette, grabbed the sheriff's wrist, and twisted, bringing the sheriff to his knees in the parking lot outside her car door with a loud *umph*.

Aragon's arm was plastered along her breasts. She gasped for air and fought for reason amid her rocketing nerves.

"Damn!" Nick muttered.

Aragon had moved as fast as lightning, like a blur, but Annette could feel his body trembling from the effort.

"Do not harm the mortal woman," Aragon said.

The shock cutting across Sam's rugged face would have been laughable were it not for Aragon's grimace of pain and the click of Sam's gun. He'd drawn it from its holster with his other hand and had it pointed in Aragon's direction. Being stuck between the two of them was like standing in the way of magma ready to blow the top off a volcano.

"Don't shoot, Sam. He's already been shot once tonight saving my ass, and he needs treatment pronto."

"Who in the hell is he?"

"His name is Aragon. He's like Jared."

"You know of Jared?" Aragon asked, frowning at her. "I am not like him, though. Jared was poisoned. I am not. I am worse."

She blew out an exasperated breath.

"Anybody want to tell *me* what's going on?" Nick demanded from the back seat.

Sam stared hard at Aragon, then asked her, "You're sure?"

"I'm sure. I've, uh, seen him change myself."

"Shit."

"That's no way to welcome him to Earth," Annette quipped, wincing with guilt over her own treatment of Aragon. Then she realized Sam's voice sounded harsher than she ever remembered, and he looked worse than hell. Had something happened? "Where're Jared, Emerald, and Erin?" she asked.

"Jared's still locked up, and Emerald and Erin are keeping watch. Nothing has happened so far. You women generate more trouble than Job ever dreamed of having." Sam looked back at Nick. "You all right?"

"Just get me out of here," Nick demanded, jerking roughly on the handcuffs. He'd probably scarred her leather interior for life.

"Aragon, let go of Sam," Annette urged. "He won't harm me, and he's the man who helped save Jared."

She could feel Aragon struggle with the decision, and she clasped her hand around his wrist as she had done before. This time the electrifying contact went even deeper. Did the man have invisible electrodes targeting her erogenous zones? "Please," she whispered past the sudden dryness of her throat. Meeting his gaze while they were this close together was a mistake. She knew it would be, but she did it anyway.

He inhaled sharply, as if he too needed more air. There was no mistaking the heat in his eyes. He released his hold on Sam and pulled back from her as if burned.

"I'll take care of Aragon, and you deal with Nick," Annette told Sam, forcing herself to move before she melted. "The handcuff key is in the glove compartment." She exited the car the instant Sam stood. Then she moved fast, intending to get Aragon out of the car and into the clinic, but Sam held her up with a hand to her shoulder.

"You've been bitten," he said under his breath.

Annette blinked. "What are you talking about?" she whispered.

He nodded at the car. "The whole Beauty and the Werewolf thing sizzling between you two. What in the hell is going on, Annette? When did you meet him? How long has he been here?"

"You're seeing things," she said, pulling away from him, refusing to face any of the answers his questions evoked. They were just too damn scary for words. "Aragon just needs help, and I'm it. We'll talk later, after I take care of him, and you can explain why you never mentioned that your deputy had been out with my sister." Two steps later she realized that she didn't need to "get" Aragon out of anything. He stood at the end of the car, arms crossed he-man style, his dark gaze centered on Sam.

"Follow me," she ordered, before either Sam or Aragon could erupt. Mount St. Helens versus Vesuvius, a no-win situation no matter what angle you tried. What was it about tonight? The thunderstorm had left way too much tension brewing in the air, and everyone seemed to be sucking it up.

She led the way inside the clinic, flipping on lights as she passed. Once in the exam room, she snatched up a blanket and motioned Aragon to the stretcher, much too aware of him as a man. In the bright light, he seemed even more larger-than-life, but also more vulnerable than ever. Pain had tightened his features and his bearing, something her hands and heart ached to change. Though as a doctor, she was familiar with the feeling, tonight with Aragon it seemed sharper for some reason.

He wasn't just a patient.

She clenched her hand. He had to be.

"Lie on your stomach so that I can look at your back," she ordered, assessing his condition so she wouldn't dwell on the heat in his eyes or the intriguing cleft in his chin. As he moved toward her, she noted the broad expanse of his shoulders, then dipped her gaze along the hard contours of his chest, past the strap of her bra holding his bandage on to his abs and—hell—riveted her eyes to the pink claw mark bisecting his torso. His chest where Pathos had scraped him wasn't the raw and oozing wound that she felt stinging along her back. Yet she was certain Aragon's injury had been worse. Rain had washed the blood away, revealing pink lines of healing skin. You'd have thought weeks had passed since he'd been injured.

With everything that had happened, she'd forgotten that Jared had also healed rapidly from injury. Still, seeing the evidence herself was miraculous—unless . . . "Turn around," she ordered, urging him about. He was so tall, six-five or taller, she thought. She had to stretch on her tiptoes to see part of his shoulders. The cuts from the glass had healed as well, only now glass was embedded in the tissue even more, which meant getting it out was going to be harder and more painful.

Snatching up the bandage scissors, she cut the elastic strap holding her pressure bandage bra on him and eased the cups back from the bullet wound. The healing process had already started there as well, which meant she couldn't delay more before getting the bullet out.

"I see the blood, but that doesn't look like a fresh gunshot wound," Sam said from behind, startling her. Nick stood next to Sam, his glare at her alternating between disbelief and "you're-a-dead-woman." Being brought to his boss handcuffed had to bite.

"Another thirty minutes, and you'll swear he'd been shot a month ago," she told them. "Aragon, I need to extract the bullet and the glass from your back. Otherwise, you'll suffer major pain in the future and may end up with a serious infection."

Aragon rolled his shoulders, making her wince. He had to be in pain. But he swung around to face her, shaking his head. "There is no need, mortal woman. I have no future to be concerned with. My time is limited. We have important things we must discuss, for Pathos will move against me, and now, I fear, against you as well."

What did he mean his time was limited? Her breath hitched as she wondered if Aragon would do the same thing Jared had tried—eliminate himself before any harm could come to another. He'd thought he would harm her while he was a werewolf, but she hadn't felt any real danger from him. Not like Pathos.

Somehow the notion of sacrificing himself as Jared had tried to do didn't fit in with Aragon's commanding presence. He seemed more the type to go out in a blaze of glory, taking as many of the enemy with him as he could.

"Pathos?" Sam asked.

Aragon grunted with disgust. "Leader of the Vladarian Order and a scourge upon all Blood Hunters' honor. He and the Vladarian vampires terrorized the mortal world a millennium ago, feasting ravenously upon Elan blood, and slaughtering many others as well. I have come to eliminate him." Aragon narrowed his gaze at her. "Are you sure you know nothing more about Pathos and Nyros, the red demon I found you with tonight?"

"A demon?" she gasped. "You mean, as in a creature from hell that does horrible things? That kind of demon?" She shuddered hard. The chill of Nyros's touch would never leave her memory. "Until they attacked me, I'd never seen either of them before in my life."

Aragon grunted. "I can see you speak true."

"I am not hearing this conversation," Nick said, backing away. "This whole *Twilight Zone* episode is not happening."

Annette narrowed her gaze at Nick. "I'm still not convinced you're an innocent in all of this."

Sam answered. "He had Sno-Med under surveillance. I trust him completely."

"Well, he isn't doing such a hot job. I heard tonight that the blood samples have already been shipped out, and tomorrow they have trucks arriving for the computers and files. Neither of you saw fit to mention that Nick knew Stef. Had, in fact, invited her out again the night before she disappeared. So what else aren't you saying? How do we even know that she didn't go out with him that night?"

"You don't trust me," Sam said, his voice low and tight.

"I trust you, Sam." She shifted her glare to Nick. "Everything else is going to have to wait until I have time to think about it. Right now I've got a bullet to dig out." Annette started gathering the supplies she needed to treat Aragon.

Nick cursed. "I told you that—"

"I'll handle this," Sam interjected. "I know he didn't go out with Stef that night because he and I went camping on Mount Kinleigh. And I advised him not to say anything about going out with Stef, because I wanted him on the case. I knew he would look harder because he knew her."

"Provided he can be trusted, I would agree." Annette respected Sam's opinion, but she wasn't ready to accept Nick's story as the whole truth. She wasn't about to accept anything at face value. Hopefully, the information she'd gathered off the computer would lead to both Stef and Mr. X. Mr. X might or might not be Dr. Steven Bryers, but just because the man's lab coat was in the office she'd accessed the files from, that didn't necessarily mean he was involved. If Dr. Steven Bryers *was* Mr. X, then it seemed incredibly stupid to leave ID lying around. Then again, someone could be framing Bryers as the culprit. And what about the demon and Pathos's appearance? Bad luck on her part, or had someone set her up?

But all the considerations running through her head would have to wait, no matter how anxious she was for answers. First she had to tend to Aragon, then get a disinfecting salve on her own scrape—something she wasn't going to do with three overprotective men around. Only then could she check out the flash drive and try and puzzle out the night's events. These past few minutes since arriving at the clinic seemed to be dragging on and on.

"I'm out of here," Nick said. "Just for the record, not a damn thing has been taken out of that building, and the only disturbance was the Moe's To Go beeping delivery. That number is what sent me scouting the perimeter and led me to your car. Lousy smokescreen. And I'm not buying this B movie bullshit about demons and—what?" He looked at Aragon. "A man from outer space?"

"Werewolf," Annette said. "Make that plural. Aragon is the second Blood Hunter to show up."

Nick gaped at her and started backing out of the room. "You're out of your mind."

Sam turned his razor-sharp gaze to Nick. "You'd best bite the bullet and chew hard, Nick," Sam said, unrelenting steel underlying his softened tone. "Or your ass will be sitting in a cell until I have time for a heart-to-heart. This shit is as real as it gets and infiltrates to the top all over the world. You're going to have to help keep the lid on it. We don't need a bunch of government bozos taking over our lives. This also has a trail to Belize."

Nick stopped his retreat, but didn't move closer. "What trail?" he demanded, harshly.

"I'll tell you later, in private." Sam cut his gaze her way, making Annette swallow hard. Not because Sam frightened her, but because she was frightened for him. She'd never seen such a look of utter pain in his eyes before. *Haunted* didn't even begin to describe what she saw. "And *you've* got less than two seconds to explain why in the hell you were at the Sno-Med Center tonight, or things are going to get extremely unpleasant really fast," he said.

Annette shook her head. Sam would have to wait; she had more pressing matters right now. "Sorry, Sam, I've already been there and done that. And things weren't just unpleasant. They were downright nasty."

She squared her shoulders in determination, then winced at the pain clawing at her back. She couldn't wait to ease the scrape with a hot bath and salve. "We'll talk *after* I extract the bullet—"

"No!" Aragon and Sam shouted at the same time, exchanging a look that made her very uncomfortable.

She held her ground, at least part of it. "I'll explain while I take the bullet out." She patted the stretcher. "Aragon, lie face down here."

"Fine," Sam said, shaking his head. "Let the woman make her magic; otherwise we're going to be here all night."

Annette groaned, thinking her chances of getting Aragon to cooperate had just nosedived.

Instead Aragon lay on the stretcher, turning to look at her with an assessing eye. "I will observe this magic of yours, mortal woman."

Annette slipped a clean lab coat over her damp clothes and set to work, giving them her spiel. "I couldn't wait until tomorrow to find out information. I went to Sno-Med, looking for information about Stefanie before anyone could take any evidence away. While I was hiding in the restroom, Pathos and his demon appeared. He sniffed the air once, then practically flew through the hall and nailed me to the wall. Then Aragon rescued me." She smiled brightly. "End of story."

"That's not good enough, Nette, and you know it," Sam said. "What aren't you telling me? As we left it this morning, we were all going to wait until tomorrow. I just don't buy you had an itch to go groping around in the dark all by yourself."

"That's what happened," she said. "And it's damn good that I went, because I just may know how they are getting things out of Sno-Med without being seen. Pathos mentioned that he'd have trucks at the tunnel's entrance in the morning."

"What tunnel?" Sam exploded. "Are you saying there's an underground exit from the research center?"

"I don't know, but it's your job to find out fast."

"I'm not letting you off the hook that easy, Nette. You didn't just decide to go out there alone."

Annette refused to look at Sam.

Aragon reached out and grabbed her wrist before she could put the disinfectant-soaked gauze to his back. His dark eyes met hers again with that deep probing look that seemed to reach all the way to her center. "She is using untruths again," he said. "They are necessary for her at this time, but I will not allow it for much longer."

Annette's mouth dropped open.

Nick laughed and shook his head. "Where is the freaking Candid Camera? You're telling me this guy can read a chick's mind?"

"I don't know, but he seems to have Annette's number." Sam snorted.

"No. I have your number," Aragon told Sam.

Sam gaped.

"But not the mortal woman's," Aragon continued, looking up at her. "Do you have a number?"

Annette smiled, trying not to laugh at the look on Sam's face. "He means cell phone number, Sam."

Sam turned to Nick. "We've got a tunnel to find, and we'll need to have the helicopter ready at dawn. Those trucks are going to have to be somewhere in the vicinity of that building, and we're going to find them."

Annette covered Aragon's bare ass with a sheet, thinking he had more than her number. She couldn't even focus with his body stretched out before her. What did he mean, untruths were necessary for her? And exactly how would he not allow them?

The man might have the hottest buns south of the Mason-Dixon line, but he had an ego bigger than the whole faction of southern males combined. Somehow, that fact was more threatening to her than Pathos and his goon.

Pathos paced over the shattered glass, seething on one hand and thoroughly intrigued on the other, which made a very interesting state for a being who'd grown practically immune to all pleasures after a millennium of overindulgence. He was sure ignorance played a large part in the woman's actions tonight, but her torch-blowing bravado had been impressive. In a thousand years, no human had ever damaged a hair on his head. Now he fisted the knotted, singed length of it in his hand, smelling its acrid stench. The heat of his rage shocked him. It had been centuries since he'd felt anything but icy determination and cold calculation.

"Why aren't we annihilating the bitch and her dog?" Nyros rasped. The demon had suffered major damage. Heat was a killer for the damned and their icy realm. That was why most of Heldon's creatures stuck to the night, rather than suffer the discomfort of the day. Fire upon Nyros's kind was like instant leprosy, causing the exposed areas to turn gray and slough off. It was amusing that Heldon kept perpetuating the myth that hell was hot, in a pathetic attempt to keep humans from discovering the weaknesses of the damned.

Pathos was luckier; shape-shifters were less susceptible to fire.

"First we find Cinatas. And I never act uninformed, Nyros, you know that. I want the details about her within an hour. We also need to discover who called and lured her here."

He followed her scent from the restroom to the Infectious Disease Department, to the desk and the computer she used. "She was in here. So get me names of people in this department." He picked up the lab coat. "Put Dr. Steven Bryers at the top of the list."

The more Pathos focused on her fragrance, the heavier his loins grew with the need of a little sport. "The bitch has a name, a reason for being here, and she's involved with Aragon. Find out why."

Anticipation pulsed through him. "You know, Nyros? If what Aragon claimed is true, the Blood Hunter is thwarting Logos to eliminate me. This will cause an uproar among the Guardians. It is perfect. All these years they've acted as if everything I've accomplished in organizing the Vladarians was of little importance. Now I know differently. For Aragon to accept an eternity of wandering, I must be seen as a force to be reckoned with, one apart from Heldon. This is excellent news."

Heady news. Stimulating news. His mind turned back to the woman and her fiery determination. He'd enjoyed the feel of her hot blood racing beneath his fingertips and the softness of her throat. It had been a while since he'd had a human slave to his desires, and seducing a woman with that much fire would be such a pleasure. He never used force. Every woman was willing once he found her Achilles heel and stroked until his commands became her every wish. A vision of her, splayed out before him like a sacrifice upon an altar, sent a rush of excitement through him. Oh, the things he could do to prime her for him.

Releasing his ruined hair, he brought the hand he'd clawed her with to his nose and inhaled the teasing fragrance of her blood. Then he slid his fingertips over the tip of his tongue to taste her. The decadent sweetness hardened more than his determination. He'd have to cut his silver mane off, and she would pay the price for it.

A sudden sucking sound accompanied by wavering distortion in the air, not unlike a black mirage seen upon a hot horizon, had Pathos whirling around, braced for an attack. He relaxed as Nyros's minion crossed the spirit barrier and fell into a submissive bow.

"We have word that Ashoden ben Shashur and an unnamed guest are housed among the black demons."

"Cinatas," Pathos replied grimly. Hell was about to get uglier—and he was the man to make it happen.

Aragon had bent the metal frame on the stretcher and probably permanently dented her nerves of surgical steel. She'd given him enough pain medication to knock out a man his size completely, but it had barely affected him. Worse yet, she didn't dare give him more without knowing his physiology.

He'd claimed she wasn't hurting him and had lain stoically beneath her knife as she'd retrieved the bullet from his scapula, extracted the glass embedded in his back, and sutured all the wounds. It wasn't until he'd left the stretcher and she was cleaning up that she'd found the evidence of how great his control had been.

Even now, as she drove up her mountain driveway through the patchy fog, he gave no indication of his pain. The bumby ride had sent her minor scrape to a just-shoot-me level of irritation, and he was in worse shape. At least, she thought he was. How much more quickly would he heal now that the bullet and the glass had been removed?

She'd had to fight World War III with Sam in order to bring Aragon home with her, a needless battle because given

Aragon's abilities, he'd go where he damn well wanted, and right now that was with her, a scary thought.

She'd just have to take every precaution to not get caught in her towel again. At least he was dressed now. Sam had shoved a clean black T-shirt and a pair of sweatpants from a gym bag at Aragon and told him to wear them or else.

"Stuck in the Middle with You" twanged on the radio as she pulled her car to a stop in front of her cabin. *"Demons to the left of me! Werewolves to the right!"* she thought. *"Here I am, stuck in the middle with you."* Even so, there had been a distinct difference between Aragon and Pathos. Aragon had been almost noble in his werewolf presence, while Pathos had been diseased and corrupted.

She sucked in air, forcing a bravado she didn't feel, and reached for her backpack, having to tug at it because she'd forgotten how heavy it was. Aragon slid his hand over hers and lifted the pack for her. His warmth and strength raced along her nerves, making her almost afraid to turn her head toward him. Almost. She shifted enough so that her gaze met his, and a slight smile curved his mouth.

She'd been trying not to think about the rest of the night. At her place . . . alone with him. Dawn was hours away yet, and Aragon had melted her into a puddle within minutes of meeting her. Now they had hours of history, and the heat seemed to be rising. Maybe the charismatic aura of spirit beings came equipped with little erotic rays that bombarded a mere human.

"Let's go inside, and *then* we'll—"

"Talk," he said for her, shaking his head and touching her cheek with the tip of his finger. "You must always lead as if you fear where others may go." Then he sighed, heavily. "That may be a good thing, for I lead only to destruction."

He turned to stare out the windshield before she could

read his expression, but she knew the guilt and despair would be etched upon his rough features just as heavily as she sensed the weight burdening his broad shoulders. His tone had struck a chord inside her that vibrated with understanding, and once they were inside and comfortable, she'd seek the reason behind them.

She swung around to exit the car and screamed at the face staring in her window.

Chapter Seven

BEFORE SHE COULD explain that her neighbor was peeking into the car, Aragon pulled her his way, crushing her backpack into her stomach as he rammed his fist toward the window.

"Wait!" she yelled, but he hit the glass anyway, causing Rob Rankin to jump back with a cry. She grimaced, thankful Aragon hadn't smashed her window. "It's my neighbor." She pulled back from Aragon's protective hold, feeling as if her back was on fire. She needed to clean the wound and get some antiseptic cream on it ASAP.

"Sorry I'm so jumpy," she told Aragon. "Rob must have gotten my messages wanting his wife to call me." She opened her car door.

"Do you always have this problem?" Aragon asked.

"Jumpy?" She paused, frowning at him. "Not until tonight."

"No. All of these men after you," he replied, sounding oddly aggravated.

Men after her?

"It's your fault," she muttered, then exited the car, backpack in tow. The chill in the night air immediately snaked down her spine, making her shiver. Honestly, there had to be something about Aragon's presence that was bringing on this man-karma.

Aragon shoved his way out of the mortal vehicle. Cars are nothing but death traps, he thought. They gave a being no freedom to move, run, or protect himself from attack. Just like the mortal woman. Being wrapped up in her gave him no freedom to run from the spell drawing him closer to her, and no protection from it either.

His fault? By Logos, what did she mean by that?

She needed an entire band of Blood Hunters to keep her safe. As he approached, he glared at the man she called her neighbor.

The moment Aragon stepped directly into the moon's light, he could feel the effects of its primal pull upon him. His sense of smell heightened, and he could smell fear coming from the man—fear and an underlying desire for the mortal woman.

Aragon pulled her closer to his side and glared at the man. Something was wrong, but his senses could discern no immediate lurking threat.

The man shifted uneasily back.

Annette glanced at her watch. "Rob, it's two in the morning." Even if he'd received the messages that she wanted Celeste to call, Annette didn't think it urgent enough for him to rush over in the middle of the night.

"Sorry," said Rob. "I didn't mean to frighten you. The electricity is out, and the power company says the storm damaged the main lines. They won't have service back up until tomorrow, and Celeste frets. More when she's under the weather. She hates the dark and worried about you being here all alone."

At Rob's "under the weather" comment, Annette's heart sank, immediately thinking that she hadn't tried hard enough to contact Celeste today.

"How is she sick?" Annette asked sharply. A headache could be a precursor to a stroke, or a leg or chest pain might indicate a blood clot. "Celeste was fine at the office the other day. I had better come check on her." Hell, in the spirit of patient privacy, Annette thought, she shouldn't even have mentioned that Celeste had been in the office. Though Celeste hadn't asked Annette not to say anything to Rob, Annette always tried to maintain the strictest of confidences. Her only excuse was that it was late, and she'd been through hell, and she had a distracting werewolf at her side.

"No. No need to check on her. Just a cold," Rob said quickly. "Uh, she came to see you?"

Now you've done it! Annette inwardly groaned and forced a bright smile onto her face. "Just a checkup," she replied. "You know, they were encouraging all of the women at the health expo last week to go have a checkup. My office has been inundated."

Rob nodded. "Yeah."

"You sure I don't need to come see her now?"

"I'm sure. Well, I better get back home," Rob said.

"Don't hesitate to call me if Celeste gets worse. And tell Celeste not to worry about me. I'm fine."

"Nor is she alone," Aragon said, surprising Annette at the fierceness of his tone. Aragon slid her backpack from her shoulder and set it on his. "Annette isn't alone," he repeated. She glanced at him, surprised. This was the first time she could recall that he'd used her name. His expression was too shadowed for her to tell anything from it; yet if she were to judge from the irritated tone of his voice, he almost sounded . . . jealous.

Ridiculous. She must be punch drunk.

Rob's eyes widened. "Celeste and I didn't know. It's good that you're moving on with your life after Stef di—"

His voice trailed off. Probably because something in her expression told him she hadn't moved on with her life. She suddenly felt very cold and very tired, and very much wanting to find her sister. "Good night, Rob."

"Yeah, good night." Rob took a step back, then another, then cautiously turned his back and hurried home.

Aragon quickly decided that he didn't like the man or the way he'd looked at the mortal woman . . . Annette. He wanted to toss the man on his ear into the nearest black hole.

The change in her had come fast, as if the man's words had drained her. Aragon followed her to her door, noting that her hand shook as she slipped the key into the lock. He slid his hand over hers, wanting to give her his warmth, his strength. "You're hurting. And not just on the outside, but on the inside even more. I can feel your pain. What is it?"

She paused a moment, staring at his hand, but didn't pull from his touch. When she looked up, there were tears in her eyes that she tried to blink away. She stiffened as if afraid to show him her hurt, and that pulled him inside out. He unlocked the door and eased it open. Then he drew her inside and wrapped his arms around her shoulders, urging her stiffness closer until he could rest his chin on the top of her head. After shutting the door, closing them in darkness, he stood still for a long while, just absorbing her, listening to her hitching breath as she fought her emotions. Slowly her body softened, and she allowed herself to lean into him, to rest against him, just a little. When he sensed that she'd calmed enough to share, he eased back to see her face.

"You can trust me," he whispered, using the same words she'd said to him. "Talk to me. Tell me what causes this anguish within you." He couldn't help her unless she opened her mind to him. He wanted her to share her hurt with him. He wanted her to want that between them.

"I'm sorry," she said, trying to pull back. "I'm fine."

"No," he said, swinging her up into his arms. "These untruths do not belong between us. You're hurting. I've seen your pain and felt it. You must tell me why." He began walking forward, unsure of where he was going but looking for somewhere to be. The doorway to his right opened onto a large room, and he moved to the comfortable sitting place in the middle of it.

She didn't resist as he sat and pulled her close, but sighed hard and settled her cheek against his chest, over his heart. Having her rest in his arms was unlike anything he'd ever known. It soothed his inner spirit as much as his hunger for her fed his passion. Everything about her affected him, as if she were a powerful moon and he a mere tide beneath her pull. And something inside him chafed at their circumstances, that he wouldn't have time to know and explore all that she made him feel. She had a different future ahead of her.

"I don't know where to start," she whispered.

"At the beginning," he said softly. Leaning back, he settled in, catching the ends of her long hair between his fingers and rubbing his thumb over its heavy silkiness. After a time, she started to talk, and he listened.

Annette meant to tell Aragon only about her missing sister. Instead she told him everything—the death of her grandmother, her drive to become a doctor, her parents' fatal accident, and her failure to be the sister she should have been even after that. "I can't help but feel that if I'd called her back that night, or even if I hadn't encouraged her into the medical field at all, she'd be alive and with me right now."

She'd never allowed herself to just let go before. To relax. To trust. She wasn't even exactly sure why. Maybe it was because she'd never met an Aragon before now.

"What did you learn from the man who called you tonight?"

She hadn't told him about that. She raised her head to look at him, her heart skipping beats as she took in the rugged angle of his shadowed jaw and dimpled chin, the penetrating intensity of his dark eyes, and the seductive curve of his soft lips. She drew a deep breath, growing heady on the scent of him and the feel of his hard body enveloping hers.

His voice rumbled deep, and tense. "I heard what he said. I didn't like it at the time, and now that I know more about you and your world, I want to . . . By Logos, it makes me very angry."

She set her hand on his chest, against the pound of his heart. "I'm fine. I'm not sure I learned anything, though. I went early, copied some information from the computer system in the department he'd spoken of, and I don't know if there's anything about Stefanie yet. I can't check it until the electricity is back on. And I don't think the man who called ever showed up. Only Pathos."

Aragon slid his hand to her lower back. "I know the scrape on your back must hurt. Do you trust me enough now to heal you?"

"What do you mean?" she asked, blinking at him. Heal her like his body healed itself?

"For me to heal you, your mind must be open to mine. I tried to help in the forest after you ministered to me, but I

was either too weak or your mind was too closed. Lean forward a little bit and let me see what Pathos did to you."

He urged her to sit up, still in his lap, her bottom nestled into the crook of his hard thighs. Before she could even
think about what to do next, he lifted her shirt up to her
underarms.

"Why do you mortals insist on wearing clothes? They are
only a hindrance as far as I can tell. They limit movement
and keep hidden your softness and your beauty."

She gasped and clamped her arms over her exposed
breasts as a shock of desire sent her pulse racing. The co-
coon of care his warm strength had created had become a
hothouse with the mere shifting of her shirt.

"Trust me," he said, sliding the palm of his hand against
her back, just along the curve of her hip. Her nipples hardened, pressing into her palms covering her breasts, and she
bit her lip. "You ministered to me. Now I must to you."

She did him, and now he was going to do her? Sort of a
tit for tat. *Not funny, Annette. No doing and no tits for tats.
He's not tat.* Everything she'd felt when he'd touched her before rushed through her again. She sucked in air to stop herself passing out.

"Annette?" he asked softly.

Angling to see his face in the shadows, she studied his
dark eyes in the play of light the moon had slipped through
the room. His rugged features were drawn into lines of concern, softening their warrior-like harshness despite the rough
edge of his beard-shadowed jaw. He earnestly meant what he
said, as if he were the healer and she a patient.

It made her feel prudish to resist taking off her shirt.
She was in the medical profession, for heaven's sake, and
by necessity dealt with nudity every day, but how could
she just bare all, with him—with the man who made her

body burn? Even the thought of it sent a fissure of fire right to her center. The combination of his sex appeal and her sex deprivation was proving to be more than she could resist.

Grabbing her shirt hem, she pulled it over her head and held the slightly damp knit against her breasts.

He set both his hands on her back, and a bone-warming heat penetrated deeply into her muscles. His touch was light, fluid, and made her ache to feel it—everywhere.

That thought had her so distracted that she missed what he was doing until she heard him speaking, low and softly mesmerizing, in a language she didn't know. He'd moved until his hands were now pressing against what she knew was her raw, scraped skin, yet she felt no pain. Instead a deep, tingling warmth spread down her spine and radiated outward in waves of pleasing sensation, sensual sensation, warm and beautiful. Her body seemed to be melting and floating at the same time, and she closed her eyes to absorb what was happening to her, feeling so good she didn't even question the why or how of it.

Suddenly, it seemed that his hands were just where she wanted them to be. She could almost imagine his mouth and tongue were claiming her as he drove the hard fullness of his erection straight to the exploding center of her entire being.

Aragon felt his spirit slip intimately around Annette's as he concentrated on easing her pain and healing the scrape that ran the length of her back. He could sense lingering traces of Pathos's scent upon her and was determined to eradicate it, soothing his touch upon her soft skin. That the vile beast had marked her angered him, made him more determined than ever to stop—

His breath caught, and his mortal flesh hardened again, as it had when she'd summoned him to her bath and his body had pressed so closely to hers. The desire grew as images exploded into his mind, images of touching her everywhere with his hands and his mouth. Images of him mating his flesh to hers, claiming her with a passion that felt like liquid fire in his veins.

He knew of mortal mating, but he'd never imagined himself doing so, not in any of his spirit forms, or even of mortals doing so with each other. It was never a part of his awareness as a spirit being. But now he couldn't see anything else. He wanted her. It was like a driving hunger inside him that urged him to know her completely.

By Logos, what was he doing? She'd trusted him, and here he was taking advantage of that trust. Just as he was about to jerk his hands off her, she groaned with such sensual satisfaction that he realized he'd melded into her mind and being so deeply within her he was seeing *her* thoughts.

She was picturing him mating with her. The sudden raw vividness of what he saw shook him, made him burn, made him need, made him want the fullness of that desire to be happening at that second and not just in their minds. He wanted to touch her breasts and mold their softness to his need. He wanted to kiss her so deeply that they were but two halves of a whole. He felt as if they were mating, that the hardness of his flesh was buried deep inside her and the world was erupting like a star bursting from a dark cloud in the heavens.

He stopped chanting and opened his eyes. The images disappeared, and he found himself as he'd been just moments ago. His hands were still pressed firmly to Annette's now healed wound, but everything was different somehow. He was different. She was different. He slid his hands up her soft back to her shoulders and pulled her back against the heat of his chest and the aching flesh of his groin. She arched against him. His lips pressed into the silk of her hair, and his heart raced like a wild wind.

He needed more of her, of her scent that was so sweetly lush and alive. Gardenia. He ran his fingers into her hair and luxuriated in the feel. It was like a rolling wave of midnight, teeming with hidden fire. Without her shirt, her skin glowed in the moonlight.

"Why do you hide your beauty so?" He buried his nose in the silky tresses, breathing deeply of their sweetness before he slid his fingers down to her shoulders and around to her breasts. She groaned and arched to his touch, filling his hands with their hot fullness. Their peaks grew hard, begging more of his touch. "What magic is this?" he whispered, brushing his thumbs over the tips.

She groaned, turning to face him. Her lips were parted as if awaiting his. She opened her eyes slowly, and he saw the core of fire he sought flaming in them. The passion, the need, the desire, were all there, staring starkly at him. But there was more, a deep and painful vulnerability that made her appear as fragile as a mist in the wind. At that moment he realized he was seeing directly into the naked heart of a mortal for the first time. And the responsibility of protecting such a treasured soul awed him, humbled him. He leaned forward, pressing his lips to hers.

Annette erupted the moment Aragon's lips connected with hers. He'd stolen the last of her sanity with his touch, luring her to such a sharp sensual edge that she could only plunge over it. She shifted in his lap, pressing against the hard jut of his erection as she brought her breasts against the firm contours of his hot chest while her tongue slid along his lower lip, then delved into his mouth. She wanted him to take his tentative kiss to the limit, and urged him every way she knew how. And after a moment's hesitation, he didn't disappoint her. His tongue met and clashed with hers, and his arms wrapped tighter around her, crushing her closer to him.

She couldn't get enough as she ran her hands along the solid ripples of his arms and the broad plane of his chest, urging him to pull off his shirt so that she could explore every nuance of him, feeling the rush of his pulse, the silk of his hair between her fingers, and the rough edge of his jaw. She pressed him back until they were lying on the sofa, both naked from the waist up, his legs spread wide with her planted between them. She arched against the hard ridge of his erection, teasing the heated flesh with the press of her sex through the cover of their clothes. She reveled in the deep, wanting groan that rumbled through him, and she drank greedily of his passion, pressing for more.

"I've never wanted anyone like this before," she cried, impatiently wanting to feel his mouth on her breasts and everywhere. She moved against him, shifting to offer her breasts to the fire of his tongue.

"And I've never known desire or this mortal mating before," he gasped, gazing at her, looking dazed and needy.

Annette blinked as the wave of cold reality hit her.

Chapter Eight

HE'D NEVER KNOWN DESIRE? He was a virgin? Good heavens. She'd rocketed right out of her mind at his touch. She'd been all over him, grinding him into the couch just like she'd imagined backing him against the wall. He wasn't a two-by-four stud looking for a screw. What sort of advantage was she taking of his innocence?

"I'm sorry," she whispered, easing back from him and out of his embrace.

He shook his head as if confused as he angled up from the couch.

She shut her eyes against the mind-blowing display of his broad chest, rippling abs, and hard erection tenting his sweatpants. "This shouldn't have happened. This is wrong. I'll be right back."

"No, wait," he said, reaching for her.

She shook her head and ran from the room, fleeing the voice inside her head that urged her to forget any sense of responsibility she might have to an innocent being, one who knew so little of her world.

Once inside her bedroom, she pressed her back to the door and froze. Not because of any pain from her injury, but because there was none. Rushing over to the mirror on her dresser, she turned her back, finding nothing but the faint lines of a healed claw mark running down her back. Only a smear of dried blood on her lower back provided evidence of how deeply she'd been scraped. She tentatively touched her spine, utterly amazed. He'd healed her. This spirit being capable of changing into a fierce beast and back again had healed her.

And changed her, she thought as she turned and saw herself in the mirror. She looked decadent. The long waves of her dark hair framed her full breasts, which still ached to experience the heat of his mouth and the torturous pleasure of his slow touch.

The searing need he'd awakened within her stunned her as much as his healing of her wound. He'd protected her at cost to himself, and how had she repaid him? Literally attacking him, then running like a coward.

Going through her private door to the bathroom, she dipped a washcloth into her scented, now cold, bathwater and cleaned her skin all over, trying to soothe the fever in her blood. It barely helped. Toweling off, she put on sweats; then, after digging the amulet out of her pocket, she dumped her jeans into the hamper. Her sweats didn't have pockets, and she didn't want to part with the amulet. She finally gave in and slipped the amulet around her neck for the first time, burying it under the sweatshirt.

Just as she was about to band her hair back into a safe knot, she realized the flash drive wasn't hanging around her neck, and hadn't been there when she and Aragon had almost made love . . .

"Hell," she cried. She remembered feeling it in place at the clinic. When had she lost it? Heart kicking into a panicked beat, she ran from her bedroom and right into Aragon's arms. He hadn't put his shirt back on, and the supple heat of him flared over her senses again.

"What is wrong?" he demanded, thrusting her behind him as if danger were fast on her heels.

She clutched his arm, sliding her fingers along his muscles longer than needed to get his attention. Heaven help her, but the shadowed profile of his stubbled jaw and rugged features made her racing heart miss a beat. His tall, dark, and dangerous sex appeal wasn't for the faint of heart.

"There's no danger," she assured him. "It's just that I have lost something very important, a string with a plastic and metal tube on it. I have to find it."

He held up his hand, dangling the flash drive by the string he'd wound between his fingers. "You dropped this as you fled."

"That's it." She reached for it, relief flooding her until he moved it beyond her grasp.

"This time I make the conditions. Tell me why you ran away just now."

"This calls for coffee."

"Coffee?"

"Liquid heaven." Unfortunately, she didn't have the electricity to fix a fresh pot. What was left from earlier would have to do. She led him to the kitchen, realizing that she was starving. Besides, they both needed something to distract themselves, and the last she'd eaten anything was a sandwich in her office hours and hours ago. Scrounging around in the dark, she grabbed some strawberries and cheese and crackers from the fridge, then poured two cups of warm sludge from the coffeepot.

Handing him the coffee cups, she took up the snack. They'd probably be safer staying in the kitchen, but they would need light and heat from the fireplace.

"Set those here," she said as she placed the snack tray on the coffee table. Then she moved over to the gas logs, lighting them. Warmth radiated, and a soft glow filled the room. When she finally turned to look at Aragon, she found him on the sofa, leaning back against the overstuffed cushions, studying her. Between the burn of his gaze and the bulk of his size, he'd turned the large sofa into an instant love seat.

She went to the coffee first. After grabbing her cup, she handed him his before she dared to sit. "We'll eat before we talk."

He frowned as if the idea didn't sit well with him, but he didn't argue. After a moment, he sniffed the coffee. "What did you call this?"

"Heaven in a cup, known as coffee," she said, taking a bracing sip. Not bad for just warm and old.

He followed her example and grimaced as he swallowed, then firmly set the cup on the table next to the couch. "You're mistaken. Hell is a more apt description for such a brew. Heaven is . . ." His gaze dropped to her lips, and he frowned again. "Why did you run a—"

"Have a strawberry," she said, picking up one, twisting off the tiny green leaves at the top, and handing it to him. "They're sweeter."

How in the world could she explain that she had a moral obligation not to take advantage of his innocence? Not to mention the fact that they'd known each other all of . . . oh, God . . . eight, nine hours. It didn't seem possible. It seemed a hundred times that. A thousand times that. What had happened to her?

His eyes widened as he bit into the strawberry. He sucked in a deep breath of air, then chewed. She watched him eat five more as if they were seductive ambrosia. She watched the way his mouth opened for the fruit and how his tongue would come out just enough to catch the juice as his teeth bit into its ripeness.

And not a damn bit of what she saw was cooling her ardor.

Just before he bit into the next one, his gaze met hers. "You're not eating? Here." He brought the strawberry to her mouth. She had little choice but to take it. As her lips closed around the fruit, he brushed his thumb over her lips, sending a jolt of fire right to her center. Her toes curled, her nipples hardened, and everything else in between went damper than before, if possible.

He made her want more than strawberries. And he wanted more than strawberries. She grabbed her coffee and gulped. Strawberries were becoming dangerous. She kept picturing him, her, and strawberries, tasting their juicy sweetness—everywhere.

"I like sweet," he said. "You're sweet. I would taste you both." He moved toward her.

She choked and set her coffee down. Could he read her mind? God, if he kissed her now, she'd be sunk.

Standing up, she moved away from him, dragging in much-needed air. She couldn't seem to stop this burgeoning desire between them.

He followed, moving up behind her. "Do you fear me?"

She shook her head. "No. It's just that—"

"What?" He set his hands on her shoulders and leaned in to brush his lips against the nape of her neck. Her knees nearly buckled.

"Why does this fire between us frighten you?"

She sighed. "Don't you understand that I don't want to cause you harm? And we, well, we barely know one another. Making love is more than assuaging the desire that flares between a man and a woman. It's an affirmation of what two people feel for one another inside their hearts. An expression of caring for another person that is given after they've spent time together and are sure about what they feel." There, she thought, feeling a flood of relief. Now he would understand.

He was so silent for so long that she had to swing around and look at him.

He stood, studying her with a sadness in his eyes that pulled at her heart.

She sucked in a deep breath. "I'm sorry. I didn't mean to hurt you."

He turned away from her and faced the fire. "You haven't. Those things of which you spoke are there—you've felt them from me, and you've given them to me. There is a connection of spirits between us that cannot be denied. Perhaps that is why you are able to summon me to your side. You must know that I ache to share more with you, to know this fullness of pleasure and the feelings you evoke within me before my time upon the mortal ground ends."

"What do you mean?" Annette's heart jolted, and her body chilled. The thought of him not being here cut at her. "How long are you here for? How will your time end?"

"I know not the answers to those questions. A day. Longer. Shorter. My fate no longer rests within my power to change. I don't even know what has given me this substance within the mortal realm."

Annette bit her lip. She had a suspicion of what had connected them, of what made his presence so strong. She slipped his amulet from around her neck and held it out to him. "Here. Maybe this will explain a lot."

He turned, and his dark eyes widened with surprise, but he didn't speak and didn't reach for the amulet. He just stared at it. "You keep it," he whispered.

"Isn't it yours?" She slid her fingers over the raised twelve-point star on the face of the dark gold disk, still awed by its iridescence and heat.

"Was mine," he replied, his voice harsh. "I proved unworthy of its honor. I left it at the Sacred Stones because I knew my brethren would search there for me." He turned away from her and paced across the room. "Where did you find it?"

"At the Sacred Stones this morning. I prayed for an answer to where my sister was, and I found the amulet in the same place my sister's backpack had been found after she disappeared. It was after Jared—"

"Died because of me."

"No! You're wrong. He's alive."

"Yes, I know, but that is only because the mortal woman brought him back to life *after* he went through the agony of death. That he lives doesn't change my own failure. My own guilt. I sent my own brother to his death."

He had his back to her so she couldn't see the pain on his face, but she could hear the jagged edge of it in his voice as if torn from him.

"How? Jared went to the Sacred Stones of his own choice."

Aragon swung around. His dark eyes were haunted. The firelight spewed macabre shadows across his face. "Did he?" he asked harshly. "Even though the other Blood Hunters wanted to give Jared more time, I refused to listen. All I could think about was how evil Pathos had become and that I'd rather Jared died, rather I died myself, than let that happen." His voice was tight with self-disgust.

"Pathos was a Blood Hunter?" she asked.

"My mentor in the spirit world. It would be like one's father upon the mortal ground. He didn't even fight the Tsara's poison. He couldn't have, for within two days he'd turned evil. It was a betrayal I couldn't forgive, and why I now seek to restore the Blood Hunters' honor as well as atone for what I did to Jared."

"Guilt," she said with a soft sigh. "I know how you feel." She slipped the amulet back on and pressed it against her heart, feeling as if a part of him radiated into her from it. Moving to him, she gazed up into his dark eyes. The pain in them echoed the one in her heart, and she wanted to soothe the sharp edge of it. She slid one hand to his jaw and along the rough stubble of his cheek. Her other hand automatically pressed against his chest, over his heart. He sucked in air, and his lips parted. He wrapped his hand around her wrist, tugging her body flush to his as his mouth descended to hers.

But he didn't claim her in a darkly passionate kiss as she expected. He stopped, his mouth a whisper away from hers. "I'm unworthy, a warrior who failed and will fade. And I may only have this moment in time. But I want you with everything within me. You make me feel beyond the shadow of my failure, and I want to know the burn of this fire you stir within me. Do you want me despite what I am?"

Want him? More than her next breath. He might be innocent, but she no longer had any doubt that he wanted her as much as she wanted him.

"Yes," she whispered, unable to turn away from his need, his passion, and this moment.

His kiss hit hard and deep and fast, stealing her breath and her sanity, for she kissed him back, her mind whirling with the dizzying sensations caused by the strength of his passion and the penetration of his spirit and mind into hers. He felt so solid and real and alive that she couldn't truly believe he could suddenly be gone tomorrow, but she reached for him as if he'd disappear in the next minute.

Aragon groaned as he wrapped his arms around Annette and pulled her body against the insistent throb of his hardening flesh, recalling vividly the images of mating he'd seen in her mind as he'd healed her. The need to know this pleasure with her consumed him. He wanted to share every part of this desire with her. He wanted to feel not only his own pleasure from her touch, but also her pleasure from his, and he sent his mind into her.

Imagine, he whispered into her mind. *Imagine what you want me to do. Imagine how you want me to make you feel. Imagine everything you want and let me share it with you.*

Concentrating with the eternal core of his being, he opened all of himself to her, even the failure that shamed him and the need that drove him to vanquish Pathos. *This is who I am. Take me. Show me all that is unknown to me.*

"Yes," she whispered, but he heard the word in her mind first. She closed her eyes and parted her lips, letting her mind and body surrender to him. He buried one hand in the soft wildness of her hair and kissed her deeply. Her images of passion came to him, tentative and slow at first, then bursting into a kaleidoscope of him touching her and her touching him. With his hand still fisted in her hair, he pressed her back against his arm and pulled her shirt up until the full round softness of her breasts was exposed. Seeing his amulet nestled between her breasts seemed right—as if the noblest part of him, even if it was a part he couldn't lay claim to, belonged to her. He wouldn't take his amulet, but he would take her.

He brought his mouth from one rosy peak to the other, relishing the satisfying feel of sucking upon them until she moaned with pleasure, arching against him. Then he lashed the hardened tips with his tongue until her breath came in short gasps, and she struggled with her need to hold onto his shoulders and her want to touch him. With his mind in hers, he could not only see her wants but also feel each frisson of pleasure that vibrated her senses higher and higher.

He too wanted both of his hands and his mouth on her, touching her, tasting her, pleasuring her, and he wanted all of her open to him.

Easing her up, he lifted her shirt over her head and pushed her pants into a puddle at her feet. Then he moved back to gaze at her soft beauty, thinking that of all the beings Logos had created, a woman was the most beautiful, and the man who beheld her the most blessed.

She reached for the waistband of his pants, urging them down, aided by an impatient shove from him. The burgeoning fullness of his mortal flesh jutted from the solid planes of his body, and she ran her hands down his chest until she cupped him, then stroked, making his heated need throb even harder. She explored the length of his legs and back up, returning to his hardened flesh. Her soft mouth and warm lips had his body trembling until he could barely stand.

With a cry of frustration at his weakness, he swung her up into his arms and carried her over to the fire, kneeling down to lay her upon the white cloud of sheepskin there. The scent of her, a mingling of lush flower and woman, was a potent combination that he couldn't get enough of. His kissed her again, delving deeply into the velvet softness of her mouth before he ventured to know all of her as intimately as their kiss. He licked her lips, kissed the curve of her chin and the angle of her brow. Moving to her neck, he was barely aware of the scent of her blood above the power of their passion, but he knew its pulsing excitement. He relished that her heart hammered in anticipation of what he would do next. Their ragged breaths and groans were a driving crescendo of passionate music, urging him to know more, feel more, claim more.

He lavished her shoulders, then her breasts, with long licks and tiny nips before he cupped the full globes of her breasts and suckled the hardened peaks until she writhed and panted. Following the flat planes and soft dip of her stomach, he kissed his way to the thick thatch of curls that covered the heady essence of her heated desire. He could smell the strength of her want centered there. It was a scent he'd never forget and struck him as his, as if the power of her arousal was for him alone and he claimed it with a kiss. But one taste wasn't enough. He hungered to lap every drop of desire from her woman's flesh. Shifting himself to kneel between her legs, he caught her hips in his grip and lifted her hot core to his mouth, delving his tongue into the sweet folds, loving the taste.

She writhed in pleasure until her breaths were ragged gasps.

"Come here," she cried, reaching for him. "I need you inside me." With her plea came an image of him driving his hardened flesh directly into the sweet core he'd been drinking from.

He was dying to be inside her. He moved up, and she arched her back off the floor, opening herself to him even more. Grabbing her hips, he drove himself deep, until he could go no farther. His body shuddered from the pleasure vibrating through her and then through him. His gaze sought hers, and his mouth claimed hers. Then she moved against him, thrusting her hips, sending more pleasure that urged him to drive into her again, only deeper and harder than before. Again and again their passion met, stroking the need and the fire until she cried out. As pleasure ripped through her, it exploded inside him. His body spasmed beyond his control, and his spirit hurtled into a heaven he'd never known before, changing him forever. She was wrapped around him in this new universe, her spirit soaring with his, for this unbelievable heaven, this unimaginable pleasure, *was her*. Was him being in her. In her mind. In her body. In her spirit. They were one.

And he wanted more.

He rolled them over until he lay beneath her and she could rest upon him. As she slept, he counted the beats of her heart, listened to her contented sighs, and saw her dream of strawberries and him, a dream that had him not only reliving every moment of their mating, but imaging just how he could have the sweetness of her and the fruit upon his tongue at the same time. His loins and his spirit burned again for the heaven of her until he lay there groaning beneath her as his hardened flesh pulsed against her softness while she slept.

Annette woke, realizing the quivering she felt wasn't in her dreams, but from the man beneath her. She lifted her head from the cradle of his chest and met the toe-curling need in his dark eyes. The sexual energy radiating from him licked teasing flames over her from the inside out. His hands slid everywhere, molding her softness to the hard demand of his desire, making her sex, her body, and her heart weep for more.

He didn't say anything. He didn't have to. Grabbing her bottom, he slid her up until his mouth reached hers and his kiss could say it all. He left her breathless, dizzy for air, dizzy for him. Arching his back as he pushed down on her hips, he entered her fast and hot and thick, filling her impossibly more than before. She groaned with pleasure as she brought her knees up to hug his hips and rose so that Aragon's questing hands could better reach her aching nipples. Their joining became a furious drive that sent her higher and higher with each thrust of his hips and stroke of his hand. She shuddered as wave after wave of intensifying pleasure washed over her, building tiny climaxes, one upon another, in a way that had her climbing to a release unlike anything she'd ever experienced. She was spinning out of control and completely helpless to his need of her and her need of him. His spirit entered her, wrapped around her, and drew her from herself, making them one in a way years of human experience could never match.

Suddenly Aragon bowed up, lifting her completely, impaling her completely, filling her, fulfilling her. His hold on her hips tightened when he thrust himself inside, and he let out a moan so deep and raw that it rumbled like thunder through the room. It shook the foundations of her heart and triggered her orgasm to a shuddering climax that rode even higher when his orgasm exploded. Her whole being felt as if it had splintered into a thousand pieces as pleasure rocked her over the edge of reason and into the arms and passion of a man she might barely know, but would never forget.

Chapter Nine

SAM PULLED IN behind Nick's patrol car and shoved his own into park. He'd told his deputy the whole story of the past week from soup to nuts on the ride to the Sno-Med Center.

"You really aren't bullshitting me, are you?" Nick shoved a hand through his short hair. "The body on the side of the road last week is really a serial killer who'd been executed two years ago?"

"Prints are an exact match. So are the dental records. The body we have is as fresh as if he'd just been wheeled from the electric chair."

"And this dead killer was what?"

"A spiritual assassin called a Tsara. It infected Jared, which landed Jared on earth. He is or was a werewolf, depending on what happens tonight. I saw him change form last night."

"And yesterday you really were—"

"Kidnapped by the renowned Dr. Cinatas. Yep, all five of us, me, Emerald, Annette, Erin, and Jared. Woke up bound and gagged on a slab in Sno-Med's morgue. The fire was a result of our attempt to save Erin. Cinatas shot wild with his gun on the roof, hit the gas tank of the helicopter, and boom. And I can't do jack shit to prove it without making it harder for us to fight the SOBs, and that would only risk more people's lives in the long run."

Nick cursed hard. "I know people who work at Sno-Med. I know people who go to their clinic for treatment."

"Me too. They're everybody's best friend."

"Dr. Cinatas and—vampires? As in bloodsucking and immortal?"

Sam fisted his hands. "Yeah, and Vasquez's name is on the list of vampires masquerading as men. But then the bastard never pretended to be anything but a monster. This changes things, you know."

Nick's sharp inhale wrenched Sam's gut. "How? My father is dead, and Vasquez murdered him. Nothing can change that."

"No, but I can damn sure take the bastard out now. I swore to the military that I'd leave the man alone. Vasquez's oil cartel is giving OPEC its first real taste of competition, and prices have been dropping significantly." Not that Sam gave a rat's ass about the price of gas, but he had to either give his word, or spend the next sixty locked up as a loose cannon. "But if the SOB isn't human, then all bets are off."

"If you're gunning for him, then I'm with you."

"Forget it." The thought of Nick in Vasquez's clutches made Sam break out into a cold sweat. Reed Sinclair had died freeing Sam from Vasquez, and there was no way in hell his son was going anywhere near Belize.

"I've been training for it ever since you came back instead of my father. Why do you think I learned to fly a bird in the first place? The only way into Belize's no-man's-zone, and the fastest way out, is by helicopter."

"No," Sam said again.

Nick shoved open the car door. The plan was for him to give Sno-Med a check, then go catch a couple of hours of shut-eye before they went searching at dawn. "Sam," Nick sighed. "You know I respect the hell out of you, but this is one thing that's going to go down no matter what you say. I'll see you at the helipad in a few. A freaking damn secret tunnel. How in the hell could Sno-Med be as big as it is and nobody the wiser?"

"I'd like to say it's because the SOBs in charge are that good, but I'm afraid it's more because the masses are blind sheep who follow anyone who gives them a free lunch." Sam's radio crackled from dispatch, spewing out a garbled message. Myra insisted on using the antiquated system despite his repeated efforts to get her to call his cell phone first. He waved Nick off and dialed Myra at the station.

"What?"

"Got complaints coming in from that geezer up on Hades Mountain."

"What? He's seeing another UFO at that Hefner-like re-treat?"

"Black clouds."

"What?"

"He's complaining that he can't see what's going on over there because a black cloud is covering the place. He says it 'ain't natural' and wants someone to ride over and take a look-see."

It was the middle of the night. All the damn clouds were black. Sam pinched the bridge of his nose and glanced at his watch. He could either go check on black clouds or face Emerald back at the station. "Call the geezer, Myra. And tell him I'm on the way."

It was laughable. He'd rather go to Hades on a fool's errand than face a pint-sized platinum blond. *Coward.* To the bone, Sam thought as he wheeled back onto the highway.

Bracing himself against the frigid waves of cold radiating from the black demons, Pathos shifted into their midst with a dozen red demons flanking him. They hovered in the air above the group that had gathered for a council meeting. The black demons, likely plotting the demise of a weaker sect, froze. Their obsidian forms were a grotesque collection of appendages from their vanquished foes, trophies attached Frankenstein-style, only more botched than one could imagine. Some of the parts—arms, legs, ears, noses, and an occasional head or two—had grafted to the host well. Others hung in useless decay, creating such an acrid stench of rot that not even the frigid air could curtail the smell.

Pathos stood, staring down upon the creatures as he waited. The weak spoke first, especially in hell.

Legion didn't disappoint Pathos. The ten-armed, double-headed leader of the black demons rose to his feet, both mouths voicing his outrage. "What is the meaning of this?"

"Come now, Legion. Surely you expected me. You have something of mine, and I am here to assure its return."

"I know of nothing. Heldon will hear of your unauthorized intrusion."

"I'll be the first to tell him." Pathos paused for effect. "For you, since you will be unable to. Is harboring Ashoden ben Shashur worth such a loss?"

Legion's ten arms shifted position as he shrugged, his greedy gaze eyeing the red demons. Pathos could clearly sense the demon's dilemma. He didn't want to bring the wrath of the red demons upon him, for they were the one faction large and powerful enough to defeat the black demons. But on the other hand, being the first black demon to acquire an appendage from a red demon would be quite a feather in his cap.

Legion capitulated, as Pathos had expected. "I didn't realize that you were here for our Vladarian guest. I'll have you escorted to him."

Pathos smiled. Extinction was the only thing a black demon was good for. "No need. I can sense exactly where he is now that I am here. I wouldn't interfere if I were you."

Pathos swung around, floating swiftly through the fetid demon realm, his keen sense of smell leading him to his offspring and the Vladarian vampire. The red demons at his back took up posts as they passed key exit points. With Cinatas just moments away, an odd tension fluttered inside Pathos's gut, catching him off guard. Someone had dared to harm his son! He clenched his fist and descended upon Shashur and Cinatas with his fangs gnashing.

They were so embroiled in their own drama that they didn't even realize they had company.

"What did you do to me?" Ashoden ben Shashur appeared to be yelling, but his voice only rasped like one upon death's door. Even for someone in hell, he looked terrible. "You will tell me!"

Cinatas was unrecognizable except for his scent and the sound of his laugh as he responded to Shashur's demand. Chained in one of the black demons' torture devices—unmatched by any of the Spanish Inquisition's instruments—he'd been burned and mutilated.

"Your license to exist had expired, Shashur," Cinatas whispered. "I am your executioner," he taunted.

Pathos exploded throughout the room like lightning, howling with rage. He ripped the machine apart and pulled loose the bands binding Cinatas.

"Pathos," Shashur gasped. "You won't believe what Cinatas has planned to do. He poisoned me during the Elan transfusion, and he's plotted to overtake the Vladarian Order."

Cinatas didn't even try to rise from the device. "Pathos! Just the son of a bitch I wanted to see."

Pathos placed his hands over Cinatas's eyes. "My son. Your pain will be avenged. Let me heal what I can."

"Your . . . son?" Shashur gasped.

Pathos looked up at Shashur's shock and smiled. "Yes. Blood of my blood. Seed of my seed." He nodded to Nyros, awaiting instructions. "Take him to the Red Demon Pits and make sure his last moments are his worst."

Warm sunlight streaming through the great room's high windows was Annette's first hint that she was still on earth, despite the heaven Aragon had carried her to several times in the past few hours. (The last time had been with strawberries, an experience that still had her creamy and hot despite her satiation.) The second hint was the sharp crick in her neck from sleeping with her head pillowed by the bulk of his shoulder. They were still naked and entwined on the sheepskin rug, all cozy and warm from the fireplace and from Aragon's heat. The thick, warm disk of Aragon's amulet sat firmly between her breasts, making her feel as if part of him still resided inside her.

Unfortunately, the third and final hint that she was still on earth was a showstopper. People were pounding on her door, sounding close to breaking it down. Sam and Emerald's voices were the loudest. "Annette! Open up!"

"Hell." She scrambled for her sweats. Now she knew how the three little pigs must have felt. Sam sounded like he was about to huff, puff, and blow her house down. Except it was too late, she thought. The big bad wolf had already eaten her up, strawberries and all.

Aragon did not look happy at the intrusion. She groaned and handed him his clothes, finding the flash drive as she did so. "Hurry and put these on," she told him, slipping the flash drive beneath her shirt. She noted that the lights were on as she passed the kitchen, so she had power, which meant a functional computer. She wanted to rush to the keyboard, and it was all she could do to force herself to answer the door.

"Great sex" had to be flashing on her forehead like Vegas neon on steroids. It had been too good, and she'd been without too long. Her lips felt kiss-swollen. Her hair was in a wild tangle, and her nipples had hardened to shameless little beggars poking at her sweatshirt, ready for more. She schooled her mouth into a tight-lipped frown and wrapped the long length of her hair around itself, tucking the twisted end to simulate her usual knot. One glance in the foyer mirror revealed her failure. She just couldn't seem to summon the tightly bound reserve she'd worn so easily before.

She'd just have to brazen it out with her friends. She was a single, consenting adult. And she wasn't the first woman to have sex with a man the same day she'd met him.

Yeah, but how many of those did it with a werewolf from the spirit realm?

But then, how many women ever connected with their lovers on such a deep level? It had been more than just sex. They'd made love, and there was no getting around it.

Had it all been in her mind? Had all of her pent-up frustrations made last night more than it actually was? She might have had a chance to find out this morning if the yoyos on her porch hadn't come barging in.

She snatched open the door and crossed her arms over her chest, tapping her foot. "It's barely seven A.M. The cocks haven't crowed yet, and I haven't had my coffee. Who wants to die first?"

Sam and Emerald took one look at her and gaped, but Annette didn't have a second to dwell on their knowing expressions.

Jared pushed his way inside, his expression grim. "Where is he?"

Erin grabbed Jared's arm. "If Aragon had made good on his pact to execute a poisoned Blood Hunter, then there wouldn't be an us."

Jared squeezed Erin's hand in reassurance. "You misunderstand. It is concern for him that drives me, not anger. Two Blood Hunters from the same band falling within days of each other? This is unprecedented, and my brethren are in deep trouble."

Annette turned to see Aragon's broad shoulders filling the doorway. The stark hopelessness in his dark eyes sucked her right to him, telling her last night had been everything she'd felt, because she knew how he felt now. She understood him and ached for him. His rugged features were so sharply grim that they stabbed through her waffling heart, pinning it in place like a moth to a board. She could still struggle, but her heart was fixed . . . on him.

"The Brethren are in less trouble than they'd be in had I continued as their leader," Aragon said harshly.

"What do you mean?" Jared asked, his eyes narrowed to points of blue fire as he pulled from Erin's touch and moved toward Aragon.

Aragon didn't answer. Testosterone-laden tension filled the room as the two Blood Hunters faced each other. Something about their posture, their sculpted, hard bodies, and the air of power surrounding them shouted their elite warrior status.

Sam didn't help to ease the mushrooming tension either. He shifted closer to Annette and spoke low in her ear. "You've not only been bitten. You've been devoured."

Emerald shook her head, slicing a sharp glance at Sam before focusing on Jared and Aragon. "Don't be a prudish gack-head, Sam. Nette can shag who she wants, what she wants, and when she wants."

Annette winced. Emerald could have left off the "what" and just said who and when. Aragon was not a *what*. He was a being, just like a man—more than a man. Annette had seen that last night. No, not just seen—she'd felt it deep inside of her.

"You weren't poisoned by a Tsara, were you?" Jared demanded. It was clear in his voice and in his face that being poisoned was the only acceptable reason for Aragon's arrival on earth.

"No," Aragon said after a very long moment. He turned his back to everyone, as if the accusation in Jared's face was too much to take, and walked to the window. "I forsook my vows and left the Guardian Forces."

"By all that is Logos's Will!" The force of Jared's exclamation shook Annette. "Why would you condemn yourself to such a fate?"

"What fate?" Annette's breath caught and her heart thudded. Condemn? "What is he talking about, Aragon?" She crossed the space between them and set her hand on his shoulder, recalling that he'd said something about his time being limited, but she thought that meant here on earth. Not permanently.

"Nothing," Aragon said.

Jared responded faster than she did. "I wouldn't call an eternity of wandering alone between worlds nothing. Why did you do it?"

Annette's pinned heart fluttered wildly.

Angry and wishing he could just disappear, Aragon whipped around to face Jared. The Blood Hunter and comrade in arms had been closer to him than any other being ever until his joining with Annette last night. He and Jared had watched each other's back through the thick and thin of war as Logos's Guardian Forces battled Heldon's Fallen Army, seeking out and protecting the Elan from those who fed upon their special blood. Aragon could remember many instances when Jared had saved him throughout the years, and it was those memories that wrenched the pain and self-disgust chokingly tight around him now.

"Don't you understand?" Aragon forced the words from his tangled whirl of emotions. Have you forgotten that it was I who urged you to sacrifice yourself at the Sacred Stones? If the Elan woman hadn't loved you so much, you would have been eternally dead yesterday morning. Under my leadership our band became divided. They were right, and I was wrong. I failed, and so I left."

Jared shook his head, his hands fisted. "By Logos, Aragon! Failure can only be determined by the Guardian Council. You know that."

"I saved them the trouble. I'll execute Pathos and move on."

"You're wrong," Jared said. "You've been poisoned, only it happened years ago. You've been gunning for Pathos for a millennium. Why?"

"Because of what he did! The Blood Hunters will always bear the stain of the bloodbaths he orchestrated in the past and the Elan he continues to kill to this day. It must end. If breaking Logos's Law to see it done is necessary, so be it." Aragon fisted his hands, feeling the chafe of Jared's disappointment in him and Annette's confusion. He could see it in her face, feel it in the emotions that seemed to be crying out inside her.

Had he known that seeking pleasure with her would have melded his spirit so intimately with hers, he would have walked away. . . . He shook his head. He wouldn't have, which told him just how dishonorable he was.

He slid his gaze over her, feeling the depth of the concern in her dark eyes and craving once again to be within the fiery core of her passion. He wanted to drive her through the gates of heaven at least once more before his time ended. Mortals had no idea how blessed they were to reach such heights of pleasure.

"The Guardians aren't going to stand by and let you do this. They can't. They will seek to punish you before your fate," Jared said.

"I expected they would."

"Then you're a fool for taking the risk. What if they reach you before you eliminate Pathos? You will have wasted your life."

Aragon shrugged. "It was my choice."

"I think you're both missing the point," the mortal, Sam, interjected.

"You don't know anything about this, Sam," Jared said.

"Nope. But I do know we had four people murdered in Manhattan, and that we're going to be added to that number shortly. We're going to have vampires, corrupted werewolves, and demons breathing down our necks, and we don't have a single plan of action established or a defensive play on the table. And the enemy is already a step ahead. There are trucks receiving loads of evidence from Sno-Med as we speak."

"You found the tunnel, then?" Annette asked. Still, her stomach sank as she realized she wouldn't have another opportunity to search for information on Stef. "I didn't get enough last night. I needed more!"

A dead silence fell, and everyone but Aragon turned to stare at her.

Sam cleared his throat. "Maybe you want to discuss that with Emerald later."

Annette blinked, started to frown, then glared at Sam when she realized how he'd taken her words.

Erin covered her mouth, but the giggle still escaped, her honey eyes bright with a knowing look that told Annette that being out-of-this-world lovers was likely common to all Blood Hunters.

"Information!" Annette clarified, holding up her flash drive, her cheeks burning. "I won't know for sure until I have a chance to look, but I don't think I copied enough information off the Sno-Med computer to help me find out where Stefanie is."

"Bleedin' hell, Nette. This happened when?" Emerald narrowed her eyes.

"You didn't tell them?" Annette glanced at Sam.

He held his hands up. "Rough night on the force kept me busy. Besides, once I mentioned Aragon's presence, everyone headed here like bats out of hell." He winced and looked at Jared. "Do they have bats in hell?"

"Underlings," Jared said.

"Fook bats and underlings, I want to know what Nette did last night."

Now that she thought about the situation and Mr. X's no-show, and since Aragon already knew, she decided to tell her friends everything. "Last night, I, uh, received an anonymous phone call telling me information about Stefanie's whereabouts was on the computer in Sno-Med's Infectious

Disease Department. I was supposed to meet the caller at midnight to get the information."

Emerald spoke. "You bleedin'—"

Sam yelled, "Why in the hell—"

"—didn't you call me?" They ended together.

"He demanded that I tell no one. And I wasn't about to blow a chance on finding out about Stef because I was too big a coward to go alone. You all would have insisted on going, and you know it."

"I don't believe this. Who was it?" Sam demanded.

"I don't know. The voice was disguised . . . muffled."

"Man? Woman?"

"Man."

"Son of a bitch. Why didn't you call me? We could have had a tracer set up on your phone by now."

"He didn't talk that long. Besides, he didn't show anyway."

"Surely this means she is alive," Erin said.

Annette shook her head. "No. It could mean that. But it could just mean where her body is, or it could be a hoax."

"A hoax to lure you to a deserted building, alone, so someone can bleedin' kidnap or murder you." Emerald paced. "After what Dr. Cinatas did to us, I can't believe that you were gack-headed enough to go. How could you?" She waved her hands in the air, bracelets tinkling with her agitation. "You, who had the bloody nerve to lecture me about meeting Erin and Jared at the Sacred Stones at dawn?"

Annette winced, recalling how much grief she'd given Emerald for picking up Erin and Jared off a mountain road and driving them to her clinic for help.

"And I was expecting them!" Emerald added. She'd had visions, Annette recalled, of Jared's coming to earth and the evil they would all have to fight. "Had moved from Ireland to Twilight just so I could!"

"You're right, Em, but this was different. I took precautions. I went long before the appointed time. I went armed, and I left you a note in your office telling you about it." She explained how she got into the facility and how she was able to get access to the computer.

"I'm impressed, Doc," Erin said.

Emerald grumbled. "No matter how bleedin' well it turned out, showing up early and leaving a note doesn't make it okay. A hundred things could have gone wrong. What were you thinking?"

"I was thinking about Stef, damn it. I have to either find her or find out what happened to her! I can't keep on not knowing! Sam, we have to follow the trucks. Not just because of Stef, but also because of all those blood samples I took from the children at the health expo. I'll die if one of them falls victim to a vampire."

"Hold it!" Sam said. "*We* aren't going to do anything. Nick has the trucks under surveillance, and he'll call when they start moving. What you need to realize is that this takes your sister's disappearance to a whole new level. I now have a trail to pick up, and I guarantee I'll find the SOB. Someone at Sno-Med was involved in either the kidnapping or"—he paused to send an apologetic grimace—"murder of your sister. That needs to play into the plan to bring Sno-Med down."

Annette sighed as the tension inside knotted almost to the breaking point. There was no way Sam was excluding her from the investigation. And she didn't have to have him point out what the anonymous call last night meant. She knew it. But hearing it spoken aloud crystallized something else in her mind. "No, Sam. We don't need to keep Stef in mind as we bring Sno-Med down. We need to find her or at least locate someone who knows what happened to her *before* we act against Sno-Med. Otherwise my sister could be lost to me forever." She looked toward Aragon. "If you take out Pathos now, it might have the same result. I could lose my chance to find my sister."

She knew she was asking a lot. Eliminating Pathos was Aragon's sole purpose for being here.

His jaw tightened as they stared at each other. It was all there between them, everything they'd experienced; it wavered like an oasis on a desert horizon, seemingly unreal. But it was; it had filled her cup to overflowing, and their connection was hotter than ever, simmering beneath the dilemma warring in him. He swung away from her. "I don't have the time to wait," he said.

She exhaled as if punched. No one else spoke. His answer stung, made her want to cry out. But then she also understood how much he needed to do what he'd vowed he would.

She could see all of them—Erin, Jared, Sam, and Emerald—also wrestle with her request. Was she being unreasonable? "Listen, I know that every day that Sno-Med is allowed to operate, it's bad news for everybody, but shifting our focus toward finding out about Stefanie for a day won't cost the world."

She watched Jared cross the room and set a hand on Aragon's shoulder. "As solid as you are within the mortal realm now, you may have the time."

"I will do both," Aragon answered. "I will find your sister and take care of Pathos."

"No, my brother. *We* will," Jared said.

Aragon turned to face Jared. It wasn't clear from his dark expression if he was accepting or rejecting Jared's words. But

Annette had a suspicion Aragon would play the lone wolf as he had done before. She and he were alike in that way.

"What did you learn?" Erin nodded to the flash drive.

Annette shoved her angst to the back of her heart, realizing that the conversation they were embroiled in might not even be necessary. What if she already had all of the answers to where Stef was in her hand? What if she learned that Stef was dead? "I don't know yet. Last night's storm knocked out the power, but it appears to be on this morning. I haven't read the files yet."

"Where's your computer?" Sam asked, reaching for the flash drive.

Annette pulled back. "This is my baby," she said. "I get to deliver." Leaving the great room, she moved down the hall and entered the small bedroom across from hers, where she had a makeshift home office. Everyone stacked in behind her, creating a cloud of tension that thickened every second it took for her to access the files. Yet there was something else; a sense of cohesiveness hovered like a spirit deliberating between worlds. Jared and Sam stayed near the door. Aragon stood to her right, positioning himself close enough to make her very aware of the heat of his body. Emerald was at her back, and Erin to her left.

The icons for X-files 1 through 200 appeared on the screen. Annette drew a deep breath and opened the first file.

"It looks like a medical record file, beginning with a patient's family history," she told everyone as she made a quick scroll down the page before returning to the top and giving a sigh of disappointment. The patient had no identifying name, only a seven-digit number that began with X-666 and ended with 1. She would have to read them all, looking for details that matched Stef's history, to find her, if her sister was in one of the two hundred files Annette had copied. She highlighted the files and selected the print option.

"I'll have to print and read all of these before I'll be able to determine any significance as to why they're in the Sno-Med system and specifically in the Infectious Disease Department."

Not a great start, considering Annette was fighting against time. Would she be better off battering down the doors of the people who worked at Sno-Med and asking questions, beginning with Steven Bryers and Sharon Wills? Even finding out what project Stef was working on from her coworkers would be progress.

"I can help," Erin said. "Having worked at the Manhattan Clinic for several months, I became familiar with their filing system and with their patient codes, though the X-666 is a new one on me. Sometimes the beginning numbers denote location. The Manhattan Clinic files all began with MC1. Here, all the Arcadia Research Center files were labeled ARC10."

"With me helping, luv, we'll have it done in a jiffy," Emerald added.

"Good. I'll list facts about Stef's medical history and our family history for you to look for, and maybe we can tag her file," Annette said, forcing a positive note she was far from feeling as she read more from the file she had open in front of her, which was dated six years earlier. That dashed Annette's hopes that Stefanie's would be among the two hundred files she'd copied; Stefanie hadn't started working at Sno-Med until last year and disappeared this year. Backing out of that file, she went to number two hundred and groaned aloud.

"What's wrong?" Emerald squeezed Annette's shoulder.

"I only had time to copy two hundred of the files. There were more. The last file I have is dated an entire year before

Stefanie began working for Sno-Med." Tears stung her eyes. She wanted to cry, but she fisted her hand instead and hit the arm of her chair. "Damn, if Pathos hadn't interfered, I might have been able to get more by waiting out my anonymous caller."

"Pathos!" Erin and Jared exclaimed at the same time, making Annette swivel her chair to face them.

"Yes," Annette said. "He had a weird-looking man with him who sort of glowed. They were having a discussion as they walked along the dark corridor." She closed her eyes, searching for the conversation she'd overheard. Years of medical training had sharpened her recall skills. "Pathos was putting Glow Man in charge of Sno-Med until Cinatas was found. No one was to enter, not even anyone from the Vladarian Order, because one of them has his offspring, and he sounded pissed about it. The trucks were to pick up any and all data, and all blood samples had been airlifted to Corazon de Rojo."

You'd have thought she'd set off a bomb, the way the men exploded.

Chapter Ten

"OFFSPRING!" Aragon and Jared exclaimed.

"Corazon de Rojo!" Sam yelled.

Annette jumped at the force of their voices reverberating in the small room.

"Son of a bitch!" Sam continued. "This just gets better and better." Sam shook his head, his face pale, his expression more ragged than Annette had ever seen it.

"What is it?" Annette asked.

Sam's laugh grated like jagged glass. "Corazon de Rojo is Luis Vasquez's compound in Belize, which would rank as a concentration camp. He's the god behind those stone walls, and even has dozens of so-called nuns serving him. You live, breathe, or die at his command."

Erin narrowed her eyes at Sam. "You should have told us more about Luis Vasquez before. If the rest of you will remember, Vasquez's name is on the list I made of Dr. Cinatas's top clients. He's a vampire in the Vladarian Order." She paced to the middle of the room. "He's one of the men who received blood transfusions at the Manhattan Clinic. I administered the blood treatment to him about two months ago. Vasquez walked in pale and weak, as if death's door was a step away. Four days later he sauntered out, looking and acting like a horny *GQ* ad."

Moving to Sam's side, Emerald placed her hand over his fisted one. "Is this what last night was—"

"Don't even go there," he said harshly. He jerked away from her touch and turned his back on her.

Emerald bit her lip and turned away, her hand clenched.

Annette's eyes widened with shock. Sam had always been gruff and irritable with Emerald, but he'd never been this hurtfully rude. What in heaven's name was going on? Neither of them would let go of their guard to connect.

But she wasn't one to preach at them. She'd never let anyone in . . . until last night. In some ways it all seemed almost like a dream. She glanced at Aragon, absorbing his solid presence, and knew that it wasn't, then focused back on Sam. Whatever his experience at Corazon de Rojo, the memory of it had etched grave lines along his brow and turned his voice to a tight rasp. "*How* doesn't exactly matter now, but I will tell you Nick's father died getting me out of that hellhole. After Annette saw fit to drag Nick into this mess last night, I had to tell him the whole story. He's with us on this, and you all can trust him."

Annette drew a sharp breath. She still had a few questions for Nick before she could come close to trusting him, but she let that go for now.

"So we know the blood is in Belize, but why?" Emerald asked.

"The place would have to have the facilities to store the blood properly," Annette said. "It could be a support center for Sno-Med, like a backup place to handle testing of the samples and transfusions to the vampires. How big is the compound?" she asked Sam.

"Big." Sam snorted with disgust. "I'd doubt they'd use transfusions there, though. Corazon de Rojo is an uncivilized hellhole. Vampires would be more likely to suck the life out of the prisoners' jugulars on a regular basis."

"Prisoners? And there are nuns there?" Erin asked.

"*Supposed* nuns in proper habits would be more descriptive. The poor sell their female children to Vasquez for 'religious service.' I'd call them Vasquez's slaves. He gets very messy with prisoners. They clean up and then spend their days upon their knees praying to Vasquez for salvation—or for Vasquez's own salvation. I don't know which, and both are hopeless. God only knows how they spend their nights—perhaps on their knees, praying for death, because of what the men are doing to them."

The more Sam revealed, the tighter the wrenching knot in Annette's stomach became. She shuddered at the thought of Stefanie being at the mercy of any of the monsters associated with Sno-Med.

"So we just sit and wait to follow a pile of trucks?" Annette asked.

"If we want Pathos, it may be our only option," Jared said. "Following him or any of the Vladarians is impossible unless you cross through the spirit barrier. They don't travel as mortals do. They shift through the spirit barrier to get to where they want to go, circumventing the rules of time and space."

"What do you mean?" Annette asked.

"One minute he could be here, and a few minutes later he could appear in London."

"Hell." Sam shook his head. "Talk about being damn near impossible to pin down."

"There are limitations," Aragon added. "Crossing too frequently will, depending on their constitution and power, cause them to incinerate on the spot."

"Then we're back to following the trucks."

"What if we lose them?"

"Four semis?" Sam gave her a disbelieving look. "I'll eat my patrol car. But no, we're through waiting. I'm setting up a roadblock, and we'll only let one of the trucks through to track where it goes. Nick could even follow it in the helicopter. The rest of the trucks we'll hold hostage. I can come up with some legal bullshit to impound them long enough to get what data we need off them and make sure the rest of the information disappears."

"It still doesn't seem like we are doing enough fast enough," Annette said, her frustration like a vise around her. But what else could they do? They needed access to the computers, and they had to locate the monsters they wanted. "What if that truck takes days to get to its destination?"

"It's a chance we'll have to take," Sam said.

"I can tell you that Pathos will seek a stronghold close to his foe," Aragon interjected. "He'll want us to constantly be aware that he is near. He will choose a place of prestige and power," he added. "Then he'll gather his forces. He is the coordinating power behind the Vladarians. They were nothing but roving beasts of the night before he took over. Without him they will—"

"—implode," Jared finished Aragon's sentence.

"Resulting in them becoming less of a future threat. But if Pathos now has an offspring—," Aragon added.

"That he has surely trained," Jared muttered.

"Then even eliminating Pathos might not change things." Annette's teeth clenched at the frustration pouring from Aragon.

Jared shook his head. "I doubt that. No one can match what Pathos has done. Under his guidance the Vladarians have become very powerful."

Erin moved closer to Jared. "Considering the names on the list, I'd give anything to be a fly on their boardroom wall now."

Emerald waved her hand, filling the room with a magic like tinkling of her bracelets. "Why can't we, luv? Bug the vermin and find out what they're plotting."

"That would be after we follow the trucks to his lair, so to speak," Annette said.

Emerald shot Sam a quick look. "And don't you dare say it's bleedin' illegal."

"Forget illegal. You three aren't going anywhere. The only *we* in action here is me and Jared"—Sam sent Aragon a guarded glance—"Aragon and maybe Nick, if it isn't too dangerous. You three will stay here and go through the medical records. Tailing the truck might be too risky. Tracking it via GPS would be better."

"You can't do either," Jared said firmly. "The devices give off sounds and signals that are audible to nonmortals, especially were-beings."

"I will follow the mortal vehicle to its destination in spirit form. I have a better chance of tracking and finding Pathos than anyone else," Aragon said.

"No," Jared interjected. "You don't know what the Guardians have decided to do about your desertion. You and I both know they won't take the act lightly. Crossing the spirit barrier could have you facing a worse fate than that of a faded warrior. There has to be another way."

Annette bit her lip. Her reaction matched Jared's response. Aragon couldn't risk it.

"That doesn't matter," Aragon said emphatically. "I came here on a quest, and I have to do whatever it takes to fulfill that quest. I am right in going for Pathos. He is the key to defeating the growing evil. I don't understand why Logos hasn't acted against him."

"You know why," Jared said. "You just don't want to accept that Logos established different laws to govern the realm of the spirit world than those for the mortal. He cannot break them, even though he has the power to do so, or order will then cease to have meaning and Heldon's chaos will have won. Assassinations in the spirit realm are against his law. A foe must be defeated in battle only."

"You speak as if Pathos is an innocent lamb that will be struck unawares. There will be a battle."

"It is the motivation behind the action that determines it. Your purpose is to kill Pathos. Eliminating evil is but an added benefit. It is impure."

"Then my decision to turn over leadership of the Blood Hunters to Sven was the right one. I am flawed, and my fate is set."

"No, it's not. You can return to the Guardian Council, tell them you erred, and seek leniency."

"My path is set."

A painful tightness settled inside Annette's chest. She understood why Aragon felt the way he did. She felt the same way about finding out what happened to her sister. Her path was set, regardless. Still, that didn't ease the reality of their situation or the gut feeling that things were about to get very bad, very fast. And she couldn't let that happen. She stood up from the computer chair and set her hand on Aragon's arm.

"We need to talk," she said, urging him to come with her. He didn't budge.

Emerald stood. "We haven't had breakfast. So until we hear from Nick about the trucks, we'll go just up the road to my place and eat while you two talk."

Aragon shook his head. There'd been enough talk, and his path was clear. The mortals didn't realize how ill equipped they were to go up against Pathos, nor how fragile their hold upon life was. And Jared was now among them. Aragon had felt his friend's mortality the moment Jared's hand made contact with his shoulder. Aragon had momentarily forgotten he hadn't been able to shift when he'd tried last. But surely if he had his amulet back he'd have enough power.

He had to make this journey alone. He'd find Annette's sister first, then eliminate Pathos. His arm tingled beneath her touch, and he flexed his muscle as the heat of Annette's hand and the scent of her skin rippled through the memories of their joining and intensified his need to do so again. The urge had been pulsing strong since the moment he'd awakened with her beside him.

"Please, let's talk," she said.

"We will talk after we mate again," Aragon countered.

She blinked at him as if she didn't understand what he'd said.

He frowned. "Is it not acceptable to set conditions for talk based upon my needs, just as you often do?"

Sam burst into laughter, an amusement that seemed to spread among the others though they covered their mouths, trying not to be heard.

"Holy hell!" Annette placed her hands over her face and ran from the room. He was amazed that she missed the walls in her blind flight. A second later a door slammed.

Aragon shrugged and sent Jared a confused look. "What is wrong? Nick speaks of mating all the time, only his word for such an amazing thing does its beauty a grave injustice. His ignorance needs correction."

"I'll tell him." Sam laughed harder. "You just might be kosher."

"He's a bleedin' prince among frogs, and we need to disappear," said the woman well named for the brilliant emerald color of her eyes. Cloaked in a mystique akin to

Stonehenge, ancient of knowledge and hidden of meaning, she was a puzzle. She was more than an ordinary mortal, only he didn't know how or why. Bracelets tinkling, she motioned for everyone to follow her out.

"We'll bring you some," Jared said.

"Bring me what?" Aragon asked.

"Peaches, for one thing," Jared said. "Just wait and see."

Aragon shrugged. "I have strawberries."

The others left the room, and as Jared turned to go, Aragon grabbed his arm. "Annette hurt Pathos trying to help me. He will come after her. I know him, and it isn't a slight he will let go, especially since a member of the red demons witnessed it."

"We'll get him first." Jared slapped his arm across Aragon's back.

"I know, but in case something happens to me before . . . you'll guard her for me?"

Jared sucked in air and stared hard into Aragon's eyes. "So it's that way for you with the mortal woman already. You have my vow. But surely you can change—"

"There is nothing to change. I chose." Even when the time came to go after Pathos, Aragon would act alone. Aragon didn't want to jeopardize Jared's future, but he had to assure Annette's safety no matter what.

For a mortal to reach the Falls, the mansion resort etched into the peak of Appalachian's Hades Mountain, it was necessary for those damnation-bound souls to travel through a tunnel that spanned the width of a large waterfall known as Satan's Ride, named so because of the deep pit and underground river it poured into. Anyone who ever fell into its treacherous waters was never seen again. Legend had it that such unlucky souls went straight to hell.

They didn't know hell already existed on the mountain's top, spreading a circle of evil, a dark cloud of comfort.

As far as Twilight's government leaders were concerned, the Falls mansion was a reclusive billionaire's folly that padded pockets way too well for them to notice anything besides the mansion's stone walls and black spires. And those could only be seen in the wintertime.

It wasn't winter.

For the damned to access the Falls, it was a matter of status. Only the upper echelon of the Fallen were permitted to pass through the fortress's walls and enjoy having their every need or desire catered to—no matter what that might be.

It had been a while since Pathos had availed himself of their services. He preferred Zion, his estate in Austria. But the Falls was convenient for now, and Cinatas needed some of the treatments that were readily available here. Shashur had tortured Cinatas to the very edge of nonexistence.

Though currently Pathos and Cinatas were the only clients in residence, by tonight all of the Vladarian Order's prime vampires would arrive for a little surprise. He stood overlooking Twilight's sun-drenched valley through the plate glass.

Far below, too far for even his acute vision, the scurrying inhabitants of Twilight's town went ignorantly about their business. And Dr. Annette Batista was among them. He took satisfaction in knowing his prey was right under his nose, and toyed with the idea of hunting her down this morning. She could provide him with some interesting interludes as he dealt with the Sno-Med situation. But first he needed time with his son, and ensuring her cooperation beforehand would go a long way toward achieving the pleasures he planned to extract from her soul a piece at a time. Tomorrow would be soon enough.

Tonight his main problem would be Luis Vasquez, now the top oil dealer within the Vladarian powerhouse.

The door opened behind him, and he turned to face his son. Mortal plastics and makeup had temporarily covered Cinatas's scarred countenance, and would have to do until they could find a mortal whose face was as close as possible to Cinatas's original. Then they would procure a transplant—whether the donor was willing or not.

Cinatas didn't speak, but crossed the room and stared out at the valley, flexing his fists. This was the first opportunity they'd had to talk since he'd dragged his son from hell. After a prolonged silence, Pathos, much to his dismay, was compelled to speak first. "Shashur has been eliminated. He is nonexistent now."

"A small conciliation, considering my losses. I would have survived the explosion, but he found me injured and sucked the blood from me until death ensued. Then carried me to torture." Cinatas kept his gaze fixed on the view.

Surprised at the news, Pathos sharpened his senses, seeking for a sign or hint of a vampiric infection in Cinatas. He couldn't detect it, yet. That wasn't to say that the virus wasn't just lying dormant at the moment. Over time there'd been other mixed beings, even a number of vampire mortals who served their sires, but Pathos didn't think there'd ever been a creature with quite the mixture that Cinatas now had, of corrupted Elan blood, were-seed, and vampire seed. "So you've the seeds of both immortals within you now?"

"What do you mean?" Cinatas turned sharply.

"Don't you remember what I said when I found you with Shashur? Aren't you curious as to why I chose you over one of the Vladarian Order?"

Cinatas shrugged. "I assumed you found my knowledge of blood proteins indispensable."

"No. Knowledge can be obtained one way or another. Even as we speak, all of your personal files as well as all of Sno-Med's records are being loaded on trucks to be brought here for examination, should you decide not to join me. What can't be so easily procured is a son from my loins."

Cinatas stared long and hard before replying. Pathos was beginning to really like the beast his son had become. Though he was young, the potential for great evil was there.

"And this happened when and how?" Cinatas asked. "I had both parents in Puerto Rico."

"Run any of your precious tests, you'll find me to be your biological father. Your mother was very heavily into voodoo, its rites and rituals, and was more than willing to bear my seed in exchange for some powerful connections from the damned."

"And why would you want that? It obviously wasn't for any familial or emotional notions," Cinatas said.

Pathos absorbed the slight sting of Cinatas's cold assessment. His son would need time to adjust to his new circumstance.

"I have a number of offspring scattered throughout the world. None specialized so brilliantly in hematology as you, which is why I activated you early and have chosen you for something very special. All of my children are learning the skills that will see my plan to fruition, and I do have a great deal of regard for them."

"How many are there?"

"Thousands. And even more are being born as we speak. Sperm banks make mass propagation easy, especially when you qualify under their genius testing. Their information is written in the Book of Life at my estate, Zion."

Cinatas frowned. "You sound like God Almighty."

Pathos smiled. "I will be. There's more to this world than lording over a tribe of vampires, and I've put the wheels in motion to get it."

That wiped the dull, undead look off Cinatas's face. "How?" he asked.

"One step at a time. Today you prove yourself to a small degree, and tonight I'll give you a little taste of the future."

"What?"

"You'd planned to take my place as leader of the Vladarians, and your hunger for power pleases me as much as your disloyalty disgusts me. It's but a small ripple between us that we'll correct over time as your fidelity improves. Someday the Vladarians will be expendable, but not yet."

"What do you want me to do?"

"Get Sno-Med off shaky ground with the media. I've scheduled a news release for later today. Nyros will have the specifics. Vamps get anxious when their blood supply is threatened, and media coverage that all is well will help. What went wrong to begin with?"

"The Elan nurse found four bodies left from Shashur's transfusion and ran, planning to cause trouble."

"Erin?" Pathos asked.

"Yes. Who is she?"

Pathos ignored Cinatas's question. Until his son proved himself, Pathos wasn't going to tell him more than necessary. And it wasn't Erin's time yet. Soon she would know who he really was to her, but not yet. "Why the body count? The whole purpose of transfusions is to limit the number of mortal deaths and the associated complications." Technology had altered the Vladarian's world. Multiple deaths were becoming harder and harder to conceal, and advances in science now made those deaths unnecessary. Unfortunately, a vampire would go on a visceral rampage and leave a mess to clean up. Shashur had been known to wipe out a village every now or then. And the Russians were bad at that, too. More fell prey to the vampire in power than to the Siberian winters.

"Shashur always demanded fresh blood. This time the donors refused to come. A message needed to be sent to the others. If a man cannot control those who serve him, then he deserves to die."

"Excellent mandate," Pathos paused for a moment to absorb it. It was exactly why Heldon needed to be nonexistent. His pride in Cinatas notched higher. "So Erin discovered the bodies and ran. What else?" Pathos asked.

"She has made friends in Twilight, two doctors and a sheriff. They are out to make trouble for Sno-Med. But more importantly, she has teamed up with someone you should know about. They caused the fire at the center."

"After you kidnapped them. I already know who she has partnered with. A former Blood Hunter named Jared. There is now also a second Blood Hunter named Aragon. You won't need to concern yourself with them. I'll be containing them." And one of them in a very special way, he thought. He pictured the dark-haired doctor splaying herself out for him and was surprised to feel a burn in his loins.

"Then why did you ask?" Cinatas frowned.

"It pays to make sure you're getting the truth by asking what you already know. Remember that."

Cinatas blinked, and Pathos smiled. His boy was catching on fast. "The second thing you will do for me today is locate a mortal woman by the name of Stefanie Batista. She is the sister of Dr. Annette Batista, one of Erin's new friends."

"Do I know this Stefanie Batista?"

"Possibly. She worked at Sno-Med."

"Hundreds are employed there."

"She disappeared six months ago. See what you can discover and check with Nyros on the list of people he has for us to question today."

"If you will indulge my asking, why do you want her specifically?"

"She's the Achilles' heel I need to stroke. Dr. Annette Batista is about to willingly provide a bedside manner that will please me in every way. I'm betting she'll do *anything*, anything at all, to protect her sister."

Pathos saw the first glimmer of real interest light his son's eyes. "You do realize that the staff here will provide anything you ask for?" Pathos asked. "Not as well as in Zion, but decently."

"Zion?"

"My estate in Austria. I'll show it to you once we've contained this problem. I've had a thousand years to build it and to perfect my plan to rule. Everything you could desire is there. And when you're ready, I will reveal it all. We'll take Dr. Batista and her sister along with us, for I don't think I'll have tired of the fiery doctor by then."

"Why even wait for the sister? Just have the doctor brought here, shackle her, and do what you want."

"You've much to learn yet to be great, son. There is power in souls. Physically forcing someone to do your will has but a weak power to it, because you gain no part of their soul. But creating a situation that makes them choose to do your will over their own takes skill and gives you more power, more of their soul. Administering pain to achieve power is for weaklings, for the one tortured retains all of their soul against such force. But to give them pleasure, make them feel pleasure when they don't want to, is to gain pieces of their soul. You'll learn.

"Meanwhile, we need to get you ready for the news conference. Have makeup apply an injury or two to your mask. Public sympathy will help the masses ignore untoward rumors. After that, we'll locate Stefanie Batista."

"You're accompanying me on this search? Do you not trust me to handle this?"

"Of course. Think of it as father-and-son time, rather than an evaluation. And who knows, while we're out, I may decide to pay Dr. Batista a visit after all. Just to whet her appetite."

Chapter Eleven

ARAGON KNEW WHAT Annette was doing even before he reached the door. Her agitated steps drummed through the quiet of the dwelling, bringing to mind his Blood Hunter brother York, whose nature often had him pacing amid turmoil while Navarre had sat quietly. The memory twisted a knot of regret inside him and brought him to a halt. He wondered what they were doing now.

After hearing Jared's reaction to his departure from the Guardian Forces, Aragon had been rethinking his decision and its repercussions. He'd been so convinced that his brethren would be better off without him that he hadn't considered anything else.

Were they suffering from his decision as well?

Yet he wasn't wrong—Pathos needed to be eliminated, and Aragon had to be the one to make it happen. Aragon knew how Pathos thought, how the were-being reacted in battle, and what he would most likely do next. In addition to his quest, another purpose to his presence upon the mortal ground had formed, one that went beyond his anger at Pathos's betrayal. *Annette.* If he had not been there to intervene, she'd be in Pathos's hands now. He'd been giving some thought to how he could find out what happened to her sister, and had come up with a plan.

When he crossed through the spirit barrier, he'd first seek

the knowledge of Logos's angels before trying to track Pathos again. The angels cared for the souls of mortals and had all the names of those who passed through their gates written in The Book. If Stefanie's name wasn't with the angels, then she'd have to be on earth, and he'd need a fix on her scent to try and find her. But he'd have to eliminate Pathos first.

As soon as they had word that the vehicles were in motion, Aragon would act before Jared and the others had time to. That would be the only way to assure himself of Jared's safety. And Aragon would get to Pathos before the evil werewolf made a move against Annette. Pathos would most likely attack by night. And he wouldn't act at the first rise of the moon; he'd wait, make his quarry sweat, make them worry, make them weaker.

Aragon knew for certain that whatever price he paid for his actions, he'd never regret melding with Annette. He had pushed open the door to her fiery beauty, and he felt his whole being go hard with the desperate want of her for more than just a moment in time. He wanted her forever, but it was a desire that would remain unfulfilled.

Pausing, she met his gaze. Her cheeks were flushed; her eyes, dark wells of hot emotion. Her mouth trembled between a frown and an invitation to kiss her that he readily recognized from last night. She had something in her hand that she'd been looking at.

"We have to talk," she said. "You need to listen to Jared."

He crossed the room and slid his thumb along the delicate curve of her jaw, sensing the tension in her, feeling the race of her pulse.

Her tongue dipped down nervously to moisten her bottom lip. She wanted him as much as he wanted her, but something was stopping her.

"I didn't ask enough questions last night. What does it all mean? A faded warrior and the Guardian Council's judgment?"

He drew in a bracing breath, tasting the sweetness of her essence on the tip of his tongue just as richly as he felt the weight of her concern wrap tightly around him. "Becoming a faded warrior is my fate. It was set before we met, when I failed in my duty to be a true leader for the Blood Hunters. I don't know when it will come, but it will, and nothing can change it."

"Don't say that," she whispered. "As long as there is time, then something can change. Maybe—"

"No," he said roughly. "Nothing will change. My fate is set."

"What about the Guardian Council?"

"They may choose a harsher punishment."

"What could be worse than wandering alone for eternity?"

"Nonexistence."

Tears filled her eyes. "Then you can't go back into the spirit world, ever. What if they try to harm you? What if you can't return? How could I help you then? It's like Stef all over again." She pressed something to her heart, and he realized she held a picture.

"May I see her picture?" he asked, setting his hand over Annette's.

She slid the picture into his hand. The woman looked very much like Annette, same glowing skin, same delicate features, same luxurious dark hair, only younger and less tense. The woman was smiling and holding a drawing in front of her that caught him completely off guard. It was an exact drawing of the Guardian Council's Judgment Hall, with twelve figures seated upon the high dais just as the

Council Servers would be. Kneeling before the Council was a Shadowman, a shape-shifter in the Guardian Forces. This Pyrathian held his shape-shifted form of a fierce winged being akin to mortal imaginings of dragons. Pyrathians were powerful warriors with a special gift. They could breathe life into those mortals whom death tried to claim before their fullness of time.

"Where did she get the drawing?"

Annette smiled sadly. "She drew it herself. Stef's love was art and the creatures she created. She kept volumes of her drawings and the stories she made up about them. I should have supported her desire to be an artist instead of insisting she have a real career."

Aragon put his arm around her shoulders and pulled her to him, searching for the right words to ease her pain. "Wait before you judge yourself so harshly. Though the path taken now may seem to have been in error, the journey isn't over. There may yet be a reason for the present."

She breathed in deeply, her dark eyes searching his. "If I heed your words, will you take your own advice as well? Will you not judge your choices so harshly? Can there be a different future for you?"

"No," he said sharply. The hope in her eyes twisted painfully inside him. "My situation is different. The consequences are set and cannot be undone. But for your sister, all is yet unknown, and you must wait until you learn the truth before you can judge yourself. Can you show me these drawings of your sister's?"

Annette nodded. "Most of Stef's sketchbooks are on the shelf here." Stepping back from him, she moved over to a bookcase and slipped a thick volume off the shelf, opening it up before handing it to him. He gave her back her sister's picture before studying the drawings.

As he turned the pages, he saw a mixture of creatures. Some of them were creatures of human mythology, like sea serpents; others were animals from the mortal realm; but there were also a number of detailed drawings of spirit beings, both those that fought for Logos in the Guardian Forces and those in Heldon's Fallen Army. He didn't know how or why, but Annette's sister clearly had a connection to the spirit world. He'd heard there were mortals who could see through the barrier, see past the twilit edges of the spirit realm, and in their visions or dreams were able to see and remember things that most mortals never even knew existed. Her scent wafted up from the pages. Holding the book close to his nose, he drew it in and fixed it in his mind.

"What is it?" Annette asked, her brow furrowed with puzzlement.

"Her scent is similar to yours, yet different."

"Her scent?"

"Each being has a unique scent, and my were-kind is very adept at detecting them." He pointed to the picture she held. "You both are very similar in appearance, but different. Scents are the same way."

Annette took the picture and ran her finger along the contours of her sister's face. "Stef's blue eyes were so dark, they usually appeared as brown as mine. People always thought Stef was a younger version of me, but that's where our likeness ended. I plowed everything out of my way with my determination to be a doctor. Even the people I cared about the most got pushed away."

Aragon closed the sketchbook and returned it to its place, then set the picture of her sister on the shelf, too. "Don't despise what you are." He cupped her chin in his palm and brought her gaze to meet his. "You're like a warrior. You pledge your life to help and protect others, and you battle every day. In the spirit realm, warriors are the only spirits that stand alone. They never meld their spirits to others, because to do so would diminish their focus and thus weaken them in battle."

She stared at him for a long moment, her gaze moving from his eyes to his mouth to his chin. She pressed her thumb to the indentation at its center before brushing his bottom lip. He closed his eyes, relishing the tingling fire she ignited with the simplest of gestures.

"What's melding?" she asked.

He opened his eyes and pulled her body flush to his. *It is a union of one spirit to another,* he said into her mind. *A connection that binds together their thoughts and experiences.*

She set her hand over his heart, and he could see the wonder of truth light a fire in her eyes. *We are melded, aren't we?* she thought back at him.

He nodded. *It is what I choose to share and give to you. Yes, we are melded. For as long as I have breath upon the mortal ground, I will be with you.*

How long? The hurt in her eyes cut him deeply. The pain she felt for him and within herself split him open as surely as a sword.

I do not know. He groaned deeply from the pain of it. "I'm sorry," he whispered aloud before tasting the sweetness of her lips. He could disappear at any moment. It could be that the only thing giving him substance within the mortal realm was her possession of his amulet. And when he took that back today, he might fade into the void to which he'd condemned himself.

If he did, that would in some ways be best for her, even though she didn't want to believe it. Given the strength of the connection that had formed between them already, more time together would only make that bond stronger, deeper, and more agonizing to break.

But by Logos, he couldn't turn away from her now. If there was any way possible to make it back to her side after he found Pathos, then Aragon would return.

"Annette, I—"

She set her finger over his lips. "Talk later," she whispered. "Just love me again. Now."

This time he was more than willing to meet her conditions.

Annette swiped at her tears. Any awkwardness she felt over Aragon's public mating declaration fell beneath her flood of concern for him. From the moment she'd looked into his eyes when he came through the bedroom door, she'd seen a care for her that no man had ever had, an honest, consuming desire. Nor had she ever felt the same driving need for any other man, this hunger she couldn't control. It was as if he'd awakened her. She'd been wrong in thinking his sharp features were too roughly warlike to be sensual. The look firing his gaze was the sexiest thing she'd ever experienced.

Melded to a warrior.

Awed, humbled, and heartbroken by the fate he could not escape, she fought back her tears and reached for him, needing him more than her next breath. He had to be wrong. Someone as vital and strong as he couldn't just fade away. Jared had been wrong in thinking he had to sacrifice himself to protect Erin, and Aragon could be mistaken as well.

For the first time in her life, she ignored her better judgment and determined to make every moment count. Starting now. Desperate jerks and awkward pulls sent her sweats to the floor first; his followed in her frantic rush to have every inch of his supple body and hard erection exposed and ready for her touch and tongue. But before she could fall to her knees and taste the fullness of his hot need, he kissed her hard, his tongue devouring her mouth even as his spirit delved into hers. A kaleidoscope of passion swirled around her.

Come with me, he said into her mind. *Touch me. Trust me. I long to give you everything. I need you.*

"And I need you," she whispered, then buried her hands into the thick wavy length of his midnight hair to pull him closer. She drank of the dark coffee richness of his eyes that seemed to roast her alive as he watched her respond to his touch.

Grasping her bottom, he slid her up until he could suckle her breasts. She braced her hands on his shoulders, shifting just enough so that he could tease each nipple to needy points that begged for more. When he lowered her to her feet, she didn't even pause before she went to her knees. She cupped his erection in her hands and brought the wet heat of her mouth to its burgeoning tip, drawing him deep. He groaned and shuddered as his hands threaded into her hair. He seemed to be urging her back up, but she persisted until his breathing was ragged and his body shivered at every stroke of her tongue.

Sweeping her into his arms, Aragon moved to the bed, his mouth devouring hers in his hunger to get inside her. As soon as her bottom hit the edge of the mattress, he had her legs spread as wide as they would go, opening her sex completely. She fell back on her elbows as he lifted her to his mouth. His tongue slid up her weeping flesh, dipping inside her before moving to the hardened knot of her erect feminine need and swirling his hot tongue over it until her hips jerked beyond her ability to control.

Then he stood looking at her a moment as if there was nothing in the universe but her. She thought he'd thrust hotly into her next, but he didn't. He leaned forward and kissed her with a slow relish that had her panting in need. He lavished the same slow burn of his tongue upon her breasts until she was moaning from the agonizing pleasure. Only then did he slide into her slowly, inching his heated erection in a little at a time before easing back out with excruciating slowness. He had the look of a man in heaven, determined to enjoy every possible second of the pleasure he'd found.

Long past the point at which she thought she could take no more, sure she either had to come or go mad, he thrust himself into her hard and deep and fast, exploding an orgasm through her that shook her entire being. Again and again he drove into her. Each stroke sent her shuddering pleasure higher and higher until she shouted and her body convulsed against his with dizzying force. The power of his resulting orgasm slammed into her mind, grabbing her upon a wave of pleasure that sent her hurtling with him. He clung to her and she clung to him, for in that moment everything disappeared but each other.

Chapter Twelve

THE PHONE RANG and Annette groaned. She couldn't move to answer it. She couldn't *think* to answer it. Aragon had shifted in the bed until she was cradled against his side. They lay on top of the thick black-and-gold comforter, with the sun from the window streaming warmly over them.

The digital readout on her clock flashed a red twelve at her. For a moment she thought they'd been making love for four hours, until she realized that the clock was flashing from the power outage last night and needed to be reset. She felt as if they'd made love that long, though. The pleasure had been unending, and she was completely drained.

"Sorry, I am unable to answer the phone right now. Please leave a message and I will get back to you as soon as possible." Her answering machine beeped, and Annette waited for the caller to leave a message.

Nothing came, though she could hear the faint sound of someone breathing until they abruptly hung up. Her eyes shot wide, and an electric charge ripped through her. Had Mr. X just tried to call her? To tell her more about her sister? Heart pounding, Annette rolled from the bed and ran to the hall where her answering machine sat on a small mahogany table. She hit the caller ID button, and her emotions nose-dived back to reality. Rob and Celeste Rankin's number appeared. Celeste must be returning her call. But why hadn't she left a message? Was she upset that Annette had revealed Celeste's checkup to Rob? Annette bit her lip.

Aragon came up behind her and pulled her securely against him. "What is it?"

"Nothing." She sighed. "I thought that the man who'd called about my sister last night was trying to call again. But it was just my neighbors."

He stiffened. "The man who was here when we arrived last night?"

He sounded agitated, and she turned to face him. "Rob. But I think it's his wife trying to call me about a blood test I need her to repeat. He really bothered you, didn't he?"

"I didn't like the way he looked at you or the way he upset you. You shouldn't speak with him again."

She wanted to ask what about the way Rob looked at her bothered Aragon, but decided to do it later when she wasn't in a hurry to call Celeste back and when she wasn't standing naked in the hallway. "We'll talk about Rob later. I need to call back now and hopefully get Celeste." She hit the dial button. Aragon crossed his arms and frowned but remained quiet.

The phone rang until the Rankins' answering machine picked up. Annette opened her mouth to leave a message, then thought better of it. She didn't want to cause Celeste any more problems. The little she'd accidentally said last night still burned.

Annette hung up. "I'll have to call back later." But the gears in Annette's mind were set in motion now, and there was no stopping them. She couldn't just sit here, looking at medical records, waiting for trucks to move. She had to do more. But she didn't want to lose a moment with Aragon, either.

"There are some people from Sno-Med I need to go and see this morning." Namely Dr. Steven Bryers, the name on the lab coat she'd found at the computer desk last night. And Sharon Wills, Stef's friend from Sno-Med who had set Stef up with Nick.

"Then I will accompany you on this mission."

"I'd like that," she said. "We need to hurry and get dressed. I'll call Emerald and let them know to contact my cell phone when they hear something. You'll have to wear the sweats Sam gave you for now. The store won't open until ten."

"Mortal clothes are unnecessary. I like you better like this," he said, gruffly, then cupped her breasts, giving each of them a sucking, nipple-hardening kiss.

She'd thought she'd had all the sexual stimuli that she could take for the moment, but she was wrong. Everything flared to an instant ready, set, and go. She pulled back from him, groaning at the urge to lie on the floor, spread her legs, and demand that he soothe the ache. Instead, she clamped her hands over her breasts and ran to the bedroom. "That's one reason we all wear clothes," she shouted back at him. "Otherwise, all our time would be spent making love."

He followed her. "Is there something wrong with that?"

She glanced back at him, laughing. *No,* she thought to herself. *Not with you.* And she felt a pang of real regret that they couldn't just do that now, and that there might never be a time when they could.

Dr. Steven Bryers reminded Annette of a praying mantis: sort of greenish in complexion, bug-eyed, tall, and so very thin that his arms seemed as if they kept folding in on each other as he fidgeted nervously in the booth. He sat across the table from her and Aragon, whining in a squeaky voice about how he wasn't responsible for the fire yesterday, and anybody who said that he had anything to do with it was just trying to frame him.

Annette hadn't even had a chance to ask her questions yet. The man had started bellyaching the moment he saw Aragon. The first words out of his mouth had been, "Listen, Detective . . ."

It was only then that Annette realized that the T-shirt Sam had given Aragon had a Police Department emblem on the left breast. Well, she wasn't about to let his assumption go unused. "We aren't here about yesterday's fire, but about the disappearance of a young woman six months ago, and your acquaintance with her."

His bug eyes bulged. "Wait a minute—I knew the girl. She worked at the same place I did, but I wouldn't call her an acquaintance. You make it sound as if there was something sordid involved."

"Then you knew Stefanie Batista?"

"Yes, I just told you that."

"Did you work on any projects with her?"

His pasty brow furrowed. "Of course not—she wasn't even in the same department as mine."

"What do you know about the X-files?"

His pale eyes shot back and forth between her and Aragon. "Was that some sort of joke?"

"No," Annette replied.

"It was a TV series a number of years ago—"

"Not that *X-Files*. The ones on your computer in the Infectious Disease Department at Sno-Med."

"What? I haven't a clue what you're talking about. There are no files in my department labeled X-files. I know that for sure. I keep a close tab on what everyone in my department does, and I don't put up with anyone wasting time or company bandwidth on movie star crap. America is sick these days. Ever since JR got shot, they let themselves get caught up in stupid television shows and don't even know how to live real life anymore."

Annette blinked. The guy looked like he was climbing onto a familiar soapbox. She didn't know if he was for real or if he was putting up one hell of a smokescreen, but she sure wasn't getting any answers. She gave it one more shot.

"Do the numbers 666 mean anything to you?"

"The mark of the beast?" he said with a snort.

"As in the first digits of about a thousand medical file numbers on the computers? Does that ring a bell?"

"Listen, you're not ringing any bells at all. Don't know what computer you've been on, but it isn't one from my department. All Sno-Med files begin with the letters of the center they originated with. Any medical file on my computer will read ARC for Arcadia Research Center. What's this all about?"

"How long have you worked at Sno-Med?"

"About nine months," he said.

"And in that time have you noticed anything strange or unusual about the research center?"

"No. I don't know what you're fishing for here, but this is the best job I've ever had. There is funding out the wazoo for anything I need. Any research that I want to do. Any equipment that I need. For the first time ever I'm experiencing what it really means to be a research scientist in infectious disease. And I'll be honest with you. The last place I worked burned, and they tried to blame it on me, saying an explosion in my lab caused it. I think they set the explosion to get insurance money."

"Well, Dr. Bryers, thank you for your time. If we have any more questions, we'll get back to you."

He nodded, slid his lanky form from the booth, and moved slowly out of the café. Annette slumped in her seat and drew a deep breath. She was glad as hell that she was a surgeon. It was a simple job, really. She diagnosed a problem, then she went in and solved it. This investigation stuff was for the birds.

"He speaks true," Aragon said. He'd been silent during the interview, though Annette noted he'd studied Bryers the entire time.

"What do you mean?"

"He is telling you the truth."

"You read his mind?"

Aragon shook his head. "I could hear his heartbeat and his breathing and feel the tension of his body. Those who lie have no control over those functions, and they immediately change pace when they do."

"Holy hell, you're a walking lie detector." She gave Aragon a big smile. Things were looking up. She could drag Aragon around and question everyone about Stef. For now, Sharon Wills was next, due to meet them at the café in thirty minutes. They had time for more than coffee. Correction. Coffee and hot chocolate. Aragon refused to try any more of her "brew," as he called it.

"We've got thirty minutes. Are you hungry?" she asked.

"Very," he replied, low and deep, then sent her nearly through the roof when his hand under the table slid up her thigh to brush a finger over her crotch. She jerked to such immediate attention that her knees hit the table leg, her nipples tingled, and her mouth went dry as everything else went wet.

"Aragon!" His name came out as a breathless hiss. "You can't do that to me in public."

"Then let's not be public." He ran his finger over her crotch again, and Annette thought she'd explode. In her mind she saw them stealing into any dark corner, any restroom, anywhere, just to ease the fire he was fanning. She'd never understood such behavior before, thought that people who did things like that were undisciplined idiots.

Hell, if the booths were higher, the lighting dim, and the room a little more secluded, she'd spread her legs and let him take her to heaven right here.

She shoved a menu in his face. "Food," she said. "We need food. And look"—she pointed to the back of the menu—"we can have strawberry shortcake for dessert." That clinched his cooperation. They ate eggs Benedict, had orange juice, and then she hit real trouble when the short-cake arrived. The look Aragon gave her as he sucked the last bit of strawberry off his spoon told her the dessert had only whetted his appetite.

Sharon Wills saved her. If the woman hadn't appeared when she did, Annette was certain that Aragon would have picked her up and carried her from the restaurant.

It was the first time Annette had seen Stef's friend dry-eyed, a change that brought her countenance from a fragile, blue-eyed blonde to a Paris Hilton gotta-get-my-hair-and-nails-done-every-day kind of gal, one that found Aragon im-mensely interesting. She barely took her gaze off him and seemed to be flashing her nails, boobs, and hair all at the same time.

"Thank you for coming," Annette said, trying to get her attention. "You look different."

"The new me," she said. "Life was passing the old me by, and after Stef . . . I decided it was too short to let that hap-pen. Look, I don't think talking about Stef is going to do ei-ther of us any good," she replied, finally meeting Annette's gaze. "I've . . . I've been trying to move past it. Went in for the grief therapy that Sno-Med has going on, you know."

It didn't look like Sno-Med was doing the girl any favors. "I have a few questions that I think only you can answer.

Someone mentioned that Stef was working on a project for Sno-Med when she disappeared. Do you know what it was?"

Sharon smoothed her brow with a long nail, as if worried about a wrinkle forming, and cut her eyes Aragon's way before replying. "I don't know for sure. It had something to do with a group study being done, treating something that I don't remember. She called it Tusk-something."

Annette leaned forward, eyes narrowing as her mind raced. A group study called Tusk-something? Like Tuskegee? The horribly unjust medical experiment had been a study of the effect of untreated syphilis on black males. The disease, colloquially known as "bad blood," had been fully curable with antibiotics at the time. But the patients hadn't been given the cure. Instead they'd been duped by medical bells and whistles into thinking they were getting the treatment they needed. "Stef didn't say anything else about the project?"

"Not really." Sharon nodded her head, then flicked her hair back into place, glancing at Aragon again. She couldn't seem to look away.

"Nothing?" Annette asked, trying to call Sharon's attention back to the conversation.

"Well, I can't remember exactly, but I had the impression she was worried about one of her friends being in the project."

"In the project how?"

"I don't know anything else."

Annette gritted her teeth. "What about other people from work? Can you think of anyone who would know about the project?"

The waitress brought Sharon a coffee and Aragon another hot chocolate, saying with a wink that she'd put extra whipped cream on it just for him. Annette had to ask for a refresher for her coffee.

"We didn't discuss work much," Sharon said as she diluted her coffee with cream, then drowned it in sugar, making Annette cringe. "She worked in the labs, and I'm a receptionist. You might try Abe Bennett from Hematology. She and Abe had been talking a lot recently, but it wasn't a boyfriend-girlfriend thing. Or you could search through her laptop. Had dragons all over it. She dragged that around with her everywhere."

Annette choked on her coffee, spilling it as she smacked the cup on the table. Aragon immediately grabbed her arm, tensing as he shot his gaze about the diner, looking for the trouble.

"I'm fine," she told him calmly. "Went down the wrong pipe." Inside she was screaming as loud as the blood rushing past her ears. *What laptop?* This was the first she'd heard of one. There hadn't been a laptop in any of Stefanie's belongings. She drew a deep breath and forced herself to remain calm. It wouldn't do to set off alarm bells with Sharon and have rumors flying before Annette could ask questions herself. And if she remembered right, Rob Rankin worked in Hematology. "What about personal relationships? Are there other friends I can ask to see if Stef mentioned anything to them?"

Sharon shook her head. "I'll think about it, but she was pretty reclusive. Preferred writing her stories over wasting time elsewhere, is what she used to say. I mean, she wouldn't even come and get her hair and nails done." Sharon looked as if that was the ultimate sin.

"I heard you arranged a date for her with Nick Sinclair. Do you know him well?"

Sharon drew a deep breath, as if she had to brace herself to speak. "Not as well as I thought I did."

"What does that mean?"

"You know what Stef was like. More interested in creating these humanoid creatures and writing stories about them than actually dating a real man. I don't think she'd been out since your parents were killed. Nick was supposed to show her that sharing dinner and a movie with a flesh-and-blood guy on occasion would be a good thing."

"He didn't?"

She shrugged. "You want the truth?" She glanced at Aragon again. "It's, uh, not pretty."

"That's what I'm here for."

"Nick wang-banged Stef that night until she couldn't see straight. I know he had to have urged her into it, because she was all about emotion in relationships, and this was just raw sex. It was too much too soon, and she regretted it. That had her all tied up in knots and sent her on a tailspin of reconnecting with her true spirit, which, I think, had her going to the Sacred Stones early Saturday morning before meeting everyone for the hike. So in a way, I kind of blame him and myself for what might have happened to her. At first I even wondered if she'd just decided to go somewhere to 'find' herself, but then I realized she wouldn't have left her sketchbooks behind. Her creatures were too much a part of her." Sharon's eyes welled up with tears again, and Annette realized how much the woman blamed herself for Stefanie's disappearance.

Coffee forgotten, Annette patted Sharon's hand and tried to digest Sharon's revelations. Nick had intimated that he'd only shared a simple meal and movie with Stef. Why had he misled her? Him having sex with Stefanie wasn't really any of her business, but in Annette's mind that constituted more than just a "no big deal" date.

Either he wasn't a kiss-and-tell guy—or he had something to hide.

"She lied," Aragon said after Sharon Wills left.

Annette swallowed the lump in her throat. Here she thought she'd finally come up with something solid to follow.

"When she said the part about trying to move past your sister, she lied. Everything else seemed to be true."

"If that's the case, then we've got some work to do. Maybe those medical files I have will look a little more interesting." Interviews over and bill paid, she led Aragon out of the diner and into her car.

"What's wang-banged?" Aragon asked as she was getting into the car. "I am unfamiliar with the word."

Her head snapped up and hit the roof. Did the man have a GPS when it came to sex? He always seemed to hone in on it. Cranking the engine, she shoved the car into drive and had crossed the parking lot before she could think of the right answer. "Sex without . . . love," she finally said as she pulled out onto the highway.

"And this is harmful to a mortal?"

How could she answer that question?

"Yes . . . in some ways . . . it's complicated."

Her cell phone rang. Emerald's number popped up.

"Hold on," she told him as she answered, listened to Emerald's plan, and hung up. "They'll meet us at my cabin. The trucks aren't all loaded yet, but Nick thinks it's close, and Sam wants to map out the best place for the roadblock. And there isn't any need for you to cross the spirit barrier. Nick is going to keep tabs on the truck from the LifeFlight helicopter. If any emergency calls come in for it, we'll figure it out from there."

Aragon sucked in a deep breath, looking as if he'd been punched in the gut. "It is time then."

Annette nodded and swallowed the emotion gathering in her throat. No more waiting. Not that she'd sat around as it was. She'd made progress this morning in looking for Stef, but she somehow felt as if she'd missed some precious moments with Aragon.

"What's that darkness?" he asked, leaning down to peer through her windshield. At six-five, he seemed to have barely any room between his head and the roof of her car.

The mountaintops across from the wide valley where Twilight made its home were the highest peaks in this part of Tennessee, and mists often covered them, especially Hades Mountain. But today, whether from a strange fluke in the weather or because other clouds were obscuring the sun at just the right angle, the mist over Hades Mountain was inky black. "Must be a storm or a trick of the light," she told Aragon.

"Has it ever been that dark before?"

"Not since I've been here."

Aragon grunted, but kept studying the distant peaks.

"Is something wrong?"

He shook his head as if he wasn't sure. They turned a bend in the road, and the mist-shrouded mountains fell behind them. He didn't turn to look at them and was quiet the rest of the way back to her place. She let the conversation lull as she tried to figure out the right answer to give him about love, and decide what she would do with the information they'd learned from Dr. Steven Bryers and Sharon Wills. She had to do something. She also tried not to think about how confused her sister must have been after her date with Nick. How she might have really needed to talk the night she'd called. The painful knife of guilt twisted a little deeper into her heart.

They arrived at her cabin before the others. The moment they exited the car, he swung her around to face him. "This love that you speak of is different for mortals than spirit beings, I think. I need to know more."

Reaching up, she slid her thumb along the cleft of his stubbled chin and ran her hand up his jaw to brush his shoulder-length hair back from his face. His eyes were intent, worried, as if the universe rested on his shoulders. The sun lit ebony fire in the dark of his hair, warming them both with its mid-morning heat. "I didn't mean to leave you hanging. Love is many things. Between a man and a woman it's feeling, understanding, a promise to care and revere, and some make a commitment to each other to honor and to cherish forever."

He returned her touch, brushing his fingers over her cheek and across her lips as if memorizing every detail. Then he dipped his hand down and pulled gently on the chain around her neck until he'd brought his amulet into the light, where it glittered a rich, iridescent gold in his palm.

"Love, then, is like an oath a warrior makes?"

"A little," she said, searching for the right words.

He leaned down and breathed deeply of the amulet. "It bears your scent," he said softly. "I would make an oath to you, then," he said, sliding the amulet over her head and holding it out between them.

"With all that I am, as unworthy as I am, I pledge to find your sister and to do all within my power to keep you safe from Pathos."

He leaned down, and she fell into his kiss, her heart thudding from the strength of the emotion flooding through her. Tears bit into her eyes, and her mouth trembled beneath the gentleness of his lips. This was different from anything she'd ever known, and the reverence of the experience awed her, left her speechless and hopelessly drowning.

He pulled back, his dark gaze hungrily searching hers. She thought he would kiss her again, this time with the heated passion that seemed to burn away anything but the desire between them. He didn't. He moved back, holding his amulet clutched tightly in his fist.

She frowned, suddenly sensing what he was going to do.

"Aragon!" she cried, reaching for him. "You can't."

He jumped back. "I must," he whispered, his expression both pained and remote. "I promise I will not fail you. Believe in me!"

"No! Don't go. There are other ways—" She threw herself at him, but he leapt into the air and vanished, leaving only the echo of a loud sucking sound behind and the stench of burned cotton as a puff of smoke filled the air. All that was left when it cleared were a few pieces of black cloth on the ground.

She couldn't believe it. He couldn't have just up and left her like this! Her insides twisted painfully, and it seemed as if her breath was frozen in her lungs.

"Aragon! Damn it! Come back!" She shut her eyes and called out to him with her whole spirit, determined to reach him somehow. She pictured him in her mind, trying to make him reappear. Nothing happened. He was gone.

She clenched her fists and pressed them hard against her chest to hold herself aloof from the hurt, the anger, and the tears flooding. Damn it! He didn't have to do this! There were other ways to follow the trucks. And he didn't need to go out there looking for Stef; she was finally making the first real progress in finding out what happened to her sister.

"Come back!" she screamed at him. But nothing happened.

She hadn't thought the well of grief she'd carried since her sister disappeared could deepen. She had been wrong.

Chapter Thirteen

HANDS CLENCHING THE X-files printouts and her stomach in knots, Annette tried to make her eyes focus on the medical case in front of her. So far, all of the women she'd read about had been marked as deceased. But there was very little information as to why they'd died, or why they were being seen for the medical study in the first place. The files so far were a compilation of patient history, physical findings from exams—but no labs were included. The diagnosis was a numerical code that neither Annette, nor Erin, nor Emerald recognized.

It was like trying to put pieces of a puzzle together with no picture on the box. She knew only one thing—it was bad. All of the women had been between the ages of eighteen and thirty-six, and all were deceased. A stomach-turning revelation itself, but when it was combined with her worry for Aragon, she thought she'd be seriously sick to her stomach.

Emerald sat calmly across the room, reading her stack, and Erin lounged on the sheepskin rug by the fireplace where Aragon had made . . .

Hell. Annette swallowed another choking lump of grief and sucked in deep breaths, but it didn't help. She had to get out of the cabin. She didn't care what Sam and Jared said about sitting tight until their return. She'd go nuts if she had to stay here. Aragon's scent was everywhere.

She had to get out. Squaring her shoulders, she looked at Erin, then Emerald. "For two women who had their panties in a wad last night, thinking that the men had left you in the investigation dust, you seem awfully content right now."

"Thongs don't wad, luv," Emerald said. "Besides, this is different. We *know* where Sam and Jared are now and what they are doing. We didn't last night. And this is important." She tapped the medical file.

"Yes, but I'm afraid we're wasting our time if we do just this and turn up nothing. I think we need to find Abe Bennett and see if there is anyone else we can question. We can even stop at my neighbor's house. I think Rob works in the Hematology Department."

"Jared will have a fit," Erin said, packing up her things. "But come to think of it, Annette is right. They're seeing all of the action, and we're licking our thumbs, reading files."

"And it's bleedin' time Sam realizes he isn't the only capable being on the planet. We'll kill two birds at the same time," Emerald said.

"Stone," Erin corrected. "It's kill two birds with one stone."

"However do you do that?"

"With damn good aim," Annette suggested. "Let's go hunting." She didn't have to say anything else before the women were out the door and piling into her BMW. When Annette pulled out of her driveway, she darted across the road and up the Rankins' drive. But the house looked silent, and no cars were in the drive, so she circled around and headed for the highway.

"Hey, did Stef have the chickenpox at age two?" Erin asked, deep into a file.

"I'm not sure," Annette said. "She had them sometime when I was in my mid-teens. Why?"

"I've got a file with a birth date that matches Stefanie's."

Oh, God. Annette squeezed her eyes shut. As much as Annette wanted to find out something about her sister, she didn't want it to be a medical file with the word "Deceased'"written at the bottom.

"Nette!" Emerald yelled. "Watch out!"

Popping her eyes open, Annette saw that a car had made a late turn onto the road. Now it was crossing the center line and about to hit them head on. She steered onto the shoulder, catching sight of Celeste's horrified expression behind the wheel as they narrowly missed colliding.

She brought her car to a stop, but Celeste kept going. Emerald launched into a diatribe about fooking idiot drivers, and Annette shook her head. Not stopping was so unlike Celeste. She started to defend her neighbor but then decided to let it go and return to the file Erin had found.

"What else is in the file?" Annette asked, praying that the woman was from Timbuktu as she pulled back onto the highway, deciding she'd try and see Celeste later. Her neighbor was obviously upset at the moment.

"Let's see. There's a note that this woman worked for Sno-Med."

Annette's mouth went dry.

"She began working for Sno-Med five years ago, and—"

"That's two years before Stefanie did," she said in a rush as the air trapped in her lungs escaped. It wasn't Stef. It wasn't Stef.

"This woman is the first not to have 'Deceased' written on the bottom of the page. There is a note that she was transferred last October to . . . Anyone ever hear of St. Anjeles in Nashville?"

"Holy hell. We finally have something solid to go on?" Annette pulled onto the side of the road, dug up her cell phone, and dialed information. "Bingo," she said as the operator punched her through to St. Anjeles. "Let me see the file," she said to Erin.

"We care for those you love when you can't," said a woman who answered the phone. "This is Melanie. May I help you?"

"Yes, Melanie. I'm hoping you can. I'm Dr. Batista. I've recently taken over a position at Sno-Med's research center in Arcadia, and my predecessor left rather abruptly. I've a number of files on my desk that I need to work through."

"Dear Lord, I heard about the fire. Dr. Helms has been trying to contact Dr. Cinatas all day."

Annette shivered as if someone had walked over her grave. Cinatas was a powerful man with connections everywhere, and only time and investigation would reveal which of those connections were evil and which were, like her and Erin, unsuspecting.

"It was awful," Annette told the woman truthfully. "Because of the damage to the building and the files, I'm afraid that something is going to fall between the cracks, and that someone will suffer."

"Yes, of course. What can I do? I owe Sno-Med a lot. They're giving my kids the best care at a price I can afford."

Annette gritted her teeth. "I have a record of a Sno-Med employee, a woman being transferred to St. Anjeles last October, but I don't have her name, just her Sno-Med file number."

"We don't get many Sno-Med employees here, so I know who you're talking about. Consuela Torres. A terrible shame to see such a beautiful woman waste away like this. But they say there's nothing there, the stroke turned her brain to mush. With no family, the staff has sort of adopted her. Do you need Dr. Helms to contact you?"

Stroke. The word left Annette with a very bad feeling. "Actually, I'll call Dr. Helms back later after I finish going through these files. But you have been a tremendous help, Melanie. What is your last name?"

"Dresher."

"Great. Thanks. I'll be talking to you again soon." Annette disconnected the phone and wrote down Melanie's name, St. Anjeles's phone number, and Dr. Helms's name. She'd have to do some more digging about the doctor. And somehow she'd have to get Melanie to take her kids somewhere besides Sno-Med for treatment. But all of that would have to wait. She didn't like what these patient files were suggesting. Deaths and a stroke. What sort of study or treatment had these women been involved in?

"It's a real honor to finally meet you, Dr. Cinatas. You have no idea how much your research has inspired us all. A cure for any cancer is just a miracle, and you are a god."

Pathos watched Dr. Steven Bryers nearly trip in his enthusiasm to shake Cinatas's hand.

Cinatas nodded his head as if receiving a small measure of his due.

"And I want you to know I didn't tell the detectives anything negative at all. Not that there was anything negative to say, but they seemed determined to come up with something wrong with all of their questions."

"Detectives?" The mask Cinatas wore didn't quite follow along with the deepness of the frown Cinatas must have been expressing, and it gave his face a surreal appearance. Pathos would have to tell him to keep his expressions neutral, especially for the news conference. Having that show up on television where people could replay and examine the footage wouldn't be good.

"Just a little while ago. They were asking about the woman who disappeared six months ago. And, if you get this, they wanted to know about 'X-files' that are supposedly on my computer. Medical files with the numbers 666 on them. I never heard of them. I just expounded on how fantastic Sno-Med's vision for research is and how I was finally getting to do what I was meant to do."

"I see," Cinatas replied. "Your enthusiasm is appreciated."

Bryers's grin seemed as if it would burst from his pasty skin. "So, how can I be of help to you today?"

Cinatas set a hand on Bryers's shoulder, and Pathos thought the man was going to faint.

"You've done a tremendous amount already. When the research center is back in operation, I can tell you are going to be a great asset to the company. In the interim, what do you think about going to the Sno-Med center in Zaire? The Infectious Disease Department there is our most advanced. You would be able to see my true vision for research."

"Are you serious?"

"Yes. You can leave soon, I hope?"

"Absolutely. When do you want me there? I'm anxious to get started."

"You sound as if tomorrow wouldn't be too soon for you. I'll arrange my private jet and have my assistant contact you with the details. I'm sure you won't prove to be a disappointment."

Bryers blinked, his protruding eyes nearly popping from their sockets. "No. Not at all."

They left Bryers and climbed inside the white limo that Pathos was indulging Cinatas in using. Though capable of crossing the spirit barrier, Cinatas was yet too weak from his ordeal to make multiple trips in a short period of time.

"Interesting exchange," Pathos said. "Would you care to explain what it was all about?"

"It would seem a lesson needs to be taught. A man doesn't deserve to live if he can't control those who serve him. Unfortunately, Stefanie Batista is either dead or as good as dead if she is in the 666 study. We haven't perfected the program as of yet."

Pathos lifted a brow. "And?"

"It stems from my initial desire to refine the Vladarians' need for Elan blood by increasing the richness of each individual supply. But if, as you say, the Vladarians will be expendable, there's no need to improve their situation."

Pathos smiled. "None whatsoever. Where are we going next?"

"To see a lab rat by the name of Rob Rankin."

The Guardian Council had decreed that Aragon be executed. Since Sven had returned, a cloud of darkness had settled over his band of Blood Hunters and into the ranks of all the Shadowmen. Usually before there were questions or concerns about a decision, all waited for Logos to either approve or disapprove the verdict, and then, because Logos was the only reasonable and all-knowing being in existence, there were no more questions or concerns. But this time, heated discussions about the council's decision and Aragon's worthiness had erupted across the spirit world.

Some believed that the Guardian Council had gone too far by superseding Logos's typical punishment for a warrior abandoning his post. Others agreed with the council that if even one among them had been willing to accept becoming a faded warrior, then the price hadn't been high enough. Such an act was as treasonous as joining ranks with the

Fallen Army, and should merit the same punishment. Some thought Aragon should be executed on sight and not even be given the respect of being brought before Logos and the council. Sven thought they were all wrong.

As news of Aragon's fate spread, many Shadowmen had gravitated to the inner circles, and Sven had brought York and Navarre to the gathering. They were the only ones who could speak for Aragon and describe what had transpired, but many were not hearing the truth.

York was in the midst of an argument with another band of Blood Hunters, defending Aragon. Navarre had reached the point of silence. The ancient calmness that always guarded his actions and responses had evaporated from his demeanor like a mist beneath an angry sun. Sven could see that Navarre was seething beneath the surface and kept close to both of his brethren.

Never before had there been so much division within the forces.

And the burden of it all rested squarely on Sven's shoulders. If he had followed through with his promise and executed Jared immediately after the Tsara had bitten him, none of this would be happening now. Aragon would still be leader, the Blood Hunters would be united, and the Shadowmen would be focused on battling Heldon rather than each other.

But then Jared would have been lost forever instead of attaining salvation for his soul.

Now, though, Aragon was doomed.

Sven stepped to York's side as a powerful Shadowman from the Pyrathian Band of warriors, Sirius, joined the argument opposing York's defense of Aragon. He spoke with the fire and conviction that enabled his kind to sway multitudes. "The council chose rightly. Aragon could have secretly longed to follow Pathos," Sirius said. "Pathos was his mentor. We all know the bond that forms in training, so this quest to kill Pathos doesn't ring true. We'll next hear that Aragon has fallen to a Tsara and into the ranks of the damned."

Sven clenched his hand, sure that York wouldn't be able to stay his temper, and that wouldn't be good. Pyrathians were shape-shifters who fought against those of Heldon's Army bent on terminating mortals before Logos's appointed time. All of the forces were in awe of the gift of life Logos had instilled within them. But when one of theirs fell to the Fallen Army, they became one of the most vile, a vampire who sucked the life from mortals, through blood or, worse, through spirit.

"How can you question Aragon's service?" York's spirit quivered with anger. "His every action has been for what he considered to be the best for the Guardian Forces. Though it was a mistake, he chose eternal punishment rather than to lead us wrongly, and rather than just fading to his fate, he's determined to fight for Logos with every moment left to him by going after Pathos to eliminate the evil—not to join it. Would that we all be able to give such a testament!"

"Those too close to truth never see it," Sirius replied. "You're blinded, Blood Hunter."

York lifted his fist. But Navarre set his hand on York's shoulder, and York turned away from the Pyrathian, marching from the gathering.

Sven met Navarre's gaze. "We've two new band members to train. I'll meet you and York within the outer circles." Navarre nodded and left. Sven turned to Sirius. "Only those who have seen and lived the truth can give testament to it. As I recollect, you were not present during the events. Had you been, I am sure the council would have called upon you to speak on the matter."

Then Sven turned to face the gathered Shadowmen, all of whom had heard both his comments to the Pyrathian and York's declaration about Aragon. Sven was angered by what was happening and burdened as well, for he'd been the one who'd set everything in motion. And he needed to be the one to bring everything back to rights, starting now.

"Brethren," Sven shouted to the group at large, bringing a hush among the gathered ranks. "In a small way, we are all guilty of what the council wishes to punish Aragon for doing, by deciding our own truth and dividing the unity of our forces. Ultimately, Aragon's heart and fate both rest within Logos's hands, and thankfully not within our flawed and unreasonable minds." He paused, then mustered his courage. "And I am more guilty than Aragon for failing in my duty. Were it not for my cowardice, he would still be leader amid the Blood Hunters, and I have informed the council of this. The difference between Aragon and me is that I failed to fulfill a promise to my brothers, whereas Aragon broke faith with the Guardian Forces and Logos.

"I've learned a grave lesson of what consequences follow when one does not act as promised, and as long as the council determines that I am fit enough to lead, I will atone for my mistake in every way that I can serve. Though what they are saying about Aragon is unquestionably false, even if it were true, then as always before our hearts should be united in sorrow at our loss and not this bickering among us. And, no matter what your thoughts, Aragon gave a millennium of service to Logos. If he is found, he should be accorded the respect of standing before Logos for punishment. To continue these discussions will only stir dissension and lead to Heldon's eventual victory. I have no time for such a defeat."

Whipping around, Sven left the gathering. There were many who were superior in rank and years of service within the Guardian Forces present, men who had taken part in the divisive discussions, and Sven was sure they wouldn't take well to his speech.

He found York and Navarre standing at the edges of the inner circle, having stopped to hear his speech. They clasped each of his hands and raised them in support and solidarity of cause, an action of unity that had been missing from their band since Jared had fallen to the Tsara. Yet even as he accepted the elation of their united moment, he knew despair waited, for whether Aragon became a faded warrior trapped in time or met his end before Logos and the council, Sven would carry the burden forever.

Before he could leave for the outer circles, a shout went up from the gathered Shadowmen, and they began leaving quickly.

Navarre stopped a fellow Blood Hunter from a different band. "Why the sudden exodus?"

"Aragon has entered the spirit realm. They seek to bring him to punishment. Your speech was true, Sven, but I don't think it will sway Aragon's fate. There is something ill brooding within the ranks of the Guardian Forces, and I fear Aragon will bear the brunt of it."

Sven only nodded. He was too consumed by the need to go and find Aragon to even trust a slight response to the news. Navarre and York were just as tense as he. How could he lead his band through this impossible situation? They were all torn between their vows and the need to help Aragon.

Aragon slipped through the spirit barrier with a sense of elation and dread. That he still had the ability to enter the spirit world told him his punishment had yet to begin, for as a faded warrior he would be truly exiled. But once he started to fade, he would be banned from the mortal realm as well. He wouldn't be able to destroy Pathos or return to Annette's side.

He shifted to the forest where he'd thrown his sword in the midst of his bloodlust last night and collected his weapon. It had been just before Annette had brought him face to face with Pathos at the Sno-Med Center. He realized now that had he had his sword with him, he might have been able to fell Pathos immediately. But he hadn't.

What had happened to him beneath the moon's pull when he'd run in the forest hunting? What had driven his were-form to such a primal state? How had that changed after he'd saved Annette from Pathos? Had her presence lessened his rising bloodlust, or had the injuries he'd received weakened him, thus lessening his were-form's strength?

And what else had happened to him from yesterday's sun's rising until now? He'd but one goal after facing his failure as a leader, and that had been to destroy Pathos. He'd accepted his eventual fate.

Now everything inside him cried out against it. He wanted more. And that *more* burned beneath his skin in a hunger for Annette. He clutched his amulet, still feeling the imprint of her touch upon it, still breathing in the sweetness of her scent, clinging to him as thoroughly as the memory of her spirit and their mating lingered in his mind. The very center of his being still resonated from the pleasure they had shared and the bond their spirits had forged. Her essence was wrapped around his soul.

He'd heard her call out to him, reach with her whole being for him, and he wanted nothing more than to turn back and bury himself within her arms again. But he had to force himself to go on. He had no forevers to promise, but he could find her sister if she was anywhere within the spirit or mortal realms, and he could stop Pathos from ever darkening Annette's presence again. He had to. And he prayed to Logos that he had time to make those things happen, because if he failed, he might as well resign himself to the darkness of the damned. He'd spend eternity tortured anyway.

Gliding along the outer circles, he kept to the shadowed fringes as he raced silently toward the host of angels who governed the transformation of mortals into the spirit realm. He had just enough time to search for Stefanie before he went after Pathos. The angels were located within the inner circles in the eastern heavens. He waited until he was parallel to their domain before he cut from the shadows.

The moment he did, he caught the scents of an unusually varied number of bands from the Guardian Forces. He paused, sensing a high degree of tension in the air, almost as if his body had to fight for the space in which it occupied. He felt that were he to relax, or if his compulsion to drive forward were not so strong, the atmosphere would force him from the spirit realm.

Everything was different now. And the difference made him know that he no longer belonged amid the circles of the spirit world. It could have been the choice he had made to leave the Guardian Forces that had altered his existence. It could have been the bond he'd formed with Annette that made the change. Whatever the cause, he was now as much an intruder within the Guardians' domain as someone from the damned, which meant he'd draw the attention of any warrior within the circle he traveled.

With no shadows to cloak his presence, he decided speed would be his greatest ally. So, abandoning caution, he flew toward the inner circles of the spirit realm, where the light grew brighter and brighter and the air warmer and warmer. Unworthy to wear his amulet where it belonged around his neck, he wrapped the chain around his hand and held the disk clutched in his fist.

When he reached the angels' domain, he took one look at the blue aura of the presiding angel guarding the gateway to their circle and knew he was in trouble. She stood at arms, ready for battle, telling him that the entire realm was on alert, and he was most likely the cause.

Without speaking, he swung away.

"What within my gates would bring a faded warrior to the arms of his execution?" she called out; melodic grace and righteous glory rang in her voice, and struck a chord of real fear within him. Her winged spirit shimmered pearlescent white amid the blue orb, and silvery bells tinkled as she motioned him her way. He was reminded somewhat of the mortal woman with the emerald eyes.

Though he'd seen one or two angels in passing, he'd never spoken to one and found now that his voice nearly failed him. "I seek knowledge of a mortal's passing into your realm. She is known as Stefanie Batista."

"And the reason you seek such? It seems there would be things of greater import for one such as you."

"My fate cannot be changed, but the success of my mission is worth any cost."

"So you seek not to alter your fate, warrior, but only knowledge?"

"I am unworthy of both," he said harshly, "but I seek your lenience in telling me what I came to learn."

"The name Stefanie Batista did come to our attention, but a Pyrathian intervened. That is all I know. You will not make the journey to your fate without great loss, warrior," she said, then slowly disappeared as she closed an invisible gate, leaving him with only her cryptic message of doom. What great loss? Surely she hadn't meant anything would happen to Annette? He felt the sudden urge to get back immediately.

As he turned, he saw a band of Pyrathians from the Guardian Forces speeding toward him and knew they did not have a friendly greeting in mind.

He couldn't afford to lose any time. He immediately spiraled down with dizzying speed and cut sharply toward the outer circles, praying the cloaking shadows on the edges of the spirit realm weren't as far away as he remembered them. It was the only place in the heavens he could move unseen.

With their warriors' cries reverberating through the air, the band came after him. Moments later another band, this time Blood Hunters, appeared to his left. He went right. With the added resistance of the atmosphere fighting his presence, Aragon wasn't able to fly as swiftly as the forces after him. They were gaining on him by slow degrees.

Aragon still had enough of his Guardian awareness within him that the amulet he clutched made the spirit connection to the other warriors' minds. He could read their thoughts, and their slanderous ill will seemed to suck his heart directly beneath their trampling feet. His valued brethren thought he'd gone to the dark, believed his pursuit of Pathos was only a ruse so he could eventually join his old mentor in serving Heldon and the Fallen Army. Though it was true he could avoid becoming faded by becoming damned, Aragon had never even considered such a horrific act.

He could bring Pathos and place him upon an altar before his brethren, and it wouldn't matter. He was now their enemy, just as much as Pathos. And only now did Aragon understand why. His betrayal in leaving the Guardian ranks had torn a hole in their faith in the brotherhood—and that hole had to be filled with something. They'd filled it with anger and disgust.

Had he known such a consequence would befall them, he would have never left as he had.

A band of three additional Blood Hunters loomed down from above him, and their presence in the chase cut Aragon to the core. Sven, York, and Navarre had joined the hunt against him. He turned again, and the change cost him. Within moments, the Pyrathians were upon him.

Chapter Fourteen

"TALK ABOUT ROTTEN IN DENMARK," Annette said as she cranked her BMW and backed down the broken pavement comprising Mrs. Bennett's driveway. They'd come to question Abe Bennett, but were SOL. "I'm not buying this whole can't-talk-to-Abe-directly-because-he's-been-transferred-to-a-secret-location-to-do-some-medical-tests-for-the-government scenario. Abe is either in on Stefanie's disappearance, or he's a victim of foul play himself."

"His mother believes it. So whoever is answering her e-mails must either be Abe or someone who knows him very well," Erin said.

"She did say that he's working so hard that he doesn't e-mail often or much," Annette pointed out.

"The gack could be not saying much because he's running scared. Which means he bleedin' knows what has happened to Stef and didn't have the balls to come to the authorities for help."

Erin sighed. "I didn't go to the authorities. I was alone and up against Dr. Cinatas and Sno-Med. I found four dead bodies in the lab. I knew if I was caught, I'd be dead too. So I had to get out of there, but also knew the second I left, the bodies and any proof that I was telling the truth would disappear."

"But you didn't run scared," Annette added. "Or you

would have hid out on a beach in Mexico somewhere rather than coming right to the lion's den."

"I figured the four dead were just the tip of the iceberg, and I'd find the proof I needed at Dr. Cinatas's research center."

"And you're right," Annette said, with a sick feeling in her gut that Stef was going to be part of that cold, hard truth. "Sno-Med has to have been doing something to those women in the X-files. There is no way that many of them died from natural causes. I wish I had time this minute to fly to Nashville and see Torres, but that's going to have to wait until I can get legitimate access to her." The feeling that if she didn't hurry all proof of Sno-Med's crimes and all hope of finding her sister would be lost hovered over her head like an ax of doom, raking her every nerve.

"What if Abe Bennett is my Mr. X, the man who asked me to meet him at Sno-Med?" Annette asked, trying to focus on the conversation and not her panic.

"I'd say you hit the nail on the right head, then. It would also mean that he's hiding somewhere close."

Annette's chest tightened, and she had to roll down her window, desperately gasping in air.

Was that why she was apprehensive? She studied her surroundings as she pulled out onto the road. Nothing hit her as being out of the ordinary. It was a perfect summer day in the rural mountains. Warm sun. Nice breeze. Farmers on their tractors in plant-striped fields. To her right four boys raced along the grassy side of a creek, a scrappy-looking puppy nipping at their heels.

"There's an off chance everything Mrs. Bennett was told is legit," Erin said softly, as if talking out loud. "I know that Sno-Med has contracted with the government before to provide medical testing, but as far as I know it's never required secrecy."

"The question is, what can we do about it? How can we get to this Abe Bennett fast via e-mail and get him to respond? Once he contacts his mother, she'll be sure to tell him of our visit, and he may run."

"No worries, luv," said Emerald. "Dr. Em has everything all figured out, provided our friend Abe is a heterosexual male."

"How?"

"Instructional porn. I'll just send him a wee message from my Dr. Em Web site, inviting him to take part in a survey. I'll ask him to view my photographic Kama Sutra book and give me feedback from a male perspective about any changes that need to be made before republication. It's a survey I have up for my clients, not just anybody. If he's heterosexual, I doubt he'll be able to resist logging on and taking a peek. Once he does, my server will have his IP address, and unless he's cloaking where he is with a long-distance server, we can get his general location."

"You're a genius." Annette laughed.

"Bleedin' hell," Emerald said sharply, turning up the radio newscast.

"WTWZ is reporting to you an earlier news release from this morning: Dr. Cinatas, head of the Sno-Med Corporation that has suffered two fires in two of their major facilities this past week, is reassuring all those receiving medical treatment from Sno-Med that they will be taken care of. Sno-Med will make a full recovery in providing quality, inexpensive medical care to all of the world's people in need."

Dr. Cinatas's voice came over the radio waves loud and clear, giving Annette a cold chill and increasing the pressure on her chest. "Have no fear. We will find and prosecute the person or persons responsible for these horrendous attacks."

The cacophony of questions being shouted by reporters quieted as soon as Cinatas spoke again.

"Yes. As you can see, I suffered injuries from which I am still recovering, but I felt it necessary as head of Sno-Med to let you know that all is well. Please rest assured that patients who have entrusted Sno-Med with their health care are our top priority during these troubled times. We already have facilities near both the Arcadia Center and our Manhattan Clinic open to care for you. Sno-Med will not let any arsonist cause our patients to suffer. We've set up a hotline for directions and help—"

"Oh, my God!" Erin gasped. "I'm going to be sick. I can't believe he's still alive."

Out of the corner of her eye, Annette saw that Emerald already had her cell phone out, calling Sam and Jared. She disconnected a moment later. "They heard. They're on the way back. And we're dead meat because we left your place."

Annette's hands shook, and her heart raced. Something besides hearing about Cinatas was wrong. Suddenly a sharp pain cut across her left shoulder and down her arm. She exhaled in a whoosh as she swerved off the road and hit the brakes.

"Fookin' hell, Nette!" Emerald braced herself on the dash.

Erin grabbed the seat back. "What's wrong?"

Annette gasped for air, shuddering with the pain. "I think . . . I'm having a . . . heart attack," she cried as the symptoms she'd been experiencing all morning fell into place. The anxiety, the tightness, the sense of doom, the radiating, sharp pain.

Emerald and Erin made a beeline for her. Erin lurched up from the back, checking her carotid pulse, while Emerald shoved the gearshift into park and cut the engine.

Just as Annette thought she was going to either pass out or be sick from the pain, it disappeared, leaving her feeling perfectly fine. "Holy hell. Never mind. No, I'm not. I don't know what's wrong."

"That's not bleedin' good enough. What's going on, Nette? You're the cardiac ex—"

"Ugghh!" Annette cried, grabbing her face as pain exploded in her left cheek. Her heart raced, and a cold sweat broke across her brow. Then everything was fine again.

"I'm calling 911," Erin shouted. "Get her out from behind the steering wheel, Em. She could be having a seizure."

"No," Annette yelled. "It was my cheek that hurt. But it's fine now. Oh!" She doubled, feeling like she'd been punched in the gut.

"Good heavens, it's as if some invisible force is beating her up."

Erin's words sent Annette's mind racing, and her heart centered on Aragon. They'd made such a connection. He'd been so into her that she'd felt his thoughts, felt his pleasure. "Oh, no! What if it isn't me? What if Aragon has been captured?"

An even deeper pain stabbed right through her—then nothing. Everything disappeared. The doom. The anxiety. The pain. Everything.

With a wrenching cry, Annette shoved open her car door and barreled out onto the roadside. She sucked in deep breaths of air and fought against the growing fear inside her. Tears stung her eyes.

Without even seeing where she walked, she crossed over the gravel and mown grass to a split rail fence where a pair of horses, one black and huge, the other slighter and gray, played in a rich, summer-green pasture. Blue-hazed mountains rolled along the tree-lined horizon, and a light breeze brushed her face, reminding her of Aragon's first tentative touch. Her heart contracted painfully.

"Nette!" Emerald cried. "By the Druids! Tell us what is happenin'!"

Erin grabbed Annette's left arm, and Emerald grabbed her right.

"It's gone," Annette whispered. "The pain is all gone."

"Thank God," Erin said.

"Uh-oh," Emerald added. "No! You can't do this!" Emerald said. "You can't!"

"Do what?" Erin demanded.

Emerald's BlackBerry tinkled. One of her patients needed some advice ASAP. For the first time ever, Emerald turned the BlackBerry off. "Sex will have to wait. Nette, you canna let yourself think that Aragon is dead just because you doona feel any weird blows."

Erin groaned. "How could I be so dense? Emerald is right! Listen, whatever is happening with Aragon, even if he has been captured or worse, your spirit crying out for his will keep you connected. If you give up, then you lose that! You have to believe. My belief might have been what brought Jared back to life. I wouldn't let him go."

I promise I will not fail you. The last words Aragon spoke to her rang through her mind. She dashed at her tears and squared her shoulders. "You two are right. Let's get back to my place and set the trap for Abe Bennett before the men arrive and mess it up."

On the return, Erin and Emerald read out facts from the medical files they were looking through, and Annette cut everything else from her mind but the project Stefanie had been working on.

She pulled into her drive and cut the engine.

What if Stef hadn't been working on a project, but had

stumbled on one and was investigating it? The X-files? What if Stef wasn't one of the medical records but had discovered them? Calling it Tuskegee would indicate that treatments had either been given to or withheld from the group of women without their knowledge. Treatments that caused death or a stroke.

She got out of the car, then froze, her gaze shifting in the direction of the Rankins' house. If the lab tests were right, Celeste was in danger of having a stroke. Celeste had been a friend of Stefanie's. Stefanie had been worried about a friend involved in the project. Celeste had mentioned that she'd received B-12 shots for anemia in the past, and that's why she'd been worried about it now.

"Nette? What is it? Is something happening again?"

"No. Hold on," Annette said and pulled out her cell phone, dialing the Rankins. The number was busy. She tossed her keys to Erin. "You two go on in. I've got to run over to my neighbor's and have her come back to my office later today to repeat a lab test that was really off. I'll be right back."

She didn't wait for Emerald or Erin to answer, but took off down the drive at a brisk walk. The fresh air would also help her think more clearly. Was she grasping at straws? Trying to make the pieces of the puzzle fit because she was desperate for answers?

"Wait up, luv," Emerald called out. "I'll walk with you. This is about more than repeating a lab test. You canna hold out on us."

"I'm not. It's just what I'm thinking seems sort of wild, but then not."

"What is it?"

"What if Celeste Rankin is one of the X-files?" Annette breached her doctor's code and told Emerald about Celeste's highly elevated red-blood-cell count. "She came in worried about anemia. If the lab is right, then her blood is no better than sludge, making her ripe for blood clots—"

"Or a bleedin' stroke. Like Consuela Torres."

"Then I'm not crazy?"

"No. Only one of the women in the files so far has been alive. How can the fookin' doctors get away with so many patients dying? People had to have realized this was happening." Emerald's bracelets jangled in her irritation.

The day was too calm, too bright. Trees swayed in the light afternoon breeze, making it seem as if all was well and good with the world.

Emerald's cell phone rang when they neared the end of Annette's drive. She looked at the display and paled. "It's Meggie's school."

"Hello? Yes, this is Megan's mother."

"Hold on, I'm losing reception." Emerald had to go back three steps. "What's wrong now? A stomachache? Yes, let me talk to her."

"I'll be right back," Annette whispered to Emerald as Emerald waited for her daughter. "If I don't go now, Sam and Jared will be here, and then who knows what we're going to be doing."

Emerald nodded. "I'll be right over just as soon as I speak to Meggie."

Annette crossed the street and dashed up the drive. Celeste's car was parked in the front with the trunk open. Several plastic bags of groceries were still in it. Annette grabbed two of them and climbed the steps to the porch. "Celeste. It's Annette." As she stepped through the doorway, the strong odor of bleach assaulted her, making her nose itch. When she brushed her nose with the back of her hand, she noticed one of the bags she carried felt mushy when it hit her arm. A quick glance told her that the ice cream had melted and leaked from its carton into the bag, making an unappetizing mess.

An odd tingling ran up her spine. She glanced around the great room of the cabin. Other bags of groceries sat on the kitchen counter. Annette's heart pounded. Was she too late? Had Celeste suffered a stroke? The doctor in Annette took over. She dropped the bags and ran to the open bedroom door. "Celeste?"

Inside, she didn't find Celeste, but her blood turned cold at what she did see. Besides the normal quilt-covered four-poster bed, dresser, and stand-alone swivel mirror, there was a desk capped by a huge corkboard, like something anchoring a police investigation. On it were pictures and articles about Stefanie. Though the Rankins had been thoroughly involved in searching for Stef, the collection still struck Annette as off—then screamed foul at her when she spied a dragon-covered laptop on the desk. The artwork was unmistakably Stefanie's.

Annette ran to the desk and snatched up the laptop; anger alone forced her brain to work through the numbing realization that the Rankins were involved with the disappearance of her sister. On the screen was an open e-mail account for Abe Bennett.

"A convenient time for you to stop by, Dr. Batista. Celeste isn't feeling well at all."

She whirled around to see Rob Rankin leaning against the doorjamb. He sounded nonchalant, as if it was nothing out of the ordinary for her to be standing in his bedroom, clutching a stolen laptop. Two steps back brought her flush with the beveled mirror, something she could easily shove into Rankin's face if he came after her.

"You called last night!" she cried, making a stabbing accusation that she hoped would fit. "What did you do to

Stefanie?" she demanded. She was too angry over his deception to pretend ignorance even for her own safety.

He smiled. "Yes, I called. Things were getting too strange even for me at Sno-Med. Yesterday I thought I'd go on record that I'd tried to contact someone about Stefanie and the X-files, just in case there was an investigation. But now it's all too late."

"Where are Stefanie and Abe?" Annette demanded.

He smiled as if he were bestowing a great gift. "Why, I simply sent them way south of the border into the *heart* of the research project she was doggedly investigating."

The X-files!

"Tell me where, you bastard."

"That seems to be my name today." He straightened from the doorjamb to face her. "Everything would have worked out perfectly fine if your sister hadn't buddied up with Celeste and nosed into her treatments and files."

"She wasn't getting B-12 shots for anemia, was she? What did you all do to her, and why? Her red blood cell count is off the charts."

His brows went up. "You'll have to ask someone else what and why. All I cared about was Celeste's poor chances of survival. Just my luck that she hung on longer than most of the others."

"You set your own wife up to die?"

"An ingenious way to collect the life insurance and retire. Sno-Med will be responsible for her death, and they're helping me pay for the life insurance policy to boot. The benefits are great."

"You're sick."

"No, just greedy. The medical minds behind the experimental study are sick."

"Interesting philosophy," came an amused voice from behind Rankin, and he swung around, surprised at last.

Annette recognized the cool voice and those arctic blue eyes. The memory of his burning cold touch crawled over her, leaving a knot of fear in her gut. "Pathos," she whispered.

"You really shouldn't leave your door open, Rankin. Any manner of creature can just walk in," said Dr. Cinatas. His face seemed different from what she remembered, but the bandages covering half of it made it hard to tell how.

Before Rankin could do anything but gape at his intruders, Pathos moved in and nailed Rankin by the throat up against the bedroom door. "Drop the knife or die this instant."

A bloody butcher knife clattered to the floor.

"Not only are you stupid." Cinatas put his face in Rankin's. "You failed. If Celeste had really survived the treatments, then I would have paid millions. Instead, I have a mess here and, it seems, at Corazon to clean up. Right?"

Rankin managed to nod. Pathos held him so tightly to the door that she knew the man could barely breathe. Not that he deserved to—but she couldn't just watch either.

"Let him go," she demanded, searching for a weapon.

"We're going to let him go," Cinatas said.

"Straight to hell," Pathos added. "See you shortly."

"No!" Annette threw the only thing she could at Pathos—Stef's laptop. He knocked it aside as if it were a fly. The computer landed on the bed, and she watched in horror as Pathos crushed Rankin's throat. Rankin slithered to the floor, death spasms wracking his body.

Pathos wiped his hand off on his pants leg and faced her. His silver hair was now closely cropped to his head, a style much less impressive than before. "Surely you were expecting me?"

Somehow in the gaze he ran over her, Annette knew he was going to make her pay for every strand of hair she'd singed, but in a very different way from Rankin. A sexual intensity burned in Pathos's eyes, one as strong as Aragon's. It raked over her, making all her nerve endings recoil with dread.

Annette forced her voice past the lump in her throat. "Yes."

He smiled, almost gently. "Good. I sense you understand your situation." He held his hand out, like a gentleman inviting a lady to dance. "Come, I am anxious for the play to begin."

"Sorry," Annette said. "I'm busy."

He lowered his hand, but his smile didn't waver. "Yes, I know. Your sister. She will make a poor substitute, but I guess I'll have to make do. Enjoy yourself, my dear. But keep in mind, your sister is only filling in until I can have you. I'm surprised Aragon isn't lapping at your heels. Give him my regards," Pathos said, and then swung around to leave.

Annette's heart and mind raced. Did Pathos have Stefanie? Was this a trick? "What do you mean? Rankin just said that he sent Stefanie somewhere."

He didn't stop, but spoke over his shoulder. "Do you really think I'm not capable of finding something when I want it?"

"Why?" she demanded, rushing to the door. "Why would you want Stef?"

Pathos turned and cocked a brow. "You know why. I want you. When you realize that I have her, I'll get you. I'll be back in a day or two. By then I'm sure you'll have discovered the truth. Meanwhile, my loins have an ache that needs to be soothed."

Dr. Cinatas chuckled as he climbed into the waiting Hummer limo, leaving the door open for Pathos.

Annette felt as if her insides were being ripped out. How could she just go with this monster? But how could she risk more harm to Stefanie if she was alive, and he had her? Even if she let Pathos walk away now, there would be no way to reach her sister in time to save her from what Pathos planned to do.

"Wait." The word barely escaped from her throat. Tears blinding her, she stumbled down the stairs, her mind on one thing: get to Stefanie and then escape. She didn't have any other choice.

Chapter Fifteen

THE FIRST FIREBALL from the Pyrathians caught Aragon's shoulder, sending a fiery pain down his arm. The second hit his cheek, and the third slammed into his midsection. He stood facing them, his sword raised but pointed to the side so that it made more of a shield than a weapon. "I've no wish to fight those whom I call my brethren," he shouted to them.

The Pyrathians paused, holding their fire, but drew their swords. "You ceased to be one of us when you turned your back upon your vow," answered Sirius, leader of the band.

"I saw no other choice for one as unworthy as I. My band was divided, and the decisions I would have made were the wrong ones."

"No!" came a cry from behind him, one so dearly familiar that Aragon's chest tightened. He turned his head to see Sven, York, and Navarre at his back, their weapons drawn against him as well.

Sven stepped forward and spoke again. "Once I failed in my promise, there were no good choices to be made. Don't you see that no matter what you did, your guilt and the dissension among us would have been the same? I am responsible."

"No! You chose rightly. You fought for Jared's life."

"It doesn't matter," declared Sirius. "The council has

called for Aragon's execution for one reason only—the desertion of his duty."

"You speak in error, Sirius," Navarre said, stepping closer to Aragon. "The council called for Aragon's *arrest*, then execution, which has yet to be approved by Logos. The council cannot change the punishment for a sin without Logos."

"Then we bring him before the council to await Logos's decision."

Aragon held up the amulet clutched in his fist, torn between both honors he must fulfill. "I cannot," he cried. "Pathos must be stopped, or great harm will come. If I am able at the end of my quest, I will return to face the council's punishment." Now that he was aware of the council's decree, his only honor lay in returning to face it.

"What belief can be given to a warrior whose word is broken? You will go to the council now, without delay, under the escort of us Pyrathians," Sirius said.

Aragon shook his head. "Mortal lives are at stake. Pathos's reign of evil upon the mortal ground reaches far wider than the Guardian Forces realize." Holding his sword at the ready, he tried one last time to reason with the Shadowmen. "I came only to learn of a mortal for whom the angels say the Pyrathians intervened. Stefanie Batista must now be within the mortal realm, or Heldon has somehow managed to claim her in another way. I must return to my quest—"

Sirius paused, and a look of confusion crossed his dark features. "Did you speak of—"

"The betrayer can tell the council his woes," said Draysius, a warrior beside Sirius. He lunged forward, his sword striking out at Aragon.

Aragon knew that if he went to face the council now, Pathos would get Annette. Before he could deflect the attack, York set his blade to block the blow. But another warrior struck from the side. Aragon had no time to twist, and the blade went right for his neck and shoulder.

"No!" Navarre shouted, thrusting ahead, protecting Aragon with his own body. The strike threw him backward.

Aragon clutched Navarre to him. "Fool!" he cried. "Do not take my punishments." Fear gripped deep into Aragon's soul. Once beneath the skin, a Pyrathian's power carried with it a soul-scorching fire.

York and Sven brought their weapons to bear against the Pyrathians, but there was a stunned air amid the fighters, as if none was sure what to do. Guardian Forces fighting amongst themselves?

Aragon pulled Navarre back, ready to join the fight. Navarre grabbed Aragon's arm, dragging him down. Aragon could see that Navarre's body shuddered violently beneath the spreading pain. "Anything for my brother," Navarre whispered. "Leave now. Fulfill your quest. Then honor your word. That is how you must help me! I will keep that truth in my heart and survive. Now go!"

Aragon looked at York and Sven fighting. How could he abandon his brothers again? He couldn't leave Navarre to suffer such excruciating pain alone, not when he could help. But he couldn't chance being captured by the Pyrathians either.

"Jared's cave," he shouted to York and Sven, knowing that they would remember where Jared had lain unconscious after the Tsara's poisoning.

"No," Navarre said, pushing Aragon away.

"Either help me or do nothing, but do not fight me," Aragon said. "Or I will perish doing this."

Navarre, weakened so much from the Pyrathian's fire, nodded and collapsed, revealing to Aragon how gravely he'd been wounded. Aragon gathered Navarre in his arms and made a dizzying plunge for the outer circles of the spirit realm. He heard cries of outrage behind him and knew he was being pursued. But his determination to help Navarre propelled him faster than any Shadowman had flown before. He crashed through the darkened fringes hiding the spirit world and blazed into the atmosphere of the mortal world, moving so fast that the air he displaced ignited, giving him the appearance of a ball of fire.

He dove through the sky, trailing white smoke behind him until he reached the forests, where he slowed his flight to maneuver his way to the earthen cave hidden deep in the Appalachians. It seemed to Aragon that he could still hear Jared's cries of pain echo off the mountains. The sorrow would grow were Navarre to be lost. Neither of them chose such a fate, but had come to it through the courage of battle, by believing in Logos's cause and forging ahead.

It made Aragon realize deep within him the error he had made by leaving the Guardian Forces as he did, for he'd come to defeat not through battle but through choice, by not believing. The Guardian Council and his brethren could not help but feel anger and betrayal.

Once inside the cave, he placed Navarre's shuddering body upon the mortal ground. Then, unwinding his amulet from his fist, Aragon slipped it back over his neck. Though yet unworthy, once he finished what he had to do within the mortal realm, he would face the council as a warrior and accept his punishment. Empowered, he pressed his hands to Navarre's wound, seeking to absorb some of the pain of the Pyrathian's fire.

Aragon's body shook, and his breaths rasped between the agonizing moans he couldn't keep himself from voicing. He sent his spirit after Navarre's, wrapping around it and shouldering the burden of the pain. They were in for a long, hard battle. A Pyrathian's fire could last several moons, a fact that had Aragon praying hard to Logos that his fellow Blood Hunters would follow. For if Sven and York didn't appear before Aragon thought Pathos would strike against Annette, Aragon wasn't sure what he would do. Until Navarre regained consciousness and was able to fight the Pyrathian's fire, his soul would suffer damage if left without help.

Time blurred beneath the blazing pain.

The closing of the limo's door felt to Annette like the sealing of a tomb. Pathos sat facing her, his long legs encroaching on her space. Cinatas sat beside him. Even knowing what Cinatas had done, she could clearly see he was the lesser of the two evils.

The chauffeur cruised down Rankin's driveway as if on a leisurely Sunday drive, so at odds with her pounding heart. Internally she kept calling out for Aragon, wanting him, wanting him to forgive her because she'd gone with Pathos. Aragon had pledged to find Stefanie, but Annette couldn't just blindly trust that promise. Aragon didn't know how much time he had left—and he didn't know what Annette knew. If Pathos really did have Stefanie, Annette would never forgive herself for not trying to save her from harm. How she was going to rescue them both from Pathos and Cinatas would just have to come later.

Sunlight, mottled by the branches of pines and oaks, fought to penetrate the limo's darkly tinted windows, but the interior remained dim. Annette searched desperately for any sign of Emerald before it occurred to her with dawning horror that Pathos and Cinatas could have harmed her on their arrival. She shot her gaze to Pathos, and he spoke before she could.

"If your friend was going to help you, she wouldn't have stayed hidden in the woods."

Holy hell. Could he read her mind? "And what friend would that be?" she asked.

He smiled. "The one you're obviously searching the bushes for. Besides, I smelled her. Her scent is unusual for a mortal, which made it stand out from the blood of the other mortal woman."

"Who?"

Cinatas spoke from the far end, almost completely shadowed by the dimness inside the limo. He sounded peeved. "It's the second time today that I've had to discard my shoes from the filth beneath my feet. How could you miss seeing such a disgusting sight? She was all over the kitchen floor. Rankin had only just started cleaning up, but as porous as tile grout is, there is no way the fool could eliminate all traces of her blood with the bleach."

She'd walked in on a murder. Celeste's murder. Though knotted into a tight ball of fear, her stomach managed to roil.

"You would have been next," Cinatas said. "So you can call us your knights in white armor." He tapped the Hummer's white leather door panel. The whole inside was white, with gold accents that only added to its coffinlike appearance.

Annette bared her teeth with a fake smile, determined to hold whatever ground she could. "Ever hear about the baby bird who was too late to fly south for the winter?" she asked, but didn't wait for an answer. "He fell half frozen into a pile of hot manure in a cow pasture. A short while later, a cat came along and dragged him out."

Pathos laughed, if one could call the rusty sound a laugh. "Let me guess. The cat then ate the bird."

"Yes. So everyone who—"

"Pulls you out of a pile of shit may not be your savior. Very amusing."

"You're not offended?" Cinatas asked, disgust peppering his voice. As he turned from the shadows to see Pathos respond, a small measure of sunlight hit his face directly, and he quickly threw up a blocking hand despite the protection of the super-dark sunglasses he wore. For a moment, Annette got the impression that the doctor was wearing a mask.

"Not at all," Pathos replied. "In fact, I'm looking forward to a succulent meal."

Annette clamped her lips together to keep herself both from being sick and from saying anything else. It seemed that the man could spin anything into his little sexual fantasy he had going. She had news for him. It wasn't going to happen.

She expected that once they hit the main highway, they would travel north toward Arcadia and away from Twilight's city limits. They didn't. The driver went about a mile closer to town and then turned left onto an unmarked road half hidden by bushes and a cluster of evergreens. The back road to Hades Mountain. The road switched sharply back and forth as it steadily climbed up the mountainside.

Thirty minutes of near-vertical climbing brought them to heavy iron gates with thick, evil-looking spikes that practically begged to have heads mounted on them. The gate groaned open at a directive from the limo driver, and they eased forward. Annette would need a Mack truck to crash through those gates. Even the Hummer would bounce back on its bumper. Escape was looking pretty dismal at the moment. But she'd come this far, and she wasn't going anywhere until she found her sister.

"I want to see Stef immediately," she told Pathos.

He smiled. "Of course you do."

"Where is she? Where has she been for the past six months?"

"The past holds little importance for you at the moment. You need to be thinking about something else entirely," he said. Before she could blink, he moved forward. His legs slid between hers, and he shoved her knees wide apart as he pressed his palm to her crotch. "You don't get anything you want until I get what I want the way I want it."

A cold burn radiated from his touch, and she tried to shove her hips back, but he had her pinned. She couldn't escape the burn, which was sickly erotic in some way, nothing like the hot desire that Aragon ignited. Her spirit cried out for the Blood Hunter, his touch, his fire. Her mind scrambled for a way to get the upper hand, but nothing filtered through the fear Pathos was pressing upon her. That cold burn had her thinking that she needed to hurry up and do everything he wanted as quickly as she could so that she could get to her sister. But deep down inside, she knew that was all wrong. So where were the thoughts coming from?

Cinatas laughed. "I can't wait to see this. Why not have her now?"

Pathos sat back as quickly as he'd attacked. "Patience, son. My little bird needs to be cleaned up first. Aragon's scent and seed is all over her. She has indeed been wallowing in a hot pile."

"Then why have her at all?"

"Because sometimes the sweetest bite is the last one."

Annette didn't know how she was going to pull it off, but she was damn sure Pathos was going to choke on her. "Poisonous bites are always your last ones as well," she told Pathos. "I'd be careful if I were you."

"I am so going to enjoy you," he said, his tone amused and affectionate.

He was so not, she thought, and then wondered who the bigger fool was, him for thinking he'd have her . . . or her for thinking she could escape.

As they rounded a bend, she caught a quick glimpse of how high up they were and saw a massive waterfall coming down the side of the mountain up ahead. Then the trees cut off the view, and suddenly a tunnel loomed before them. As they entered it, a loud roar filled the car despite the limo's extra insulation. She almost panicked, looking in every direction for the train that was surely about to hit her, until she realized from the seeping water along the tunnel's walls that they were actually going underneath the waterfall.

It was as fascinating as it was daunting, for it added another almost insurmountable element for her to conquer if she and her sister were able to escape by foot.

Provided Stef was alive and able to escape. Once through the tunnel the horizon opened up to an expansive, almost level gap through the double peaks of a mountain that housed a castlelike gray stone structure so large it would take days to search through every room. Annette's heart sank even more. Oh, God, this was not working out right at all. How could she have predicted this?

"Welcome to the Falls," Pathos said.

The lump in her throat was too large. She couldn't say anything at all.

Before they came to a stop, Cinatas pulled a white hooded cloak from a concealed compartment and slipped it on, covering his head like a grim reaper.

A circular drive, sparkling fountain, and sweeping marble staircase rising to a columned portico gave the entrance an appearance grand enough for any opulent palace. The moment the limo came to a stop, the massive doors at the top of the stairs opened, and men in crisp black tuxedo-style uniforms exited and unrolled a red carpet from the portico down the stairs and all the way to the limo.

After bowing, the men stood at attention, staring straight ahead, never once looking at her, Pathos, or Cinatas as they exited the limo and climbed the stairs. At the entrance, a bevy of formally uniformed staff had lined up on each side of the door as if they were servants greeting royalty. No one spoke. Pathos and Cinatas didn't even glance at the people who bowed or curtsied as they passed. Finally, when they'd reached the end of the line, a man sporting decorations to rival a four-star general abruptly dismissed the servants, then bowed, cleared his throat, and spoke to Pathos in a quiet, self-effacing voice.

"Sir, you may wish to know that Señor Vasquez, along with Samir from Arabia and Wellbourne from London, have arrived early. They declined special services and have gathered in the Olympus Room, awaiting your arrival."

Where was Stef in this dramatically ostentatious hellhole? A Vladarian vampire was here in Twilight! Annette recognized Vasquez's name—the name that had cut deeply into Sam—from Erin's list. But neither Samir from Arabia nor Wellbourne from London were on Erin's list. Were they here for the ride, or were there more vampires than those Erin had given transfusions to?

Pathos frowned, clearly irritated at the development. "Leave us, Ungar, and send Lotus and her women to oversee my companion's grooming," he told the man, nodding Annette's way.

When the man left, Pathos turned to Cinatas, then began to pace. "Why is Wellbourne with Vasquez? I wanted to wait until tonight before introducing the order to you, their new leader, but we'd better start now, especially if Wellbourne is going to side with Vasquez about Ashoden ben Shashur. Due to his oil leverage, Shashur had close ties within the Vladarian Order, and his demise will cause trouble. The sooner we stamp it out, the better. Don't make me regret choosing you over Shashur."

Cinatas drew back the hood of his cloak. "Meaning?"

It was the first Annette had seen him without shadows hiding his face. The full light revealed that he might really have on a mask, one with bandages on it. Odd.

Pathos's smile was deadly cold. The air even seemed to turn frosty. "I'll give you power, my son, but if you ever try to take it from my hand again and betray me, what you suffered from Shashur will be a pleasure in comparison to what I will do to you."

Cinatas didn't respond. He only stared back at Pathos. All was not rosy in hell, it would seem.

A door opened, and six women of different races and heights seemingly floated into the room. Each wore a black silk dress, simply cut to hug a perfect hourglass figure, and black slippers that made no noise upon the marbled floor. They didn't speak and kept their gazes focused on the floor.

"You know what I want. Do not fail me," Pathos said.

Annette was in the middle of rolling her eyes when the women converged on her.

"Forget it," she said, backing up, holding them at bay with her raised hands.

"Then our lives would be forfeit," said a woman from behind her.

Before Annette could swing around, a soft hand pressed against her neck and a sharp prick followed by a burning rush along her vein and a fuzzy feeling in her head told her she'd been drugged. She ran two steps, but within seconds her muscles lost their ability to hold her upright no matter how loudly her mind shouted at them to move. The women caught her before she hit the floor.

Irritation ate its way up Pathos's spine as he walked into the Olympus Room, where Vasquez and Samir waited. With the exception of seeing his global plan evolve, he had few pleasures and rarely any anticipatory excitement. Centuries of indulgence had stolen any real enjoyment. At least, until he'd met this woman and her little makeshift blowtorch.

He ran his fingers through his short hair to remind himself how much she owed him. Now that he had his little bird in hand, watching what the women would do to her, seeing their hands all over her helpless, naked flesh, readying her for his enjoyment, would be an added pleasure he hadn't known he would enjoy until he saw the look of total panic in her eyes as she succumbed to the drug. He so wanted her to know he was watching everything being done *to* her *for* him.

But the instant Pathos met Vasquez's gaze across the room, he knew Shashur's execution was going to be a bigger problem than anticipated.

Vasquez wore his full military regalia, and like the two Vladarians flanking him, the anger in his gaze bordered on mutiny. "Wellbourne, Samir, it is good to see you. What has you gentlemen unable to wait until the meeting tonight to speak to me?"

Vasquez reared his shoulders back, realizing that Pathos had deliberately refused to address him.

"What is this I hear?" Vasquez bellowed. "Shashur's gone? One day he calls me and *mi amigo* is well, then he's *nada*?"

Pathos smiled sadly, but his right hand balled into a fist. "I went to see him, found him ill, and sent him for help, but his existence ceased before anything could be done."

"That is unfortunate," Vasquez said, gravely.

"Yes, Shashur was a valued member of the Order. He will be missed."

"No. You misunderstand me, Señor Pathos. What is unfortunate for us all is that I heard a different story about *mi amigo*. One that I would not have believed at one time. But there are other things happening, no?" He shot Cinatas a cutting glance. "First, you and El Doctor have been slowly commandeering more and more of Corazon for your experiments, expecting Vasquez to hide the many that die. The jungle covers secrets well, but I tire of this intrusion. Now there is this new trouble with El Doctor. And I say to myself, Vasquez, there is something not right here. Still, I have faith, no? But now the black demons come to Vasquez and tell a very disturbing story about Shashur. That my fearless leader has had *mi amigo* executed."

Cinatas stepped forward, somehow managing to twist his masked face into a disapproving frown. "You dare to question Pathos? He has brought all of you from groveling beasts to contenders for world power. Have you no respect? No appreciation?"

"*Si*, El Doctor. That is why Vasquez is here for an explanation *before* taking action."

"Interesting." Pathos turned his back on Vasquez and sauntered across the room to sink comfortably into an overstuffed black wing chair that put him at the head of the room with his back to the wall. Stretching his feet, he leisurely rolled his shoulders and gave Vasquez an affable smile. "I've always considered you to be highly intelligent,

Vasquez. So you'll have to forgive me if I'm finding it difficult to believe you'd take the word of beasts with no more
intelligence than to sew rotting appendages to themselves
and parade like grotesque gargoyles. Why Shashur went to
them thinking they could treat his strange illness, I don't
know. The disease must have affected his mind. The truth is,
Shashur was past the point of saving due to the black
demons' incompetence, but I sent him to the red demons
anyway, hoping they could keep him alive long enough for
Dr. Cinatas to discover what was wrong."

Cinatas moved to stand beside Pathos's chair. "What I
fear, gentlemen, is that Logos may have tainted the blood of
the Elan. Two of those who supplied Shashur's transfusion
last week were young women who hadn't been donors
before, but their foster parents have been with us for a
long time."

Pathos eased a smile across his face. The sheer brilliance
of his son astounded him. The vampires were now on the
defensive and threatened, but not by either him or Cinatas.
In fact, they could eliminate any of the Vladarians they
chose to with few repercussions. Genius!

Real fear struggled with Vasquez's bullish antagonism, his
expression twisting as if a noose had just tightened around
his neck.

Wellbourne frowned. The Brit rarely showed emotion or
involved himself in any of the oil-rich vampires' drama. It's
why Pathos occasionally had him out to Zion. His appearance with Vasquez was a slap in the face.

Samir moved forward. The principal owner of SINCO
Oil, the slick shark never had the spine to do anything but
ride either Vasquez's or Shashur's wake. "What do you
mean, 'tainted the blood'?"

Cinatas sighed as if greatly troubled. "I'm still investigating, but my preliminary impression was that the proteins in the Elans' blood have been altered to be lethal to a Vladarian's system. A bit like *E. coli* poisoning for vampires."

"You're trying to tell me that after all this bloody time, Logos has changed the game on us?" Wellbourne demanded.

Cinatas shrugged. "Shashur's demand for fresh blood, not frozen, left him open to something like this. As to why now . . . who can fathom Logos's mind? Perhaps he's threatened by our growing strength within the mortal realm."

"Vasquez must see your proof! I have little trust at the moment," Vasquez said.

"Unfortunately, any proof burned in the Manhattan fire. But rest assured I am investigating this and will notify all of the Vladarians of my findings. Until then, we'll only be able to use frozen Elan blood from longtime donors."

Wellbourne paced away. "The neurotic Euro vamps are in a panic over something as simple as the two fires. Couldn't even wait until midnight for the answers. This is going to send them through the bloody roof. When were you going to tell us?"

Pathos smiled. This was going better than he could have imagined, and Cinatas had them all in the palm of his devious little hand. "Tonight—when I turned over leadership of you Vladarians to my son. I grow weary of your lack of appreciation for all that I do."

All three of the vampires' fangs flashed as they snarled in outrage and shock.

"Bloody hell," yelled Wellbourne. "You must be joking."

"Your son?" gasped Samir. "Who?"

"Gentlemen, you're already very well acquainted with him. Dr. Anthony Cinatas. The man who has been a savior of sorts to you already."

Vasquez let out a long string of Spanish curses. "El Doctor? You are very mistaken if you think to turn your leadership over to him. He has already proven himself to be most difficult. Corazon is mine, and he commandeers everything as if he has the right. The Vladarians *vote* for their *jefe*."

"Well," said Pathos, "then perhaps we'll take a vote at the meeting tonight. And depending on the results, maybe Cinatas will be compelled to discover what killed Shashur."

The dead silence that followed his words was like music to his ears. He'd never achieved that among the Vladarians. Never.

"Until tonight then, gentlemen." And on that note, Pathos exited the room, Cinatas silently following behind him.

Chapter Sixteen

SAM GLARED AT the sky before nailing Emerald with an angry glare. Erin and Emerald were lucky they weren't dead. He didn't know about Annette, but he hoped to God they had some time before the werewolf tore into her. He was more than pissed that they hadn't followed orders and stayed put. He felt as turbulent as the mother of all thunderstorms that seemed to be brewing overhead. It appeared out of nowhere, tearing through the sky, ready to demolish everything in its path. He could relate.

"You didn't do anything to save her?" Sam shouted above the thunder at Emerald. She sat on the front porch of the Rankins' house, looking as sick as he felt and clutching a dragon-covered laptop to her breast. Pieces of Celeste Rankin were all over the kitchen. He'd known a lot of hard shit in his life, but nobody could face that kitchen and stay detached.

"No, I dinna," Emerald said, her voice no more than a whisper. She didn't look at him, but kept staring out at the whipping trees and down the darkening driveway, as if she was still watching the limo Annette had supposedly climbed into of her free will.

"Why?" he demanded again. He sucked in several deep breaths and clamped down on the rising lump in his throat. His deputies would be here at any moment, and he prayed to God the storm would hold off long enough for them to search the perimeter of the cabin for evidence before the storm destroyed it all.

He knew he wasn't just shouting to be heard over the storm, too. He was shouting because he was just so damn mad that the women hadn't done what he and Jared had asked.

He really was glad Emerald hadn't tried any foolhardy heroics. Really, what could one woman do to stop a were-wolf and an insane doctor? It was just that her mystical mumbo-jumbo ticked him off so much that he had to shout at her about something. Either that or pull his own hair out.

"I already told you. Meggie had a vision. If I had done anything other than bleedin' hide, they would have fooking taken me with them, and then it would have been vera, vera bad."

A vision! A freaking vision ruled her actions. Not reason, not intelligence, but a vision relayed to her by a young girl who apparently had never had a vision before. Sam pinched the bridge of his nose, thankful to hear the approaching sirens.

"Well, I hope to hell Nick doesn't lose sight of the truck we 'let' past the roadblock, or Annette will be seeing her sister sooner than any of us thought. They'll both be pushing up daises. That truck is our only link to Pathos, and hopefully Annette will still be alive by the time it reaches him, provided that's where it is headed."

"Don't you dare say that!" Emerald erupted from her seat and swung around. The fire in her eyes seared right through him, making him feel more of a worthless bastard than he already was. He knew she had to be feeling worse than hell that Annette had been taken, and he shouldn't be adding to it. But damn it, at some point they had to understand that an order to stay put was just that. The whole freaking U.S. military would implode if soldiers didn't obey orders.

"Stefanie is alive!" Emerald shouted.

"Stefanie!" Sam was sure the pounding in his head and the blood roaring in his ears meant that he was in the midst of a stroke. How could she be arguing over Stefanie's demise right now? How could she even be thinking about Stefanie at a moment like this? Annette had just been taken—he was still puzzling out the went-without-force scenario.

The woman was whacked, and he looked with fervent relief at one of his deputies tearing up the drive. "Rankin just hacked his wife up. Are you telling me he didn't touch a hair on Stefanie's head? She's probably buried in the backyard in as many pieces as his wife. Go get in Rand's squad car," he told her when the deputy skidded to a halt in the gravel. "I'll drive you over to Annette's as soon as I talk to him about what needs to go down here. That computer you're choking is evidence, but I'm going to ignore that for a few minutes until we get a copy of what's on there. We don't have time for red tape if any of the data can lead us to Annette."

"I'll walk," she said.

Lightning cracked across the sky, trying to split the world open. Sam got in Emerald's face. "You'll ride either in the car or over my shoulder, but there is no way in hell you are walking down the damn road."

She looked up at him, and the tears swimming in her fierce green eyes nearly sent him to his knees. "We canna stay in our homes anymore, Sam. And I canna protect Meggie anymore without more power, not even in our home. I canna let anythin' more happen to Meggie."

Sam reached out to pull her into his arms, but at the last second only set his hand on her shoulder. "Nothing is going to happen to Meggie. Do you hear me? Nothing."

She shook her head and stepped away from his touch. "It already has. Her vision was vera bad. And I'm afraid we canna stop what's coming next."

He turned his back to her before he said the words clamoring to escape from his screaming tension. He'd turned away before he told her to wake up and deal with the real world, to unbury her head from the mystical sand, before the world ate her ass up—words he wouldn't have hesitated to say before last week and his realization that werewolves and vampires were real. Before he gave in to the even stronger need to kiss her.

Through the pain scorching his spirit, Aragon began to despair. Instead of growing stronger and regaining consciousness, Navarre became more delirious, weaker. And Aragon didn't know if it was because he was losing his own power, becoming more and more a faded warrior, or if Navarre's soul was being damaged, and thus he was losing his spirit to live and fight. He knew he'd already missed his opportunity to follow the mortal vehicle to where Pathos might be. But all might not be for naught; the dark cloud hovering over the mountain told him that something more was there.

A heavy hand fell on Aragon's shoulder. "You must go."

York's voice seemed to be coming from a long tunnel. Aragon shook his head. "I can't leave Navarre. Not like this."

"You must! You must finish helping the mortals you pledged to aid and then return. Sven has gone to the council, requesting you be absolved and that your execution punishment be placed upon him."

"What?" Aragon reared back, shocked to the center of his being. "Why? He can't do that!"

"Sven saw it as his only honorable path. The fight with the Pyrathians convinced him that only atonement will bring peace amongst the brotherhood. He sees all of this as his fault and hopes to convince the council of it. He went in peace with the Pyrathians so that they could all face the council with their actions. You know the council will wait the sacred three sun cycles before deciding upon a matter of such import, but we've no time to waste. You must go, now."

Navarre began to shudder again.

"How? Navarre isn't surviving the pain." Aragon grabbed York's hand and pressed it to Navarre's wound and then set both his hands over Navarre's heart. "Together we might save him."

York groaned, his arm shaking from the searing pain. Then he thrust his other hand over Navarre's heart, and the energy exploding from him shocked Aragon. York's nature had always been fervent, but Aragon hadn't realized how passionate or how strong. "I can do this alone. And if necessary, I can take him to the Pyrathians. They can help heal those they've burned if they choose to," he said. "Now go."

Aragon hesitated, but when he felt Navarre responding more to York's energy than he had to his in all the time he'd been with him, Aragon stepped aside. He started to tell York that he was already becoming a faded warrior and might not be able to return to the spirit realm, and that Sven's sacrifice would be in vain. But he didn't. York needed to think of no one other than Navarre. Aragon set his hand on York's shoulder. "I will save Sven."

He left the cave then, walking into the fading afternoon light. A storm brewed above, dark, angry, and fierce. The Guardian Forces had gathered to fight the growing concentration of Heldon's Fallen Army. A battle in the spirit realm was about to explode and rain down upon the mortal ground. Their blood would fall from the heavens and pour upon the earth in iridescent droplets so powerful that all of life survived upon it.

Aragon stood for a long moment amidst the thunder and the lightning, torn between seeking out Annette or following through with his plan to find Pathos. The difficulty he had with his spirit form and traveling through the spirit realm gave him no choice. He had no doubt he was fading. There was only one thing he could do, and he ran hard in that direction, gasping in the high mountain air as his body strained for substance in the whipping wind that cut at him. He couldn't seem to breathe in enough air, and the earth beneath his feet didn't feel as solid. The scents of the forest—pine, fresh green, and fecund soil—though still there, weren't as strong as they had been yesterday. He could smell the blood of the creatures, though, telling him that some of his abilities were strong yet. He clenched his fists and gritted his teeth, raging against the fate that he feared was ripping away his last chance to be a measure of the warrior he'd thought he'd be. Crossing the spirit barrier seemed to have drained more of him away, and his heart cried out for Annette, for a chance to know once more the pleasure and the fire of her embrace. He prayed to Logos for just a little more time.

He needed her, and his spirit called out for hers, seeking the connection they shared. But he found no answering cry, and wondered if he'd even make it to her side before he faded completely.

He ran faster. He ran by instinct to the mountain with the hovering dark cloud, one that was even darker than the storm forming overhead.

Annette fumed. She was splayed like a plucked turkey, basted in some sort of tingling oil, ready for a feast. All Pathos had to do was jerk the red satin sheet off. The women had placed her before a large wall of windows that torturously overlooked the valley where the small city of Twilight sat, unknowing of her predicament or of the storm clouds rolling toward them. In fact, given a pair of high-powered binoculars, she might be able to pick out a building or two and find the road that led to her cabin . . . and her friends and . . . Aragon.

Oh, God. She finally let herself face what she had been trying to avoid ever since she realized that she was virtually paralyzed. She was not going to be able to find Stefanie. And she was not going to be able to stop Pathos from doing whatever he wanted to do. The knowledge that Pathos was going to violate her and rip away all of the pleasure Aragon had left simmering inside her made her soul cry out.

I'm sorry! She should have believed in him. She shouldn't have tried to do this all alone.

Aragon!

The drug they kept administering to her rendered her voluntary muscles just weak enough to be totally ineffective. She could still feel and think, but she couldn't move. She wasn't sure how long her bathing session had lasted, but having someone else take total control of her body had been a humbling and harrowing lesson in what she expected of patients almost every day as a surgeon. Granted, all of her patients had been completely knocked out, but that powerless feeling had to be the same.

The women, though respectful, had done everything imaginable to clean her inside and out. They'd sensitized every nerve and denuded her of every hair from the neck down, then slicked her up.

She wanted to cry, but wouldn't let a single tear leak through her resolve. She would focus completely on Aragon and not give Pathos the satisfaction of reacting to anything at all. Besides, as poorly as her vocal cords and swallowing reflexes were working, she'd likely choke on her tears.

The sound of a shutting door and muffled footsteps sent her heart pounding. Pathos appeared at the foot of the divan, and his perfect features relaxed into an amused smile. "You smell delicious," he murmured.

She glared at him.

Pushing aside the sheet, he ran a finger up the sole of her foot. The cold touch was torturous in that she couldn't move from it, and her nerves jumped, lodging a sick erotic feel in her loins.

He frowned when she didn't react. "Don't think you can put me off. Believe me, I have many ways to make you feel things you've never even imagined could be pleasurable." He slid his finger up her leg to her open sex, pressed painfully hard on her most sensitive spot. "I just left your sister's side. She has skin as soft as yours. Shall I have her first?" Then he backed away, clearly disgusted.

Stef! Annette's heart cried out, wondering what her sister was suffering. Pathos sounded as if Stefanie was in the next room. Annette desperately tried to struggle, tried to move, but couldn't.

The door opened. "I came to enjoy the show," she heard Cinatas say.

Pathos cursed. "She's still drugged. And can't move."

"But she can feel, so what's stopping you?"

"I don't want her to just succumb to the pleasure. She's going to strain for it. I'll bathe, and by then she should be . . . in working order."

"Mind if I amuse myself a bit? Adrenalin will hurry her recovery."

Pathos's smile when he looked down at her was answer enough. Cinatas would violate her as well.

A hard knock sounded at the door. "What now?" Pathos said.

"Forgive the intrusion, but I thought you should know. Only one of the trucks has arrived. The rest are being detained by the law. The sheriff from Twilight is at the iron gates and insists on speaking to you both. Should I let him pass? If necessary, accidents do happen frequently on the road to the Falls."

"I'll handle the sheriff," said Cinatas. "I have a score to settle."

"No, not yet," Pathos said. "Once Sno-Med is back on steady ground, then we'll settle some scores. Tell the sheriff we aren't here, and he needs a search warrant to pass through the gates."

"Very well." The man's reply was followed by the door shutting.

"He's likely here for her," Cinatas said. "He won't go peacefully. By morning he'll be back with that warrant."

"Then we'll welcome his search. Why don't you go hear what he says, then come back?"

"What about her?"

"She's on our side. She'll betray her friends when the time comes. I'll even free her in the morning, and tomorrow night she will come back for more of my kind of pleasure. The good doctor will do anything for her sister, right?"

Annette stared at him, horrified, and he slid his palm over her baby-smooth crotch. "What? You thought this would be a one-night stand?"

She blinked, fighting back the tears, aching painfully where Pathos had touched her. Not because he hurt her, but because the pain of that evil touching her after knowing Aragon's pleasure was too much to bear. And the agony of having her sister so near and being unable to help was just as bad. The clouds moving across the horizon were darker than ever.

She cried out with her whole heart and soul. *Aragon!*

Annette's cry slammed into Aragon and stopped him in his tracks. It echoed louder than the thunder, crossing the distance separating them, joining his spirit to hers. The call from her was even stronger than his warrior's bond, for though the heavens rumbled with a brewing battle between the Guardian Forces and Heldon's Fallen Army, he could barely hear them.

And it came, heart-stoppingly, from the direction in which he was headed. From the black-clouded mountain and the sense of pervasive evil that grew with his every advancing step.

By Logos! Had he miscalculated what Pathos would do? Did Pathos have Annette? He ran harder. He ran until his blood pounded so hard that he could taste it in his mouth, until his breaths were so ragged pain lanced his sides with every gasp. Even his warrior-honed muscles screamed from the strain. He reached a huge stone fence capped by black iron spikes and a thick gray mist, and nearly doubled over from the rank stench of Underlings. There would have to be hundreds of them around for him to smell them this strongly and not be within their midst.

But Underlings weren't normally able to cross the spirit barrier into the mortal realm. Some dark magic here, or a heavy concentration of evil, must have weakened the spirit barrier to a thin layer. He shuddered. Almost any depraved creature from Heldon's realm, no matter how lowly, could cross the spirit barrier at this point. Why hadn't they wreaked havoc on everyone in the area, attacked and devoured the mortals while they slept in their beds?

He didn't know. Maybe they were only able to exist within the cloud of evil shrouding the mountaintop. He did know one thing for certain. The stench was so strong that he had little doubt the number of Underlings was more than he could fight alone—and he had no brethren to call upon for aid.

His heart hammered with a fear greater than any he'd known before. Annette was in the middle of this hole from hell. Her life, her spirit, and her soul were in grave jeopardy. He'd have to cross the spirit barrier to get to her. But that left two problems. First, he wouldn't be able to bring her through the spirit barrier to get her out. That meant they were going to have to find a way beyond the evil barrier before the Underlings caught them. And second, the gathering storm in the area meant the spirit realm was crawling with the Guardian Forces. He'd escaped once. He didn't think he'd be as lucky a second time.

Thunder and lightning lashed through the sky as the growing energy from the gathering forces filled the entire Appalachian area. It didn't surprise him to see that the Guardian Forces had moved in. They would have had to be blind to miss this mushroom explosion of evil on top of the mountain. He had to move swiftly and carefully.

At every passing second the turmoil surrounding him worsened. The growing energy of the coming battle danced in the air and whipped the wind, adding to the darkness as the storm and the coming night choked the light from the day. Already he could feel the moon's pull upon his were-form, urging him to give in to his baser desires, and it wasn't even visible in the sky yet. He wondered if the surrounding evil could amplify the effects of the moon on him.

Grasping his amulet, he leapt, but instead of being smoothly sucked into the spirit world, his being seemed to lodge partway, as if he didn't have enough power to make the shift. He wavered between the realms, his being straining itself beyond its limits, growing hotter and hotter, scorching him.

Please! his spirit cried to Logos. *By all that is good and pure! Help me!* He fell to his knees, his eyes squeezed shut.

As a Shadowman, a warrior within the Guardian Forces, Logos's power had been free-flowing, and unquestionably his to draw upon. Now there was a cold, agonizing barrier between him and that power.

When Aragon hit the ground, it wasn't the rough earth he expected, but an amazing softness and the heavenly scent of Annette amid the fetid odors of Pathos, Vladarians, Underlings, and more. Opening his eyes, he stared into hers as a flood of relief and deep emotion knocked him down.

The difficulty he had in crossing the spirit barrier told him his fate of fading had truly begun, and he cried out against it, realizing there was something greater within the world than war and eliminating Pathos, and he was drowning in her dark eyes at that very moment.

She lay on a cushioned bed, her creamy, soft skin partially covered by red satin and her mind in a panicked whirlwind that roared around him.

He could hear the sound of water, smell the steam and Pathos's stench, and knew the evil werewolf was in the shower, giving Aragon hope that he'd be able to whisk Annette away undetected. No being, whether mortal or spirit, could smell through water or its thick vapor, for the iridescent blood of the warriors cleansed away filth and absorbed all scents.

Aragon! Annette's mind shouted at him. She didn't speak or move, but tears filled her eyes, and he could feel her entire being cry out to him. He gathered her in his arms, yet she lay limp within his grasp.

Drugged. Can't move. Can't speak. Thank God you came. We must hurry. Pathos is in the shower, and Cinatas will be back in a few minutes as well. Sam is at the gates.

Shh. He brushed his lips over hers. *All will be well,* he told her.

Taking off his amulet, he slid it over her neck, giving it back to her in part to comfort her, to mark her as his, and hoping her possession of it would renew the solidity he had felt while she had it before. He couldn't tell if it made any immediate difference, but seeing his amulet on her made his heart beat with more assuredness than he'd ever felt before.

He gently laid her back so that he could gain his feet and swing her, covering sheet and all, solidly into his arms. That she had been reduced to such a helpless state sent a fiery rage burning through him. He wanted to tear Pathos apart from limb to limb.

Searching for a way out, he stepped into the next room, where a wall of glass doors led outside to a stone parapet. The evil gray mist hung thickly over the place, but he didn't see any Underlings yet. Quickly he moved into the descending night. Rain began to sprinkle the mortal ground, thunder reverberated, and lightning crackled across the sky, signifying that the battle in the heavens had begun—the chill of Heldon's cold army was rushing against the heated mass of the Guardian Forces.

Wait! We can't leave! Stefanie may be here! I must find her! And what about Sam?

Stefanie here? Aragon paused just outside the door. He remembered the essence of Annette's sister's scent from her book of shape-shifters and were-beings, an insight into the spirit world that said Stefanie saw more than most mortals, or at least imagined more. He didn't note that essence now. Was he losing even more of himself and his abilities? Becoming even more of a faded warrior?

They couldn't linger. Once Pathos discovered that Annette was gone, he would raise the alarm, and they'd be trapped by the number of Underlings surrounding them.

Where? Where did you see her?

I haven't. Pathos said he had her, would use her as a substitute for me.

He could have spoken falsely.

I know.

He wouldn't be able to carry Annette to safety and then come back again. Not only did he fear that another crossing through the spirit barrier would be his last, but once the alarm would be sounded, they were lost. He had to look for Stefanie now and get them both out.

Stepping back into the room, Aragon drew in another deep breath, focusing completely on the scents inside the domain. *I don't detect her scent among those here.*

Are you sure? Pathos said that he had just left her side. Almost as if she were in the next room.

No. I would know for certain if she were as close as that.

She must be here. Maybe tied and drugged like me. He said her skin was as soft as mine. She has to be here.

He touched her?

Yes.

Aragon would know without a doubt if he were to smell Pathos's clothes. It was a risk, but one he felt he had to take just to ease the wrenching pain inside Annette's heart. She'd sacrificed everything to save her sister, and he needed to do everything in his power to help.

He laid Annette just inside the door. *I'll be right back.*

Stealing back through the rooms, Aragon slid to where Pathos bathed, surprised to see the steam billowing within the room. Most from the realm of the damned couldn't tolerate heat, and he wondered what Pathos had done to change that fact for himself over the past millennia.

A sudden surge of anger coursed through Aragon's body, and he clenched his hands. He could kill the beast now. He'd already condemned himself in order to fulfill that quest. But then what?

Any scenario besides immediate escape would make Annette pay the price. And she'd pay with her life and her soul. He couldn't take the chance. He picked up Pathos's clothing and carried it to Annette. He sniffed over every foul inch of it.

Nothing. There are other mortal scents, and blood, and even the scent of the man you call your neighbor, but none of Stefanie.

Rob Rankin?

Yes.

Tears filled Annette's eyes, but they narrowed with an angry determination that seemed akin to his own. *Pathos lied. What about Sam? What if he forces his way in?*

There is too much dark magic. Sam won't be able to get in until they want him to. We have to leave now. It may already be too late.

Let's go.

As he stepped out into the night with Annette secure in his arms, he sensed her despair at having believed her sister near, only to lose her again.

I'll find her. And he would. He could do no less.

Annette drew a breath of night air into her lungs. She didn't know if the drug was starting to wear off or if Aragon's presence had eased the knot of horror inside her, but she seemed to be breathing more deeply now. Either way, she welcomed the damp coolness, the taste of the gathering storm, and the scent of pine forest.

And of course the sensual aroma that belonged to Aragon alone. It wasn't something she could put her finger on, but it was real and comforting, and as alluring to her feminine side as the warrior himself. She met his gaze, seeing the commitment of his heart in his promise to her. There was a tentative quality to his gaze that made her heart ache, making her realize more than ever that he was as vulnerable and needy as she—all of the mixture of emotions and dreams and desire that made her human now lived and breathed within him.

Yes. We will find her. Her spirit assured his. *And you will change this fate of being a faded warrior.*

Before he could respond, she caught a movement out of the corner of her eye and stared in horror as a black, winged batlike creature the size of a jaguar came at her with claws slashing and razorlike teeth bared.

Aragon swung around, shoving his broad shoulder between her and the attack. He stumbled at the impact, and the creature screeched; a sound so unholy that her entire body shuddered with a cold chill. Then Aragon pulled away and ran.

The creature flew after them. Annette could hear the fleshy slap of its wings in between its screams loud enough to awaken centuries of the dead. She struggled to do anything to help Aragon, but could only shift her head closer to the warmth of his shoulder.

Aragon leapt onto the stone railing of the balcony, and her breath gushed out in a spasm of fear. Pathos's rooms had been on the fourth floor. Lightning ripped sideways across the night sky, as if headed directly at them. She couldn't shut her eyes, she couldn't scream—all she could do was reach out with her whole spirit, wanting to wrap her arms around

Aragon. He jumped just before the lightning struck. It seemed that as they fell toward the ground, a storm burst wide open with a deafening thunderclap. Hard-hitting pellets of icy rain stung her skin.

He hit the ground with a jarring thud and didn't even stumble as he broke into a run. Trees and bushes passed in a blur as he wove among the dense growth that protected them slightly from the raging storm. Sometimes he ducked low, sometimes he jumped high, but no matter how fast he ran, she could hear the growing number of screeches following them. The sound of hundreds of flapping wings was a cross between the roar of a train and the menacing drone of swarming killer bees on the attack.

The only thing holding the creatures off was Aragon's speed. She could hear the felling of trees and brush behind her as the creatures tore after them. Suddenly the forest ended, opening to a clearing that would surely lead to their capture. Hard drops of rain, almost like bullets of icy hail, stung her everywhere.

Go back to the trees, she cried. This time she could clasp her arm closer to her pounding heart. The drug had to be losing some of its effect.

No. You can't ever let Underlings surround you. You have to stay ahead. No matter what.

That no-matter-what came in the form of a cliff.

Chapter Seventeen

PATHOS SNATCHED HIS clothes from the floor by the balcony's door. Aragon's scent reeked amid the lingering essence of the woman he'd had readied to feast upon. He could almost taste her on his tongue, he wanted her so hotly. Never had he had to wait this long to slake his desire, and the painful burn of it angered him.

Underlings were after Aragon and the woman, and once caught, they'd rip her to shreds before consuming her. She'd vanish without a trace. Aragon would be another matter. They'd drag him into Heldon's freezing fires and feast upon his soul until there was nothing of Logos left, and only Heldon's hellish image could be seen in the warrior.

The triumphant screeching of Underlings in the distance told him that they were moments away from capturing their prey. He turned to leave her to her fate, deciding that he'd have Cinatas retrieve her sister for his pleasure, provided she was still alive. Cinatas surmised that Rankin had sent the woman to Vasquez's hellhole in Belize.

She'd probably be nothing more than a broken shell. Nothing like the fiery doctor who defied him at every turn. Pathos roared in frustration. The doctor *would* serve him! The nerve she'd stroked to life inside him by scorching his hair wouldn't let her escape him again, even for death.

He whirled into his were-form. Ignoring the raging battle overhead, as he always did, he drew in the cold wet air and howled, splitting the night with his command as he raced through the rain to the gathered Underlings. He'd have her the second he got his hands on her.

Aragon paused on the precipice of the cliff and adjusted his hold on Annette. His shoulder burned where the Underling's talon had punctured the muscle of his back. The blood inside him throbbed through his body. He suddenly felt strange and feverish. A waterfall rushed by them, so powerful that the cooling mists billowing upward nearly blinded him as he set his keen sight on the deepest part of the pooled water below. He prepared to jump, gauging the distance from his position to the jagged rocks he needed to leap past.

Then he heard Pathos howl for the Underlings to wait and knew the moment he'd sought for so long, to meet his betraying mentor in battle, had come. An overwhelming, answering howl clawed through his throat. He and Pathos would fight, and one would die. He loosened his hold on Annette and turned to set her down as an urgent savagery ripped through him.

The moon and the surrounding evil permeating the air jerked at his were-being, sharpening his senses and thrusting his bloodlust to a needy edge that had his were-form bursting into view despite his efforts to fight the shift. Never before had he been unable to control the power and magic in his body. It was as if his entire body was being overcome. His teeth ached, and fangs jutted painfully into his lower lip. His muscles bulged to an excruciating point as hair erupted everywhere. His awareness of anything but satisfying the lust of his desires dimmed.

He wanted Pathos.

He wanted blood.

The howl he'd been trying to stifle exploded from his gut, tearing its way through him. He could taste Annette's blood scenting the air and wanted to sink his teeth into the hot rush of it beneath her silken skin, just inches from his mouth.

He had to have blood. He needed blood. He wanted blood. Any blood. His body burned for it.

The Underlings halted the attack, swirling about them, lashing out at each other with screeching snarls, barely restraining themselves from their desire to kill. One of them lashed out, drawing a thick splattering of blood from another, and a group of them converged, devouring their own. Its nearly flesh-bare bones fell to the ground. Their frenzy fed Aragon's lust for blood. His mouth watered, his heart pumped hard with anticipation, and he tightened his hold on Annette. Just one taste of her sweetness was all he needed. He brought her neck closer, then shook his head hard, searching for sanity.

By Logos! He would not succumb.

What was wrong with him? What was happening to him? Another minute beneath the influences raging at his were-form, and Aragon knew he'd forget about saving Annette completely. He'd bite her and then go after Pathos, even if it meant leaving her to the Underlings; such was the strength of the bloodlust in him.

He didn't waste a moment. He let Annette's feet slide to the ground as he anchored her body against his, his arm holding her tightly to his chest. Then, grasping the sheet, he wrapped it around his back, under his arms. Doing the same to her, he next tied the sheet tightly so that they were completely anchored together.

Pathos broke into the clearing, howling that no one had ever or would ever escape him. Aragon met the werewolf's crazed gaze across the distance and growled in triumph, realizing that he'd won the battle over Pathos at this point, if not the war. Aragon jumped over the cliff with Annette into the mists rising from the deep pool at the bottom of the waterfall.

She screamed, her voice vibrating with terror.

Aragon fought for his sanity, squelching down the lusts that his were-form thrust upon him, and focused his mind on Annette and her need. He wrapped his arms around her and forced his spirit to surround hers. *Trust me,* he told her as they fell.

A second howl cut through the forest, this one more bone-chilling than before. It sent a shiver of terror up Sam's spine. God! Annette was being devoured by that beast, and he and Jared had just barely made it past the stone wall closing in the place like a fortress. The stench of the place was unbelievable.

"Sam! We have to leave now!" Jared shouted.

Sam could barely hear Jared over the bursts of thunder and an ungodly screeching ripping his eardrums apart. "No!" he shouted back. "Not without Annette!"

He'd tried to get to the top of Hades Mountain with the power of his badge. That failed. Now he'd do it through sheer force of will, or die. Before Nick had had to abort tracking the truck from the helicopter because of the storm, he'd pegged it as heading up Hades Mountain. And he'd been right. It was with a sick feeling in his gut that Sam drove up to the high stone-and-iron gates leading to the reclusive mansion. The place that everyone laughed off as a billionaire's folly. The place he'd been warned about.

Old man Hatterfield wasn't a redneck drunk on moonshine after all. The geezer had actually realized that there was something very wrong on Hades Mountain, and Sam had been too blind to see it. He was the freaking sheriff of Twilight, sworn to protect those he served, and evil had been camping right under his nose.

"It's either too late, or Aragon has escaped with Annette."

"What do you mean?"

"The first howl was Pathos commanding the Underlings not to touch whoever it is they are chasing, that the victory was to be his. This second howl was pure rage. So either Aragon has or is about to escape with Annette, or the Underlings didn't obey his command. If we stay here or go farther, we'll be dead too, and all that will be left to face the evil will be Erin and Emerald. It's not a risk I'm willing to take, especially since I think Aragon has Annette. We need to go back."

Suddenly the high-pitched screaming became louder, and the awful stench grew so strong that it started crawling nauseatingly down his throat. He started to cover his nose with his arm, but Jared grabbed him. Frantic.

"Underlings!" Jared screamed, pulling him back to the stone wall. "Run!"

"What?" Sam glanced in the direction of the rising sound and saw a teeming herd of flying black beasts ripping up everything in their path. He didn't even take time to breathe before he started hauling ass. Pumping his arms as hard as he could, he was still losing, big-time. The creatures were gaining on him at light speed, fangs and claws slashing in anticipation. His eardrums felt as if they were rupturing from the sonic trauma. He palmed his gun, even though it was as useless as a gnat's dick against the force after him.

Sam was five feet from the wall when he felt the creature's cold, fetid breath reach him and heard the tree he'd just passed ripped in half. He was a dead man.

Jared had made the wall, jumping high enough to grasp onto one of the iron spikes topping its fifteen-foot, dark-mist-riddled height. Swinging one leg up, he hooked the top of the wall and reached out his hand.

Sam jumped for Jared's hand, shooting his gun blindly behind him, fanning out the spray of his bullets until he'd unloaded half the magazine. Jared caught his wrist and with an impossible burst of strength swung Sam up to the top of the wall. The screeching behind him turned even more chaotic, and as Sam gained his feet to jump to the other side, he saw that he'd drawn blood on three of the creatures, who were now being eaten by the horde.

There was barely a moment's pause before the front line of the remaining creatures looked at Sam and Jared and then lunged. The evil bloodlust coming at him was cold enough to freeze the blood in his veins. Sam wasn't even sure if he'd jumped from the wall or if his knees had simply given out. The creatures lashed out, but seconds before their claws made contact, they incinerated, blasting Sam with burning hot air.

Trust you? Annette whispered in her mind. She wasn't sure what was happening to Aragon, but the change was scaring the hell out of her. His were-form was slightly different than before, less manlike, a little more wolfish, and a lot more savage. The dark glint of hunger in his gaze as his fangs dug into his lip seemed to reflect the mindless blood-lust of the creatures that had circled them on the cliff's edge. Then he'd shaken his head, and she'd felt Aragon's spirit, the same that she had known so deeply inside her. It was the Aragon she knew, though his were-form was more frightening than she remembered. She reached out to him with her own spirit.

Yes, she told him, even though it seemed as if they were freefalling to hell itself. She shifted her head tighter against his neck and closed her eyes. All she could do was hold her breath and believe in him.

They sliced deep into the chilly water. She could feel it pressing in on her, trying to force the air from her lungs. Its rushing turbulence whipped them around in a dizzying circle. They were being sucked into a powerful whirlpool that drew them deeper and deeper. Her heart hammered, and her body screamed to breathe again.

She could feel Aragon fight against the impossibly strong current forcing them downward. He struggled, his werebody shuddering from the effort as his strong limbs fought the pressure. Just when she thought she would pass out, he broke free and propelled them both to the surface. Blessed air. She gulped in a lungful before the current dragged them down again.

In her mind, she heard Aragon cry out, and with a burst of strength, he rammed through the treacherous whirlpool sucking at them and thrust them into a rushing river. The roar of the waterfall faded to the droning rain and the hum of a river molding the face of the land with a fluid hand and a relentless will.

Annette wasn't sure how much time elapsed as he navigated downstream, somehow able to see and avoid large boulders and sharp rocks despite the rain and the descending night. Slowly, the heaviness keeping her from moving eased as the last of the drug wore off and her adrenaline kicked in.

She should have been cold, chilled from the water and the dropping temperature of the sweet mountain air at night. But she wasn't. Aragon's heat and presence warmed her to her soul.

Aragon shifted from his werewolf form with an arching cry and became . . . normal. That his body was capable of such a vast change was almost incomprehensible to her, yet it was true. Frightening and . . . magical.

After he changed, he had to strain harder to keep them afloat and to fight the swirling current, making her realize that his werewolf form, the savage part of him, is what had saved them from death and evil.

He seemed to be growing weaker, and though she wasn't strong enough to swim, she thought she could walk, and she told him so.

Before answering, he swam in a circle, searching the night sky through the misty rain. "The water masks our scent and keeps the Underlings and Pathos from being able to trace our path. It would be best to find shelter now so the storm can wash away the path of our scent." He pulled them to the side of the river and untied the sheet binding them together.

She had felt so natural, warm, and secure with her naked body against Aragon's that it was moving away from him that felt awkward. He helped her gain her feet and wrapped the wet sheet around her shoulders.

Though extremely shaky, Annette managed to stand on her own and hug the sheet to her suddenly chilled body. Even though the sheet was wet, it kept the cold rain from directly hitting most of her skin, giving her a small relief from the discomfort. "What shelter did you have in mind? I don't know anywhere that will be safe from those horrid banshees. How can things like that exist, and no one knows?"

"They are Underlings. I've fought them many times within the spirit realm, but have never had to battle them upon the mortal ground. You know from the imaginings of others and the reports of things unusual that occasionally creatures from the spirit realm find a way into your world. But I think right now it is a dark magic allowing their presence. Remember the black cloud hovering over the mountain peak that I asked you about earlier?"

She nodded, and Aragon explained that a pall of hovering dark magic could thin the spirit barrier enough to allow creatures from the damned to cross through. "But if they try to go past the boundary of the black magic, they will implode."

"Kind of like people can only exist in the earth's atmosphere. Please tell me we are out of range of those Underling things."

"Not quite. I'm not as concerned about them as I am about Pathos. He likely didn't follow us over the cliff, because he cannot see or smell us in the water. Nor can he trace our scent on the mortal ground as long as it is raining. But as soon as the rain stops, he'll be after us with a vengeance."

"Then we'd better get moving, fast." She groaned and took a shaky step.

He scooped her off her feet, and she wriggled in protest. "I can walk."

"But I can run. There is a cave where we'll be safe until sunrise if we can get there before the rain stops."

Annette wrapped her arm around Aragon's neck and huddled into his amazing warmth as the dark shadows of the forest passed in a blur. There was something very different about his embrace compared to when he'd run from the Sno-Med Center. He carried her closer to him now, held her tighter, yet more gently.

Before she had much time to contemplate his embrace, he entered a warm, lit cave—one that he seemed familiar with, for he immediately turned left from the entrance, and another section of the cave opened up to become a very warm chamber with a hint of wood smoke flavoring the air.

"Where are we?"

Aragon didn't seem to hear her. He set her on her feet and swung around, searching into the shadows beyond the firelight. Annette blinked several times, half wondering if Aragon had conjured the place by some miraculous method.

The light came from a small fire in the middle of the cave and revealed a pool of misty water. The air held the strong, earthy smell of minerals that she'd noted at hot springs purported to heal patients who bathed in their waters.

"They are gone," Aragon said with such despair that Annette immediately stepped to his side.

"Who is gone? What's wrong?"

He sighed. "Navarre and York, which means either that Navarre didn't survive the Pyrathian's fire, or that the agony became too great, and York needed help to save Navarre." He then told her about how his friend and fellow Blood Hunter had suffered harm in protecting him. That Aragon had brought him to the cave, and how York was seeing to Navarre while Aragon went to finish his quest.

She could hear his pain and guilt, and she didn't know what to say. That he'd had to leave his friend to help her humbled her and tangled every part of her heart up with him. All she could think to do was to wrap her arms around him and hold him tight as she pressed her cheek over his heart. For too long a moment, Aragon didn't respond. He just stood still.

"I'm sorry," she whispered. "If it wasn't for me, you wouldn't—"

"No." He slid his hands to her jaw and shifted her face toward his. "If it wasn't for you, I wouldn't know this wonder that fills me. Before you, I had only one desire within me: to kill Pathos. Jared was right. My anger at Pathos's betrayal drove my every action, spurred me to be a flawed leader of the Blood Hunters, and led me to turn my back upon all I had sworn to uphold."

"No, you—"

He slid his finger to her lips, stopping her denial. "With you, I learned there is something more, something greater than my driving need to eliminate evil at all cost."

She was standing dripping wet, naked but for a sheet, in a steamy cave with a warrior who'd spent his whole life training for battle and fighting a war. Gazing into the deep, rich darkness of his eyes, she saw an inner light that blazed right to her soul. Her heart flip-flopped, and her mouth turned so dry, she had to lick the moisture from her lips and his finger.

The fire in his eyes burned brighter.

"What?" she whispered, needing to hear him say what his gaze had already shouted.

"This thing called love," he said just before his mouth claimed hers in a kiss so passionate that not only did the earth move beneath her feet, but her world tipped on its axis, opening a whole universe to her that she'd never known before. The raging storm outside the cave couldn't come close to the power of this man's passion.

Tears stung her eyes as he threaded his fingers into her hair, brushed the long tresses from her face, and kissed her cheeks and forehead, making her feel cherished.

"You're so soft, so beautiful—"

"So are you," she whispered, kissing the cleft of his chin and the droplets of water beading his thick lashes before brushing his lips with hers.

He seemed to hesitate a moment, as if surprised, then he slid the sheet from her shoulders and stepped back to look at her. She lifted her chin and met his gaze with her back arched, offering herself to him without reservation as she pressed his warm amulet between the swell of her breasts.

He seemed to understand. Spreading the sheet on the ground before them, he held out his hand to her. She set hers into the large, heated strength of his. "Mine and yours," he whispered, so moved that his body trembled as he pressed their clasped hands over his heart. "For now."

He kissed her hard then, shedding all semblance of control as his tongue delved so deeply into her that she couldn't tell where one kiss ended and another began. Fire ignited between her legs, and a hot need made her breasts ache. He kissed her until she thought she would scream if he didn't touch her somewhere else right that second or die if he didn't keep kissing her again and again. She arched to him, thrusting against him, wanting every part of her in contact with the fluid heat of his passion. She needed and wanted him everywhere.

Leaving her mouth, he ran his tongue to the edge of her jaw, down her neck, then slowly to her nipple. She watched the tip of his tongue circling her hard peak several times before finally taking her into his mouth and lashing the needy point until she shuddered in his arms. She groaned deeply, urgently, clasping his shoulders as her knees went weaker.

Pressing her back over his arm, he gave the same treatment to her other breast, then both of them until she was a puddle of seething, edgy need. He started to move lower, and she knew that once he did, she would be lost, and all of those sweet droplets of water slipping down his hard, delectable body would be wasted.

Urging him back, she kissed him, ran her tongue across his bottom lip and sucked upon its softness before she slid her tongue down the rough cleft of his chin. She licked up beads of water, sucking kisses along the supple skin of his neck and the hard planes of his chest. When she flicked her finger over the disk of his nipple, his body tensed and his breath caught. She did it again and again until his hips jerked against her. Then she teased him with her tongue and teeth as she kissed her way down the ripples of his abdomen to his pulsing erection.

He was hard and needy. Falling to her knees on the satin sheet, she sucked the long length of him into the warmth of her mouth, then slowly pulled back, slipping her tongue back and forth across his sensitive tip. She ran her hands up the sculpted contours of his thick legs and kneaded the taut muscles of his buttocks before gently caressing everything that made him so powerfully male.

He cried out in pleasure, his legs shaking from the force of it.

"Enough!" he said, falling to his knees before her.

"There's more," she said.

"I know. You." He pressed her back onto the satin. Then he brought his mouth to hers in a searing kiss that started at her lips and dragged down to her slick sex. That she was completely bare there didn't seem to hinder him at all. In fact, it seemed as if he took extra enjoyment in lapping and nipping every plump nuance of her exposed sex, suckling every contour, running his tongue and teeth over every smooth inch. Her cries of growing pleasure echoed through the cave.

"Aragon!" she shouted, and told him she couldn't take anymore without him being inside her.

He smiled, settling himself between her legs until the thick, burning tip of his erection teased the opening of her sex. "Nothing compares to sharing this journey with you as it was meant to be," he said roughly.

He cupped her breasts together and branded each tip with the heat of his tongue before he drove himself deep inside her. She sighed, locking her legs about his hips and arching her back to meet the power of his every thrust. He held her hands captive beneath his, palm to palm, giving her no choice but to lie back and fully absorb every sensation he gave. He thrust into her hard and fast, angled to glide teasingly along her hot spot. His chest brushed her sensitized breasts as he stroked her to the very core of her womb, making her whole body strain and shudder from the force of the building pleasure. Then he eased out slowly, his gaze never leaving hers as he repeated his thrusts again and again, driving her desire past the point of reason, past the point of caring about anything but the wild eruption of pleasure consuming and binding them together. She didn't know the exact moment that his spirit penetrated hers again, she just knew that he was there in her mind, experiencing her pleasure and sharing his. The simultaneous rush of her climax and his hit her in an overpowering ecstasy that entwined her mind, body, and soul with Aragon's. And the flood of it thrust her pleasure to a new height, one that she knew Aragon shared completely, down to the very essence of his warrior's soul.

Pathos wanted to rip out every one of the Vladarians' throats. They were the reason he wasn't doing what he wanted to be doing at that moment. Well, not exactly. Aragon was the primary reason. The bastard had had the balls to invade his domain and steal what Pathos was dying for. His only consolation was that Pathos had trained Aragon.

But the Vladarians were why Pathos was stuck in a room full of pompous asses, listening to them bemoan Shashur's fate, listening to their panic over the possibility their future supply of Elan blood would dry up. They had divided into either regional or financial factions. The Western Europeans with Wellbourne sat in one corner, the Russians in another, the oil magnates together—a mixture of nationalities that included the Latin Vasquez and the Arabic Samir. Then there were the royals, who considered themselves above the rest. But no matter how lofty, vicious, or depraved, there was one element that reduced them all to the level of beasts.

Mortal blood. And they were now fighting over which faction would store the reserves of Elan blood. Pathos had shipped the stock of Elan blood to Corazon last night because it was the closest facility, and would ask the fewest questions. Now Vasquez was threatening not to allow the other Vladarians access to the blood if they didn't follow his bid to become their new leader. Word had spread, as Pathos knew it would, that Pathos wanted Cinatas to become the next leader of the Vladarians. That had the factions of the oil-rich and the royals up in arms.

Elan blood, the sweetest and most powerful blood of the mortals, gave vampires a dynamic charisma and allowed them to go longer between feedings. He also had heard the infusion of the blood was an orgasmic experience beyond compare.

Orgasm. Something he hadn't had in years. Hadn't even wanted in years. Until now.

He clenched his fists, feeling the burning in his loins increase. She'd been prepared for him. He'd had his hands on her plump, succulent flesh, so ready for the taste of her, so ready to twist her soul to his pleasures. He closed his eyes, but instead of seeing himself thrusting into her, he saw Aragon.

A roar of rage exploded from him.

The room went deadly silent, each faction of the Vladarians reacting differently.

"Enough!" Pathos stood, sweeping the room with a furious glare. "Enough bickering and sniveling. My patience is at an end. As soon as the Arcadia Research Center is repaired, the blood will return there. Cinatas will continue your transfusions from the frozen supply of proven donors. No one will be accorded the luxury of fresh blood. Cinatas will now take over the task of directing you ungrateful beasts. Those who are in agreement with this will stand."

Vasquez cursed, jumping up from his seat.

"I take it you are voting for my son, Vasquez?" Pathos asked with a deadly calm that he was far from feeling.

"No! Vasquez will be in charge of the Vladarians." Vasquez charged to the front of the room.

"Very well," Pathos said, smiling. "Those in favor of Cinatas will stand, and those for Vasquez will remain seated. But first, my son, will you tell the Vladarians what you will do for them as their leader?"

Cinatas stood. "I've always made miraculous strides to meet the Vladarians' need for Elan blood. As leader I will discover what in the fresh Elan blood sent Shashur into nonexistence."

"Now, Vasquez," Pathos said, looking at the Vladarian with distaste, "what will you do as leader?"

"Vasquez will restore the Vladarians' power and future back into the hands of the Vladarians and out of a were's."

"Since you've already threatened to withhold Elan blood from those not in accordance with your will, we can all deduce that you mean *your* hand, and *your* power. It is time to vote, gentlemen. Those for Cinatas stand."

Pathos was encouraged to see that Wellbourne was the first to stand. Others followed, until only a few besides the oil lords remained seated. The majority ruled, and Cinatas had it.

"The Vladarians have chosen. Gentlemen, I suggest you avail yourselves of the pleasures the Falls has to offer. In the morning we will discuss the details of this new rule, and Cinatas will address you as your new leader. EVERYONE will be here."

Then, before he could get dragged into any of the erupting arguments, he exited the room. For the rest of the night, he was going to hunt, and his red demons were going to help. They'd leave no bed unturned, and no friend of hers free. He'd find Aragon and Annette wherever they were hiding. Then he'd send Aragon to suffer the tortures of the damned, and once he'd taken Annette, he'd claim her soul for Heldon, imprisoning her for eternity.

Chapter Eighteen

SOMETHING WAS WRONG.

Aragon awoke suddenly at the feeling clawing at his insides. He relaxed slightly as he heard the storm continue to lash the mortal ground. The battle raging in the heavens was one of the fiercest he'd ever heard, telling him that the concentration of evil surrounding Pathos hadn't been just in the mortal realm. Hopefully that was why York and Navarre had left the cave, and not because Navarre was failing.

Still, something else nagged at him, and it wasn't the fading sensation he'd been experiencing since journeying through the spirit barrier. Nor was it the hungry vibrancy that had him in a constant state of hard need for Annette.

His shoulder, which should have healed by now, still stung where the Underling had gouged him, and something he couldn't describe coursed through him. It was as if the bloodlust that had raged almost out of control earlier had gained a foothold in him and wouldn't let go. He felt tarnished, somehow less than honorable.

Had evil somehow infected him?

He shook off the thought. Underlings were not like Tsaras.

Maybe it was angst over Navarre that had him feeling this way. Concern for his fellow Blood Hunter ate at Aragon's heart. Or maybe it was his dread of telling Annette about the Guardian Council's judgment.

For that weighed very heavily on his heart, too. She needed to know they had even less time. He didn't have the luxury of lingering to discover how long it took to become a faded warrior. As soon as he assured her safety and located her sister, he would have to return to face the council.

Annette stirred. Nestled snugly against him, she reach to caress his rough cheek with her palm. "I sense your worry," she said.

"Many things are as they should not be."

"And you feel as if you have to change them all. Put them right." She wasn't asking a question, but making a statement.

"I must. Partly because I am responsible for some of the wrong, and partly because I am the one who can best do what needs to be done." He pulled her closer to him, wondering how to tell her about the Guardian Council's verdict. Having his brethren at war overhead made him feel comfort at their closeness and regret that he'd driven them apart with his obsession. But none of those feelings compared with the stabbing grief of having to leave Annette and face the punishment of the council.

He wanted and needed her with a force greater than his will. And it was only because he didn't have to walk away at that moment that he could even imagine he'd have the strength to do so when his time upon the mortal ground ended. Giving her the amulet was now having some effect upon his being; either that or physical contact with her had heightened and sharpened his senses. He felt more alive.

"Why?" she asked quietly. "Why must it be you to put things right? Why can we not just forget it all and disappear after we find my sister? Find some place safe, and just be? You haven't faded yet. Maybe it will take a long time, or it may never happen. Just as Jared found redemption from the damned, maybe you too can be freed from the fate of a faded warrior."

He exhaled deeply, hearing the yearning in her voice, the need, and the want for things to be different than they were. "Were that possible, it would still be impossible for me to live without honor. I have but these moments to give."

She didn't say anything, but twisted to bring her lips to his. When he tasted of her, there was a salty dampness edging her soft mouth that brought a bittersweet ache to his heart. He needed her more than the essence of his own life, and as long as the storm raged, he planned to fill that need as deeply and as greatly as he could.

He filled his palm with her soft breast and teased the tip of it until it hardened beneath his fingers. She pressed closer to him, her back to his chest, so that the swell of her bottom rubbed against his surging flesh, urging him to fit himself more tightly to her.

She arched her back, and his hard arousal slid enticingly along the groove leading to her smooth, heated sex. Groaning, she shifted and brought the hand he had resting on her hip to her sex, showing him just where she wanted his touch. She was wet and warm with her unique scent of woman and desire; the fragrance would forever bring pleasure to his mind and a hot heavy need to his groin. He buried his face in the sweet silk of her long curly hair and thrust inside her heated core. Then, rolling onto his back, he brought her to rest on top of him, spreading her legs wide to give him access to every part of her. Slipping his spirit into hers, he sensed exactly what touch she needed to take them slowly back to the heaven he'd found within her. She responded to his every touch, to his every desire, until there truly was no end to where he existed and she began. They were as one, bringing a completeness to his entire being and a satisfied peace that he'd never known before.

A terrified scream jerked Sam up from his chair. Lightning flashed in quick succession, strobe-lighting the room before the bombing roar of thunder shook the foundation beneath his feet. Momentarily disoriented, he first thought it was his own scream from a flashback until he realized he was at Emerald's, and it had been a child's cry. He and Nick were keeping watch. They couldn't do anything toward finding Annette until the storm passed and dawn came—except pray that she and Aragon showed up.

"Em!" Sam took the stairs three at a time as he raced to Emerald and her daughter, but he wondered if they could even hear him, between the fury of the storm and Megan's continuing cries. By the time he reached the top step, Em's daughter had stopped screaming, and Emerald's soothing burr reached his ears, sultry and soft. It was the same tone she'd used to comfort him after his flashback until he'd trashed her efforts to reach him.

"Meggie. Doona worry. We're going."

"They're coming, Mommy. The red monsters are coming."

Sam burst into the room. He expected to see Emerald in bed, comforting her daughter. Instead they were both throwing on clothes. Emerald looked his way. "Doona argue. Get Nick, Erin, and Jared. We have to leave now." She shoved her feet into shoes and slung her purse over her shoulder before she grabbed a blanket off the bed.

"Now, Sam, or we're vera dead."

"What in the hell is going on!" Nick called from the bottom of the stairs.

Sam drew a breath, met first Megan's, then Emerald's terrified gazes, and dug out his cell phone. "We're leaving now." Megan was a miniature version of Emerald, silvery blond, green-eyed, only more petite and delicate. Her tear-stained face wrenched him wide open. She shouldn't be involved in this ugliness, and he half wondered if Megan's cry was because they were giving her nightmares, and not because she really was having visions of bad things. Even if it was just a bad dream, it was worth leaving just to ease her mind. And hell, he'd seen monsters himself tonight. They hadn't been red, but the burn on his arm where one of them had incinerated proved it.

Within a minute they were in the car, racing farther up the drive in the pouring rain to get Erin and Jared from Silver Moon, Emerald's cabin. It was more than cramped quarters with all six of them in the squad car, but Emerald held Megan in her lap, wrapped up tight in a blanket with the seat belt around them both. Not ideal, but it would have to do for now. They went racing back down the drive and out to the highway. Even with the wipers at full throttle, he could barely see the road. Still, when they flew back by Emerald's cottage, it looked as dark and quiet as it had when they'd left. Not a red monster in sight.

"We'll go to the station," he told everyone. It was the safest place he could think of, and he had access to an arsenal of weapons there as well.

"No, we canna. We'll only cause people to die," Emerald said.

Sam clenched his teeth. How in the hell could she say that? He sucked in air. Enough was enough. They'd wanted to leave, he'd gotten them out. And he'd damn well take them to where he could keep them the safest.

Emerald spoke again before he could. "We're needin' a place with power, lots of it."

"That's the station. I've got plenty of firepower."

"Guns willna do much good against the forces coming," she said.

Sam opened his mouth, then shut it as he recalled how useless his gun had proven to be on Hades Mountain earlier. Sure, he'd popped off one or two of those hideous creatures, but if the damned things hadn't hit some supernatural barrier, he would have been eaten alive.

"There's the electric plant on the road to Arcadia," Nick said. "This time of night you'll have power out the wazoo because nobody will be using it."

"We're needin' magic power, no man can make it."

"The ancients did," Jared said. "At the Sacred Stones. There are millennia of magic built upon one another there. Enough power to hold back or even destroy evil."

Sam shot a glance at Jared in the rearview. The Sacred Stones had almost destroyed Jared.

"We are needin' to be there now," Emerald said.

"No!" Erin cried, turning to Jared. "You are not going back there. Even if it is the safest place on the planet, I'm not taking the chance that you'll be hurt. I can't even believe you suggested it."

"I would have returned to the Sacred Stones soon, Erin, love, for there my spirit can commune with all that I was for so many years as a spirit being. Don't fear that I will be harmed again, only cleansed."

"Cleansed! After what happened there, you might as well guzzle poison."

"Don't worry," Sam interjected between clenched teeth. "We are not going to go up on a deserted mountain in the middle of the night in what has to be the freaking storm of the century."

"We've no choice, Sam," Emerald said.

"Yes, we do. I'm driving." With that said, Sam made a beeline for the station house situated in the middle of Twilight's nonexistent "downtown" area.

"Mommy?" Megan cried.

"Hush, my little angel. Doona worry. I'll make it all right. I promise," Emerald whispered, making Sam feel like hell.

Son of a bitch, what was he supposed to do? Take everyone to an isolated place in the forest where they'd be nothing but sitting ducks for anything after them because a little girl had a bad dream? Red monsters?

His gut clenched. He'd seen black ones.

"Nick, where would you go?" Sam asked.

"Station house."

"Jared?"

"Sacred Stones."

"Erin?"

"Station house."

"Sam, you canna decide on what feels right. You have to bleedin' choose what has the power to save us. What happened to Jared there is all the proof that I'ma needin' to believe."

Sam felt as if he were in a torture vise. Everything in him said that it was beyond stupid to go out into the woods in the middle of the night, unprepared and unprotected, with supposedly God knew what was coming after them. Those black creatures had been in the woods. They were in town, less than a mile from the station, and all looked well with the world. Not a creature was stirring. "We'll go to the station house first and then decide. There're weapons that I want a little closer at hand." Hitting the gas, he turned the corner and zipped into his empty parking space.

His night deputy and Myra, the night dispatcher, were already in-house.

Before he could open his door, a heavy thud sounded on the roof of the car, and a man's face appeared in the windshield amid the distorting rivulets of rain. Only it wasn't a man, but a grotesque, red, glowing caricature of one. The creature tore the wipers from their sockets.

"What the hell is that?" Nick yelled.

"Red monsters!" Megan screamed.

"Oh, my God!" Erin shouted. "Jared!"

The back passenger window shattered into tiny cubes. Rain poured in with the creature, but Jared nailed the thing in the face, knocking it back hard. Sam shoved the car into reverse and stomped on the gas.

Two more were behind the car, and he didn't hesitate to plow them down as his tires spun and squealed. The one that had been on the roof tumbled to the hood and managed to hang on as Sam threw the car into drive and floored the gas. It smiled with a cold and evil assurance.

The creature slid to the driver's side as Sam careened onto the highway.

"Hold on!" Sam shouted a few blocks from the station. He jerked the car hard to the right, then left, before he slammed on the brakes. The maneuver sent the creature tumbling onto the highway. Sam punched the gas, hitting the creature before leaving it in their exhaust.

"What in the hell are they?" Sam demanded.

"Red demons," Jared said.

"Can they fly?"

"No, but they can cross the spirit barrier and appear at any destination within moments. Good thing is that once the sun rises, they'll retreat to their frozen domain in hell."

"Frozen?" Nick asked.

"Later," Sam said, promising an explanation he couldn't really deliver.

"Sam?" Emerald said, and she didn't have to say any more. He understood the plea in her voice, heard it as deeply as he heard Megan trying to bravely suppress her tears and terror.

"We're going, Em," he told her. "Right now." He couldn't believe he was really going to go hiking up to the freaking stones. They'd either be struck by lightning or catch pneumonia from exposure—if they were lucky. If the goons pegged their location, they were dead meat.

There was about a quarter-mile walk to reach the damn stones. And Sam still had no real idea what the stones could do to protect them from the creep show rearing its ugly head in Twilight. In his book, they were about to jump off a boat to swim through a shark frenzy for an island that might or might not be quicksand.

Thirty minutes later, his take on the situation wasn't far from the truth. They'd reached the top of Spirit Wind Mountain and were halfway down the path to the Sacred Stones, drenched and running like drowned rats, when three red demons appeared like glow-in-the-dark Frankensteins. The air instantly turned subzero, turning the rain into sleet and the ground into a sheet of ice.

Sam pulled his gun, unloading two bullets into one of them, knocking it down. Nick did the same with the second. And Jared went after the third with his bare hands. They slid on the frozen ground.

He was about to order Nick to take the others and run for the Sacred Stones when the two demons he and Nick had shot rose back up with more menace than ever. Icy air blasted from their nostrils. The shit was deep, and they were in it to their eyeballs.

Emerald thrust herself in front of him, and Sam nearly buckled beneath the shard of fear stabbing through his chest. He couldn't even yell or breathe. She held her fists up in the air, shaking them like New Age maracas, and started spinning around so fast he couldn't get hold of her to jerk her back. Her bracelets more than tinkled now. The sound of silvery bells rang, growing louder the faster she turned.

The demons stopped and stared at her; even the demon fighting Jared turned to watch Emerald. The air about them became warmer and started to swirl, and the demons took another step back, their faces twisting with rage. Moments later, the demons started running in a circle around the perimeter of the wind Emerald was making, an area that enveloped the six of them. Then more and more of them began to appear out of nowhere. Three to sixty in two-point-five seconds.

Well, this was just fine and dandy, Sam thought. Emerald would last all of ten minutes before she expired from exhaustion.

"We must get her to the Sacred Stones," Jared said, moving up beside him, his gaze on the speeding demons.

"What in the hell is she doing?" Sam demanded. "And how is she keeping back shit that my gun can't take down?"

"I don't know," Jared said. "She has some sort of magic. If we get her closer to the Sacred Stones, it might help her."

"How?"

"Maybe if we as a group slowly edged that way, she'd be able to inch forward as she spins."

"Worth a try."

Organized into a tight group, they moved toward the Sacred Stones at an agonizingly slow pace. But Emerald seemed to sense their plan and edged with them. Sam was sure that her power was growing. They had covered about ten feet when a sudden roaring came at them from the direction of the Sacred Stones, sounding like an oncoming train.

Chapter Nineteen

Sven approached the Guardian Council expecting to receive a strong reprimand for the altercation with the Pyrathians over Aragon. Sirius waited just outside the Guardians' hallowed circle for his turn to confess the errors of his band of Fire Warriors, but by the time Sven finished saying what he had to say, he didn't think the Guardians would need more. They stood at stiff attention in a semicircle at the end of a long glittering corridor known as the Judgment Hall. There were twelve across the vast hall, all aged warriors who helped carry the burden of Logos's fight against evil with a zeal unmatched by any warrior within the realm. Though their countenances were simply garbed in misty white, their usual combined light of energy was almost blinding in its intensity, but this time Sven didn't have to shield his gaze. It was as if something had dimmed the power of the council, and their grave expressions confirmed that. Sven knew without asking that the dissension among the Forces was responsible.

All warriors strove to be chosen to fill a seat upon the council. Only Logos determined who would serve and for how long. It had been Sven's secret wish to one day be so great a warrior that he'd be chosen, but those hopes were gone, fallen beneath the trampling heels of his own cowardice.

He slid to his knees before them, his head bowed. He was a fool to think any part of him was worthy enough to serve their justice, but it was all he had to give.

"Rise, Blood Hunter, and speak what truth you may," directed the leader of council, known only as First Council Servant. His tenure of service within the council was the longest. Then the others followed in order, Second Council Servant, Third Council Servant, and so on until the Twelfth, who had served the shortest term. Once united with the council, personal names lost their importance. The councillors lived and breathed their service with an unrelenting diligence.

"I come in hopes the council will see the truth of my guilt and accept me, Sven of the Blood Hunters, as worthy enough to pay for my sins."

"And to what guilt do you refer?"

"My failure to do as pledged. The current schism within the Guardian Forces can be directly traced to the moment I not only stayed my hand from executing the poisoned Jared of the Blood Hunters, but also stayed the hand of Aragon of the Blood Hunters. My brother Aragon may have chosen unwisely, but I caused him to fall. He is now saving the lives of mortals from the claws of Pathos and will return to the council to honorably accept his execution, as the council has judged necessary."

"The council is lightened to hear of Aragon's honorable intentions."

"Then I ask the council to consider my honorable intent as well. For the first time ever there has been fighting among the brethren. And I personally led my band of Blood Hunters to defend Aragon against a band of Pyrathians, who were only seeking to enforce the council's decree."

"If Aragon's intent is to be honorable, why did he not come to the council himself?"

"Mortal lives, for which he took responsibility before learning that the council had amended Logos's punishment, were in imminent danger. He will return once he has seen to their safety. When he arrives, I'm asking the council to place their punishment for his abandonment upon the guilty party, me, and submit a mercy plea for Aragon's fate for Logos to decree. This act will unify the forces again. Justice will be served, and Aragon absolved."

"While the council fully understands the burden that you see as yours to bear, the council's perspective is one of law and order and cannot be subjected to emotions of the moment. As leader of the Blood Hunters, Aragon had both the responsibility of Jared of the Blood Hunters and the honor of his position within the Guardian Forces. His decision to forestall Jared of the Blood Hunters' execution, and then to abandon his post, are his alone to bear. So while you are more than worthy, we cannot honor your request. Nor can we afford to needlessly lose a warrior during these troubled times. Aragon's fate is already sealed. He is lost to us, but you are not."

Sven's throat tightened around a knot of frustration and disappointment. Did only law and order determine truth? Though he saw the logic of it in his mind, his heart cried out against it. Was not Logos more than law and order? Were not love and sacrifice and forgiveness greater truths than law and order?

"What of my defense of Aragon against the Pyrathians?"

"We will bring the matter to the table and summon you for our decision when ready."

Sven bowed his head and slowly backed from the presence of the Guardian Council. That he had even questioned their wisdom only worsened the burden he felt. He sent his mind out in search of York and Navarre as he headed for the outer circles of the spirit realm, a place where the darkened shadows of twilight hid the boundaries separating the spirit realm from the mortal realm.

As he hurried, his concern grew. His attempts to reach York and Navarre kept failing, which meant Navarre had to be in a very bad state.

"Sven of the Blood Hunters, we must speak."

Sven turned to see the Pyrathian Sirius bearing down upon him. He didn't look happy, making Sven wonder if the Guardian Council had chosen to blame the Pyrathians for the altercation between his band and Sirius's.

Sven nodded. "Speak quickly, then. My time is short, for I must locate my brethren, who are in need. I accepted full blame for the disturbance between our bands and petitioned the council to punish me."

"A deed you should not have done, for I am to blame as well. The council wouldn't even give me an audience to explain, but immediately adjourned to a private session after you left. You must come with me. Your band of Blood Hunters are within the Pyrathian camp, and it is not good."

Had York lost his mind? Sven wondered as he grimly followed Sirius.

Dawn came, and with it the glaring fact that Aragon couldn't keep the world or evil at bay any longer. Outside the cave, the storm's rage had subsided to a drizzling mist. He'd already scoped out the area and determined they were well beyond the spell of dark magic that gave Underlings a pathway to the mortal realm. So all he had to concern himself with was in what direction Pathos would vent his rage. Pathos would attack with a vengeance, and Aragon had to be ready.

Kneeling beside Annette as she lay sleeping on the red sheet, he lifted a handful of her silky hair and ran his thumb over its softness, watching the curls twist around his fingers before he brought the ends to his lips. He hated to wake her, for their shared passion had both filled and drained her, but their idyll had ended.

Scooping her into his arms, he walked to the steamy pool, absorbing its clean, rich mineral scent as he immersed them both in the liquid warmth. Though his body continued to feel overwarm, the heat soothed the soreness of his shoulder where the Underling had attacked.

Annette's eyes fluttered open, and the sultry light that filled them the moment she met his gaze made something inside him tighten so painfully that his eyes stung. A soft smile curved her lips, one that welcomed both him and the warmth of the water.

"What time is it?"

"Dawn. The worst of the storm has passed, but it's still raining."

"That means a wet, cold walk down the mountain without an ounce of coffee to fuel me." Her horrified expression brought a smile to his spirit. "You've almost convinced me," she said, sitting up in his arms.

"Of what do you speak?" he asked, liking her amused tone, for he knew her heart was heavy with a great sadness and pain that her sister had yet to be found.

"That making love is better than coffee."

He frowned, lifting a doubting brow. "You can't even begin to compare that vile brew to—"

"In fact, I'm sure you could completely win me over with"—she twisted to straddle him and slid her hand beneath the water to caress and palm his sex—"a cup of hot Aragon right now."

His flesh leapt to her touch, and he groaned. "Annette, we need to—"

"Love once more," she whispered, kissing him with a tenderness and a desperation that he couldn't deny. "I love you," she whispered.

He could feel the tears in her soul and the need in her heart, and he wrapped his arms tighter around her, freely giving himself over to her, giving all that he had to give.

Annette didn't care if it was logical to love a man in so short a time. It didn't matter if the entire world thought she'd gone insane. All that mattered to her was this man. The tenderness and passion he'd shown her surpassed what some women spent a lifetime praying for from their husbands. And she was willing to give this moment her all. She felt him in her soul and in the trembling of his touch. His kiss told her that he gave his all.

She wanted to love him once more. When they left the cave, their time alone would end; a few minutes more before facing the cold rain and colder world weren't going to make that much difference.

This time she led Aragon into the passion and made the magic happen. Sliding forward until she could take him inside her, she wrapped her arms around his neck and threaded her fingers through his midnight hair, pulling his full mouth to hers. Her breasts, with the warm amulet dangling between them, brushed his chest, and her knees hugged his hips. The sultry water caressed her skin, heightening her senses with whisper-soft, liquid fingers. She kissed him hard, then gently, then wildly, rocking her hips to drive his want and their need to a physical satiation that stripped them so completely of anything that there was nothing but total acceptance of one another left.

"And I love you," he whispered as he pulled her against his pounding heart. "No matter what."

She laid her head in the crook of his shoulder, wanting to think of nothing more than the pleasure, but the unbidden image of last night and the cliff kept replaying in her mind.

You can't ever let Underlings surround you. You have to stay ahead. No matter what.

Last night it had been a cliff. She didn't know whether to take comfort or fear in Aragon's "no matter what" promise.

The magic was gone too soon, sweeping their pleasure away with a growing wave of reality. The time to leave had come, and she could no longer delay. As soon as they hit the outside world, both barefoot and draped in torn halves of the red satin sheet, she didn't have time to worry about what would come. One hundred yards from the cave's entrance, Aragon stopped and motioned her to stand still. The rain had ended, putting them both on alert.

He listened intently before his brow narrowed with concern. "They're searching for us," he said. "Though they're too far away to be an immediate danger, I can hear them and smell them." Taking her hand in his, he urged them down the mountain at a faster pace than they had been moving. Pine straw and the mush of wet fallen leaves softened the brunt of the dirt and rocks on her bare feet. "Humans and dogs are part of the search," he added a moment later. "I didn't expect Pathos to make his failure so public. I thought he'd either—"

"Be waiting at my place for me to reappear, or . . . dear God . . . he'd be more likely to really get his hands on my sister, give me irrefutable proof of it, and make me come to him. Something that would make me pay with my soul. We need to really hurry." She picked up her pace.

He swooped her up. "I can hurry better than you can." She

didn't argue as he broke into a run. "In realizing the true nature of Pathos, you are already halfway toward defeating him. You'd make a good warrior," he said, only partially winded.

"What makes you say that?" she asked, pulling her hair off the nape of her neck so that the breeze his speed generated could cool her skin. The rising of the sun had caused the forest about them to emit a steamy air, one that seemed to be dampening the spirits about her, for barely a bird chirped or a bee buzzed.

"Your selfless courage and dedication. Your instinct to put another's needs before your own."

"It's not true," she said, shaking her head. "You have no idea how much my selfishness has cost those that I love."

"Because you chose to be a doctor over—"

"Over loving, over giving anyone I cared about priority over my own goals."

"Are you a doctor for glory and prestige, or are you a doctor to save the lives of those in need?"

"No one in her right mind goes through what I went through to have a wall trophy."

"Then I suggest you rethink who you are. No battle is waged without cost."

"Only if the same rule applies to you as well," she said.

"There's no comparison. Anger didn't spur your actions."

"There's no way to convince me the hero's heart that has done nothing but protect and defend mortals you didn't even know two days ago, at extreme cost to yourself, hasn't always beaten within you. So maybe neither of us is as bad as we think. But it doesn't matter. The consequences of our actions were too high a price, and now we have to do what we can to fix it."

He looked as if he was about to argue, and she pressed her finger to his lips to stop him. "It's true," she insisted, but before she could say more, the *whop* of an approaching copter thrummed in the air. Pathos had not only let the dogs out, he'd called in the heavy equipment as well.

Aragon darted beneath the covering of trees and kept to the shadows as he rushed down the mountain. Annette tried to make herself as unburdensome as possible. If there was any way she could have ditched the me-Tarzan-you-Jane routine without jeopardizing their safety, she would have. Instead she had to rely upon him again, which chafed a bit, and kept her looking for a way to help.

He reached a clearing and, instead of running directly across it, began skirting the edge. Just as he bent to escape the circling copter, she caught sight of it, instantly recognizing the LifeFlight blue cross emblazoned on its side.

"It's Nick," she told Aragon. "Hurry into the clearing and try and get his attention."

Aragon dashed into the open just as the helicopter swooped over. Annette waved her arms, struggling quickly out of Aragon's embrace so that she could run too. That's when she saw Sam nearly hanging out of the door with a pair of binoculars. He signaled that he'd seen them, and the helicopter swung around.

"Let's give them some landing room." Annette grabbed Aragon's hand, pulling him to the side of the clearing. By the time Nick brought the copter down, she and Aragon were almost already to its side, their heads ducked low against the punishing blasts of wind from the blades. She had to hold her sheet in place, or it would have been whipped right off her body.

Nobody tried to speak above the roar of the engine and slicing blades. Nick took off the moment Sam slammed the door shut. Had it been anyone but Pathos after them, she would have closed her eyes in relief as Nick circled around.

The helipad was next to the ranger's station near the Smoky Mountain National Forest, about twenty miles north of Twilight, and didn't seem far enough to escape Pathos's rage. Then again, was there anywhere in the universe that was possible? She kept waiting for claws to grab her and the deep chill of his touch to burn her soul.

"Do we need an ambulance?" Sam asked, his blue gaze grave.

She shook her head no, forcing a reassuring grimace. If Pathos had gotten to her, she didn't think there was much modern medicine could have done to help her.

Sam looked as if he'd spent every hour of the night in an agony of anxiety. It made her feel guilty for the time she and Aragon had shared. But given the ferocity of the storm and their unprotected state, they'd had no choice but to seek shelter.

Sam picked up the radio, and Annette grabbed his shoulder.

"Everyone safe?" she shouted.

He nodded this time.

"Where?" After everything that had happened, she doubted any of them would be safe in their homes again. But considering Rankin's part in this, she realized safety was nothing but a relative deception anywhere.

"You'll see."

Annette shrugged and leaned back into the seat next to Aragon. She'd find out soon enough. If Sam wanted to be cryptic, then she'd let him. Aragon wrapped his arm around her shoulders and drew her closer to him. Then she felt him stiffen.

"Are you hurt?" she asked, getting close to his ear to be heard.

"Scratch on my shoulder," he said. "It will heal."

Thinking a tree limb must have harmed him during the run down the mountain, she nodded and closed her eyes to rest for a moment. She would look at Aragon's shoulder once they reached safety.

It was good to see both Sam and Nick. She still needed to talk to Nick about Stef, but now that she knew Rankin was behind Stef's disappearance, she decided her sister's night with Nick wasn't exactly her business anymore. The conversation she'd had with the son of a bitch was still hot in her mind.

"What did you do to Stefanie and Abe Bennett?"

"Why, I simply sent them way south of the border into the heart of the research project she was so doggedly investigating."

Annette had a sick feeling that she might know where "way south of the border" was.

Sooner than Annette expected, Nick circled and began to descend. She leaned to the side, peering out the copter's window. They weren't anywhere near the LifeFlight helipad. And the horizon tilted sickeningly as the sight of the Sacred Stones grabbed her insides and twisted.

"What are we doing here?" she shouted at Sam, hardly able to make herself heard over the copter's noise.

"It's safer. Em and Jared will explain."

Annette widened her eyes but didn't voice her opinion as she looked out over the mountaintop. To her it was the least safe place for miles.

Seeing the ancient stones from the air made her realize that there was a pattern to the placement of the pillars and lines of the flower beds. She grabbed Aragon's amulet from where it rested upon her chest, glanced at the twelve-point star, and compared it to the Sacred Stones.

Either her imagination was working overtime, or there was a strong similarity. She made a mental note to ask Aragon what the symbol meant and how the Sacred Stones tied into the spirit realm. She hadn't asked before, and she should have.

Past the stones, a thick grove of trees in a green almost too vibrant to be real gave way to a lush clearing. In the center of it sat a faded cement pad edged in tall dark grass lashed by the force of the driving blades.

Annette didn't know exactly why the forest surroundings seemed Hollywood odd to her, but they did. It was as if they weren't quite the way they were supposed to be, and she blinked several times as Nick zeroed in on the pad. Shielding their faces from the wind, Emerald, Erin, and Jared were a welcome sight. After landing, Nick began shutting down the engine, and Sam popped out of his side of the copter, motioning for her hand to help her out.

Aragon steadied her from behind with a hot hand on her shoulder and hip as she wobbled a moment before stepping down into the bright of the morning sun. Exiting the helicopter and trying to stay decent in her half of the red satin sheet became a cover-up scramble brilliant enough to make a politician's day.

Emerald grabbed her the moment they met, just past the worst of the pummeling copter wind. "Bloody fooking hell, are you okay?" she shouted, trying to hug and shake the daylights out of her at the same time. Tears fell from Emerald's red-rimmed eyes, their green depths stark with emotion, and Annette's own eyes watered in response. She felt awful that her friends had worried so much.

"You shouldna have gone with the bastard. No matter what he said. We could have doon somethin' to save Stef." Emerald dashed at her tears with a rough hand and glanced back at the copter. "The bastard dinna have Stef, did he?"

Annette hugged Emerald back. "No, he didn't, and I'm sorry." Emerald cried harder, and Annette hugged her tighter. "I'm really okay. Aragon has great timing." Glancing to her right, she saw that Aragon was with Jared and Sam.

Emerald pulled back and gave a wobbly grimace. "I know. What has me so fooking wrung out now is that if it had been my daughter, if someone said they had Meggie, I would've doon the same."

"Where is Megan?"

"Here," Emerald said, urging everyone to follow her even farther away from the whip of the slowing copter blades. "For now."

When they were free of the wind, Erin slid her arm about Annette's shoulder and gave a welcoming squeeze as they walked. "I'm so glad you're all right. I kept thinking about what I went through with Cinatas."

"You and Jared had it worse. Aragon found me before Pathos did anything bad. Pathos is different from Cinatas. Not as sadistic, but more chilling. He'll find a way to make you do what he wants rather than use pain or force. Somehow that makes it worse."

Erin shivered.

Annette sucked in a bracing breath. Even the air smelt sweeter and fresher here. They were headed for a cluster of concrete block buildings at the end of the pebbled dirt path. Nothing about the buildings' bark-brown paint or brown tin roofs was surreal. The drab colors blended into the pine-straw-strewn earth, which only made the unrealistic shades of green coloring the trees, bushes, and grass even more odd. She blinked several more times at the forest surrounding them. Was there something wrong with her eyes? She shook her head and focused on the dirt beneath her feet. While it was a normal brown color with a smattering of pebbles dotting its surface, the earth felt unusually soft to the soles of her bare feet. It was solid ground, though, and she shoved the oddity to the back of her mind, wondering if something about her experiences during the past twenty-four hours had her seeing things differently.

"What exactly happened at the Rankins' house?" Erin asked.

She explained what happened. "He had Stefanie's laptop, and he's been e-mailing Abe's mother."

"We know, luv. I found the laptop, and there are records and dates on there about the X-files that are going to go a long way in helping to bring some of the doctors at Sno-Med down. Sam has it locked up in safekeeping."

Annette hoped it wasn't on a dusty shelf at the station house where sticky fingers could easily nab it. She made a note to ask him later. She wanted to see it, touch it, find some connection to her sister. But for now it was good enough to hear that Stefanie had collected evidence that would help bring down the evil she'd uncovered.

"Sam says Rob killed his wife," Erin said.

Annette shuddered. "Yes, and he would have gone after me, except Pathos and Cinatas showed up and eliminated him. Rob had Stef and Abe Bennett sent somewhere because they discovered he was using Sno-Med experimental treatments to kill his wife for the insurance money. I think I may know where he sent them."

"Whoa there!" Sam grabbed Annette's shoulder, swinging her around to face him.

She told them all about what happened with Rob and his comment about sending Stef and Abe way south of the border into the heart of the research project. "Couple that with the fact that all of Sno-Med's blood supplies and samples went—"

"Corazon de Rojo," Sam said gravely.

"Yes," Annette whispered.

"She's as good as dead," he said harshly.

Though she'd considered that in the very back of her mind, Annette still felt her heart sink with despair. Aragon must have been completely attuned to her, because his arm wrapped around her shoulders, helping her to stay upright.

"DOONA SAY THAT!" Emerald shouted. "She's not. And we've got to get her out."

"We'll go," Sam said. "We'll go fast. As in today. But don't be wearing any Pollyanna glasses about what we'll find."

"Pathos may be after Stefanie as well," Aragon said. "He will use or harm whoever he can to get to Annette."

"He already tried," said Jared. "Last night the red demons were out in force, determined to get to us. Before sunrise nearly one hundred had gathered."

Annette shuddered, looking at all of her dear friends. It would kill her inside if something happened to them because of her. "What did you do?" she whispered.

"Not we," said Erin. "Emerald. We had almost made it to the Sacred Stones before they attacked. Emerald stopped them with some sort of magical power, but it wasn't until we got closer to the Sacred Stones that she kicked supernatural ass. Her power blasted the demons back a hundred yards and kept them back until sunrise."

"Doona make it more than it was. We're needin' to get to Stef."

"I will get her," Aragon whispered.

Annette slid her hand over Aragon's to let him know they were in this together. "How are we going to get to Belize? A flight from Atlanta with a major airline would take too much time, even if we could get seats at the last minute. Besides, Aragon and Jared don't have a passport or any identification yet. And what are we going to do when we get there?"

"Not a problem," Sam and Nick said at the same time.

"I've got friends in high places," added Sam. "They can fly you anywhere you want to go."

"And I've got 'em in low," replied Nick. "I'll get the passports, and you get the transpo."

"What's this?" Sam narrowed his gaze at Nick.

"Geeky low," Nick clarified. "They can do anything with computers, though they usually don't, but I think this falls under *necessary.* Jared and Aragon need identities."

"I'll be stayin' here feedin' the magic," said Emerald. "Until the concentration in the atmosphere is stronger, I canna leave, and I canna leave Meggie, either."

"There's no reason for any of you to go," Sam said, pointedly looking Annette and Erin's way.

Annette narrowed her gaze. "Are you so sexist that you will leave a qualified doctor and nurse behind so that your he-man machismo can exercise its muscle? From what you've said about Corazon de Rojo, Erin and I are essential."

"They have to be a-goin', Sam," Emerald said. "So you best not waste precious time arguin' aboot it."

"What do you mean?" Sam demanded.

Emerald shook her head. "I can't say more because I don't know more. Now let's be giving them some food, and you put your mind to getting to Belize."

"It's entirely too convenient for you to mutter, 'They have to be a-goin', Sam,' and expect that to be law. Corazon is a death camp that I don't want any of you getting near."

Emerald's eyes sparked with fire. She planted her finger in the middle of Sam's chest and backed him up with each of her points. "Convenient?" she said. "Do ya think it's easy knowin' evil is a-comin' and bad things are goina happen and not be able to do a thing aboot it, now? Do ya think I like only seein' a piece of the trouble, and never knowin' exactly what it is? And what about Meggie? Do ya think she wanted the burden of a vision no child could even hope to understand and shouldna ever have to face? Do ya think that's convenient?" Emerald's last words were choked with heavy emotion and wrung Annette's heart.

"Em," Sam whispered, looking as if his eyes had just opened for the first time.

"Doona speak to me," Emerald said and swung around, marching to the first building on the right.

Annette followed on Emerald's heels, with Erin right beside her. Annette glanced at the dormlike living quarters— bedrooms and a bathroom shooting off from a central living room—then focused her attention on Emerald. "What happened with Megan?"

Emerald put her fingers to her lips and tiptoed to a closed door, cracked it open, peeked inside. "Meggie's sleeping," she said, shutting the door softly. Crossing the room, she spoke low. "She didn't sleep at all last night. Remember the phone call from the school yesterday on our way to the Rankins'?"

Annette nodded.

"She didn't have a stomachache, but pretending to be sick was the only way she could get the school to call me. She had a vision. Of you and me. Of Rankin and what he did to his wife. Of Pathos and of black creatures with wings eating me alive while you had to watch it all so that you could see what would happen to your sister if you weren't good. She told me that no matter what, I could not go to where I was going. That I had to go right home."

"But you didn't." Annette shuddered. "You followed me."

"I couldn't just leave you, but I couldn't stop them from taking you either."

Annette shook her head. "I pray to God that there is never a next time, but you have to promise to do what Meggie says next time. Pathos knew you were hiding in the woods. He could smell you. I have no doubt that had you been with me, and Pathos had captured you, he would have done exactly what Meggie dreamed, but slowly, a piece at a time, whenever he wanted me to do something 'willingly' for him. The black creatures are called Underlings. There were hundreds of them flying around the place where Pathos took me. Thank God, according to Aragon, the Underlings can only exist in a limited area under special conditions."

"You didn't tell me all of it before, Em," Erin cried.

Emerald swallowed hard, as if she were having trouble even speaking. "I didn't want you to worry aboot it all when I wasn't completely sure about the details. Meggie's never had a vision before. I didn't have my visions until I was older. Eighteen. I canna imagine what this is doing to her. She is still so innocent. She's barely ten."

Annette went and wrapped her arms around Emerald. "I am so sorry that she went through it. Is there any way to make them stop?"

Emerald shook her head and pulled back from her. "The Druids are never kind."

"Can these monsters get any more evil?" Erin gasped, her face pale with the impact of it all. "Tsaras, Underlings, undead zombies, demons—Heldon and his army seems too big. There's no safe place for any of us."

"That's where you're wrong, luv," Emerald said. "I swear on me mother's angel wings that there's more good than evil aboot us. And they are fighting every minute against anything that would steal away goodness and life. Then there's the good magic. You can see it growing stronger around us."

"Yes." Erin sighed.

"Is that why the trees and the grass and the bushes are all so unbelievably green?" Annette asked.

Emerald nodded.

"What is this place, anyway?"

"An old, retired ranger station. Sam came up with the idea of using it this morning. Because it's so close to the Sacred Stones, I can pull from the power of the ancients and the spirits on Spirit Wind Mountain to protect us here. Now we best get you two ready to go to Belize before the men sneak off without you."

"They wouldn't dare," Annette muttered.

"This is Sam and Jared we're talking about," Erin said.

"And Aragon," Annette added. "You're right, Em. Though patterned differently, all three of them are cut from the same macho cloth."

"After what he said today, I'm hanging Sam out to dry," Emerald said.

"Believe it or not, I think he got the point," Annette replied.

Emerald shook her head. "It doesn't matter. I don't have the strength to argue with him. I can't allow him to hurt me anymore. I have to focus on Meggie and on the magic now."

Annette didn't try to change Emerald's mind at the moment. She could see that her friend was doing all that she could, and it wouldn't hurt Sam to be out in the cold a bit either. But then, they all might just end up like that, she thought, recalling Pathos's chilling touch. Belize might be a tropical locale, but Annette had a feeling that their destination would be a freezing hell.

Chapter Twenty

SAM BIT DOWN on his bottom lip hard, drawing blood. He watched Emerald march away, a mass of hurt that he'd laid open. His body was covered in a cold sweat. God. The thought of Vasquez getting his hands on any one of the women did more than leave Sam filled with dread. It eviscerated him, exposing all of the agonizing fear that shackled him to his nightmares. He already bled with his every breath. How could he take any more?

The slow burn at the base of his skull sent a ripple of pain down his spine. Shit. It was freaking daylight. That he wouldn't even have the shadows of night to hide in this time seemed to cut him off at the knees.

"I'm scouting the perimeter," he muttered to Jared.

"Need help?" Jared asked, narrowing his gaze at him.

Sam pretended to be checking something out in the sky. "No. I can handle it. Be back shortly." He didn't wait for a reply before he took off at a dead run. He ran until he couldn't breathe. He ran until the pain stabbing down his spine paralyzed his legs and rendered him a convulsing mass of agony on the forest floor. Pine needles bit into his face and dirt ground between his teeth, but it was the stench of death and suffering that had him gagging. And the vision of the poor woman he'd seen staked to the ground that had him dying inside.

She'd tried to help him escape, and for two days, he'd been hanging in a tree watching what the men and the animals did to kill her as painfully and as slowly as possible.

By the time he'd relived her death, he was sobbing. He'd rolled into a fetal ball and could do nothing but cry. He was scared shitless and wasn't even sure he could crawl back to camp, much less walk like a man.

He'd thought his life became a living hell when he'd sworn to keep his hands off the one man who most deserved his revenge. But he was wrong. Living hell was finally getting the chance to kill that man and realizing he didn't have the balls to face him.

A string of Mozart's concertos played softly in the darkened room where Pathos reclined in a meditative state. He'd let his lust and his rage get the best of him, and it was time to reclaim himself from the doctor's scorching grasp. He'd still have her, but the possession would be a cold deliberation and not a hot slaking of desire.

First he had a battle to fight. Vasquez had left in the middle of the night—a slap in Pathos's face, one that now forced Pathos to eliminate him and take the Elan blood supply back from the bastard.

Pathos had learned the merits of centering oneself before war long ago. Listening to the intricately composed melodies with his eyes closed brought back memories of that golden time in his earthly existence when as a predator he'd reigned supreme. In Europe his senses had been at a peak; the late-night soirees and courtly games, followed by nightly hunts to satisfy all of his fleshy hungers, whether as a beast rampaging through the forest or a man slaking his lust. Those were the times— times that could never be recaptured, now that technology and culture had altered man and his world past such vulnerability.

As his mind drifted, searching for the icy calm that served him so well, he found himself recalling a different life in another realm. He'd existed as a creature of both good and evil, and he always excelled, simply because he could do no less. Both sides were all about possessing mortal souls. Logos, of course, was hot for purity, Heldon for cold evil. Pathos didn't see the point in either, and he knew neither would win. In the end his way would prevail. Moderation was the key. On the whole, mortals were a selfish, lazy lot and would prefer not to have to make a choice between anything. Pathos would give them that option. He'd perpetuate an existence in the middle where no path had to be followed but for one: his. He required neither purity nor evil to be propagated, but subservience to his will was essential, a fact he had to reaffirm now with the Vladarians.

"It's time to leave," Cinatas said, stepping into the room.

"Good." Pathos stood, his fist clenching like a vise.

"Samir left with Vasquez, as well."

"Excellent. I'll enjoy getting rid of the spineless prick now. Any others?"

"No."

"Wellbourne?"

"Is content for now. But we'll have to watch him. I think he suspects Shashur's demise wasn't from tainted Elan blood. So I'll just have to come up with several Elan and 'taint' them to give him the proof he needs."

"You don't need to explain yourself to him," Pathos said, scowling.

"No, but it will strengthen my power to have them shaking in their fangs."

Pathos clasped Cinatas's shoulder. "I'm really looking forward to your reign, son." Life hadn't been this interesting in centuries, he thought, and what he would do to teach Dr. Batista a bedside manner she'd never forget made it even better.

He knew where she and her friends were now. They thought they were safe. Thought they had enough power to fight him. But they had no idea what he could unleash. He'd show them just as soon as he returned from Belize.

Having bathed and dressed in what he'd been told were "jeans" and a "pullover," Aragon went in search of Jared. While not binding his every movement, the clothes chafed at his body and spirit, inhibiting his freedom and exacerbating the tension inside him.

Something was wrong. But then, having to tell Jared how right he'd been about Aragon's obsession with Pathos twisted his insides in knots. He could now see how it had skewed his actions as a warrior and his decisions as a leader.

He found Jared in deep concentration near the spot where the power of the ancients was being funneled to fuel the green-eyed woman's magic. Aragon stood quiet a moment, absorbing what Jared had to be observing. The magic flowing past them was like a fierce wind. He had to brace himself against the strength of it, at odds with the calm in the mortal world, where only a slight fluttering wind riffled through the trees. The fullness of the sun hit directly overhead, warming the creatures with the bounty of Logos's creation. Even the petals of the soft-hued flowers growing amid the Sacred Stones barely swayed as they basked in the life-giving light.

Without turning, Jared spoke. "What do you suppose the source of her magic is? When I first met her, I feared she might have a connection to Heldon's power. Those upon the mortal ground have been so easily deceived by following the lure of his misuse of magic. Yet at every turn she has proven herself true. Still I question. When I suggested that the Sacred Stones might provide sanctuary, I had not expected this. She kept the strength of her power well hidden, which makes me question even more. Any thoughts?"

Aragon paused as a dearly missed sense of the familiar wrapped around him. He and Jared had always sought each other's opinions, and as leader of the Blood Hunters Aragon often relied on Jared's consensus before bringing a plan to the brethren. That Jared still sought his counsel after all the mistakes Aragon had made was humbling.

"It is a warrior's responsibility to question the unknowns until they are known. As to her power . . . after we spoke last, I crossed the spirit barrier and went directly to the eastern heavens. I stood before the gates of the angels' domain in the heart of the inner circle. I went to inquire of Annette's sister and spoke directly to an angel—something I've never done before."

"Nor I." Jared turned to face him then. "Has any other warrior even gone to the angels' gates?"

Aragon shrugged. "She knew of my shame and showed no surprise at my presence until she learned of my quest. I tell you this because the tinkling bells of the angels *exactly* matches the sound of the magic woman's bracelets. That can mean only one thing." No heavenly tone could be heard on earth unless it had been bestowed.

Jared's eyes widened. "Angel power. I hadn't even considered it possible. That would mean either Logos has placed her upon the earth for a purpose, or . . . she's like me. Fallen."

"An extremely rare situation, as the angels haven't been in battle since Logos elevated them to their roles as Soul Keepers."

"True. So if the source of her power truly is the heavens, then why does she speak of the Druids so often?"

"Perhaps she does not want the true source of her power revealed."

"It is something to consider, and a better explanation than any I have determined. It would account for the strength of her magic and why it could even temper the moon's pull on my were-being."

"Then this pull to savagery beneath the moon is common? I never experienced it within the mortal world until this time."

"Nor I until I became . . ." Jared sharpened his gaze before he finished his sentence. "Mortal. Do you think that before punishment a faded warrior becomes mortal?"

Aragon grunted, thinking about all the things he'd felt since throwing aside his amulet. "It is possible. I experienced things that I have never before, as if my presence upon the mortal ground was more solid than ever. But then, I think Annette's possession of my amulet has something to do with it as well." His gaze drifted to the Sacred Stones, where everything between them had started just a little over two nights ago. As many millennia as he'd lived, and as many experiences as he'd known, still nothing compared to her, and he barely knew her.

"I saw that she had your amulet when we left the Sacred Stones that day," Jared said.

Caught by surprise, Aragon jerked his gaze back, wincing at the muscle in his shoulder that pained. "You did? And you let her keep it? Why?"

"Well, as tightly as she held the thing, it would have taken a full-scale battle to pry it from her hand. And perhaps in the back of my mind I thought you and the good doctor needed a dose of each other, should your amulet open a communication channel between you as it does between the brethren. By the looks of things, it did." Jared's words were tempered by the glint of humor in his gaze.

"It did more than that. Did you know the amulet had the power to call me forth to whoever is in possession of it?"

"Truly?" Jared's eyes widened, then crinkled with laughter. "She called you to her?"

"Several times. The second time she inadvertently shifted me, right in the middle of an attack on Pathos, into her bath." Aragon paused, then frowned. "I had the fulfillment of my quest in the palm of my hand, and then it was gone." He narrowed his gaze at Jared. "So you could have prevented all that has happened between me and the mortal woman? I have you to blame for everything?"

Jared's brow lifted. "No more than I have you to blame for my involvement with Erin."

Aragon stared hard at Jared, who stared hard back. Then Aragon flung his head back and roared with laughter, managing to cuff Jared playfully on the arm. "She's the best thing I have ever known. Do these mortal men know how good they have it?"

Jared shook his head, grinning from ear to ear. "It doesn't seem as if they do." He drew a bracing breath. "So you are not angry?"

"No. You were right about my obsession with Pathos. There are more important things than eliminating evil. For a warrior not to see that, he must be partially blinded by evil himself. I will find Annette's sister and then seek out Pathos. And when I meet him in battle, I will do all within my power to vanquish him, but I will not sacrifice greater things for the opportunity to do so. After, I will go face the Guardian Council's punishment for my actions."

"What was their decision?"

"It doesn't matter. I am honor bound to face it, and there are more important things I need to tell you. The mountain fortress where Pathos carried Annette is so saturated with dark magic that a pathway to the damned has formed. Hundreds of Underlings prowl the grounds. There are too many congregated there for so few of us to face. I fear tonight we may encounter the same."

"I know. Sam and I were there, trying to get to Annette. We were nearly food for the Underling horde. As for their presence in Belize, we'll have to see. Pathos will not be expecting an attack upon the Vladarian Vasquez. Surprise will be in our favor. From what I have learned, Vasquez is heavily immersed in the military, but also very comfortable in his little kingdom."

"In this fight you are the few against the great many. Logos needs more warriors who are aware of the real battle being fought upon the mortal ground."

"My opinion exactly, and I have to wonder if my journey to this point was not predestined."

"You mean Logos had you poisoned by a Tsara?"

Jared shrugged. "Let's say he may have simply let happen what Heldon had orchestrated. Who knows? To fight this evil we will need to target the Vladarians one at a time and create as much dissension as we can among their ranks."

Aragon grunted. "You mean attack in our were-forms and make them think Pathos is behind it?"

Jared sighed. "Would that I could. My death and rebirth at the Sacred Stones altered my were-form. I can't shift into my wolf's cloak anymore, but I still have the heightened senses and some of my were-strengths, especially during the moon's pull."

"I have noticed the moon's effect upon me," Aragon admitted, then hesitated. "It seems to be growing worse."

Jared leveled his gaze on him. "Worse how? With me, the combination of the Tsara's poison and the effects of the moon made me mindless. I had no control over any of my were-magic, and the only thing that eased my situation was

Erin's touch and presence. Are the effects of the moon beyond your control?"

Rolling his shoulder from the nagging Underling injury, Aragon replayed in his mind what had happened to him on the cliff. Surely his lack of control was due to the dark magic saturating the area. "No," he said. "I can control it." Besides, he had a gut feeling that tonight would be the last time he'd need to suppress any savage urges. Once Stefanie was located, all that remained between him and the council's judgment was Pathos. And Aragon knew where to find him now. "Then we'll strike at the moon's zenith tonight, when our were-gifts are the strongest?"

"Just before midnight," Jared concurred. "The hardest part will be making Erin and Annette stay out of it. I war between deciding if they would be safer with us or apart."

Aragon shrugged his shoulders, wondering why Jared considered something so routine to be difficult. "I would think there is more danger in battle with us. We are the warriors. We will just command them to remain where they are safe."

"You and Annette haven't spent a lot of your short time together talking, have you?"

"We've spoken some."

Jared couldn't supress a bark of laughter. "It's time for lunch, and I'm starving. Peach cobbler's in the oven, and you don't want to miss that. Let's head back, and I'll tell you about the creature known as mortal woman. To command is the kiss of death, but if you seduce her into what you want, make her think it is her idea in the first place, you'll get what you want plus all the heaven any being can take."

When Sven arrived with Sirius at the center of the Pyrathian circle, they found York and Draysius in a heated argument. Navarre lay still as death on the ground between them. Other Pyrathians had gathered around them, but none were intervening in the situation.

York shouted, his anger so hot that sparks flew from his spirit form, "I know you can do it. Take back your fire before his soul is too damaged to survive. I cannot save him alone, and he doesn't deserve to die at the misguided hand of a supposed brother!"

"Misguided!" Draysius cried. "It is he who interfered with the fulfillment of the council's decree. One as foolish as that deserves whatever death his folly leads him to!"

"He but protected a beloved friend from the impetuous actions of an irrational being! Honor demands that you—"

"Do not begin to speak to me of honor!" Draysius roared. "Blood Hunters have been disgraced beyond—"

"Enough!" Sirius commanded. "This dissension within the Guardian Forces is to end immediately. The Guardian Council is content to await the return of Aragon. Should its Forces do no less? Free the Blood Hunter Navarre from the torture of your fire, Draysius. York is right that honor demands it, though his accusations against your character are as misguided as yours against the Blood Hunters."

"Is there to be no consequence then, Sirius? Must I bear the brunt of his foolishness?"

Sirius sighed.

Sven spoke. "I have taken full responsibility for the incident before the council and await their punishment. I am the leader of York and Navarre, and they were but following my lead to protect their brother from harm. Everything that has happened, even Aragon's decision to leave, is a direct result of my failure. There will be a consequence, and I will pay it."

"And you, Draysius," Sirius said, walking to his fellow Pyrathian and setting a hand on his shoulder. "You were but following my lead." Sirius then faced Sven. "It would seem

I've learned great lessons in leadership today from a great leader. Sometimes there is more honor in compassion than in judgment."

Sirius then slipped to his knees near Navarre's head and set his hands upon the fallen Blood Hunter. He placed one hand upon Navarre's head, the other upon his heart. A bright field of fire surrounded Sirius's body, and he began to shake as if in great pain.

"No!" Draysius cried, falling to his knees as well. He tried to thrust his hands through the wall of fire, but was deflected.

Moments later, Sirius collapsed, and Draysius gathered Sirius from the floor into his lap.

"What is it?" York asked. "What happened?"

Draysius looked up, grieved and angry. "Sirius did as you asked. He withdrew the Pyrathian fire from Navarre."

"But what is then wrong?"

"He will now suffer the fire. He will survive, but his strength as a warrior will now become lesser. To recall the fire comes with a price."

"I didn't know," York whispered.

Draysius stood with a shaking Sirius in his arms. "Take your brother and tend to him. He should wake eventually and be whole once he has healed inside, but it will take time."

Sven helped York lift Navarre to carry him to the Blood Hunters' circle. The repercussions of his failure were growing wider and wider. He had to find a way to end it before all of the order and goodness within the heavens unraveled. The effects everywhere would be devastating, but worse upon the mortal ground. Evil would rule absolutely.

Annette studied the men from beneath her lashes, wondering if something was up. The planning session for their attack on Corazon de Rojo was too basic. By dark they were going to have an observation point set up. At a set time before midnight, Jared and Aragon would circle the border of the compound, sniffing for Stefanie's scent. If they found it, Sam would set off a distracting explosion, while Jared and Aragon penetrated the compound and extracted Stefanie. Sam would search for and destroy the Sno-Med blood that had been flown in from the research center. Afterward, Jared and Sam would free any prisoners and kill Vasquez while Aragon led Stefanie and Abe Bennett to the helicopter where she, Nick, and Erin were to have it set to go and all of the medical equipment at the ready.

Sam had special ops training. He'd been a Delta Force team leader for years. She imagined that on those missions every operation had been timed to the last second. That maps and diagrams had been drawn, and that ammunition selection and supply had been discussed. But none of that had happened here. Maybe there wasn't time.

Or maybe they'd run through that plan to keep her and Erin pacified, and they really were going to sneak off without them.

Maybe she was being overly suspicious because she needed something, anything, to take her mind off Stefanie. There was two hours still to go before they left for Belize, and she was climbing out of her skin. Aragon seemed to be avoiding her.

Or maybe he was just really getting into his first hamburger, french fry, and peach cobbler experience. He hadn't said much since they sat down to eat at the picnic-style table. She shifted her gaze to Aragon, only to have a wall of heat slam into her, making her throat tighten, her toes curl, and every muscle in between jump.

He'd just slid his tongue over the back of his spoon to get the last bit of the peach cobbler and ice cream from it before he dipped it back into the bowl. The look in his eyes was almost as orgasmic as when he slid into her, all hot and ready.

After watching him suck away three more bites, her mouth watered and everything south heated and grew damp as desire shot through her. She clenched her legs together, trying to ease the sudden need, but only succeeded in making herself ache more. How could she think about that when she was going after Stef in two hours?

Because she had two hours, and she was going crazy.

His eyes shut, and he inhaled as if he couldn't get enough of the taste and the flavor to satisfy him. She bit her lip, trying to keep herself from leaning across the table and grabbing him. If they were alone, she'd be in his lap in a heartbeat. Then he opened his eyes, a lazy half slit that barely let her see his dark gaze from beneath his thick lashes.

"Can you make this with strawberries?" he asked, melting her completely with one sentence.

A sudden bombardment of images of her covered in strawberries and him licking her as thoroughly as he had his spoon intruded into her mind, and she knew he'd slipped the erotic pictures inside her mind, as smooth and hot and as filling as his arousal penetrating her to the core.

Her wet mouth instantly went dry. She just nodded.

He smiled, luring her heart right out of her chest and into his sensual spell. She completely forgot about any sort of Delta Forces operation planning. Maybe a short walk would do her and Aragon some good.

Aragon stood, shoving his not quite finished bowl of cobbler aside. "Come," he said. "We must—"

"Talk!" she interjected, fearing he would publicly declare his intention to mate again. She stood and chose not to look anyone in the eye. Any comments that were made about their abrupt departure she ignored, too. Aragon's music was the only thing she wanted to face right now.

"Thanks," Aragon said, tapping an absorbed, cobbler-eating Jared on the shoulder as he passed.

Jared only grunted.

"Thanks for what?" Annette asked as they hurried through the door.

"Advice about the mortal realm," he said.

The door had just slammed shut behind when Aragon grabbed Annette by the waist, swung her around, and backed her to the wall. His mouth came down on hers, all peachy and creamy and hot. His thick hard thigh shoved between hers, sliding along her needy crotch, and his hand immediately found her breast with a nipple-flicking thumb. The first spasms of her orgasm started by the time he ended the kiss.

He backed away and grabbed her hand. "Come."

She took one step on wobbly knees. "Can we hurry?"

"I can do that," he said with a grin and swung her up into his arms, then winced with pain.

"What is it?"

"Nothing, just a cut on my shoulder that will heal soon."

"The same cut from this morning?"

He shook his head. "Last night."

"And it hasn't healed yet? Let me take a look at it." With everything that had happened, she'd forgotten about his shoulder.

"Later. Right now there is something else I need," he said roughly, before claiming her mouth with his. He managed to steal her breath when he trailed kisses down her neck, but when he lifted her breast to close his mouth over her cotton-covered nipple, her mind went blank. The rush into the cover of trees passed in a sensual blur. Barely a hundred yards from the camp, Aragon pushed her up against a tree. Their lovemaking was furious, elementally raw, and gloriously abandoned. He undid the front clasp of her bra and jerked up her shirt. His shirt and her jeans ended up wadded and wedged between her back and the tree trunk. His jeans went to his ankles, and she wrapped her legs around his hips as he thrust deep inside. With his hands anchoring her hips, he pumped fast and hard into her needy heat, driving her to a feverish explosion of pleasure. And in that moment, when his soul wrapped around hers in the ecstasy of their release, she realized something was wrong. She could feel it in his heart and see it shadowing the dark fire in his eyes.

"What is it? What are you not telling me?" she whispered. He shut his eyes and she felt his instant withdrawal from her spirit, even though he was still inside her, still hot and full from their passion.

He leaned forward to kiss her, to distract her, and she pushed him back, lowering her legs. "Tell me."

He released her with a sigh. She pulled her shirt back down, and tossed his over his shoulder as he was snapping up his jeans.

She didn't waste time on underwear or socks. She stuffed them in her pockets and went commando, slipping into her jeans and tennis shoes. "Talk," she said, folding her arms across her chest.

He drew a deep breath, broadening his shoulders as if to brace for the burden he now had to share. "Once Stefanie is found, I must leave for good."

Her heart sank as a sharp pain shot through her. "Why? You're not fading yet." He'd been just as hot and powerful a lover a moment ago as he'd been the first time.

"It's not a matter of waiting until I fade now. I don't have a choice. The Guardian Council has changed the punishment for leaving the forces, and I must honor their judgment."

She paused, as her heart and breath wrapped around his brick-hard words and sank beneath the total conviction in his voice. He was a warrior, and there was no question of what he should do. "You learned this when you went back yesterday, didn't you?"

"Yes."

"You shouldn't have gone. I knew it." She shut her eyes against the flood of shouldn't-haves and tried to breathe, but her chest was too tight with pain. "What is the punishment?"

"Nonexistence."

Not even her crossed arms could keep in her pain. She pressed her hands hard against her breasts, fighting to breathe. Tears filled her eyes, and her throat would barely work. "They've called for your execution."

"Yes," he whispered, reaching for her.

"No!" she shouted, backing away, shaking her head, refusing to accept what he was saying. "No. It's not right. Forget about them. You left the forces to do something important. They, this council, are no longer important. You don't need them. You don't owe them."

"Yes, I do. Whatever wrong choices I made, I am still a Blood Hunter and a warrior. I didn't know the full repercussions that my leaving would have upon the forces. Things are bad, and even if they weren't, honor demands that I respect their decision."

"Honor?" she cried, wanting to strike out at anything. "Is there any honor in the senseless act of executing a good, loving, courageous, and honorable man?" She swatted at her tears like flies, nearly bruising her cheeks in her anger. "Is there any honor or sense in blind obedience?"

She smacked his chest with the palm of her hand. "You are smarter than that. You left the forces because you knew the only way to stop the evil Pathos has been creating was for a lone man to go after him. You're already honorable."

He grabbed her shoulders, trying to pull her into his embrace. "Was it really the only way?" he asked softly. "Or was it the only way I could see in my hatred? Annette, please, I must return. I'm sorry. During this time of passion with you, I, who have been in existence for millennia, learned what it meant to truly live and love. Nothing and no one, not even time, can take that away from us. I love you. No matter what."

"No matter what," she whispered, falling into his embrace, unable to believe that this would be the end of their love. "No," she said, pulling back from the emotional storm consuming her. "You're wrong, Aragon. Honor doesn't demand you follow a senseless edict. Honor demands that you do what is honorable, what you do so well, which is love and protect others. If you really loved me more than an army that has no respect for you, then you wouldn't go back."

Aragon stiffened, sucking in a ragged breath of air and then exhaling as if punched. "How can you say that? This is who I am, what I do, and what I must be. I failed once. I won't fail again. If you really loved me, then you would understand."

Annette pulled from his arms, tears blinding her. "I don't understand," she cried. "I don't." She ran, and he let her go, a fact that made her pain even worse.

Chapter Twenty-one

A SENSE OF VICARIOUS déjà vu filled Annette as she watched the endless canopy of trees zip past the copter's window. She'd been a teenager when *Romancing the Stone* hit the big screen, and though it had been a thoroughly enjoyable movie, she'd thought the adventure Joan Wilder had been forced to take with Jack Colton had been highly improbable. Now, here she was, south of the border, looking for her missing sister with a *werewolf*, whom she loved and wanted to shoot at the same time.

After copious amounts of tears and tissues amid Erin and Emerald's advice, Annette had squashed down the pain over Aragon's decision in favor of being pissed off. The pain was still there, buried inside her, but anger made it easier to breathe.

How could he just accept execution as his fate? She couldn't. It went against every single fiber of her mind, body, and soul.

She glanced at him from the cover of her sunglasses, which considering the falling twilight looked ridiculous. But she wasn't ready for anyone else to see her pain yet. She didn't think she would ever be ready. Here at her most anxious but also her most anticipated moment, the moment when she might find her sister, Annette wanted to pound something. She wanted to shout and vent and change the world. She wanted a fairy-tale moment!

She was a fool.

Nick kept a low profile, flying stealthily over Belize's Cayo district as they headed for an area near the remote Mayan ruins of Xunantunich. Sam knew of a secluded field Nick could land in that would put them within a mile of Corazon de Rojo. There were no public airstrips in the jungle, and they didn't dare land closer. Dusk shadowed the evening sky, giving them good cover but allowing them to see the terrain below enough to make a safe landing. Xunantunich's Archaeological Park had closed at four, and everyone had their fingers crossed that by this time in the evening, not a soul would be around to get curious about their landing close to it. Nick came prepared with a few tools to fake a mechanical problem if anyone did.

It appeared the plan was just as they'd plotted in Twilight, but everyone was still tense, apprehensive over the unknown variables. A lot was riding on Sam's recollection of the routine and layout of the Corazon de Rojo compound.

Nick landed in the field minutes before a blanket of darkness slipped over the jungle. Not even a ribbon of the sunset remained on the tree-dense horizon. The air was heavy with the humid scent of rain, and dark clouds crept across the moon, pilfering bits of its light. The first thing Sam did was hand out flashlights that were practically weapons—their strobe effects disoriented attackers, their high beams made the entire area glow as if the moon were just a few feet away, and their weight could fell a man with a single blow. He showed everyone how to signal for help with them.

Next, the men immediately began rechecking the equipment and pulling out the real weapons, stashing them at hand but out of sight should anyone happen upon them. It was at that point the full import of what they were about to do hit. This wasn't a movie. This was real. Though their

James Bond, seat-of-their-pants method and their *Mission Impossible* goal to bring down Sno-Med and the Vladarian Order seemed like a Hollywood fantasy, the bullets and the danger were real.

And so was Sam's trouble. Whatever had happened to him here, he was dragging it with him like a mushroom cloud. His pupils were dilated, sweat poured off him, and Annette swore that his hands were shaking.

"Are you okay?"

He jerked around. "Why wouldn't I be?"

She held her hands up and backed away a step. "Forget I asked. Why don't you tell me just what kind of guns those are?"

He seemed to force himself to relax. "The best my contacts could get. Mainly a couple of M-16s, one that will launch my supercharged door-buster bombs—guaranteed little babies that will burst their way through any door or gate and then some. Big Bang and Big Fire. I'm counting on that as being our ace in the hole if Stefanie is there. From forty meters away, I can create some serious damage to the gates on the compound and maybe inside on the steel door to the prisoners' huts."

Annette swallowed hard. One hundred fifty feet didn't sound like much leeway, but Sam was clearly ecstatic about it. After making a few appreciative comments, she moved to where Aragon stood on the edge of the forest, staring into the dense trees and brush. She felt as if she had to say something, or do something, more to make him understand.

But when she reached him, she found he was panting as if out of breath from a run. He'd never done that before, which, as many times as he'd carried her as he ran, meant that something was very wrong.

"Aragon?" she said softly. She set her hand on his shoulder and found that even through the cotton of his shirt his temperature was burning hot. He flinched from her touch. "Good Lord, Aragon, you're sick!"

"I don't know what this dark fever is." His voice was raw, as if scraped by broken glass.

"Let me see your shoulder." She pulled on the back of his shirt, tugging it up. A reddened, angry, swollen area surrounded a barely scabbed-over wound. "You have an infection. What happened here?"

"An Underling claw caught me. Whatever is wrong, it's causing me to shift." He turned her way, and she could see that fangs were beginning to press into his lower lip. His dark eyes were tortured, almost wild. "It's making me feel things that I can't seem to control."

She grabbed his arm, ignoring the mat of erupting hair. "Come with me. Maybe it's just the fever causing this to happen. I can help." She didn't know what was causing the sudden onset of his symptoms. She'd been seated next to him for hours, and though she thought something was off, no hint of this crisis had shown.

He set his hand over hers. It was still smooth. "Your touch is already helping." His voice sounded slightly less pained.

She took his hand firmly in hers. "Hurry." Jared, Erin, Nick, and Sam came up as she led Aragon to the helicopter where her med kit was.

Nick's eyes were wide with shock. Annette figured seeing Aragon suddenly half werewolf, half man had pretty much eliminated any lingering disbelief for him. She did note that thankfully his favorite expletive escaped him at the moment of his greatest need.

Jared took one look at Aragon and cursed. "By Logos, what's wrong?"

"He has an infected wound on his shoulder. It's from an Underling attack last night," Annette said, then gave him a quick assessment. "His lymph nodes are swollen, too." She snapped open the oversize tackle box that held an emergency kit worthy of a war zone. First she gave him a megadose of Tylenol to help fight the fever. Then she pulled out vials of an antibiotic and a steroid and popped out a syringe. Mixing the antibiotic, she drew up as much medication as she dared; then she remembered how little effect the painkiller had had on Aragon's system before, and drew more antibiotic into the chamber. The hottest buns south of the Mason-Dixon line were about to get a shot.

"What can I do?" Erin asked.

Annette gave her a half-humorous, half-painful grimace. "You don't suppose warriors faint when they get shots?"

"Get ready to find out," Erin said.

Aragon shuddered. "I can't seem to stop myself from shifting," he gasped.

"You'll have to stay here," Jared said. "You can't go if you can't control yourself. It's too dangerous. The moon's rising, and its pull is probably not helping. It's only going to get worse the closer it draws to its zenith."

"No! I must go," Aragon said harshly. "You and Sam cannot do it alone. You need my strength."

"Not if we can't count on what you'll do. We'll change plans. We'll forget any thought of an attack. We'll only find Stefanie and get her out, making as little disturbance as possible."

"No. You said yourself that your were-talents aren't as strong as they used to be. You might not be able to scent Stefanie at all, and we'll not know if she is there or not. This whole trip will have been wasted. I can do it," Aragon insisted, groaning. Even as he spoke, his legs shifted, ripping the seams of his jeans from the thighs down.

"We don't have time to argue," Annette said. "If I can get some medication in his system to fight the infection and fever, it might help."

"What can you possibly do in forty-five minutes to help?" Jared asked.

"Watch me," Annette said, snatching up a small bag of IV fluids. Since they were short on time, she'd go right to the vein with the medication. She injected the antibiotic into the IV bag and then set up an IV port into the back of Aragon's hand, having to go mainly by feel to locate his vein because of the thickness of the hair erupting all over him. Then she started another line in his right hand, hooking up a bag with a steroid dose big enough to address his body's inflammatory response.

"Check his vitals every five minutes and let me know if there are any major changes," she told Erin. Annette knew she was taking a risk by giving Aragon the medications without knowing how a werewolf's cell structure differed from a human's. But her instinct told her there wasn't that much difference—that what happened to shift Aragon from man to beast was more in the realm of unexplained magic than logical science.

Then she set up a small surgical table. "Brace yourself," she told Aragon. "I'm going to let the poison from the wound." She applied a liberal amount of a topical anesthetic to the area.

Jared looked over at the exposed wound. "Underlings are not supposed to be poisonous. And this is not like a Tsara infection, either. I've never seen such a problem before. All of the Guardian Forces heal quickly from nonlethal injuries."

Annette frowned, worrying her tongue over her teeth as she thought. "Your experiences are from the spirit realm. There, you might not even have germs, but here on earth we do. Maybe Underling scratches on earth cause fevers and infections. Or maybe your immune system can't fight pathogens that we have here." She prayed that the latter wasn't true. It would cause a lot of serious problems for Aragon.

"Instead of cat scratch fever, we now have Underling fever," Erin said.

"Good way to put it," Annette replied.

Nick managed to recover enough to join the conversation. "So there really is such a thing as cat scratch fever? I thought it was just a Ted Nugent song about sex."

"Men make everything about sex," Erin said, rolling her eyes.

That got Aragon's attention. Jared's too.

"They do not," Nick said.

"Is that a bad thing?" Aragon asked.

"Name something they haven't," Erin shot back at Nick. Then she frowned at Aragon. "There are more important things than sex."

The look Aragon and Jared exchanged was comical. Erin had a fight on her hands if she was going to bring them around to her point of view. Realizing Erin was very adeptly distracting her patient, Annette ignored the talk and worked on easing any infection from Aragon's wound. He didn't even flinch under her ministrations, though she knew it had to hurt. Using her skills to help someone in need eased some of the pain inside her, made her feel as if there was something that could be done to stop the craziness of killing one so good and noble.

Within thirty minutes, she'd infused the medications and cleaned and bandaged his wound. Aragon's temperature was down, and between the medication and her touch, he'd brought his were-being back under control.

"You should have said something earlier about your wound, and we might have avoided all this," Annette said, giving Aragon a stern look.

He lifted a brow, one that managed to push every hot button she possessed.

"I had more important things to attend to at the time," Aragon said softly, melting her anger. Oh, God, she loved him.

Ignoring the hot flush of her cheeks, she met Aragon's gaze head-on. "I'm going with you to the compound."

"No!" Aragon and Jared spoke simultaneously.

"Hear me out! It's what I do. Who I am," Annette shouted back. "You need Aragon, and I can give him additional medication if the need arises. Not necessarily IV, but an injection, which would be better than nothing. If there is any delay in the plan and the medication in his system wears off, we could be facing another crisis. There would be the added benefit of my touch in helping him maintain control as well. I think this must have happened to him last night in some way, and all he had was me."

"She's right, Jared," Erin said. "And you know it. There isn't any reason for her to stay here other than male ego. We're all adults in this, and with what we're fighting, there's just as much risk sitting here in the middle of the jungle as in going to the compound. She should go."

Aragon grunted as if he wasn't happy about what had just been said, but he didn't have an argument against it either.

Jared opened his mouth to say something, then shut it and slowly nodded his head in agreement. "She is right about the danger. Unless they're under the kind of magic

Emerald is wielding near the Sacred Stones, we can't predict or stop an attack, not without Guardian Forces hovering over us at all times. It's as I mentioned before—they may be safer with us than apart."

"I don't believe this!" Sam said with disgust. "Let's just all march up to the gates of Corazon and have a party! They aren't trained to react in combat. She'll only slow us down."

"I didn't get to be a surgeon without learning early to follow instructions and to react fast in situations. Sam, neither of us can move as fast as Aragon and Jared can, but I'll keep up." And she would, or die trying. "And I don't have to go inside the compound. Just be close enough to do some good if I'm needed."

"I say she comes," Jared said. "Aragon? Sam?"

"She comes," Aragon's gaze centered on hers. "It's what she does and who she is. I understand that now." She could see that he still warred with his concern, but that he was willing to let her go. The burden of his words washed back over her. *This is who I am, what I do, and what I must be. I failed once. I won't fail again. If you really loved me, then you would understand.*

She hadn't. And now there wasn't time.

"You've less than two minutes to gather what supplies you need," Sam said.

Annette didn't waste a second. She grabbed up her field bag and dumped saline, syringes, and one vial each of all the emergency meds into a small pack. She didn't voice her inner fears that prompted her to have every medical solution at her fingertips. But more than being there for Aragon drove her. If Stefanie was in bad shape, Annette would never forgive herself for failing her sister twice. Annette had to do everything she could do the very moment she could do it.

"I'm ready," she said a minute later. The men stood near, weapons in hand.

"Wait a second," Nick said. "I don't scare easy, but you all can't just take off leaving me in the dark. Just exactly what do I need to be on guard against from this spirit realm, and what do I fight them with?"

"Don't worry, I'll bring you up to speed," Erin said, from where she stood at Jared's side, having just given him a kiss he wasn't likely to ever forget.

Jared slipped his amulet off and hung it on Erin's neck. "When I get back, I'm going to finish what you started."

"I can't wait," Erin said, then brought Jared's amulet to her lips.

Jared faced them, looking as if he was ready to conquer the world. "Let's go, then."

Annette turned away, tears in her eyes as she clutched Aragon's amulet to her breasts. Her gaze met Aragon's, and a stab of pain went through her at the smoky desire and pain in his dark eyes. She knew he wanted to do and say more about a future with her, but couldn't.

"Fire works well on demons because, despite information to the contrary, hell is really a very cold place," Annette told them and turned away, thinking that unless she thought of a way to save Aragon from his fate, her life on earth was about to become a very cold place indeed.

Chapter Twenty-two

"I'M READY." Aragon turned from the stark pain and the fruitless hope in Annette's sad gaze, wishing that she could hold him as tightly as she held his amulet, for it seemed neither heaven nor earth could separate her from it. He'd heard and felt every cry that her heart made and had no answer to comfort her, so he'd kept silent as he picked up the weapon Sam had given him and joined Jared. He felt extremely unsettled inside, and preferring the feel of his spirit sword to that of the mortal gun wasn't why.

Walking away from Annette with her last thoughts being so sad was what worried him. The magic of her medicine still coursed through him, making him more amazed at her gifts. His first instincts had been to protect her from all harm and put her someplace safe. But he now realized there was a greater place for her to be—a place at his side, where she could use her skills and he his, for there was just as much worth in what she could contribute to the battle as in what he could.

I was right, he said into her mind. *You make a good warrior woman, especially with a blowtorch.*

You're with me? She swung around, clearly surprised to find him in her mind.

I am always with you.

I have to tell you. I understand, okay? Even if I can't accept it. I understand.

Thank you, he said, feeling her spirit back with his.

"We'll meet you at the north checkpoint in thirty minutes," Sam said. "It won't hurt for me to plant a charge on a bridge leading to the east. It's the main road from the compound to civilization, and we may want them to think we're escaping in that direction."

"Good. There's nothing left to do but go." Jared turned, walking into the dark forest.

Aragon paused before following. *I am always with you, no matter what, remember that,* he whispered to Annette's mind. Only then did he feel ready to join Jared. They were to travel ahead to the compound, search the perimeter for Stefanie's scent, and be positioned for the next step by the time Annette and Sam reached them. He had Stefanie's sketchbook in his pack, so there would be no question as to her scent.

Though he could feel the fever inside him, hungering to be unleashed, the medicine kept a tight hold on it. And the denseness of the trees overhead blocked much of the moon's direct light, thus easing its pull.

"So what are you going to do about her, about your future?" Jared asked softly as they moved toward their target.

Aragon sighed, his heart heavy. "There is nothing to be done."

"What does that mean?"

"It means that my fate has been set. Tomorrow will see its end."

"The council has called for your execution, haven't they?"

"A punishment is a punishment, be it that of a faded warrior or nonexistence," Aragon said with a stoicism he was far from feeling.

Jared cursed. "No, it isn't, and you know it. At least with existence there can be a hope of change."

"What has been done is done."

"Then Logos has agreed with the council?"

"I won't know until I return. Hopefully Sven will have failed."

"You spoke to him when you returned? Why would you wish Sven failure?"

He'd said too much, and now he had to tell Jared everything that had happened, and about Navarre's possible death in protecting him. Aragon gritted his teeth, feeling the bite scrape against the insides of his cheeks. He was the father of so much harm. He told Jared the full story. "I have no recourse. Honor and courage demand that I face the council's decree. I couldn't stop Navarre, and I pray to Logos that he will survive, but I can see that Sven doesn't fall. No warrior will sacrifice his life for mine."

"You chose well for the Blood Hunters' leader."

"Why?"

"For he is doing no less than you or I would. Will you deprive him of his duty?"

Just as Aragon was trying to twist his mind enough to even comprehend Jared's logic, his friend threw another wild element into the mix. "There is something else you are forgetting."

"What?"

"It isn't final until Logos speaks. Don't you remember the twelve Guardians whom the council demanded be executed for their failure to protect Logos's own?"

Aragon shook his head. "That was over two millennia ago." Though Aragon wanted to reach out and take that glimmer of hope and breathe fire into it with his very soul, he didn't, for he realized that there was a flaw in Jared's reasoning that had never been there before. Jared was thinking like a mortal now, and though the spirit and mortal world blended together within the twilit shadows of the outer circles, that's where their similarities ended. The logic that ultimately ruled the laws of the spirit realm differed greatly from the mortal.

Aragon? Are you all right? I felt pain. His warrior woman had found her way to him without him opening the channel.

I am fine. Would be much better were we . . . He sent a lusty image of the two of them.

In return she pictured a strawberry placed strategically on her body, and Aragon tripped on a large stone in his path. Jared grabbed his arm to keep him from falling.

"Don't ask," Aragon muttered to Jared. "I'm fine, and no, I don't need any medication. I'm in complete control of my were-form." It was something else that he was having a problem with.

"We're almost there," Jared said a short time later.

"Let me shift and fix upon Stefanie's scent before we get closer."

"No. Considering your situation with the Underling fever, I wouldn't shift unless there's trouble and we need your extra strength. The pull of the moon should heighten your were-senses enough to detect Stefanie in your warrior form."

"It will." He pulled her sketchbook from his pack, breathed deeply of it, and then gave it to Jared. When Jared had fixed the scent, Aragon replaced the book, and they went directly for the compound, moving so fast that they appeared only as a dark blur.

The moment he left the canopy of the trees, Aragon felt a light, misty rain falling. His stomach knotted as he wondered if he'd be able to detect Stefanie's scent. If the rain fell harder, he wouldn't be able to. Hurrying, he carefully slid to the wall and began moving around it. Situated in the middle of dense jungle, only the red-tiled rooftops of Corazon de Rojo's buildings could be seen above the high red clay walls. Hexagonal guard towers rose at each corner. The center north tower climbed to a point well above the canopy of the forest. Each tower was manned with armed guards, but nobody was located at ground level all around the outside of the wall. There were only four exits, situated at the exact north, south, east, west coordinates. Their steel doors were locked tight with no visible guards present.

Circling the perimeter of the compound left Aragon very disturbed. "By Logos, the evil and the decay are overpowering. I hear so many moans of misery that even I can hardly distinguish one voice from another."

"Sam said if there was a hell on earth, this would be it."

"How can the many within this world allow the few to perpetuate such horror?"

"I haven't discerned the answer to that yet."

"There is so much wrong to be righted." Aragon shook his head sadly. "The mist makes it difficult, but I may have detected Stefanie's scent about the middle of the west side. I'll need to get closer to be sure. The vampire scent is strong. There is more than just Vasquez here."

"According to the map Sam put together," Jared said, "the housing for the nuns is located near that section of the west wall. My bet is to search there first. We'll circle again to be sure, then move to the north point where we are to meet Sam and Annette."

After circling and verifying their impressions, the Blood Hunters moved out from the compound's perimeter to the meeting point. Sam had chosen well. With the north's observation deck being so high above the jungle canopy, it left

Corazon slightly vulnerable to ground activity. A white gravel road glowed like a pearlescent path, and they positioned themselves with it in sight.

"This time I could hear more conversation above the painful moans," Aragon said.

"I, too," Jared said. "Furtive tones, speaking apprehensively about a Vladarian war?"

Before Aragon could answer, the distant hum of an approaching vehicle rose above the noises within the compound. They slipped farther into the shadows. It would be disastrous to be detected by a Vladarian's sharp night vision.

A few minutes later, a white Hummer and a dozen trucks appeared. Inside the Hummer they could see Pathos, Cinatas, and the red demon Nyros, plus two others. The rest of the trucks were open and filled with armed men, some mortal and some demonic.

Pathos was here, and Annette was on her way. Aragon exploded beneath the rapid rush of bloodlust and fear shooting fire to his every cell. The memory of what Pathos had done to Annette, how he'd rendered her so helpless, raged inside Aragon. His fangs cut into his lip, and his muscles bulged, tearing apart seams. His barely leashed control cracked. All Aragon could think of was eliminating Pathos now before there was the slimmest chance that Annette could be harmed again.

Jared grabbed his shoulder as Aragon stepped into a fleeting beam of moonlight, but Aragon shrugged it off. *No matter what, I'll eliminate the threat to the woman I love.*

No matter what.

Annette heard the harshly uttered words, and this time, rather than comforting her, they sent her heart racing with fear. "Something's wrong, Sam! We need to run faster."

Already her side ached and her lungs were raw with the effort to breathe in enough of the damp oxygen to feed her body's need.

"What do you mean?" Sam gasped, picking up his pace to move ahead of her.

"It's Aragon."

"Hell, we can't afford for anything to go wrong. We're still ten minutes away from the checkpoint, at the very least. We'll have to abort the mission. Maybe try again tomorrow."

"Make that ETA five minutes," Annette gasped, adrenaline forcing her past her ability. She reached out to Aragon with her mind. Maybe her spirit could touch his and help.

Aragon! . . . Aragon?

No answer.

All she could feel was a solid wall of roiling emotion. She tried to run faster but was already straining harder than she ever had. Her muscles seemed to be losing their ability to function.

"Dear God, please," she cried, tears negating what little visibility Sam's light shed on the ground. Positioned in front of her, he moved quickly down the path people had worn between Corazon and the Mayan ruins of Xunantunich. Then she tripped and fell, hitting a sharp rock that cut painfully into her forearm and forced a sharp cry from her as her breath exploded from her lungs.

Something slammed up against the savage flood in Aragon's mind and made him pause, stopped him from rushing after the vehicle in which Pathos rode. He had to shake his head hard to clear it enough to understand what it was his mind had heard.

Annette. She was hurt and near. He could feel her desperation.

What's wrong? he asked harshly, forcing his mind to work above the bloodlust filling his desires.

Need you. Come.

Aragon went to move, and only then did he realize that Jared had him on the ground with his legs pinned. How had that happened? He sucked in air, searching through the savage fog in his mind, but came up empty. He must have been truly out of his mind, a very frightening thought.

"Jared. Let me rise."

"No. Not until you shift."

"Annette needs us. She's called me to her."

Jared stirred. "If you start running for Pathos again, I'm going to render you unconscious."

Aragon grunted. "You can try." He hoped the playful tone of his voice would reassure Jared that he had his senses back.

Jared let him up.

Aragon leapt to his feet and began running back into the jungle, away from Pathos. He heard Jared's sigh of relief. Apparently his brother had doubts that he would be able to back up his threat. Amusement helped Aragon rein in more of his were-being, but his wolf form was still in full force.

A minute later he found Sam and Annette crashing through the jungle. Annette didn't pause or hesitate; she launched herself against him and wrapped her arms around his neck. "You need me," she said.

"Yes, he did," answered Jared. "I wouldn't have been able to hold him another five seconds. He would have gone after Pathos and practically eliminated our chances of getting to Stefanie."

"She's here? He's here?" Annette backed from Aragon's arms, her whole body wrenching with both hope and apprehension. Her mouth went dry as her heart hammered with joy and apprehension. "We have to get to her before Pathos does. We have to hurry!" She started to run, but Sam grabbed her arm and swung her around.

"You go off half-cocked without a plan, you're only going to get us all dead. We have to think. What area do you think Stefanie is in, and what is Pathos doing here? Something doesn't sound right."

"Stefanie's scent is strongest at the midpoint of the west wall," Aragon said.

"We're going to search the nuns' quarters you've indicated are there," Jared added. "Pathos and an army of demons and mortals were at the north gate, and from what I could hear, they aren't welcome. All is not well within the Vladarian Order."

"When did all of that happen?" Aragon asked sharply. "I didn't hear—"

Jared set a hand on Aragon's shoulder. "You were too caught up in the craze. I've been there. Nothing was able to reach me when the moon was out. Speaking of which, unless we come up with a new plan and act fast, we'll lose the time of our greatest strength."

"Why change plans?" Sam asked. "We were going to create a diversion anyway. Pathos's arrival with armed men only makes it better. Just let me get up a tall tree with this little door buster, and we'll send Vasquez's gates and doors to steel heaven. North, south, east, and west, here we come."

"I know Pathos," Aragon said. "Last night, Annette and I got the upper hand, with hundreds of Underlings as witness. Once he catches wind of our scent, he'll be relentless in his pursuit and have every demon after us as well."

"I knew I needed a blowtorch," Annette muttered. Just the thought of running into Pathos and Nyros again filled her with dread. That dread turned cold at Aragon's next sentence.

Aragon looked at Jared. "This isn't bloodlust speaking now. It's time. I will stop Pathos tonight."

Sam got into perfect position. The tree he'd shimmied up was high enough to give him a damn good view of Corazon. Too good. Memories started edging in at the sickening familiar scents of human suffering and despair. The pressing, humid heat set every muscle in his body aching. The burning at the base of his skull started. His hands trembled as he raised his doctored M-16, putting the north gate in his sights.

But the gate wavered, shimmering like a vision on the desert. Sweat poured into his eyes, carrying a stinging bite that blurred his vision even more. He set the gun across his lap and mopped his brow with the sleeve of his shirt. That's when the first pain shot down his spine. His body drew up, and he nearly fell out of the tree. He had to latch onto a branch, cutting his hand on a spur. Blood ran down his arm, a river of red that sent a second shard of pain ripping down his spine.

No! His mind screamed at him. *No!* This was not going to happen.

He jerked the gun up, gasping for air to no avail. Resighting did little good. The gate, the limo, the gate, the limo—they kept merging as the horror of the past crept closer, determined to steal his mind.

He pulled the trigger, and as the little bomb exploded in a flash of light, filling the air with the screams of burning demons, Sam felt a steady calm wash over him. Reloading his next little surprise, he took aim again. Years of fear fell beneath a wave of cold rage that had been welling in his gut and choking him since he'd escaped the death camp below. He was going to raise all hell and then mow the bastards down.

"Why are we sitting here at the gates as if we can't eliminate Vasquez and any other Vladarian who dares to side with him?"

Pathos drew in another breath of the misty air before shutting the soundproof car door and turning to face Cinatas. He wondered if the rage still burning in his gut had him imagining Aragon's scent, but he was sure the Blood Hunter had been here. Recently. He smelled him the moment the car door had opened. "Aragon the Blood Hunter is here. And another as well. I can smell them both."

"Jared and Aragon are here with Vasquez?" Cinatas asked. "Has Vasquez switched allegiance from the damned to fight us?"

Pathos shook his head. "I don't even think that's possible, once you've crossed. But what if Logos is trying to destroy me by manipulating the damned? It seems too coincidental that after a millennium, not one but two Blood Hunters are suddenly working on the mortal ground. Both against Sno-Med. Vasquez could be easily duped by one of the Blood Hunters."

"I see."

"If you're seeing as clearly as I am, then you'll realize we're going to play a little game with Vasquez. Find out as much as we can before we act."

His cell phone rang, and Pathos curled his lip with amusement. "My friend," Pathos said.

"You say that? Vasquez thinks not. You come with an army!"

"What do you expect? You left like a thief. Left before hearing my son this morning. It was very rude of you."

Vasquez grunted. "Perhaps I did not hear you speak of the meeting this morning. Vasquez was angry over the unfairness of the vote."

"Unfairness? Why don't you tell me what you are doing with the fallen Blood Hunters? Then maybe we will talk," Pathos said, hating the concession. He itched to move in and rip Vasquez to shreds.

Suddenly the gate in front of the Hummer exploded. Shrapnel and fire peppered everything with scorched metal, even doing damage to the bulletproof glass.

A long string of curses blasted over the phone line. "This is how you talk, Señor Pathos? Vasquez will show you. I will burn everything before you can touch it." The line went dead.

Pathos looked out to see several demons in the truck behind writhing as the fire melted them. The damned were so vulnerable. "We've both been set up," he told Cinatas, thoroughly amused. A line of machine-gun-firing soldiers came scrambling from inside the compound and were picked off by his men, who used the trucks for cover. "Let's move."

Moments after Sam blew open the west gate, Aragon, with Jared at his side, penetrated the compound. The heat scorched at his wolf's cloak, and small pieces of debris still rained down, sizzling in the mist. There was more on fire than seemed possible if Sam had only blown open the gates. Screams, moans, and shouts of fear and confusion filled the smoky air, but the loudest sounds were the frantic cries of many terrified voices, begging, "Free us! Free us! Free us!"

Many were trapped in the buildings. Aragon's insides twisted with the need to answer the desperate voices. *By Logos! Can't you hear them! Help me to help them!*

He and Jared rushed to free those trapped by the fires.

Closely timed third and fourth blasts farther away drowned out the people's cries for a moment and distracted the armed guards from Aragon and Jared's presence, letting them free prisoners unhindered. Aragon saw that some of the armed men carried torches and were randomly setting the place on fire. Billowing, acrid smoke filled the area, making Aragon's eyes burn and his lungs heave. He tried to escape it, tried to locate Stefanie's scent in the air, but either the misting rain masked the scent, or the smoke was too thick. A lot of the smoke came from a very tall cathedral-arched building in the center.

"I cannot scent Stefanie anymore," he shouted at Jared.

"Nor I. Keep moving. We'll find her."

Going to the left, he and Jared tore down more doors and ripped iron bars from the windows, searching through every building for Stefanie. They met desperation at every turn. Men. Women. Children. The pain in their eyes was agonizing.

Aragon saw a man with a gun shooting those trying to escape. Howling with rage, claws slashing, Aragon went after him, ripping the gun from him and raking deep grooves in his face. The man ran off, screaming, blinded by blood. He'd carry the scar of his cowardice forever.

Amid the mist and the smoke and the screams, chaos ruled.

They'd been through six buildings, and still no Stefanie. Then he heard a number of cries coming from women to his right, and he pulled Jared in that direction. A long white building with bars on the windows loomed ahead. Women completely draped in black were beckoning from between the bars. He went to them. But when they saw him, they shrank back, shrieking with terror, holding out the crosses chained about their necks.

Stunned, Aragon froze, wondering if he was causing them more harm by trying to help. Some seemed frantic enough that it was a wonder their hearts remembered how to beat. Annette had never responded to his were-form like that.

"Ignore their fear," Jared shouted, surging past and grabbing Aragon's arm. "Help me break open the bars."

Together they tore open one window and moved to the next, then the next. As the women began emerging, Aragon searched. He knew he would know Stefanie. He'd scented her earlier. She had to be here.

Jared began grabbing the arms of women as they passed, halting them for a moment, saying "Stefanie Batista." Over and over again he called. The women would shake their heads, pull away, and go running.

Aragon wondered if he had been mistaken before. No. He'd been sure. Jared had been sure. She had to be here. He was turning for the next building when he saw a woman struggling to carry another woman, an invalid, out a window he'd just torn open. Dressed head to toe in black, they were unidentifiable, except that they needed help. He rushed over to lift the invalid from the struggling woman's arms. The moment he touched her, he could feel that she had but moments left to live.

The woman who'd been carrying the invalid looked up in surprise, but didn't shrink back from his were-form. For a second, he took in her dark hair, and eyes, and hoped that he'd found Stefanie, but the scent was wrong.

"Marissa," the invalid woman whispered. "Marissa? *Por favor*, tell me?"

"*Si, abuela.* We are freed." She took the woman back into her arms and sat upon the ground in the middle of the chaos. She must have sensed the invalid would live only a few moments longer, and chose to spend those moments comforting another rather than trying to flee the death around them.

Aragon didn't want to leave them alone, almost felt compelled to carry them out of danger, but he had to find Stefanie first.

"Where is Stefanie Batista?" Aragon asked. The helping woman's haunted eyes widened. She shook her head sadly and lifted a shaking hand, pointing it at a tower in the arched building centering the compound—the one in which the entire lower floor was on fire. It explained why he hadn't been able to catch her scent after entering the compound; she'd been higher up, and once the heat and smoke started rising . . .

By Logos! Aragon started running.

Chapter Twenty-three

SAM SWUNG DOWN from the tree, hot to see that he'd left every gate smoking. He shoved the door buster over his left shoulder and went gunning for the compound. Once he'd destroyed the blood supply, he'd make sure Jared and Aragon had found Stefanie, and then he was going to hunt down Vasquez. Entering Corazon from the opposite end Jared and Aragon had, Sam made a beeline for the "infirmary."

Once he reached it, he blew the metal doors wide. The staff inside was running around in confusion. Sam grabbed one man and put a gun to his head. "Any sick patients in here?"

Sam doubted it; if any of the prisoners got sick, they were left to die. But he still had to check. The man shook his head no.

"You've got less than two minutes to clear everyone out, because this baby is going to blow." He shoved the man away. Then, to set him into action, Sam fired his M-16 at the floor. The man jumped and started yelling as he ran down the hall for the exit.

It was time to get trigger-happy. Entering the first lab, Sam found a refrigerator stocked with bags of blood and started shooting. Blood splattered everywhere, running in rivulets across the floor. And it felt damn good. Demolishing the testing equipment with a spray of fire, he moved to

. the next room, doing the same. It was going to take a little longer than he thought, but there was nothing like a little blood to cleanse the soul.

After a soundless blast of petrifying cold, the red demons shattered the door to Vasquez's hidden chamber. Pathos sauntered casually into the room. Cinatas followed, and the red demons flanked them both.

In were-form Pathos stood chest, head, and shoulders above all others. While the door's collapse revealed a cowering Samir, surprisingly, Vasquez was nowhere to be seen. Two of the other oil-rich Vladarians were, though, along with one Vladarian who had turned himself into a religious guru and had a large following among the mortals. They looked up in surprise.

"Pathos! Thank God."

"We're being attacked."

"What is happening? Luis should have already returned, we must help him," Samir said.

Pathos couldn't detect any overt mutiny in their expressions. They genuinely thought he was here to save them.

"We *are* under attack," Cinatas said, moving to Pathos's side. "From within the order, it would seem."

Shocked denials echoed through the chamber.

"Who would dare?" demanded Samir.

"Vasquez and you three, perhaps?" Pathos suggested.

The Vladarians blanched.

"No!"

"We are here to buy Elan blood!"

"Vasquez has promised to sell to us. He is getting the blood now . . ."

"Did not my son and I promise that the transfusions will be as they were before?" Pathos demanded.

"Yes, but . . . surely Vasquez has not betrayed you. He is angry and will—"

"Do you think we lie?" He stalked toward the Vladarians, sniffing for the scent of guilty fear. After passing by them all, he curved his fleshy lips with satisfaction.

"Then you won't mind me watching you torture Vasquez into nonexistence for his betrayal. I'm sure each of you has a fate worse than death to share with everyone else. This is a fair judgment for betrayal of the order, isn't it?"

He didn't wait for their murmured replies. Once they'd tortured one of their own, they'd be forced to staunchly support Cinatas's rule; without Cinatas's protection, they'd be food for the other Vladarians. He sent Cinatas an amused glance. "You'll wait with them, make sure they each have a hand in Vasquez's demise, while I go take care of a little problem?"

"It will be my pleasure," Cinatas said.

Pathos turned to Nyros before leaving. "Find Vasquez's cowardly ass and drag it back here."

Then he went hunting. The tangy smells of battle permeated the air—smoke, chaos, charred mortal flesh, and the sweetness of spilled Elan blood. Aragon was out in that battle, and Pathos was going to find him. He headed in the direction of the north gate, where Aragon's scent had been the strongest.

Traveling up the white gravel road, he found the spot where the imprint of the Blood Hunters was heavy, and where the surrounding vegetation lay crushed and broken as if there'd been a skirmish. Trapped in that mortal vehicle Cinatas insisted on using, he'd driven right by and hadn't even smelled them.

The scent led to the west, into the jungle. The moment he stepped into the cover of the trees and out of the rain, he caught a sweet aroma drifting on the light breeze, and his loins swelled. Aragon hadn't come to the jungle alone. The good Dr. Batista was very, very near. He loved the way fate played right into his hands.

Aragon ran to the burning building with Jared on his heels. Even with his were-strengths, it appeared to be impossible to reach the upper level of the tower—not with so much of the building on fire. The smoke escaping through the tower windows was choking and thick. It would be a miracle if Stefanie were alive.

He latched on to the side of the building, punching handholds in the plaster as flames lashed painfully at his skin, burning through the thickness of his hair, blistering and searing his flesh. He kept climbing higher.

Jared waited below. Someone would have to be able to carry Stefanie out of the compound if, when he finished, Aragon's injuries were too great.

In the very top room, he ripped the bars from the window and found a single woman crumpled upon the floor next to it. He lifted her up, shuddering not only from the pain of his burns but from the scorching heat of her body. Even her clothes seemed to be smoking from the inferno she'd been trapped in.

As soon as he saw her face he knew it was Stefanie, a softer, more delicate version of Annette. "Stefanie!" he yelled to her, shaking her. *I have her,* he told Jared, who waited below.

Her eyes fluttered open. "You came," she whispered. "Save Marissa. Too late for me."

Her body trembled badly. He could feel the flutter of her heart grow fainter.

"No!" he yelled at Logos, fate, anything that might be listening. "This will not be!" He tried to send a part of himself into her to help heal her, but although her heart struggled a little harder, it wasn't enough to save her.

"Stefanie!" he shouted, trying to reach her fading spirit with his as he tightened his arms around her. He'd failed. She was dying, and he'd failed. He'd lost the power to heal, was becoming more and more a faded warrior.

Annette paced and cursed. She'd agreed before coming that she didn't have to enter the compound. Hell, it had been one of her bargaining chips. But she hadn't counted on being left in the dark of the forest with a heavy gun in one hand, a flare in the other, and not being able to see what was happening at the compound. What was Pathos doing here with armed men? Was he after Stefanie?

Annette's stomach cramped at the thought. Had Aragon and Jared found Stefanie first? Was her sister really alive after all this time? She could hear the explosions. And screams. The explosives were just a diversion. There weren't supposed to be screams.

A foolish supposition on her part. Anytime you used guns and bombs, people got hurt. She knew there was aid she could give, but also knew it would be the height of stupidity to rush into the compound totally ignorant of the setup, no matter how her medical training and her heart urged her to act. She'd help more of the injured by waiting, but that didn't make it easier.

The snap of a branch brought her whipping around. Aragon's name died on her lips.

"Pathos," she breathed.

He smiled.

The chill went to her core. She didn't move, but tightened her hand on the heavy pistol as she wondered if bullets had any effect on werewolves, though he wasn't in wolf form right now. Was there anything that stopped werewolves dead in their tracks?

Legend would suggest silver, and she didn't have an ounce on her.

The comforting warmth of Aragon's amulet hung between her breasts, but she didn't dare interrupt the rescue. And even if she could call Aragon to her, she wouldn't, not with him weakened by the Underling fever.

She was on her own with a flare, a gun that might or might not do anything to him, and a pack of drugs hanging on her shoulder. If she ran, he'd catch her in a flash. She sat down, set the flare and gun close to her, and slipped the pack of drugs into her lap. "So what brings *you* to the jungle?"

Apparently having expected her to run, scream, or attack, Pathos hesitated before lifting a brow and replying. "Decided to take a walk and smelled something very sweet."

She flipped opened the medical field kit, her brain scrambling for a solution, her heart pounding. "I've noticed that the jungle has a variety of flowers, all pretty, usually sweet-smelling, but I hear some are deadly." Annette pulled out the silver sulfadiazine burn cream and the silver nitrate eyedrops.

"You know there is nothing that can stop me. And if you're thinking about eliminating yourself, forget it."

"Nothing so dramatic. Just putting on some hand cream. These jungle walks can be rough on your skin." Annette slid open the cream and rubbed some on her hands and face, wishing she could take a bath in the stuff as she eyed Pathos. Where would he be most vulnerable to the silver solutions? "Doctors train themselves to make the best of bad situations. You've got me. So what's next? Should I take my clothes off?"

Pathos laughed. "Please do."

She pulled off her shirt, leaving her lace bra on, and rubbed more cream over her arms and torso. When she finished she made sure she had a blob of extra cream in the palm of her hand. Then she stood, secreting the silver nitrate drops in the back waistband of her underwear, and unsnapped her jeans. Why wasn't Pathos advancing toward her? Why wasn't he attacking?

Annette. Aragon called out to her just as her hand moved to the zipper of her pants. Her heart hammered. She didn't dare answer, yet. He would know something was wrong. She had to hurry. She picked up the gun to distract Pathos with as she walked to him. "Do you want to render me helpless like last time? Does that make you feel all he-man werewolfish?"

Annette!

She pushed Aragon from her mind. She had to do this. Silver solutions had to have some effect on werewolves.

"We'll get to that eventually. When we've more time." Pathos's gaze zeroed in on the see-through lace of her bra, and his smile widened. "I wouldn't use the gun if I were you, unless you happen to be packing silver bullets. It's only going to make me very angry, and I might hurt you then. Take off the rest, then turn around and bend over."

Annette smiled, moving to Pathos's feet. Kneeling in front of him, she reached for his zipper. "Why don't you show me what you have? Let me feel it with my hands first."

Aragon felt Stefanie's heart stop and a coldness begin. Cut to the quick to have come so far only to lose her spirit at the last moment, his spirit cried out with rage. He had to get

Stefanie to Annette, to the magic of her medicine. He yelled for Annette, but received no answer.

No! Help me save her! Aragon's mind shouted, crying to the spirit realm, to anyone who could hear him.

The fiery spirit of Sirius the Pyrathian shimmered before him. "I caused you harm, Aragon of the Blood Hunters. I was wrong. Keep this one safe, brother. She is special," Sirius said, his tone completely unlike that of the angry warrior Aragon had faced a short time ago. Sirius reached out and touched his fiery hand to Stefanie's heart. Then, before Aragon could even thank the Pyrathian, he suddenly disappeared, as if he'd lost all power to appear within the mortal realm. Stefanie gasped. He heart thudded once, then again and again. Each beat grew stronger and stronger. She began coughing at the amount of smoke choking them. Aragon stepped out onto the window ledge. It was farther than he'd ever jumped before, but he didn't hesitate.

He landed with a jarring thud and would have lost his hold on Stefanie, but Jared stepped over to help steady them.

"She needs Annette's medicine," he told Jared.

Jared nodded. "Take her. I can free the rest."

As Aragon turned, the woman he'd spoken to, who'd been helping the invalid, stumbled up to him. "Is she all right?"

"She needs help," Aragon said.

"I will come with you to help." She wobbled on her feet. "Please, *por favor,* you must take me with Stefanie. El Diablo, my uncle, will kill me. I can walk, see?" She took several unsteady steps. "I am Marissa Vasquez. Please do not leave me behind."

Aragon didn't have time to deliberate. Stefanie must have meant this woman in her whispered plea. He knelt down beside the woman with Stefanie still cradled in his arms. "Grab my neck and hold on tightly," he told her.

Her sigh of relief was so great that she appeared as if she too were going to lose consciousness.

The woman leaned against his back, locking her arms about his neck. He winced from his burns. A battle cry from red demons rose above the chaos, a sound Aragon never imagined he would hear upon the mortal ground. And a spray of bullets hit the building, sending chips of concrete and dust flying into the smoky air.

Aragon broke into a run, pumping his way back through the shattered gate amid the thick screen of smoke.

Annette! He reached out to her with his mind, but no answer returned to him. *Annette!* He pushed harder with his mind and suddenly slammed up against her attempt to push back. In that second, he registered the fearful thud of her heart and the wrenching of her spirit. Something was very wrong. Then it hit him. Pathos. Not once amid the shouts and screams at the compound had Aragon heard or scented Pathos.

Rushing to the north, Aragon crossed the path he and Jared had taken to meet Annette and Sam earlier. Pathos's scent clung to the vegetation and filled Aragon with anxious rage. He knelt, lowering both the woman on his back and Stefanie to the ground.

"You must wait here with her. There is danger ahead. I will be back." He left the instant the woman released her hold on his neck, not even taking time to answer her desperate questions as to what the danger was.

Pathos watched Annette unsnap and unzip his pants. He wasn't fool enough to believe the good doctor had resigned herself to her fate, but he still hadn't picked up on her angle yet, and the puzzle intrigued him.

His bulging sex spilled out from the confines of his pants. Her eyes widened, but it was the conquering smile on her face that had him reacting fast. He grabbed her hair, jerking her back from him hard enough to scare the hell out of her, but not enough to break her neck. Not yet.

She cried out and swung at his sex, smearing a white cream over his penis from stem to stern, then blinked expectantly up at him as if he was supposed to melt or something. Had she tried to poison him with something from her arsenal of medicines? He laughed at her failed attempt.

"Open your mouth," he demanded, jerking on her hair, snatching her his way.

Mouth clamped shut, she pivoted and tried to lunge away from him, pulling strands of her hair.

Suddenly, his penis began to itch, then burn as if doused in liquid fire. He grabbed at his sex with his other hand, trying to swipe off the cream and hold on to her at the same time. The burn worsened. And his hand began to itch and burn, too.

"What in the hell did you do?" he screamed, throwing her to the ground as he whirled into his were-form, where his regenerative abilities were the strongest. He'd take her as a wolf and kill her in the process. He lunged for her, determined to assuage the burn of his penis by violating her every way he could.

Holy hell. I should have used the gun, Annette thought, trying to gain her feet as she scrambled away from Pathos. His roar of rage shook the jungle. The silver in the burn cream wasn't enough to melt him like water did the Wicked Witch of the West, just enough to piss him off worse than ever before. She was going to die. She'd gambled and lost.

I love you, Aragon. No matter what! Her heart cried, filling her with something that transcended what was happening at the moment. Something greater than herself, and greater than the evil.

She'd fight to the end. She pulled the silver nitrate drops from the waistband of her pants. Though a measly 1 percent, an eyeful of it ought to do him good. Too bad she hadn't thought of making up a lethal injection of a silver solution ahead of time. Before she could get the top off, Pathos landed on her, knocking her flat on her face. The weight of his were-form crushed her into the ground. Dirt filled her mouth. She couldn't breathe.

Crashing through the foliage, Aragon's soul chilled at the rage echoing in Pathos's howl. Annette's cry reached him, and he burst through to find Pathos on top of her, one hand closing around her neck as he ripped at her pants.

Leaping, Aragon wrapped his hands around Pathos's throat, jerking him away from Annette as he twisted his body hard, trying to snap Pathos's spine. Pathos rolled with him, roaring, arching to claw him off. Aragon held on, tightening his hold on Pathos's neck, shoving his knee against the werewolf's spine. His muscles quivered, and a sweat broke out all over his body as never before.

"Run to Jared," Aragon commanded Annette, who had gained her feet and backed away from them. He could tell a marked difference in his strength from when he'd fought Pathos before at Sno-Med that first night. He'd weakened, and Pathos knew it. A triumphant growl burst from Pathos as he threw Aragon off.

Aragon slammed into a tree, cracking its trunk. His breath exploded from him. Sharp needles of pain ripped up his side, and his vision blurred. Before he could recover, Pathos hit him again with a bone-breaking kick to his chest, making the pain in his side worse. Aragon shifted as he gained his feet, ready to grab Pathos at the next kick, knowing that his old mentor would keep hitting at the same point of weakness he'd gouged into Aragon.

But Pathos had found an even weaker point. He was attacking Annette again. He had her by the hair and was dragging her toward Aragon as he clawed off her bra, leaving bleeding marks over her skin. "I'm going to take her and kill her right in front of you, and you've not the power to stop me," Pathos taunted. But instead of standing at his full were-height, Pathos was crouched over as he dragged Annette, who twisted and pulled, trying to fight him.

Aragon launched himself toward them, feinting as if he were going to hit Pathos low. Pathos laughed and went to kick Aragon. Aragon twisted at the last moment, shifting his focus from Pathos to Annette. He grabbed the rope of her hair that Pathos held and jerked it free as he kicked the bottom of Pathos's foot, knocking him off balance. Then Aragon rolled with Annette, feeling an odd burn where his body touched her skin.

She shoved something at him. "Silver," she said.

He shook his head as he rose to attack Pathos. "Keep it and run, and keep running no matter what," he told her, putting himself between her and Pathos. If he failed, she might need it.

"Won't run, no matter what. You might need me," she said, snatching her shirt from the ground.

Aragon cursed, loving and hating her stubborn devotion, but he didn't have time to argue. As he expected, Pathos was stalking toward them, but oddly he had one hand pressed to his genitals as if in great pain. More wolf than man, with a tail and protruding snout, he was now a caricature of a

Blood Hunter. He had no stature of truth, or shimmering cloak, or fluid, muscular grace.

"She's mine, and you're both dead. No woman silvers my dick and lives."

Aragon sent Annette a quick glance, amazed, and drew strength from her undaunted spirit and from deep within himself. She'd put on her shirt and stood ready to help battle. He might be weaker than Pathos, and he might be fading, but he still had heart and the courage to choose right, and a warrior woman by his side. "Think again, Pathos. It's your turn to face Judgment Day."

Aragon charged. Pathos's hold on his genitals set his counterattack off center, giving Aragon the edge he needed. He plowed Pathos back so hard that the protruding edge of a branch pierced Pathos's left shoulder. Roaring with rage, Pathos ripped free and went for Aragon's throat. Aragon got his hands around Pathos's first. They rolled to the ground, and Aragon managed to get on top, gaining the edge.

Then suddenly three sharp bursts of pain exploded in his back, and he heard Annette scream.

A brightness flooded his vision, and a power greater than his own began sucking him upward from the mortal realm. Sucking Pathos up too, for Aragon refused to let go of the evil were.

Annette screamed his name over and over again, but a searing wall of fire stood between them. Aragon's soul cried out to her. *I'll always love you. No matter what.* As he looked down at her before the mortal realm disappeared, he saw that she had his amulet clutched in her fist and was shaking it at the heavens, her face torn with pain.

Chapter Twenty-four

ANNETTE COULDN'T BELIEVE what was happening. One moment Aragon was winning the fight against Pathos, the black fur covering his body shimmering, as if the moon itself had found a way through the dark jungle canopy to give Aragon its power. The next moment the light intensified to a blaze around them. Then the rapid fire of a machine gun erupted behind her, spraying both Aragon and Pathos with bullets. Screaming, she ran to Aragon, trying to see if he was hurt even as she was trying to see who in the hell had shot them.

Suddenly a searing force threw her back, and they were sucked upward. She could feel its power pulling on her skin, hair, and clothes, and though it was hotter than anything she could remember, it didn't burn her. She grabbed Aragon's amulet in her fist and thrust herself against the force, calling Aragon's name and demanding that it take her too.

I'll always love you. No matter what.

She felt his spirit intimately brush over hers, and then he was gone.

Tears and anger spilling from her, she whipped around at the hearty laugh behind her.

"This is fun, is it not, Risa?" said the man, his voice heavily accented. "The *gringa* silvered the werewolf's dick. Vasquez thinks it is something he should have thought to do. The silver bullets worked much too fast, no? I shoot, and then poof, they are both gone." He laughed again and pushed the woman who stood in front of him, hard.

Silver bullets! Annette's insides wrenched. ARAGON! She wanted to thrust through every dimension that stood between them and cut the bullets out herself.

Dressed in black from head to toe, the woman called Risa barreled forward and fell to her knees with a sharp cry.

"Please," the woman cried. "I had to leave Stefanie, or he would have shot us both."

"Stef!" Annette cried, trying to grapple with her grief over Aragon and word of her sister. "Where?" she demanded, stepping toward the woman.

The man pointed the machine gun at Annette. "Not so fast, *gringa*. Vasquez needs time to think. Who is responsible for destroying Vasquez's *casa*?" He flashed dagger-sharp fangs, and his eyes turned red, instantly changing him from a petty despot to a nightmarish beast. "Was it Pathos, or perhaps you?

"I will have answers, now." He pointed the gun at the woman on her knees. "Have you ever seen someone's head blown apart, *gringa?*"

Annette's stomach heaved.

Sam plowed through another freezer of blood with his machine gun and headed upstairs. What had at first given him immense satisfaction now paled beneath the sick realization that all of this blood had been taken, possibly unwillingly, possibly even at the cost of death, from people, from *children*. He could take heart that he was striking the vampires at their weakest spot, but unless they could get all of Sno-Med's records, the vampires would just find more to feed on.

He ran up the stairs, ready to rock on the shit up there, when he heard a door snap shut just ahead of him. Inching his way forward, he plastered himself against the wall and popped the door open.

He smelled it then, the sickly strong cologne with which Vasquez drenched himself.

Inside, he found the room empty, but realized he'd found an office. Vasquez's office. Where in the freaking hell could the bastard have gone to? It had to have been Vasquez whom he heard. But there was no way out of the room. So where did he go? After searching the room thoroughly, Sam readied all of Vasquez's computer equipment for the junkyard. As he turned to leave, he spied a piece of paper on the floor, half under the bookcase.

As a prisoner here, he'd heard that if he dug deep enough beneath his cell, he'd connect to escape tunnels that ran under the compound. Moving as far as he could across the room to minimize the heat from the bomb, Sam angled his altered M-16 into place. A little door-busting bomb was exactly what the doctor ordered.

Suddenly his breath frosted in the air, and he whipped his head around to see three red demons coming up behind him. The creatures cracked open their mouths.

Sam smiled and pulled the trigger. Though he shot in the opposite direction, the resulting flash of light and heat had the red bastards rolling on the ground, screaming in agony. "Glad I could make your day," he said before ducking into the tunnel he'd blown open.

The smell of soil, stale air, and Vasquez's cologne washed over him. He drew in a breath and then moved into the darkness. A tingle of anticipation rippled up and down his spine, and the taste of revenge sweetened in his mouth. It had taken years longer than it should, but Vasquez was finally a dead man.

The tunnel went for about a hundred yards before Sam could see the glow of light indicating its end. He began to run, cursing his luck. The bastard had made it to the jungle, where tracking him was going to be hard as hell. Sam didn't have that much more time before he was to meet up with Aragon and Jared. A cold sweat broke out over his body. The thought of Vasquez getting free sent a burning pain to the base of Sam's skull.

That pain shot a fiery dart down his left leg just as he was climbing out of the tunnel, and he fell back inside. Cursing, he wrapped a chokehold on some roots hanging down, spitting out the dirt plastering his face. He pulled himself up out of the tunnel and lay gasping at its mouth.

For a moment he lay there, taking stock. Finding Vasquez at night . . . suddenly gunfire erupted not far away, and adrenaline had Sam's body fighting to escape the pain. He gained his feet and limped toward the sound.

"Tell me now, *gringa*. I've no more time. Who has attacked Vasquez?"

"Me," Sam said, stepping up behind Vasquez and putting a knife to the Vladarian's back. "Drop the gun and don't move. The blade is silver, and it's inches from your heart."

Vasquez's curse warred between surprise and rage. "Who is *me*?" he demanded.

"Sheridan. Sam Sheridan."

"Who?" Vasquez twisted, trying to see him, but Sam jabbed him in the back hard.

The putrid, bitter gall of memory twisted in his gut. "You don't remember shooting down a reconnaissance copter and taking me and two others captive to torture at whim? You don't remember planting enough cocaine in the wreckage to bury our reputations for life? Nobody asked too many questions or looked too hard for corrupt men, right? Delta Force or not. I owe you for the deaths of Waters, Angelo, and Sinclair."

"Sinclair? He's not—" The woman's words were cut off as Vasquez kicked her back onto the ground. Then he shifted, grabbing Sam with almost superhuman strength and sinking his fangs into Sam's neck. Screaming with rage, Sam shoved the knife into Vasquez's heart, then pushed him away. Vasquez fell to the ground.

The scent was making Sam sick. He felt dizzy. Blood rushed down his chest, and he pressed his hand to his neck, feeling really weird.

"Sam?" he heard Annette call, but he couldn't think to answer her at that moment.

"Sam?" Annette called again, rushing to his side. She pushed his hands aside and put pressure on his wound.

"He has been bitten," the woman said. "It is very bad. Very bad." She sounded as if she wanted to run away.

Annette tried to look at the woman and at Sam at the same time. "Stefanie! Where is she?"

The woman gained her feet. Her lip was bleeding, and the side of her face was already turning purple. She stared at Vasquez's fallen body, the knife still protruding from his heart. "He's dead, isn't he?" she whispered. "I can't believe it."

Sam seemed to come out of his stupor. He kicked at Vasquez. "Hell, yeah, he's dead."

"Sit still," Annette told Sam. "You've two puncture wounds gouged into your neck, but he missed your jugular. Hold pressure here and let me get some gauze." She ran for the med kit, slipped out a package of gauze, and handed it to Sam.

LURE OF THE WOLF

"I'll put a pressure dressing on it when I get back. I have to find Stefanie first." She turned to the woman. "Please, take me to Stefanie! She's my sister, please."

A crash in the underbrush had the woman jerking free, but before Annette could cry out or the woman could run, Jared burst through, grim-faced and cradling a woman in his arms. "By Logos!" he yelled. "We need to hurry."

Please God, let this be Stefanie, Annette's heart cried as it pounded harder. The woman had her face turned away and was shrouded in black from head to toe. She seemed unnaturally still, given all that was happening. Annette was too scared to move.

Jared came to an abrupt halt when he saw Vasquez on the ground. "Vasquez's men are looking for him in the direction of the Mayan ruins. Erin and Nick are sitting ducks."

"Stefanie?" Annette whispered.

The woman stirred, turning her way, and Annette gazed into her sister's blue eyes, eyes that she'd never thought to see again. Everything froze, as if life hinged on that moment; even her heart seemed to pause as she waited for her sister's answer.

"Nette? I knew you would find me," Stefanie whispered.

"Yes. I found you," Annette cried over the raw lump of emotion choking her. Her sister was emaciated, like a concentration camp victim, as if the tenuous thread of life holding her to this world was about to snap. She cried out, hugging her sister, desperate to say everything in her heart that needed to be said. But she had to wait. Stefanie seemed to understand. Within that embrace, their hearts connected as never before, and Annette vowed never to let go again. No matter what. She took Stefanie's pulse and found it stronger than she expected.

"What about Abe Bennett, Stefanie?" Annette asked. Stefanie shook her head. "He . . . didn't . . . make it." Her voice was so raw, so tortured, that Annette didn't ask anything else for right now.

"We must go," Jared said softly. "Where's Aragon?"

"Gone," Annette whispered, her vision blurring even more. "When Vasquez shot them with silver bullets, he and Pathos were sucked up until they disappeared in bright, fiery force."

"The hand of Logos!" Jared whispered reverently, looking grim.

"What does that mean?" Annette pulled back, blinking at her tears, trying to read Jared's face for answers.

"Logos has the final word for all fates. He sought Aragon and Pathos with his own hand, which means the matter was grave enough that he will see to their judgments. I'm sorry." The sorrow in Jared's gaze said it all. "We must get to the helicopter quickly."

Annette nodded, shoving her heart aside as the doctor in her took over, the part that flawlessly performed no matter what turmoil she faced. She pressed her palm to Stefanie's pale cheek. "Jared is going to take you to the helicopter fast. A nurse named Erin is going to get an IV going and give you some electrolytes. I have to put a pressure bandage on Sam's neck, and we'll be right behind you, okay?"

Stefanie smiled and nodded.

Jared sent Sam a questioning glance.

"Go," Sam said. "She's right on. We'll be right behind you."

Annette told Jared what fluids and medication to give Stefanie. He nodded and left.

She applied cauterizing paste and a pressure bandage to Sam's neck. He seemed a bit different, as if he were weakened somehow. But in the short time since Vasquez's attack, he couldn't have lost that much blood. Maybe he was just stunned.

"All that crap about vampires turning people into vampires is bullshit, right?" Sam asked. "Jared said that vampires were fallen Pyrathians from the spirit world. So they weren't once human, right?"

Annette met his gaze and shook her head, her hand automatically falling to Aragon's amulet and her heart squeezing with pain. "I don't know anything anymore, Sam."

"No," the woman said, looking at Sam fearfully. "It's true. My uncle went from a respected man much loved by many to a beast. It does not happen overnight, but it will happen." She set her gaze upon Vasquez's body. "A knife to the heart is not good enough. You must cut his heart out," she whispered. "You must be sure."

"We'll burn him," said Sam. "I don't want to dirty my hands anymore. See if you have anything flammable in that medical bag," he said. "Meanwhile, I'll gather anything that will burn."

The woman snatched off the black cloth covering her head and stripped off the dress as well. She wore white undergarments that were like a gauzy T-shirt and shorts. "These will burn. And I never want to see them again."

A few minutes later, they left. A fire, encircled by stones, burned bright behind them.

Nick had the helicopter ready, and Erin had Stefanie situated securely in the helicopter, IV going. They were in the air without incident within minutes of returning to the field. The seven-hour trip back to Twilight, and the ordeal of getting Stefanie and Risa to a nearby hospital was a nightmarish blur. Since they had no passports, Sam circumvented the public airport by calling in huge favors from some private and some military contacts. With Erin's help, Annette kept a watchful vigil over her sister, her heart rejoicing that she had her sister back and grieving that she'd lost the man she loved. She didn't know what was happening in the spirit realm, but she did know Aragon. No matter what, he'd return to the Guardian Council and face his execution.

"You two are still here? Have you not heard of the command for all available forces to go immediately to the Guardian's Arena?"

Sven looked up from where he and York watched over Navarre's lifeless body to see the concerned face of Flynn—the youngest warrior yet to pass the grueling training to become a member of the Guardian Forces and an elite Blood Hunter.

"Thank you, Flynn. We will hurry."

Flynn glanced at Navarre. "Any change?"

"No, but there is hope. Sometimes that is all that is needed."

Flynn nodded and left.

Sven had heard the stir of activity about the Blood Hunters' camp, but had chosen to ignore it so far. Navarre's need was greater than any excitement among the forces. But a command to the arena sent fear darting through his spirit. Only matters of great internal import were addressed within the arena. And the greatest matter facing the Guardian Forces now was that of Aragon. He stood.

York rose as well. Sven could tell by the pain on York's face that he too feared that this gathering would be the fulfillment of Aragon's punishment. Aragon must have returned. "York, one must stay with Navarre. As your leader, I ask that you remain."

"We both know that a Guardian Aide can be called to watch over Navarre. We will go to the arena together."

"You're sure?"

"I am a warrior. There is no question. I will bear all that must be."

Sven nodded. With an aide at Navarre's side, Sven and York joined the many others going to the arena. Everything within him fought against Aragon's punishment. The guilt belonged to Sven, and every step he made sent torturous spurs of regret burning through his spirit. He'd worried about York acting rashly, but in truth it was his own control that was on the verge of rebellion. How could he watch Aragon fall? He couldn't. He had to act.

"I must see the council first. I will come to the arena and find you."

York paused, then placed his hand on Sven's shoulder. "Must you? Will you leave me to walk alone, wise leader?"

From the shadows darkening York's spirit, Sven knew that York was speaking about more than walking to the arena. Nor had York called him a wise leader before. York knew Sven felt he had to do something to stop this judgment, and was gently reminding him of the responsibility of his position.

The gentle nudge touched Sven's heart and sent his conviction wavering. Wherein was the truth? What should he as leader do? Go with the council's decree and live forever with his failure burning inside? Or force a way to exchange his life for Aragon's?

Just as he was about to leave York, Draysius the Pyrathian joined them. He looked grim and not in the least triumphant that Aragon would face punishment. "I need to speak with you," he said to Sven.

Sven nodded. He was running out of time to help Aragon. "Speak then."

"It is Sirius," Draysius whispered. "I cannot find him."

"What do you mean?"

"I left him in his inner circle to heal from the return of the fire, and when I returned, he was gone. I haven't said anything to the other Pyrathians yet. He was delirious and kept saying he had to right the wrong to the Blood Hunters. I thought perhaps he'd come to you?"

"No," Sven said. "But York and I will help look for him."

A disturbing roar of surprise exploded from the direction of the arena, filling Sven with dread. "But first we must hurry to the arena."

Chapter Twenty-five

PATHOS BURNED. Fire ate at him, curling around every part of his body, inside and out. Excruciating pain agonized his every second. He was locked not only within Aragon's stranglehold but within Logos's pure beam, yet he hadn't instantly disintegrated. Did that mean a greater punishment lay ahead? Were all of his plans upon the mortal ground to be lost? He focused his entire power on reaching Cinatas. *My son! Listen. You must go to Zion and take Nyros. He will show you all that I have ready. You must make it happen. And you must find a way to save me!*

Heat poured into Aragon's spirit, comforting in some places, scorching in others, but his greatest pain lay deep within his heart, where his love for Annette burned. He wished he could have done more, given more, helped more, and loved more. The evil that she and the rest would be facing was so great, he didn't see how they would survive, much less win. At least he still had Pathos in a death grip.

Suddenly the flame holding them disappeared, and they fell. Still, Aragon did not let go of Pathos, even to save himself from whatever unknown fate lay below. He landed with a stunning thud on his back with Pathos on top.

ARAGON, RISE.

PATHOS, RISE.

Aragon's soul fluttered. Logos had spoken. He released Pathos's throat. Pathos looked stunned and, terrified, jerked back with a cry, twisting about to see where they were.

Aragon already knew. He could tell by the roar of the Guardian Forces that they were within the Guardian Arena— the place where judgment would fall. Aragon rose to his knees and bowed his head enough to see his brethren but not Logos. He'd seen the bright, all-encompassing spirit of Logos only once before. He'd never forget it, and was not worthy to see it now. He waited in silence, unlike Pathos, who stood and bared his teeth at the surrounding men, men he'd once called brethren, men he'd once led and taught. He'd fallen so low that it was excruciatingly painful to see him here now.

The forces fell silent, as if realizing their fate might one day be to reveal dishonor before all upon the arena's unforgiving floor.

ARAGON. THOUGH YOU VOWED YOUR SERVICE, YOU FOLLOWED YOUR OWN COUNSEL AND LEFT THAT SERVICE BEHIND. A FADED WARRIOR YOUR FATE WAS TO BE, ONE WHO HAS NO PLACE WITHIN HEAVEN, HELL, OR EARTH.

"I accept the consequences of my folly," Aragon said. Though he spoke softly, his voice rang throughout the arena.

"No!" shouted Sven.

Aragon turned to see his brother walk toward him as the forces parted. "My actions led him to his choice. I wish to take his punishment."

SVEN SEEKS TO TAKE YOUR JUDGMENT, ARAGON.

Aragon stood and faced Sven. "It is a sacrifice I cannot accept, for the flaw was within my own heart, not his. He sought to save. My heart was too full of my need to destroy to see the paths of salvation."

SVEN, HE SPEAKS TRUE. GO FORTH IN PEACE AND BE THE BRIGHT LIGHT OF GUIDANCE AMONG ALL THE SHADOWMEN.

With his pain and guilt etched deeply into his spirit, Sven turned and stumbled as he left. He would have fallen had York not caught his arm. The Blood Hunter nodded to Aragon.

We are with you always, York said.

Aragon braced himself for his fate, his only regret being that he would never again know the fullness of the love he held for Annette. His hands shook as the pain of it tore through him again, and his whole being cried for one more chance.

PATHOS. YOU SERVED ME WELL. YOU FELL AND SERVED ANOTHER. YOU WILL TAKE ARAGON'S FATE. YOU WILL WALK THROUGH ETERNITY AS A FADED WARRIOR.

Pathos's cry of denial was cut in half as he disappeared.

Aragon stifled a cry from his own heart. He didn't want even Pathos to take what punishment was his.

THOUGH YOU LEFT THE FORCES, ARAGON, YOU CONTINUED TO SERVE ME BY FIGHTING AGAINST THE EVIL IMPERILING THE MORTAL REALM, PROVING YOUR MERIT. TO ALLOW THE COUNCIL'S JUDGMENT OF NONEXISTENCE TO STAND WOULD BE UNJUST. YET TO LEAVE YOUR ACTIONS UNPUNISHED WOULD BE UNJUST TO OTHERS WHO SERVE WITHOUT QUESTION. DO YOU FORFEIT IMMORTALITY AND POWER, OR DO YOU FORFEIT LOVE?

Aragon fell to his knees, tears falling, heart hammering. Give up all that he was as a warrior? Could he choose a life as an ordinary man?

Chapter Twenty-six

EXHAUSTED, ANNETTE LEFT Risa calming Stefanie and slipped from the room to find Erin, Jared, Sam, and Emerald congregated in the outer room. Stefanie's screams had awakened everyone, but it was no surprise that Nick was absent. Every time Stef saw him she would say she was sorry over and over again, but wouldn't explain why, and he couldn't take it. He was likely out walking the perimeter, checking for problems and planning on going back to Belize. Risa's story about a drug dealer operating under the name of Sinclair had convinced Nick his father was alive, even though Sam swore Vasquez had gunned down Reed five years ago.

They'd been back from Belize for two days and every time Stefanie fell asleep, she woke up screaming. Even sleeping aids didn't break the cycle. They only made Stef harder to calm down, and the only one who could really calm Stef was Risa. Given those factors, the hospital doctors, after stabilizing both women, had been quick to release them into Annette's expert care.

"Is she all right, luv?" Emerald asked, her short hair spiked from a hellish night. Earlier, Megan had had a nightmare about red demons again. Emerald was already strained to the max by having to maintain the constant flow of magic to protect them. Annette was worried about her.

"I don't know," Annette said. "Physically Stef's recovering, but unless she can get some sleep, I don't think all the nutrition in the world is going to help. People have lost their minds because of sleep deprivation. If she would just open up and tell someone what happened in Belize, we could help her. That she won't makes me want to scream, too."

"Just leave her the hell alone," Sam said, and Annette gritted her teeth. The vampire bites on his neck had him so edgy that he kept jumping down everyone's throat. "You pushing her to talk is making it worse. Give her some time and she'll open up."

Annette shook her head and had to bite her tongue to keep from pointing out that Sam had had plenty of time and was as closed as a sealed tomb.

Emerald had no such restraint. "*That* gack-head strategy has worked well for you, hasn't it, Sam? You doona have any idea how to help Stef so stop dishin' out the advice."

"Time out." Annette held up her hand, wondering how long she'd be able to keep it together. From the moment Aragon had disappeared she'd had to be on as a doctor and sister and friend. And she was dying inside. Reaching up, she clasped his medallion to her chest. Aragon was gone, and her heart hurt so badly she could hardly draw her next breath. But nobody seemed to realize that. Everyone was so involved in the aftermath of their crushing blow to Cinatas and the Vladarians. Jared and Nick were searching through the medical records on the trucks and Stef's computer—

A heavy hand fell on her shoulder and Annette found Jared had silently crossed the room. His uncanny eyes, like burning coals of blue topaz, searched hers. "It's about to be dawn," he said. "The power of the Sacred Stones is greatest then." Erin joined them, sliding her arm around Jared's waist. Her eyes were full of love and deep compassion.

Erin knew, Annette thought. Erin understood her pain. Somehow it made the knife in Annette's heart hurt worse, as if empathy let her bleed more. She had to grit her teeth to focus on what Erin was saying.

"Jared and I thought if you were at the Sacred Stones during the sun's rise that maybe you could reach Aragon through the spirit barrier."

Annette's pulse paused then thudded. She swung around to look at the door to her sister's room.

Emerald stepped in front of the door. "Doona worry, we'll watch over her. You go."

"This is real good," Sam said. "She's already lost him once. Now you're going to make her go through it again?"

"Shut the fook up, Sam. Your disbelief doesn't have to poison everythin'."

"No," Jared said. "Sam is most likely right. Once Logos has spoken, nothing will change that. But there may be time yet for her to speak with Aragon one last time."

And maybe her heart could change Logos's will before he speaks, Annette thought. She had to try.

Grabbing a light, she ran along the rough ground to the Sacred Stones, the cool air burning in her lungs. The mists of Spirit Wind Mountain swirled around her feet and her flashlight jolted wildly from her haste, making it almost impossible to see where she stepped. She stumbled. Her ankles twisted. Tree limbs and shrubs tore at her, but she neither stopped nor slowed her speed.

The first fingers of dawn were creeping across the grass when she reached the center of the stone pillars. With both hands clinging to his medallion, she searched the heavens.

"Aragon! Can you hear me?"

Spinning in a circle, she shouted at each of the pillars,

calling his name over and over, but only silence was her answer.

And the sun kept rising.

"Please!" she cried, falling on her knees, bringing Aragon's amulet to her lips. She prayed with her whole being, with her whole heart, with her whole soul. "Bring him back to me." Her voice, growing hoarse, broke on a whisper that still seemed to echo through the silent stones.

"Why Aragon? Why did you have to take him and leave behind evil like Cinatas? Aragon is honorable and courageous and loving and loyal. He is worthy!"

God, how she missed the power of his gaze on her, the feel of his rough cheek against her skin, the sweet, burning tenderness of his passion. His odd humor and even his stubborn code of honor. Every part of her ached to hold him.

"Please send him back to me!"

The wind swirled, moving faster and faster around her and through the trees, and her heart leapt in a rush of anticipation, feeling the kernel of hope she had buried deep, deep inside her come alive. The wind made her feel as if the spirits on the mountain were answering her.

She jumped to her feet and ran the circle, calling his name. She'd been able to call him to her before, she could do it again, especially at the Sacred Stones.

But nothing happened. The wind died down. The sun rose. And the heavens remained as silent as the stones.

She fell to her knees exhausted. She'd had only snatches of sleep since they'd gone to Belize. She'd eaten little, and all she wanted to do was curl into a ball and escape the pain. All she wanted to do was to send her spirit in search of his, to leave this earth behind and find him wherever he was. But she couldn't.

Stefanie needed her. Sam and Emerald and the rest of the group needed her. They had to stop Cinatas and the Vladarians once and for all.

When she gathered enough strength to move, she returned to the camp. After checking on Stefanie, she told Emerald what happened and then decided she had to have a bath or she'd not live another minute. A hot washcloth in front of a hospital sink was the only cleanup she'd been able to do over the past two days, and the doctor was prescribing a good soak in a hot tub.

She sank into the steamy water and closed her eyes, letting wave after wave of relaxing warmth seep into all the aches, but her heart wasn't having any of it. The hurt there grew as her tense muscles eased. It was as if by letting down her guard, she'd given her pain free rein to rip her apart.

She wanted Aragon to come barreling across the bathroom and fall into her tub again. She ached to change his fate the way she gave her patients another chance at life through the miracles of medicine.

She wanted the no-matter-what love of his arms wrapped around her. She wanted him to take her heart places she could never go alone.

Her eyes burned and tears welled as she dipped below the water.

It was soap. It had to be soap, because she couldn't let herself cry.

If she did, she might not ever stop.

A knock sounded on the door, and her heart slammed hard in her chest. "Ar—who is it?"

"It's Em."

Annette sighed and gulped back the flicker of false hope. Just because he'd appeared once when she was in the tub didn't mean it would happen again.

She didn't want to talk to anyone. Didn't want to see anyone.

"What is it?" she asked, trying to get a grip, but failing.

"Some lady is ringing for you on the bleedin' gack's cell. Why anyone would call Sam to get you I don't understand."

"Well, who is it? Tell them I can't talk right now," Annette said.

Emerald cracked open the bathroom door. "I'm sorry, luv. I know you want to be alone right now, but she says it's vera important. You have to go to Sam. The telephone reception is bad, and it's an international call. Sam said to hurry."

Quickly drying and dressing, Annette rushed over to the building Sam had designated as his office. She was not in a good mood. "Hell, Sam. Who is it?"

"She won't say. Hurry up, though."

"Hello." Annette rolled her eyes and turned her back on Sam.

"Ees this Annette Batista, no? You are sister of Santa Stefanie Batista, *si?*"

"Yes." Her insides scrambled with a mixture of pain and worry at the heavily accented voice. It would be a long time before she could put Belize behind her. But . . . "*Saint* Stefanie"?

"Thees is very important. You must come get *el hombre* before he cause big war here."

Annette frowned at the phone. "What? Who? What war?"

"You talk to him. You tell him to be quiet until you come get him, or there will be big trouble. He want to change everything. I tell him world cannot be perfect. He cannot fix everything."

"Who?" Annette demanded, her heart thudding with hope she couldn't voice. "Tell who to be quiet?"

"Annette?"

Her knees went weak, and she sank to the floor with a thump. "Aragon," she whispered. "Is that you?"

"Yes and no," he said after a long pause. "I'm here on the mortal ground, but I seem to be unable to leave this country without money or proper documentation. And if you don't have clothes on, everyone thinks you are *loco*."

"Where are you?" She couldn't believe she was talking to him. That they were using a telephone to communicate.

"I was returned to the mortal ground shortly after Logos pulled me and Pathos away. He sent me back to the same place in the jungle I'd been taken from, and I have been trying to get to you."

"You're in Belize?" She swung around and saw that she had Sam's full attention.

"At a place near the Mayan ruins."

"We'll get you out," she told him. "Are you all right?"

"Yes and no. We'll talk as soon as we're together."

His "yes and no" sounded much like an answer that someone who was half here and half not here would give. Was his fate to be that of a faded warrior after all? Annette quashed her apprehension and prayed she'd make it to him in time. It didn't matter how faded he was, or how little time they had. He was back. That's all that mattered. She spoke to the woman and got the full information of where Aragon was and how to get to him. Then she had a five-minute argument with Sam. He wanted her to sit tight and wait for Aragon to arrive in the States via his contacts. She wanted to go charging to Belize. He won; she'd see Aragon faster his way. And despite her impatience, she had to be impressed with Sam's speed, because several hours later a military transport helicopter was landing on the washed-out and overgrown pad.

Everyone had gathered to meet Aragon. Though the copter blades were still churning the air and punishing the ground, Annette rushed forward. Aragon climbed out of the copter wearing a military flight suit stretched to the breaking point across his broad chest. His hard jaw was covered in stubble, and his dark eyes were questioning. She threw herself into his arms and burst into tears. He kissed her hard and long. The blades had nearly wound to a stop by the time he paused.

"No wonder he was in such a hurry," commented one of the military men who stepped off the copter. "I would be, too. How about you, Mikey?"

"Would have sprouted wings," said the other man.

"What happened?" Jared asked, moving closer.

"The whole story will have to wait, but you've got yourself another permanent brother for the war you fight on earth," Aragon said, swinging Annette up into his arms. "Only this mortal man has something very important to do first." Annette wrapped her arms around Aragon's neck, completely unconcerned that everyone watching knew what was going to happen next.

It was early afternoon, and the fullness of the sun shone down upon the unnaturally green forest Emerald's magic had created. Even lush flowers had bloomed in their absence. The landscape looked like the setting for a Disney movie. Aragon threaded his way through the trees, kissing her, then whispering her name, and kissing her again.

Finally he stopped and let her legs slide to the ground. "I have something I must tell you, and then I have something to ask of you."

"Anything. It's yours," she said, dashing at the tears that kept seeping from her eyes.

He cupped her cheeks in his hands and met her gaze squarely. Passion blazed in his eyes, all hot and dark and consuming, but there was something else, an unexpected hesitance. "I am no longer a warrior. I am now mortal. I have no gifts, no strengths, no powers from the spirit realm. Do you understand what I am saying?"

Annette sniffled and nodded. "Yeah, I do. You're trying to tell me that you're no longer Superman. But that's okay, because you're still Aragon. You're still the man who melts my knees and can take me to heaven with the depth of his love and passion. You're still honorable and loving and courageous. You're still all of those things that make you who you are. That's who I love."

Then Aragon knelt before her and took her hand in his. "Annette, I would be honored to have you for my wife, to walk by my side and be what you were meant to be. Will you marry me?"

"Yes," she whispered. "Yes!" she shouted, embracing her very own fairy-tale hero as he rose and kissed her, letting her know that what he wanted next wasn't going to make a PG rating.

YOU CHOSE WELL, MY SON.

Aragon released Annette and looked up into the heavens. "What is it?"

"Did you hear that?"

"What?"

He smiled. "How much I love you," he said. "I'm sure it can be heard to the ends of the universe."

And he was right.

DESIRE LURKS AFTER DARK...

BESTSELLING PARANORMAL ROMANCES FROM POCKET BOOKS!

NO REST FOR THE WICKED KRESLEY COLE

He s a vampire weary of eternal life. She s a Valkyrie sworn to destroy him. Now they must compete in a legendary contest—and their passion is the ultimate prize.

DARK DEFENDER ALEXIS MORGAN

He is an immortal warrior born to protect mankind from ultimate evil. But who defends the defenders?

DARK ANGEL LUCY BLUE

Brought together by an ancient power, a vampire princess and a mortal knight discover desire is stronger than destiny...

A BABE IN GHOSTLAND LISA CACH

SINGLE MALE SEEKS FEMALE FOR GHOSTBUSTING.... and maybe more.